MADELEINE D'ESTE

License Notes

CHAPTER ONE

WASP WOMAN.'
A glob of spit thwacked her cheek. Her eyes flashed but she clamped her jaw shut as the guards dragged her into the Great Hall of the Eel, past the throng of townsmen.

'Sinner.'

They hacked and snarled at her, their disgust striking her face like rain. She held her chin high but with her hands secured behind her back, she couldn't wipe her face clean.

'Murderess.'

Foul-smelling fishermen, goat-herders in hessian, callous-handed blacksmiths and even merchants dressed in silk shoved and jostled her as she struggled through the crowd.

'Filth.'

Hands grabbed her hair. Strange fingers tore at her grubby clothes and groped her breasts. She gasped through clenched teeth, her heartbeat pounding in her ears.

But she said nothing.

Soon she would speak and they would be forced to listen.

'Traitor.'

The guards shoved her into a chair in the centre of the room beside the others. She grunted as her elbow struck the hard wood. The Masters of the Shield and the Scion sat in front of her. Behind them was the low dais where the High Table sat and the forest green, gold and terracotta tapestry woven with the eel sigil of Ambrovna covered the wall.

The side door opened, hushing the mob and the Duke entered, his golden brooch glinting against his terracotta-red surcoat. The guards thumped their swords against their shields to announce his arrival, a deafening metallic din rising up to the vaulted ceiling. The pushing stopped and the townsmen bowed their heads.

Her belly clenched like a fist.

As he sat on the carved wooden throne, the blank-faced Duke nodded to the Master of the Shield. Lord Kalin lifted a dark eyebrow and began.

'Men of Ambrovna. According to the laws of the Kingdom of the Four Rivers and the Duchy of Ambrovna, Gerthorn Nyvard, the thirty-fourth Duke of Ambrovna is present in this Great Hall to hear the accusations made against these women. In this realm, the Duke's decision is final and justice will be served today.'

She rolled back her shoulders and lifted her chin. She was ready.

PART ONE

THE RETURN

CHAPTER TWO

Seven days earlier.

'THEY'RE HERE! THEY'RE HERE!' CHILDREN'S voices carried down the doglegged Alleys and through the open door of Rabel's dirt-floored wooden shack. Horns blasted and the Temple bell pealed as merrily as at the Festival of the Father.

'Come on, Ma.' Rabel's eldest boy grabbed her hand and dragged her towards the door, grinning. Her sandy-headed four-year-old twins pulled at the hem of her hessian tunic, too young to understand but caught up in their older brother's excitement. She wiped her brow to hide a grimace.

'He's home. Hurry, Ma,' Teo said, the nine-year-old's eyes were big and grey-green like his father's.

With the floors swept, the blankets neatly folded away, the table dusted, the water jug full, the chipped bowls and dented pot rinsed and drying, she could not delay this moment any longer.

Tying her kerchief around her head, Rabel shooed her other two children out of the shack door. And all the while, her stomach churned.

'A perfect day for a homecoming,' the Duke said, admiring the last gasp of summer, as green turned to amber under a cloudless blue sky.

On horseback, in a terracotta-red surcoat, he led the procession of men, smiling and joking as they wound their way through the rocky red hills towards Ambrovna and the sea. Their pace was brisk despite the bleary eyes from last night's stop in Bolsk where the cider flowed freely. They were war heroes after all and they were almost home after nearly two long years.

A freckle-faced boy scuttled out from between the rust-coloured boulders onto the dirt road, followed by his flock of three shaggy goats, bells clanging around their necks. The boy's eyes glistened as he studied each man marching by. 'Pa?'

A man with a jagged raw scar across his forehead broke away from the pack and placed a hand on the boy's shoulder. 'Tavoy,' he said, shaking his head.

The boy ignored him. 'Pa?' he said again, his voice fading but his eyes still scouring the waves of passing men, not even recognising the Duke in his search for his father.

'I'm sorry, Tavoy,' the scarred man said. 'He was brave. He's in the Land Beyond the Sunset now. His fightin' made the Father proud.'

Tavoy's face crumbled.

'Chin up. You're the man of your house now. You need to be strong. Protect your Ma and sisters.' The man patted him on the back and the boy, no older than seven, gulped. 'Don't disappoint the Father. You must follow in the footsteps of your Pa and show courage.'

Tavoy stared blankly at the ground. The man slapped his narrow back once more and joined the rest of the returning warriors, leaving him to stand alone by the side of the road, his head bowed. His goats wandered over the boulders and out of sight as the first tears trickled down his freckled cheek.

The Duke rubbed his goatee and sighed. The day would not be sweet for all.

'They are coming, m'Lady,' her stout maid said from the window.

Agata smoothed her terracotta-coloured tunic, adjusted her gold tasselled belt and danced over to join her maid. The view from her bower in the castle keep stretched over the red hills, beyond Ambrovna and into the surrounding lands of the Vorosy Clan. A caravan of horses and men on foot streamed past the grass-thatched brick cottages of the goat-herders at the far outskirts of town.

'He is almost here.' Agata twirled around, patting her black braided hair coiled on top of her head. 'How do I look?'

'Lovely, m'Lady,' Sira said, with a smile but the warmth did not extend to her eyes. Her birthmark splashed diagonally over her left eye and cheekbone, the violet stain making her blue eyes seem all the icier. 'The Duke will be very glad to see you.'

'And I to see him.'

Agata squinted into the golden autumn sun, searching for her husband among the small figures but they were still too far away. She grinned and fidgeted. She couldn't wait to drink in his warm familiar scent and tell him everything of the past year.

'It will be good to have the men back, m'Lady. In the eyes of the Father. Life can return to normal. It will be a weight off your shoulders.'

Agata chewed on her lip for a moment. 'The dais is ready? The pennants are all up and the wine?'

'Yes, m'Lady. Everything is in place.'

'Fetch my cloak, Sira. I must be there waiting for him when he arrives in the Square.' Agata picked up her skirts, dashing out of her bower door and along the brick corridor, her stomach fluttering.

'Welcome home, brave men!' hollered a toothless old man at the gates of the Brickworks, dropping to his knees before the mounted Duke. 'And you, m'Lord.'

The red soil of Ambrovna was perfect for bricks but since the death of King Rados and the inevitable declaration of Civil War, the bustling brick-makers had fallen silent. Thick spider webs covered upturned wheelbarrows and the furnaces were stone cold.

'Thanks to the Father for bringin' you home,' said his flint-haired wife, her eyes lowered as she traced the circular sign of the Father on her forehead.

'Tomorrow, once your heads have cleared,' the old man yelled, hobbling alongside them, 'come back and I'll give you work. All of you.'

The men cheered.

'No one is complaining about blisters now,' said Lord Kalin with a smirk, the Duke's life-long friend on horseback beside him.

The Duke beamed.

The dirt road became paved red brick and the cottages gave way to carpentry workshops, potters' kilns and tin smiths, all built from the same bricks. Their doors and windows were firmly shuttered, closed for business like the Brickworks.

At the roadside, a barefoot tawny-headed girl handed out fist-sized purple plums to the passing parade of soldiers. The Duke stopped his horse beside her and she curtseyed deeply.

'M'Lord,' she stuttered, holding the basket above her head. 'Welcome home.'

He nodded as he reached for a plum. 'Thank you, girl. How I've missed our fruit.'

Sneaking a glance at the Duke, the little girl gasped. She fumbled to cover her mouth and almost tipped over her basket.

The Duke smiled weakly.

'Does it hurt?' she blurted.

Kalin flung out a gloved hand but the girl ducked in time. 'How dare you speak to your Duke.' His eyes were cold and grey. 'Learn your place, girl.'

'Kalin. She is only curious,' the Duke said, frowning. He smiled down at the girl. 'It did hurt. Very much. But with the Father's blessing, I am healed and strong once again.'

The girl nodded, averting her eyes. She curtseyed once more before bolting away.

The Duke sighed.

'What cheek. And you were too lenient,' Kalin grunted. 'If this is any indication, the rest of the town will be in a fine mess after a year under your woman.'

'I will have to get used to it,' the Duke's voice trailed away as he flicked the reins. He swallowed hard, picturing Agata's face when she finally laid eyes on him, or what was left of him.

'You missed a spot, Irina. Get up there and scrub it right now,' Froma said. 'Your master will give you a thrashing when he comes home and sees this filth.'

'Yes, Mistress.' Irina scuttled up the ladder, the wooden bucket swinging from her skinny arm.

Froma squeezed her generous nostrils closed. 'And wash yourself once you are finished. You reek.' She paced up and down the street in front of her merchant store, running her fingers along the lead-lined window panes, tutting. 'Do I have to do everything myself?'

Two middle-aged women in jewel-toned silk tunics and matching headscarves walked by, arm in arm. Froma wiped the dust from her finger, adjusted her own headscarf under her chin and plastered on a smile. 'Lady Reyna. What a pleasure. Isn't it a lovely day?'

'Oh, Mistress Plesec. I did not see you there.' Lady Reyna peered down her nose despite Froma's towering stature. 'The Father must be pleased with our men to put on such a beautiful day for their return.'

'In the eyes of the Father,' Froma said, making a circle on her forehead.

'You are not heading to the celebration?'

'Soon. Everything must be perfect for his return, Lady Reyna. I want to show him how well I have managed his interests while he has been away.'

'Quite. But you will be glad to have Master Plesec returned home safe and well?' Lady Reyna flapped her lace fan.

'Of course,' Froma said, a little too quickly. 'I must say what a splendid tunic, my Lady. The colour is so becoming.'

'I have been saving it especially for today. Although my dressmaker...' Lady Reyna sighed heavily. 'Lazy churl almost failed to finish it in time.'

'How awful. Good help is hard to find.' Froma glanced up at her maid scouring the window sills. 'But the afternoon winds, my Lady? Very chilly this time of year. You would not want to fall ill. Perhaps I could interest you in a cloak. I have a lovely plum one inside lined with squirrel fur, perfectly suited...' Froma gestured to the open door of the store.

Lady Reyna smiled coldly. 'Not today, Mistress Plesec. Today is not a day for trade.'

'Of course,' Froma lowered her eyes.

Cheers erupted in the distance and Lady Reyna turned away.

'Perhaps we shall meet in the Square later, my Lady.'

'Perhaps.' Lady Reyna shrugged and strolled away, her companion giggling behind her fan. 'The gall of that woman,' Lady Reyna said without lowering her voice. 'Trying to sell me a garment, today of all days.'

'Disgusting. What do you expect from a foreigner?' her companion replied.

'Thank the Father the men are back. Put her in her proper place. Along with the Duchess and the others in that Committee.' She shook her head and tutted. 'Carrying on like a man. Shameless.'

Froma narrowed her eyes and glared at the backs of their colourfully covered heads as they disappeared into the crowd. The clomp of marching boots and men in song drifted around the corner. Froma sucked in a breath and ran her finger down the crooked line of her nose. They said war changed a man. Froma hoped this was true.

'Haven't you finished yet?' she yelled up at the maid. 'Useless girl.'

CHAPTER THREE

A GATA SKIPPED DOWN THE CASTLE keep stairs, over the bricks worn smooth by a thousand years of the Nyvard family. Her feet travelled so fast even Sira struggled to keep up. Finally, after a long year of rattling around the castle on her own, she would see his face and hold him again.

Her belly fluttered and yet she cringed, recalling her behaviour on the day before he left.

While Ambrovna had bustled with war preparations, Agata had hidden away in the solar. The stream of golden sun through the windows and her intricate needlework had not been enough to quell her nerves and a few wayward tears had splashed onto her stitches.

'Here you are, my dear,' the Duke had said, sitting by her side. Sira had curtseyed and in her unnerving way, faded like smoke into the background. 'Now now, no need for tears.'

Agata had sniffled, forcing a smile. 'You are the one going to war, my Lord. I should not be the frightened one. Are you all prepared?'

'Almost. There is one more task. A serious matter I must discuss with you.' The Duke gently took the needlework hoop from her and placed it on the green embroidered cushions, leaving her empty fingers squirming in her lap. He clasped her hands in his and her eyes moistened once more.

'I have a problem,' he said, clearing his throat.

'Anything I can do to help you, Husband?' She squeezed his hand.

'This is highly unusual.' He peered at her intently.

Agata swallowed hard.

'But with last month's terrible accident...'

'In the eyes of the Father,' she muttered.

'Someone needs to rule Ambrovna in my absence.'

Agata's lips trembled as she nodded. Could he see her heart thumping through her tunic?

'My dear. It must be you.'

She had slipped her hands out of his grasp and tried to hide the tremors inside her trumpet-shaped sleeves.

'I know your time here has been short but the people have already shown a great fondness for you.'

'Not all of them,' she said with a weak smile.

'I cannot shirk my duty. I must heed Prince Absalom's call to arms. The Vorosy Clan must take the throne.'

'My Lord, there must be someone else?'

'You are the only one.'

'My father is more broad-minded than many. I know my letters and numbers and your language but I am not as educated as--'

'I know you are only a woman but you are the next in line. The House of Nyvard has suffered its unequal share of death. And we have not been blessed with new life in our short time together.

'Why not Lord Sylwin? Your uncle is too old for war and he is so very wise. Isn't he the right person to take on this responsibility?'

The Duke shook his head. 'He is only my mother's uncle. He is not of the House Nyvard. It must be you. This is the duty you accepted when you took your vows. Although I admit I didn't expect to lose Uncle Moinn so soon.'

Agata fidgeted with the silver tassels at her belt, his words resting uncomfortably on her shoulders. Suddenly she was eight summers old again, the first time she felt the weight of her high-born position, the crack of the birch switch still loud in her ears.

'I have made my decision,' he sighed.

'What if I do something wrong, my Lord?' she said, her voice cracking. 'I could wreck it all.'

'Nothing should go wrong,' the Duke smiled weakly, patting her knee. 'The fighting is far away on the borders of Tramissa and Nithese.'

Agata pressed her lips tightly. Sun-soaked Tramissa was her homeland but with the upheaval of Civil War and the jostle for the throne between the Four Clans, Agata must keep her fears for her family to herself. This was not the time to remind her husband she was born into the Neven Clan.

'The battles should not cross the Jahan Ranges. The town will be safe. All able-bodied men are obliged to come with me. Except for the Fatherhood, of course. The Scion will continue his role as spiritual adviser to the Duchy. He will be here to support you.'

She shivered at the thought of a personal audience with him. In peacetime, Scion Zavis would not lower himself to meet with a woman alone, even the Duchess.

'Do not worry about Zavis. I have known him all my life and he has always been a crop of prickles but he is also very wise. Actually...' the Duke rubbed his fingers through his goatee. 'Yes. This has been done before. A hundred or more years ago. If you are so unwilling...there is another option. The Scion could preside over the Duchy while I am gone?'

'No,' The words catapulted out of her mouth before Agata even finished the thought. Her heart thundered as she realised she had no other choice. She must make her mother proud. She lowered her head. 'I will take on the task, my Lord.'

The Duke nodded, placing his hand on her shoulder. 'With the assistance of the Scion and Lord Sylwin, you will manage Ambrovna well.'

Agata pictured herself sitting on the carved throne in the cavernous Great Hall of the Eel with an old man on either side telling her what to do and say. If only she had a wise sister or aunt or mother-in-law in the castle, but she walked the corridors alone. 'Could I ask some of the other women to assist? Maybe Lady Reyna. And other capable women. A committee? We could work together.'

The Duke frowned. 'A group of women presiding in the Great Hall? It would be irregular.'

'This is war.' She held her body still, her eyes wide. 'We must make do.'

The Duke rubbed the back of his neck. 'I suppose there could be no harm in it. Although the Scion will likely have a different view.'

'I would be wise with their counsel.' Agata nodded heartily.

'Remember the final decision lies with you,' the Duke said. 'These women cannot influence you. You have a position to uphold. You are the House of Nyvard in Ambrovna. You are me.'

'Hurry back,' she had said breathily, clasping his hand.

The procession marched towards the town Square past the finer homes and stores with their curlicued eaves and red geraniums swinging in baskets. Women and children in fine silks and threadbare hessian streamed into the streets, crying and singing, cheering and grinning.

A gust brought the first taste of sea air and the sounds of jaunty fiddles and pipes to the Duke. His heart swelled as he watched the town embrace their returned men, thrusting mugs of cider into their hands, slapping their backs. Tears of relief and joy flowed freely. Until this moment, few knew the true fate of their fathers and sons.

One side of the Square led to the blue sea where the wooden jetty was lined with moored fishing boats. A gnarled tree, which was older than anyone remembered, dominated the centre with its trunk as thick as the Temple columns. Shiny ravens, their keen eyes watching over the proceedings, cawed from the twisted branches, which were looped with terracotta eel sigil pennants.

Further ahead, the steep avenue led up to the Duke's castle, which was carved into the red rocky cliffs. The tower, like a sentinel, proudly thrust into the sky overseeing his lands below. This was the longest time the Duke had spent away from the familiar sheer red-brick walls wrapped in verdant ivy, his home since birth.

'Pull back,' shouted Lord Kalin and the men shuffled into rows. The Duke guided his horse to the head of the procession for the final steps into the town Square, a smile on his lips but a tightness in his chest.

Rabel loitered by the cotton merchant's store away from the crowd while Teo squeezed to the front.

'Pa? Pa?' he cried, his voice drowned out by the singing and cheering. His was only one of many calling out the same words.

Rabel held her breath, the knot in her stomach pulling tighter with each wiry man with shaggy honey-coloured hair that passed. But Rabel didn't scour the crowd with longing or anticipation.

'A sin in thought is as real as words or deeds. A true follower's mind is as clear as a sunny day, with only the light from the Father, the Sun.'

Closing her eyes, she circled her forehead, but the all-knowing Father already heard the wickedness in her heart. He knew what she wished for.

Rabel would be happier if she never set eyes on her husband again.

CHAPTER FOUR

A BREATH CAUGHT IN AGATA'S CHEST and her cinnamon-coloured eyes lit up. Perfectly positioned on the dais in front of the Avenue, she saw him the moment he entered the Square. He was so handsome and tall as he led his charge of men. The townspeople burst into song, the song of Ambrovna.

> *'Ambrovna, the town the Father has blessed,*
> *Our Duke in the castle, the eel on his chest.*
> *The red rocky cliffs, the bountiful sea,*
> *The Temple, the hills and the Old Man Tree.*
> *Our men stand strong, our women obey*
> *And with every breath to the Father we pray.*
> *Ambrovna, the town the Father has blessed,*
> *Our Duke in the castle, the eel on his chest.'*

The townspeople's proud words bounced off the cobbles and brick buildings. Everyone sang along, even the small boys and girls. Everyone except for Agata. She could only mouth the words, her time in Ambrovna had been too short to commit the song to heart. This was yet another reminder she was an outsider.

As her husband passed the Old Man Tree, he looked up to the dais and their eyes met. He smiled, he was not yet thirty summers old but his face was gaunt and etched with new wrinkles. What horrors had he seen in the past year? Deaths, maimings and worse still, the politics of the new court of King Absalom in Sulun? Sulun, the capital of the Four Rivers Kingdom, sat at the conflux of the five rivers. This was neutral territory where the five rivers met, including the border with the independent and wild territory of the Akull, the fifth clan.

Unlike his men who were more like a troupe of vagabonds with their scruffy tunics and torn hose, the Duke's beard was trimmed and his tunic was clean. Agata averted her eyes as wives rushed into their husbands' arms and kissed them passionately. No matter how much she missed him, no matter how much she yearned, a Duchess must remain on the dais and smile. Their own reunion would be behind closed doors. She wet her lips. Only a few more hours.

Begrudgingly satisfied with the cleanliness of the store front, Froma joined the rest of Ambrovna in the town Square, her nose high in the air. She pursed her mouth as all around, the lower classes humped and groped like animals. She curtseyed long and low as the Duke passed but his eyes were firmly trained on the dais. And on Duchess Agata.

Froma, whose stature was advantageous, searched the battalion of returning men, her heart battering under her chemise. Her belly pinched at the sight of a rusty-headed burly man on a chestnut mare at the rear. Danis. His cheeks were even rosier and his fish lips thicker than she remembered. Froma gulped as their eyes met and she forced a smile. He waved in her direction but continued on, following the procession towards the stage. She twisted her gold betrothal band around and around her finger as the townspeople rejoiced.

'Mama. Mama,' Teo cried, forcing his way back through the townspeople. The broad grin on his little face made his big eyes appear even bigger.

Her heart dropped like a stone as a honey-headed man appeared behind him.

Iwan.

'Look at you.' Iwan pinched the twins' cheeks. His chin was covered in bristles, his nose as red as an apple. 'Not babes anymore.'

The twins scurried away from his reach and hid behind Rabel's patched skirts.

'Forgotten your old Pa?' he teased, pulling them out by the hands. Aula immediately burst into tears and Jorn looked up with a trembling lip.

'Pa's a hero,' Teo told his brother and sister, puffing out his skinny ribs. 'Tell us. How many Hende Clansmen did you slay?'

'Only done my duty, son. One day you'll get to do the same.' Iwan turned and leered. 'Lost your tongue, wife? Aren't you glad to see me?'

'Course I am,' Rabel said with a slight purse of her lips. She leaned in and kissed his rough cheek, her stomach turning at the familiar sickly scent of his cider breath. 'Thank the Father for your return.'

She willed back her tears as his hand clutched her bottom.

'Not much there,' he grunted. 'But enough.'

Rabel's whole body drooped. Life was returning to normal. The Father never listened to a sinner like her.

The Duke's bay mare approached the pennant-trimmed dais and Agata's pulse thundered in her ears. Giddy as a child, she clenched her fists to force herself to remain still. Today was like her betrothal day all over again.

The Master of the Shield rode closely behind her husband. Lord Kalin, the keeper of law and order, with his stern face and jet-black hair. His colouring was unusual for an Ambrovnan man, much like her own.

Kalin slipped from his horse first and stopped in front of the Duke. Agata raised an eyebrow. Had a year at war given Kalin a new set of manners? The Duke held his friend's forearm and Agata gasped, her hand flying to her mouth as she saw the real reason for Kalin's kindness. The Duke's left stocking was empty.

Stinging tears sprang to her eyes but she bit down on her lower lip and crushed her fingers together on her lap. The eyes of the town were upon her.

The Duke hobbled off his horse, resting on Kalin's shoulder. Kalin gestured angrily and a squire scurried over with an iron paddle. The jovial crowd fell silent and bowed their heads. Men nodded to wives and children as the Duke struggled up the three steps to the dais. Agata gripped the arms of her carved chair, holding herself back from rushing to his aid. She was worldly enough to know bringing attention to a man's weakness was never appreciated. Why were his letters silent about his injury? Why did he keep the secret until now?

The Duke limped towards her and his throne. She jumped to her feet, curtseying deeply and he smiled down at her, his slate-grey eyes shining with a strange mix of pain and happiness. Beaming back, she blinked away her tears and gestured to his empty throne. He waved her away and turned outwards, facing his subjects.

'People of Ambrovna. We have returned triumphant.'

The people cheered and hollered. Horns tooted.

'We lost many Ambrovnan men and many fellow Vorosy Clansmen in our campaign. They fought bravely for the Clan and the Father welcomed them into the Land Beyond the Sunset with all our past ancestors and warriors.'

Some people stared blankly, others dropped their heads to mask their sniffles and muffled sobs.

'I am thankful to be back in my town of Ambrovna with the sea, the red cliffs and my beautiful wife.' He turned to Agata. 'As you can all see, I have had my own minor loss. A leg severed in a battle with the Hende Clan. Although I may not be quite the dancer I once was, let me assure you, this changes nothing.'

He smiled and his men chuckled. Agata fixed a smile on her face while her heart squashed like a wine press.

'I am alive and well and will continue to serve as your Lord as we enter into a new era under a new King. One of our own, the head of our Vorosy Clan. I was lucky enough to meet with King Absalom on a number of occasions in Sulun and he thanked me for your bravery, assuring me he was a friend of Ambrovna. Tonight, we celebrate but tomorrow we return to our old way of life. The life we love.' The Duke turned on his crutch towards the red brick Temple and Cloisters on the Western side of the Square. The bald, eyebrow-less Scion and fifteen similarly hairless Cousins stood in a row, their arms tucked inside their bronze-coloured tunics. 'Scion Zavis, will you say a prayer for our fallen men?'

The Scion, as gnarled as the Old Man Tree, moved to the stage with the swiftness of a much younger man. The people kneeled and the Duke sat in his throne next to Agata. She grasped his hand until her knuckles were white.

'Be gentle, dear wife,' he whispered and she instantly dropped her grip.

The gnome-like Scion cleared his throat, his circular pendant swinging at his neck. 'The Father watches over us all. The Father blesses our land with his radiant benevolence which we call the Sun.'

Scion Zavis scoured the crowd with murky green eyes hidden under drooping eyelids. The lack of eyebrows made his stare seem razor-sharp and Agata knew the weight of his glare well.

'He is a good Father when we are good children. All-knowing and wise, he rewards us when we respect his wishes and punishes us when we betray him. He protects our men in battle but in the end, he rewards the faithful by inviting them to join him in the Land Beyond the Sunset.'

The Scion's words were full of the love and forgiveness of the Father but Scion Zavis was as uncompromising as the surrounding brick walls. Agata's first introduction to the Fatherhood of Ambrovna on her betrothal day had left her speechless, yet no one else seemed alarmed when he sermonised about a man cleansing the diseased soil of a woman. How often was she reminded? *A woman's body is sinful and there is a place in the Land of Eternal Darkness for the unclean who do not abide by His rules.*

'The Father is pleased by the valour and bravery of the men from Ambrovna and we are forever grateful to him for our victory and the return of so many. We shall repay him with our hard work, our obedience and respect. In the eyes of the Father.'

'In the eyes of the Father,' the townspeople echoed. Agata and the Duke drew the eye symbol of the Father with a swirl of their fingers on their forehead as did all the townspeople.

'Bring him forth,' the Scion said.

The crowd hushed and parted as four men carried a shrouded body on their shoulders towards the jetty. The men unfurled the wrappings and lay the death-blackened blood-smeared corpse on a raft.

'We send our departed Lord Eimel to the Land Beyond the Sunset to join the Father and all other soldiers who gave their lives selflessly. He fought bravely for Ambrovna and we ask the Father to welcome him.'

The men lowered the raft into the water and pushed the naked Lord Eimel out to sea.

'In the name of the Father,' the Scion said and Ambrovna repeated his words.

Agata's heart clenched. Her husband could have easily been the one floating out to sea. She said her own private heartfelt thanks to the Father as the waves carried Lord Eimel away.

'Now we celebrate!' shouted the Duke.

The crowd roared. A squire scampered onto the stage with a silver tray and the Duke and Agata charged their goblets as joyous tunes on fiddles and pipes filled the air.

Agata reached over to her husband and whispered. 'Why did you not tell me?'

'I did not want you to worry.' He patted her hand.

'Welcome home.' The Scion interrupted without bowing. Two Cousins stood behind him. 'The Father is pleased with your offering and he has rewarded you with life.'

The Duke lifted a red-gold eyebrow. 'I thank the Father for saving my life, but my leg is long gone.'

'Maybe it is in the Land Beyond the Sunset,' Kalin said with dark eyes twinkling.

Scion Zavis narrowed his eyes. 'The battlefield has not taught you any humility, it appears.'

Kalin shrugged, holding out his empty goblet to the squire.

'Now you are home safely, I must insist the old order is replaced as soon as possible. The Advisory Council must meet tomorrow. It is imperative.'

'Within the next day or so.' The Duke waved his hand.

'The war is over and normal life must resume. Everything must be returned to its rightful place.'

'I have some--' Agata started but the Scion silenced her with a glare.

The Duke sighed. 'We have been travelling for ten days, Scion, and I can only think of my own bed.'

'Another day of ungodliness may be the undoing of this town.'

'I disa--' Agata tried again.

'Tomorrow. I urge you. Do you wish to give the Father a reason to show his displeasure? Look around at the state of the town.'

Kalin snorted. 'The ivy is rather thick on the castle walls.'

'Tomorrow, then.' The Duke's shoulders slumped. 'But in the afternoon. Leave me now and we shall meet in my Cabinet after luncheon.'

Agata breathed out slowly through her nostrils, her cheeks burning.

'Excellent.' The Scion stepped away with a flicker of a smirk in her direction. 'The Father will be pleased that all is returned to its proper place.'

'You are absolved of your duties immediately it appears,' the Duke said to Agata, tapping her forearm. 'This should be a relief. You were not keen on the responsibility when I left.'

Agata paused. She had so much to share.

'Yes, my Lord.' She smiled weakly, clasping her hands in her lap. 'I am glad you have returned.'

The Duke lifted his goblet in the air, laughing and pointing to a rubbery acrobat tying himself in knots. Agata collapsed into her chair and into the background, where the Scion thought she belonged.

CHAPTER FIVE

FROM HER PLACE IN THE far corner of the dais, Sira watched the Duchess crumble. Last night her mistress' eyes had gleamed with hope.

'It will be a new era,' she had said, her Neven Clan accent labouring every "r". 'The Duke will be ever so pleased with the state of the Duchy. I expect he will invite me into the Advisory Council permanently. Won't it be wonderful, Sira? Women and men working together on important matters and making use of all our talents. Ambrovna will be the greater for it.'

Sira had said nothing, waiting as she always did, as steady and still as the silver suits of armour in the Great Hall. Ambrovna would return to normal, back to the way the town was and always would be. Women and men, nobles and merchants, fishermen and farmers, goat-herders and servants, all in their proper place, like the Sun in the sky and the sea in the East.

The Duchess spent too many long winter nights huddled over dusty pages in the Cabinet. She had offered to teach her to read but education seemed like a curse to Sira. All those words and thoughts brought her mistress needless misery. The Scion's sermons taught her all she needed to know.

'I wish you would speak your mind, Sira,' the Duchess had said, a line she repeated often.

'I don't know what I think, m'Lady,' Sira replied, blinking. 'In the eyes of the Father.'

'Nonsense. Of course, you do.'

Sira had shrugged with her servant's smile but the Duchess was right. Sira knew exactly what she thought about many things, including the Duchess herself. But twenty years of boxed ears under the old Duchess had taught Sira more than how to pronounce her words properly. She knew her place, and as the Scion said, it was more pious to say nothing and smile.

'*Never speak with tarnished thoughts. A true follower of the Father knows their words are gold.*'

The young Duchess had done a better job than Sira expected, for a woman. At first, she had been fearful of a town without men. Who would protect them? How could they manage alone? The corridors of the castle and the town were so empty and quiet without them. But as the weeks and months passed, Sira enjoyed walking the cobbled streets at night as a Singlewoman without the fear of strange hands grabbing her from the shadows. She never dared say it aloud but she almost preferred the new Ambrovna.

But the freedom couldn't last.

The Duke was home, back on his throne where he should be, his wife by his side. Despite her high-born position, the Duchess shouldered the same expectations of married women that had existed since the Sun first rose. As the Scion taught, a woman's only purpose was as a vessel for life. It was her duty to produce heirs and nothing more.

From her place at the edge of the dais where she always stood, Sira watched the drink flow. As the songs grew bawdier, she spied a familiar face chugging down a tankard. Her breath caught in her windpipe and slumped. Everything *was* returning to normal. The bad was back along with the good.

The Duke settled back into his chair with a chuckle and another sip of rich red wine. For the hundredth time in the past hour, he thanked the Father for his return home but not everyone was as joyful. He caught glimpse of a hollow-eyed woman leaning up against the Old Man Tree, tears streaming down her face.

He beckoned to Lord Kalin. 'Find out how many war widows are left.'

Lord Kalin nodded and whispered into the ear of his squire.

The Duke returned to watching his people make merry. There were more veiled faces than he remembered. Goodwives often wore kerchiefs or scarves secured under the chin, although Agata followed the bare-headed fashions of the ladies in the capital court of Sulun, but only the truly pious covered their noses and mouths with a veil. Commitment to the Father must have strengthened during the war, the women obeying the Scion's every word to ensure the protection of their husbands and sons. He turned to comment to Agata, when he recognised a face in the crowd.

The Duke froze. His goblet slipped from his fingers. Wine splashed across the wooden dais like a splatter of blood. Him? Here in Ambrovna?

'Clumsy,' he said, forcing a laugh. Within moments his valet appeared with a replenished cup.

'Are you ill, my Lord?' Agata said, biting at her lip.

'It has been a tiring year.' He faked a smile.

She nodded. 'But you are home now.'

He smiled again but under his tunic, his heart galloped, and he scoured the Square for the face again. But the man was gone, lost among the throng.

Was he ill? His eyes tricked by the light or the wine or the long journey home?

The Duke dropped his smile, deep in his marrow he knew it was true.

Even in his worst nightmares about that day, he'd never considered the man was Ambrovnan. One of his own subjects? This meant the man knew precisely who he was and he'd known all along.

The Duke closed his eyes, a lifetime of worship taught him the Father never rewarded weakness.

CHAPTER SIX

'WHERE'S PA?' SAID TEO AS Rabel laid the stew pot and hard bread on the table.

After the Duke's speech, Rabel had dragged Teo and the twins back to the shack. Rented from the stable master, it was a single, windowless wooden room with a leaky thatched roof, legions of fleas and the persistent stink of horses from next door. With the whole town rejoicing, there was no one else to watch over her small ones and anyway, she did not feel like dancing. Once night fell, it was better to be off the streets. No good came to a woman alone in the Alleys at night, even a Goodwife.

'With the other men. Celebratin',' she said, wiping Aula's nose with her apron.

'I thought he'd be home for dinner,' Teo said, slumping on the bench.

Rabel shrugged and spooned the watery fish-head and turnip stew into a wooden bowl. Even before the war, Iwan was rarely home for dinner.

'I wanted to hear his stories.' He pouted in between shovels of stew.

'Plenty of time for war stories. Your Pa is home now,' she said, holding back a sigh. 'Forever.'

Jorn yanked his sister's hair and Aula shrieked, smacking her pudgy fist into his chest. Jorn wailed and Rabel pushed the twins apart while Teo sat eating, lost in his own thoughts.

The door burst open, striking the wall with a crash and Iwan staggered into the room.

'What a racket.' He grimaced as he strode over and grabbed Rabel's bony bottom. 'Here's somethin' nicer for a man to come home to.'

She pulled away with a frown. 'Leave off.'

'I've been on the battlefield for a year,' he said, leaning over her with his sour breath. 'A husband deserves better treatment.'

'Pa. Tell me about the war. Did you kill lots of Hende and Sopter Clansmen? How big was your sword?' Teo said with wide gleaming eyes.

'Later, son. Where's my grub, woman?'

Iwan pushed little Jorn out of the way and took his seat at the table.

'I'll serve up,' Teo said.

'What's your Ma been teachin' you while I've been away? Women do the servin'. Woman?'

Rabel gritted her teeth and pushed a bowl of stew, followed by a hunk of yesterday's bread, across the table.

Iwan took a greedy slurp. He stopped, his mouth twisted in disgust and sprayed soup across the table.

'What's this muck?' he sneered.

'Fish stew.'

'Worse than army food. What kind of homecoming is this?'

Rabel shrugged. 'All we could afford.'

Iwan narrowed his eyes. He cupped the bowl in his hand, and pulled his arm back to throw. Rabel cowered, waiting for the splash of hot liquid.

She waited and waited, but nothing. She lifted her eyes to see his contorted smile. He placed the bowl down gently with a snort and dunked his bread in the stew.

'Where's the kitty?' he said with his mouth full.

'I don't have anythin',' she stuttered.

'Don't lie to me, woman. I know you.' He slammed his fist on the table and got to his feet. Aula began to cry and Rabel clutched her girl to her breast.

'Believe me, there's nothin'.'

'I've known you since you were fifteen summers old, woman,' he scoffed. 'You've got coins somewhere. You always do.'

'No,' she said.

He knocked all the bowls and empty jars from the make-shift shelf onto the dirt floor. Rabel flinched and Aula wailed louder.

'Shut that thing up,' Iwan said.

'Please stop cryin', little one,' Rabel said, her voice raspy and shaking but Aula kept blubbering, snot and tears trickling down her face.

'Bloody useless mother. Control your babes. Or I'll shut 'em up myself,' he snarled and crossed the room. He rifled through the blankets and winter cloaks, throwing them everywhere. 'Where is it?'

'Please, Iwan,' she said between Aula's sobs. 'There's nothin'.'

He turned back to the broom and a clay pot in the corner. Rabel held her breath as he picked up the pot.

'Liar,' he said with a wallop and the pot shattered across the table. The startled twins whimpered as Iwan sifted through the broken pottery shards. Empty handed, he moved on with a huff. He stood, hands on hips in the middle of the room, eyes narrowed and Rabel gulped.

Iwan slapped his open palm on the table next to Teo. 'Where does your Ma keep her coins?'

'I-I-I,' he stuttered.

'Leave him alone.' Rabel put Aula down. She moved around the table to shield her son.

'Are you going to lie to your Pa, too? Like a woman.'

Teo's eyes darted towards his mother.

'Where are your loyalties, boy?'

Teo swallowed hard and Rabel pressed her lips together.

'Come on,' pressed Iwan.

'There's a hiding place...' Teo bowed his head as he pointed towards the wall stud. 'Over there.'

Iwan hurried over and reached into the gap between the stud and the thin wooden wall.

'Ha.' He pulled out a felt purse and shook it in the air.

He squinted as he tipped the contents onto the table and a handful of coppers rolled out.

'We need it,' Rabel pleaded.

Iwan lunged and grabbed her by the chin. She flinched, her lip trembling as his fingers crushed her jaw.

'This is the way you treat a man back from war. Your own husband.' He shoved her head away. She stumbled backwards over the bench, cracking against the edge of the wooden table.

Pocketing the coins, Iwan stormed away, slamming the door behind him. The flimsy door rattled on its hinges.

With a sigh, Rabel squeezed her eyes tight.

'I'm sorry, Ma.' Teo reached out his hand, his cheeks wet.

'It's not your fault,' Rabel sighed.

'He's my Pa,' Teo said, his young forehead wrinkling. 'I didn't know what...' Teo rested his head against her breast.

'I know.' She patted his hair.

'Why is he so mean to you?'

Rabel smiled wearily and wrapped him in her arms.

Rabel's shack was silent for the rest of the night while all around Ambrovna, the streets echoed with shouts of joy and laughter.

Froma sat tall at one end of the long dining table dressed in her finest tunic, a pine-green silk with gold embroidered neck and cuffs. Candles flickered from the centre of the table and shadows danced over the dark wood-panelled walls. 'Are you glad to be home, husband?' she said, interrupting the quiet chewing and scraping of knives.

Danis grunted from the opposite end and poured himself another goblet.

'I am glad to have you home. Fit and well. Unlike the poor Duke.'

Danis nodded his big red head and wiped his mouth. 'The Duke is an example to us all.'

He reached for another hunk of roast goat as Froma picked at her plate. She had a bird-like appetite despite her ample figure. Her roiling belly had improved a great deal over the past year but tonight the pangs were back with a vengeance.

'I hope you will be pleased when you look over the ledgers tomorrow,' Froma said with a smile. 'I used to help Papa with his accounts. He always said I had a knack for the abacus.'

Danis narrowed his eyes and kept chewing.

'While you were away, I worked very closely with the Duchess. I was a member of her Interim Committee. We became close friends. I even helped her with matters of administration and trade. To keep the town going. Some of the Seneschal's tasks.' Froma smoothed her hair.

Danis laughed a short bark and shook his head. 'Women running the town.'

'We did our best, given the circumstances.' Froma pursed her lips. 'The town is in a good state. Don't you think, husband?'

'But now the men have returned. And you will go back to embroidery or whatever you spend your days doing. Spending my money,' he said with a sneer. 'Not giving me heirs.'

'I was hoping...' she said, placing down her fork. 'I could continue to help you with the business. I have a few ideas on how to expand into different grades of--'

'Enough.' Danis slammed his goblet down on the tabletop. The candlestick and plates jumped. Froma closed her mouth and held her breath as a wave of heat rolled from the other end of the table. 'I don't care what you *think*.'

'But I...'

'No more of this talk. I am back. This is my house. My business. I don't listen to women. I would get more sense from this jug.'

Froma opened her mouth. 'I have...'

The empty wine jug hit the wall, porcelain shattering all over the floor. Froma flinched as red liquid splattered her walls.

'Irina. Fetch more wine for your master,' Froma said through tight lips.

The pasty girl appeared from a dark corner with a new jug and as soon as his goblet was replenished, Danis poured the contents straight down his throat. His face was almost as scarlet as the wine as once again, he held out his empty goblet for more.

Froma pressed her hands against her stomach. She knew she was walking along a precipice but she could not stop herself. She'd worked hard, spent long nights understanding and protecting his interests. Other men would be grateful for such a dedicated wife.

'I did my best to ensure your business was returned to you in good shape...'

'Stop.'

This time he threw the full goblet at her. Red wine splashed across her face as the goblet bounced off her forearms and smashed against the tabletop. She cowered.

'You think you are better than me.' He grabbed the curved carving knife from the platter of meat and stepped towards her, his eyes hard, his thick lips wet with saliva. Froma's heart thudded against her ribs.

'Do I need to teach you some respect?'

'I have every respect for you, husband,' Froma stuttered.

'I was at war for a year,' he bellowed. 'And this is how you welcome me? Wittering on with your empty-headed woman thoughts. This is my house. My business. I do as I please. You do not get a say.'

He thrust the knife deep into the table and stomped away. 'Irina, bring more wine to my cabinet.'

Froma's hands shook as she wiped the drops from her face. Tomorrow after he slept off the wine and checked the ledger, he would change his mind. He would even be proud. The figures would prove she was a capable wife and not the useless burden he claimed. She smoothed her hair and forced a smile to her lips. Tomorrow he would thank her.

CHAPTER SEVEN

AGATA WAS ALONE IN HER chamber as she had been every night for more than almost two years.

She gazed over the slate and thatched roofs of Ambrovna and out towards the hills blanketed in darkness, the moon lounging lazily in the sky. One by one, the town lights extinguished until only two torches burned brightly in the Square, illuminating a handful of rowdy stragglers.

Agata paced up and down the rug-covered brick floor barefoot, her black hair hanging loosely down the back of her chemise. She'd dismissed Sira hours ago, in readiness for her long-awaited reunion with her husband. But where was he?

Her ears rang with the Scion's undermining words and her husband's quick yielding to his demands. She sighed at the lifetime of empty days stretching ahead of her filled with needlework and watercolours. She could do so much more. Feed and clothe the children, reform the poor women of Guts Alley, flatten and rebuild the festering passageways.

With each step, she vowed she would be stronger next time. That whatever the Scion or Sira said, the world did not need to return to the old ways. The past year had taught her one lesson: she and the Scion rarely saw eye to eye.

A fierce storm had hit Ambrovna at the tail end of the previous winter. All night Agata had lain awake, listening to the groaning winds, the hammering hail and the savage sea, worrying about her subjects in their flimsy shacks. The next day dawned with an icy blue sky and an eerie stillness, and there were many bleary eyes around the ancient High Table in the Great Hall of the Eel.

'Let's begin,' Agata had said to Lord Sylwin and the six women of the Interim Committee, all wives of prominent members of the Merchant and Craft Guilds. She took her chair at the head of the High Table in the Great Hall, the walls behind her covered in polished swords and armour. This was a place where decisions were made, alliances forged and feasts celebrated. Portraits of past Dukes of Ambrovna hung on the wall, row after row of disapproving male faces looking down on her. The Duke's throne had remained vacant, another reminder that Agata's position was only temporary.

'My Lady, the Scion is not here,' Lord Sylwin said.

'We shall start without him,' Agata had said firmly. Two of the Interim Committee members pursed their lips and shared a disapproving glance. 'We cannot wait. What is the damage, Lord Sylwin?'

Sylwin cleared his throat, his eyes yellow and rheumy. 'Four fishing boats were dragged out to sea.'

'We told the wives on numerous occasions to move the boats further inland,' tutted Gala, the full-figured grocer's wife.

Agata was the only noblewoman at the table after Lady Reyna and Lady Ashka condescendingly declined to join. At the time, their snub had offended Agata but now, as she looked around the six eager faces, she was glad.

'Where were they supposed to move them?' said Jadzia, a shipwright's wife, crossing her slender arms. 'It's not as easy as you think. These women have now lost their livelihoods. And what will the men do when they return?'

'Are you suggesting compensation?' Froma said with a raised brow. The wife of a mohair merchant, Froma had an unfortunately bent nose and the frame of a man.

'If the Duchy wants fish to feed its people...and of course, the taxes,' Jadzia said.

'It's their own fault,' said Froma.

Despite the seriousness of the conversation, Agata suppressed a little smile. The earlier meetings of the Committee were never this heated.

Jadzia pointed across the table at Froma. 'Where do you think your dinner comes from?'

'We cannot protect people from their own laziness,' Froma said.

'Go hungry.' Jadzia tossed her mousy-brown hair. 'Or perhaps learn to fish yourself.'

'There are always others--'

The great oak door scraped along the brick floor and the Scion rushed in, his ankle-length bronze-coloured tunic flapping. Two Cousins followed close behind. The Committee straightened their postures, and Karolien and Randvi quickly secured the veils over their faces and circled the sign of the Father on their foreheads. Agata nodded politely as Zavis took his seat beside her but he only stared vaguely in her direction.

'There was considerable damage to the Temple roof last night,' he said, without an apology for his lateness. 'We need--'

'One moment, Scion. Lord Sylwin is giving a report on the damage across the town.'

Zavis narrowed his eyes and pressed his mouth closed. Agata's heart hammered in her chest as she forced a calm expression on her face.

Sylwin continued. 'The Bakehouse lost its roof and the ovens are ankle deep in rainwater. There will be no bread today, my Lady.'

'No fish and no bread,' said Jadzia with a tilt of her head.

'People are needed to help remove the water, fix the shingles and get the ovens firing again,' Sylwin said.

'I need volunteers,' the Scion said, leaning forward, prodding the table top with his finger. His eye of the Father pendant swung from his throat. 'As soon as possible.'

Agata pursed her lips. 'We must provide bread for our people, Scion Zavis.'

'The Festival of the Father is four days away. I do not know what you Neven Clansmen do but here in Ambrovna, we take our celebrations very seriously. This is the first major storm in years. The Father is obviously unhappy with Ambrovna. We cannot be complacent. We must make amends.'

'We also celebrate the Festival of the Father in Tramissa. We are not as frivolous as you may think,' Agata said through clenched teeth. 'There are simply not enough people to do both repairs at once. May I remind you, there is a war and our numbers are limited. We must focus on the greater need. First the Bakehouse and then the Temple.'

'It appears you do not understand the seriousness. It is the fasting season,' the Scion scoffed. 'For the pious, food is not important. This affects the spiritual health of our people. Do you want to further anger the Father? '

The others around the table remained quiet, their eyes lowered to their laps or darting across the room. Agata gritted her teeth. She could not allow the children to go hungry.

'How long will it take to fix the Bakehouse?'

'Two days at least.'

'Who has the skills to repair the roof?'

'There are a few old thatchers left and a couple of girls have shown themselves quite adept with a hammer.'

'Excellent. Focus all volunteers on the Bakehouse today and in two days' time, send the group to the Temple.'

'If there is more rain, the Temple will be ruined,' said the Scion, his glare white hot.

'The skies are clear today. Perhaps the Father will bless us.'

'The Father does not forgive laziness...'

Froma nodded at Jadzia, who squeezed her lips into a long thin line.

'...or stupidity. The Duke always respects his duties to the Father. He would understand the gravity of this situation. He would never put anything before his duties to our Protector.'

'The Duke is not here. I am in his place.'

The Scion's blazing stare was unwavering. 'With my counsel.'

'And Lord Sylwin's,' Agata replied, her thighs shaking under the table. 'But the final decision lies with me.'

The Scion blinked very slowly, his eyes never leaving Agata's face. 'Let it be on your head then.'

'Lord Sylwin, please arrange for all volunteers to be sent to the Bakehouse first. Once this is fixed, the Temple roof will be mended.'

'If you command, my Lady,' Lord Sylwin said quietly.

Agata drew her shoulders back and held her head high. 'I do. Provide me with an update at luncheon.'

'Yes, my Lady.'

'Now back to these fishing boats...'

Later that morning, Agata had stood by the big windows in the solar, surveying the town below. A broken branch lay on the cobbles underneath the Old Man Tree but he was unperturbed having faced far worse storms in his long life. Agata stretched out her arms and with a deep breath, she smiled. Her worries were unfounded. It had not been so difficult to stand up to the Scion after all. But her happiness vanished as her eyes were drawn to a movement on the Temple roof. She cupped her hands against the glass. Three bent figures were hammering shingles.

Agata flew out of the solar and ran down the brick stairs.

'Where is Lord Sylwin?' she demanded of every servant she passed.

By the time she found him in the main bailey chatting with one of her grey-headed guards, her nostrils were flaring.

'How is this morning's progress, Lord Sylwin?' she said, her voice shaking.

He limped towards her, an old injury from the last Civil War thirty-five years ago.

'Very good, my Lady.'

She narrowed her eyes. 'Is the work at the Bakehouse complete? Is that why people are mending the Temple roof?'

Lord Sylwin rubbed the back of his neck.

'I gave the instructions,' Agata insisted.

The old man bowed his head with a half-shrug.

'I am the ruler of Ambrovna.'

Lord Sylwin wet his lips and looked away.

'Am I not?'

'My dear Duchess. I tried. Believe me, I did.' Lord Sylwin said with a sigh. 'It is not so easy. You are young. You have much to learn.'

Agata picked up her skirts and fled inside, hiding her shameful tears. Each time the Scion thwarted her, she promised he would not win again. But his attacks were like a battering ram. As Agata let the tears fall, she wondered whether her efforts were futile and the Scion was right all along.

As the last of the celebratory torches went out in the Square, Agata sighed again, rubbing her eyes. Where was her husband? Her four-poster bed called out to her and she stopped her pacing. Snuffing out the candle, she left the bed curtains ajar and yawned as she slipped under the eiderdown embroidered with the eel sigil. The bed was soft and welcoming but the bed-warmer was stone cold. Despite her feet being like frost, she dozed off quickly in the darkness.

The door hinges creaked and Agata woke with a start. Dim candlelight crept into the room and the Duke hobbled inside, his iron crutch thumping on the brick floor with every step.

'Come, husband.' She patted the feather mattress.

He smiled wearily but stayed standing. 'It has been a long day.'

'And a long year. Come and lie beside me.'

He did not move. 'You appear well, Wife.'

'My only complaint was missing you,' she said.

'The responsibilities were not too great, I hope.'

Agata sat up. 'It was not easy. But Sylwin was a wise advisor and my Committee women proved talented and capable. It gave me a chance to see--'

'And Zavis?'

She grimaced. 'It is obvious what he thinks of me.'

'He is true to his faith.' The Duke shrugged.

'I was scared at first but now-- I have many ideas of how--' She leaned towards him.

'Have you received word from your father?'

Agata stopped short, shaking her head. 'Nothing,' she said in a small voice. 'I do not know if he is alive or dead. Or Taraz.'

The Duke chewed on his lip.

'There is news?' Agata gulped as she grabbed for his hand. 'Please, tell me.'

'In war, there are many stories. It is hard to know what is true.'

'Go on.' Her chest tightened.

'They say he aligned himself with Lord Hugon.'

Agata grimaced. The vainglorious Hugon, the great nephew of late King Rados, had been leading her brother astray since they were boys. What immature prank had Hugon roped Taraz into this time?

'There were rumours of a plot. Hugon wanted to challenge Prince Celso's claim to the throne.'

Agata squeezed her eyes shut. Treason? Foolish Taraz. Disloyalty during a Clan war was far more serious than gambling debts and drunken buffoonery. This was a scrape her father could not rescue him from.

'Is he in the dungeons?'

Her husband cleared his throat. 'His head ended up on a spike. At the capital gates after the fall of Sulun.'

Agata covered her mouth with her hand, her mind flooded with bloody images of her brother's dismembered head. 'Who did it?'

The Duke shook his head. 'No one knows. The Hende? One of our Vorosy battalions? One of his own Neven Clansmen?'

She lowered her chin, composed herself as best she could. 'And what of my father?' she choked.

'Your father is a clever man. I hope he has gone into hiding,' he said, patting her arm as she gripped her hands tightly in her lap.

'And what of us? Now the Neven are no longer on the throne, will I cause problems for you? With my accent and my complexion, they will always see a Neven woman.'

'Our Clans have been allies for hundreds of years. This time the Vorosy has triumphed but the alliance stands.'

'But the relationship is not always smooth. And if the stories of my brother are true...'

'You are a Vorosy woman now of the House of Nyvard,' the Duke said as he bowed to kiss her on the forehead. She leaned back her head to reach his lips, but he tilted his head away.

'I am tired, my dear. So much work ahead of me,' he said with a sigh. 'Sleep well, Wife.' He lumbered out of the room and closed the door softly behind him, leaving her alone with her tears.

With her head in her hands, she wept for her beheaded brother, her missing father, and her crippled husband. But mostly, she wept for herself. The men had been home for less than a day and her new-found courage had vanished.

'I tried, Mother,' she whispered. 'But I can never be the woman you hoped I would be.'

CHAPTER EIGHT

RABEL WATCHED IWAN SNORE AS he lay on the leaf-stuffed mattress while the rest of the family rose for a new day. Always small framed, he was now skin and bone. His face was sunburned and flaky making him even uglier than she remembered.

Hushing the children, she stoked the fire and heated up the last of the stew. There were barely two bowls in the pot, let alone enough to feed five hungry bellies. Clutching the pocket knife in her cracked red hands, Rabel sliced up the hard bread. When she was young, her hands had been pretty and delicate but now she was just as worn and ugly as him.

'I'm hungry, Ma,' Teo said.

'I know,' she said, serving him the largest portion.

'Thank you.' When his hand lingered over hers as he took the bowl, Rabel's heart clenched. Teo scoffed down the stew then scampered next door to muck out the stables. Her nine-year-old boy off to work while his father lay flat on his back, snuffling like a hog. If only Iwan had stayed away.

As soon as the thought crept into her head, she scolded herself and covered it up with the Teachings. *A sin in thought is as true as words and deeds.* But like Iwan, her sinful thoughts always came back. Pa had always said she was rotten to the core. Riddled with sin. '*A woman's body is sinful. A woman's thoughts, words and actions must be as pure as the sun.*

Iwan jolted upright and yawned loudly, scratching his groin.

'Get me some ale, wife,' he bellowed as he swung his scabby feet out from under the blanket.

'No ale, husband. Only water.'

'What?' He grimaced. 'The army had weevils in the bread and rotten meat that made you dribble shit for days, but there was always ale.'

'Well, there's none here. I've got water.'

'Pfft. Water is for goat herders.'

'Do you think we're the Duke and Duchess,' she muttered.

'I heard that. None of your cheek, woman. Where's my breakfast?'

'Give me a copper and I'll get some bread.' She held out her hand.

'Coppers?'

'The coins you took last night. There must be somethin' left.'

'Are you daft, woman? I don't know what you're talkin' about. My pockets are empty.'

She breathed out through clenched teeth. 'The money you took from the kitty.'

Iwan leaped up and grabbed her by the elbow. 'Watch your mouth. You don't talk to me like that.' He shoved her and she stumbled towards the wall. Her eyes narrowed and angry words bubbled inside her. She knew better but she could not bite her tongue.

'I hear old Orvald is lookin' for men at the Brickworks,' she said.

'I've just come back from war, woman. You think it was all drinkin' and marchin'?' he said. 'I saw mates sliced clean in two. Grown men wailin' like babes with their guts hangin' out and their arms lopped off. I saw rivers of blood and corpses piled sky high. You think I can go shovellin' dirt for Orvald after that? I'm grateful to be standin' here, with my head and both my legs. Coin can wait.'

'If coins can wait, so can the ale.' Rabel pressed her chapped lips.

'Shut your mouth.'

'What are we supposed to do? Teo only earns four coppers. That'll never feed all five of us. And your debts...'

He narrowed his eyes. 'How *have* you been payin' my debts, wife? I thought you said you had nothin'? Been whorin' yourself?'

Rabel glanced across at the twins playing with Iwan's boot in the corner of the shack, grateful they were too young to fully understand his words. There was a kindly older man, a trader from Neros. She liked his company and he gave her gifts. That was different.

'I did some work for the Plesec Merchants. But it's over now. All the work goes back to the men.'

'Get some silver from that sister of yours.'

'No.'

'Starve then. I'm goin' out.' He tugged his boot away from Jorn and tied the straps as he hopped out the door.

Rabel clutched her head and bared her teeth. She refused to go to her sister. She would not beg again. She slumped, sighed and started to fold up the blanket from the bed, the wool still warm with his body heat. What other choice did she have?

'Bad man,' said Jorn, his lip thrust out.

Rabel's eyes welled as she rushed to her twins and took them in her arms. 'We don't say things like that. He's your Pa. He must be respected. The Father doesn't like it when we say mean things about people, especially--'

Rabel jumped as someone knocked so hard, the door rattled on its hinges. She patted Jorn's sandy head and lifted the latch.

'Mornin' Rabel,' said the shrivelled woman in the doorway. A bald man twice her size loomed behind her.

'Sabet,' Rabel said with a watery smile, her pulse galloping. 'Is it that day already?'

'You should know better than that.'

'With all the excitement...'

'Business is business.'

'I see your son is back?'

'In the eyes of the Father. Now I can go back to my fireside and my knittin'.' Sabet's wheezing chuckle made Rabel's stomach flutter. This time it wasn't hunger.

'I am sorry, Sabet,' she said with a clumsy swallow. 'I've got nothin' for you today.'

'Rabel. Rabel. Rabel,' the old woman tutted, shaking her grey head from side to side. 'That will not do. I am very disappointed in you. One of my best. So good with your payments.'

'We spent too much celebratin' Iwan's return.' Rabel shrugged.

Sabet narrowed her eyes. 'Straight back to his old tricks. I heard he lost a load on the cocks last night. I won't be the only one chasing him today.'

Rabel clutched her hands. 'I can pay you tomorrow, Sabet. I promise.'

'But I need payment today. Who knows what the Father will bring? At any moment I could be dead in my chair with debts unpaid.'

'I'm sorry.' Rabel bowed her head.

Sabet's son pushed past Rabel and into the shack. He searched the table and rifled through the shelving along the back wall. Rabel didn't move to stop him. She knew he'd find nothing of value; she'd tried selling everything many times before.

'Because I am a generous woman and you have been so good, you've got until midday.'

Rabel bit down hard on her lip.

'Thirty-three coppers. Come and find me at the Seaweed Arms before the bells of midday service. If you don't --'

'Nothin' here worth taking, Ma,' Sabet's son said, his voice deep and slow.

'There are always things to take, my boy,' Sabet said, reaching out a finger to stroke Aula's cheek. 'You just need to look closely.'

Rabel pulled Aula close against her chest. 'Thirty-three?'

The old woman hobbled out of the door. 'Midday, Rabel. Midday.'

Rabel slammed the door closed and slumped down on the long bench, her head in her hands.

Two days earlier, Agata's Interim Committee had met in the Great Hall of the Eel but today, the women who'd run Ambrovna for the past two years were shoved back into the solar like a sewing circle. The absence of Lord Sylwin and the Scion was particularly glaring.

'Now our men have returned triumphantly,' Agata said. Her face was composed but her fingers fussed with the tassel in her lap, 'our Interim Committee is disbanded. We must go back to the way life was before.'

The six female members nodded. Disappointment hung in the air, despite the more comfortable cushioned surroundings of the warm solar. Even the moist golden almond cakes sat untouched on the platter.

'I would like to thank you for your guidance and counsel. The men are of course too proud to say...'

Karolien and Randvi gasped. Their faces bare and their beige veils hanging loose over their shoulders, they made the round sign of the Father on their foreheads.

Agata lay her hand across her breastbone. 'We have left the town in a good state. I believe we have proven ourselves capable in the eyes of the Father.'

'In the eyes of the Father,' the women chanted in reply. Some more enthusiastically than others.

Clawa, the wine merchant's wife-now-widow, sniffled into a white handkerchief. Agata had her own grief but she knew better than to mention her brother Taraz, the name of a traitor in the new Ambrovna. She feigned a smile and stretched out to pat Clawa's forearm.

'It was fun while it lasted,' said Jadzia with a hint of a sigh. 'What will you do now, m'Lady?'

'Babes,' said Gala, the grocer's wife, a mischievous smirk on her plump cheeks. 'Lots of babes.'

Jadzia laughed heartily while others giggled behind their hands.

'Mind your tongue,' Froma said, pulling herself to her full height. 'You cannot speak to the Duchess in such familiar tones now.'

Agata smiled. 'Thank you, Mistress Plesec. I want us to remain as friends. I have grown fond of you all over the past year. I would hate for us to part now the war is over.'

'Hear, hear,' said Gala.

'I would like us to continue our gathering. Perhaps in another form? Poor Clawa reminds us that not everyone celebrated last night. This morning I had an idea. We could help the widows and orphans. They must be looked after, given the sacrifice of their men.'

'Excellent idea,' said Froma.

'This is proper work for women,' Clawa said, dabbing at her eyes. 'We can ask the Scion. Work with the Fatherhood?'

'A Women's Circle,' Karolien said and Randvi nodded vigorously. Agata smiled through a clenched jaw. There was no escaping the Scion.

The door creaked open and a servant girl slunk over to Sira who was seated in the corner.

The Circle members rediscovered their smiles with their purpose revived. They exchanged ideas and tucked into the cakes and wine.

'I've heard rumours,' said Gala in a low voice. 'About an Allotment.'

Jadzia gasped. 'No? Now? I thought the Allotment was a fairy tale to frighten young girls.'

Agata frowned. She opened her mouth to ask Gala to explain when Sira appeared silently at her side. 'May I go to the gates for a moment, m'Lady?' she whispered in her ear. 'My sister is here to see me. The goblets are full and there are plenty of cakes. Kellma will stay in case you need anything.'

'Only for a few moments. Is something wrong?'

'Probably m'Lady,' Sira said. 'I saw that fool husband of hers in the crowd yesterday.'

'Hurry back.'

Sira nodded and slipped away. Agata bit her lip. Unlike the others, Sira was close-lipped, rarely speaking about herself and her own troubles, no matter how much Agata coaxed and probed. But over the year, she'd picked up scraps about the ne'er-do-well brother-in-law. Sira's downtrodden sister was exactly the type of woman she longed to help.

'Enter.' Lord Kalin looked up from his desk in his dim room inside the barbican.

His second in command, Seliv stepped inside, the burly man filling the doorway.

'Another one, m'Lord' Seliv said as he handed over a grubby piece of paper covered in ink blots and smudged penmanship. Lord Kalin held it between his fingers like a soiled handkerchief.

'Duke. I will tell.'

'It was in among the Seneschal's papers.'

'This is the second?'

'There could be more.' Seliv shrugged. 'I almost threw away the first one. What should we do, m'Lord?'

Kalin scrunched the paper into a ball and tossed the note into the fireplace. With a whoosh of flame, it was gone. 'Not worth bothering the Duke about.' Kalin rubbed his chin, silently watching the flames for a moment before shaking his head.

'Right, what else have we got today?'

'A pickpocket and a poacher, m'Lord.'

'How dull,' he sighed. 'Come on then. I suppose we should deal with them.'

He strode out of the door and into the dank dungeons, sword clanging at his hip. Seliv followed, struggling to keep up.

Sira's sister stood outside the iron gates, wringing her hands as the yawning guards leaned on their pikes. Rabel's dry skin stretched taut over her high cheekbones accentuated her already long reddened nose. Sira grimaced at her sister's brittle frame and sucked in her own rolls of well-fed flesh.

Rabel smiled, her eyes middle-aged before her time.

'What's wrong?' Sira frowned, her sister's bony-handed grip was like iron.

'I'm so glad you came,' Rabel said, a shake in her voice.

'The Duchess is kind but I cannot stay for long. What is the matter?'

'I'm ashamed to ask.' She bowed her head.

'Coins. What has he done this time?'

'The same as always.'

'I thought you'd paid off his debts?'

'I was so close. A few more months and it would have been gone. I didn't miss a payment. But I forgot and then Sabet came this mornin' and I had nothin'.'

Her sister's life was straight from the Teachings. '*A woman's life is filled with suffering*'. The path all women must endure. Sira sighed. 'How much do you need?'

'Thirty-three coppers.'

Sira's eyebrows jolted skyward. 'That is the payment? How much did he lose?'

'You don't want to know.' Rabel shook her head. 'Sabet is a shrewd one.'

'She makes short work of stupid men like Iwan.' Sira pursed her lips. 'What are you going to do about him?'

'I don't know,' Rabel choked. 'I don't know.'

'I am sorry.' Sira's chest tightened. 'All the coins of the Duchy went to the war. Our payments were stopped.'

Rabel nodded, tears in her eyes.

Sira lowered her voice. 'But I do have a silver hidden away. I can give it to you.'

'Thank you, sister.' A tear escaped down her face. 'I hope it's enough.'

'No tears. Please. Do you have food?'

Rabel shook her head, her eyes downcast.

'I can help with that, too. Go now. I will meet you under the Old Man Tree.'

'Thank you, but please hurry, I have to pay Sabet before the midday bells.'

The sisters embraced. Rabel's hard ribs poking through her coarse tunic. Her children were not the only ones in need of a meal.

Sira slumped inside the gates. If only she could do more. But no one listened to a Singlewoman, especially one who dared to interfere with a man and his wife. Offering food and a few coppers seemed so small and hollow and did nothing to quieten the crushing feeling that she'd failed her sister. Again.

Crossing the main bailey, she passed guards joking and arguing. Groups of men inspected wheels, braying horses and armoury stocks. The Seneschal scowled and pointed with his long-nobbled finger before scribing in his thick ledger. A boy up a ladder poked at a nest in the eaves while three men bellowed instructions from below.

Sira winced. She had forgotten how noisy the world of men could be. She stepped through the kitchen door into a wall of heat. An enormous fire roared in the hearth at the far end. A kitchen girl turned hunks of roasting meat on spits while another frantically swatted away a buzzing wasp with a cloth. More girls darted from the domed baking oven to the long dented wooden tables, sweaty hair pasted against their foreheads. Sira smiled. Theirs was a life she knew well. Her time in the kitchens had started soon after her first bleeding when her Pa decided a life in service was the best Sira could expect with her stained face. His words still rang in her ears. 'Never forget, my girl. Without the Duchess's charity, you'd be back there hidden away with the rest of the Unwanted.'

Sira crossed the gleaming grey flagstones to a tiny red-headed woman who was tossing a handful of salt into an earthenware bowl big enough to bathe in. 'I need a basket of yesterday's food.'

'Given to the pigs already.' Majvi shrugged then barked at one of the scurrying kitchen girls. 'Get me the juniper.'

'You must have something,' Sira said.

'Didn't you get enough almond cakes in there with the other ladies?'

Sira rolled her eyes and Majvi winked. 'You're lucky. The men were too busy drinkin' to eat all the food last night. Let me guess. Rabel? Take some cold goat and a bit of cheese. If you're quick, you might catch Wintrud for some stale bread before she feeds the geese.'

Sira nodded. The cook tutted, giving Sira's plump arm a quick squeeze before she turned back to her pot and licked sauce from the spoon.

Rabel's trouble had begun one Sunday luncheon after midday service many years ago. Sira had been shelling peas with her Ma on her free afternoon and catching up on the babes, deaths and betrothals of the street when Pa burst in the front door, dragging Rabel by the elbow.

'Rabel,' Ma gasped, darting from her seat as Pa threw her to the floor.

'Leave her,' said Pa and Ma stopped short. 'I caught her with that fisherman. Again.'

'Rabel. You must listen to your Pa,' Ma said, shaking her head and wringing her hands. Sira sat, her mouth open, not moving or saying a word as Rabel lay face down, her brown hair strewn like a carpet on the floor, her skinny back heaving as she sobbed.

'How many times have I warned you? Yet you disobey me again and again,' Pa bellowed. 'I should've known three daughters and no sons would bring me nothin' but trouble. I saw you touchin' him like a harlot. For all of Ambrovna to see! This is the last time you disrespect me and the Father. I won't have you in my house any longer.'

'Pa,' cried Ma.

'No. Not Rabel too,' Sira said.

Rabel stopped bawling and lifted her head, her eyes round and wet.

'You heard me. I want you gone. Let him have you. You are no daughter of mine.'

Sira desperately wanted to rush in and stop the fighting but her feet were stuck to the floor. When she daydreamed of Sunday family luncheons as she peeled parsnips and scrubbed the kitchen flagstones, there were no banishments and arguments. Her family would sit together happily as the Father wanted. Sira did not move to stop her Pa. Instead, she covered her ears with her hands and stared down at the ground between her elbows.

'I love him,' Rabel said, her eyes flashing with defiance.

'See.' He pointed to Ma, his hands flying up in dismay. 'She admits it.'

'And I am with his child.'

Ma's knees buckled, her face in her hands.

Pa's cheeks blazed as he loomed over Rabel. 'After all the years I worked to clothe, feed and house you and you repay me with sin. I always knew I was cursed with three daughters. And two of them Fatherless harlots. Now I only have one.' He flung open the front door and shoved Rabel onto the street with a kick of his boot.

'Pa,' Sira said, finally finding her tongue but her voice was thin and feeble. She looked to her Ma whose eyes were glassy, her hands clutched at her chest and fat tears filled the bags under her eyes.

'Good riddance,' Pa said, slamming the door. 'I don't want to hear her name again in this house. Understood?'

Sira nodded but inside her unvoiced protests were like knives in her belly.

'Let's eat.'

Obediently, they returned to the table in silence.

Each time Rabel asked for help, Sira relived that day. If only she'd intervened as an older sister should have. If only Rabel had chosen Juok instead of Iwan. If only. But all the wishes, gifts and daydreams couldn't change the past or make amends. When it mattered, Sira had done nothing.

With a basket of kitchen leftovers on her elbow, Sira hurried inside the castle keep and up the well-worn servants' stairs to her small room adjoining the Duchess's bower on the top floor. The tiny room had two doors, one leading to the service stairs, the other into the Duchess's room. Sira thanked the Father every time she closed her door, grateful for the day she was chosen as the Duchess's personal servant. The private room was more precious than any coin. Although the Father would not wholly approve, she'd won the heart of the Duchess through her hair-braiding skills, her nimble fingers well practised from years of pastry plaiting and lace-making.

Sira lifted her straw bed, revealing the floor beneath. She prised out a loose brick and grabbed a grey-velvet pouch containing a single silver coin and a thin chain, her only remaining keepsake of her Ma.

The Duchess's bower door burst open.

'There you are--'

Sira jumped, dropping the pouch and swiftly shoving her foot over the hiding place in the floor. She plastered a smile on her face and stood as still as stone. 'M'Lady.'

'Why is this food here?' The Duchess pointed to the basket.

'I am helping out the needy. As you suggested, m'Lady,' Sira said.

'Your sister?' The Duchess folded her arms.

'Yes, m'Lady.' Sira bowed her head. 'Her children go hungry.'

'And the pouch?'

For a moment, Sira dropped her mask and grimaced. The Duchess was more observant than she realised.

'She needs coins, m'Lady. I must go to her. She's waiting for me.'

'You cannot keep helping her like this, Sira,' the Duchess said.

'What else can I do? I am the only one she can turn to. Even when my Ma and Pa were alive, there was only me. They disowned her.'

'There has to be another way.'

Sira shook her head. 'She cannot leave him. Under the old Duke, deserting wives were flogged in the town Square.'

'But he is dead. Surely we are not so barbaric these days.'

Sira half-shrugged. 'This is our way. It's what the Father teaches. Suffering.'

'And how is this fair?'

Sira sighed. 'If only he had not returned from war.' She flinched and circled her forehead. 'In the eyes of the Father. He has laid a thorny path for Rabel. This is what she must endure.'

Her mistress tilted her head. 'I could talk to Lord Kalin? If Rabel's husband is as bad as you say, he will be up to other wickedness.'

'Could you, m'Lady?' Sira sparked up, picturing the guards dragging Iwan away to the dungeon, but then she shook her head. 'She would still have to pay for his upkeep. And how long could they hold him?'

The Duchess pulled at her bottom lip, her eyes far away. 'Yes. Something more lasting.'

Sometimes Sira did not understand her mistress's Neven ways but today her words made sense. Bread and coins were not enough.

Someone needed to put an end to Rabel's troubles. Sira shuddered as an answer flitted through her mind like a dark moth. She shooed away the thought with a vow to attend today's midday service.

'May I go, m'Lady?' Sira said, edging towards the door. 'She is waiting. I will hurry back. Please do not concern yourself with my problems. The Father will provide an answer.'

Her mistress nodded with a frown and absent-mindedly waved Sira away as she exited through her bower door. Sira grabbed the pouch and basket and rushed down the servant's stairs. With each step, she circled her forehead and repeated 'in the eyes of the Father' under her breath.

CHAPTER NINE

F ROMA BUSTLED HOME, HER HEAD bubbling with ideas to help the war widows. She smirked, convinced she'd return to the castle with the finest suggestion.

A strong friendship with the Duchess would serve her very well and silence that Lady Reyna. Froma had few friends. Most women in Ambrovna were too common or too dull. The Duchess was refined and graceful but she was an outsider after all and could not claim all of Lady Reyna's airs and graces. With King Absalom settled on the throne in Sulun and the Vorosy Clan back in control, the Duchess's position was even more tenuous. And then there were the vicious rumours about her brother.

Froma clutched at her belly, the almond cake tossing inside. The best remedy was a nip of plum brandy and luckily she was already on her doorstep. Her lip curled as she spotted rust on the front door hinges. The iron gnawed by the insidious sea air.

The bell tinkled as she entered the shop and headed towards the residence at the back. She walked past bushels of white mohair, bales of dyed woven cloth, skeins of yarn and sample cloaks. Her first task was to find Irina and send her out to scrape away the rust with a wire brush.

A voice cried out from the other side of the shop.

'Mistress Plesec. There you are!' Vinko, a trader from the neighbouring port of Guelen, stood by a bushel of second-grade mohair. Danis was beside him with a tuft of fluffy white wool in his hand. 'I was disappointed you were not here to greet me when I first arrived.'

'Master Vinko. How fortunate we are to have you back.'

Vinko, his thinning hair scraped across his age-spotted head, took Froma's hand and kissed it with a slurp. Froma smiled calmly. He was one of their best customers after all.

'I was just telling your husband what an asset you are to him. And what a hard bargain you drive.' Vinko barked out a phlegmy laugh.

'The price was fair, Master Vinko.'

Vinko swatted her away with his hand. 'Will you join us? I would like to hear your opinion on this season's yield. Is it as good as last?'

Froma smirked and stepped towards the bale. 'Of course, Master Vinko. While the waft is not as thick as last year, the strength is far superior--' She glanced up and noticed her husband's tightly held jaw. She immediately closed her mouth.

'Please excuse my wife, Master Vinko,' Danis said, stepping between them. 'She has many other errands to attend to. Don't you, Wife?'

His stare was as hot as a branding iron and Froma fought the urge to narrow her eyes. Instead, she dropped her head and nodded.

'Running a home is a never-ending task. Or so my wife tells me.' Vinko laughed and his guffaws turned into coughs and splutters.

This time Danis chuckled with him and waved his hand. 'Fetch us some brandy, Wife.'

Froma forced a smile and hurried through the side door into the residence, gritting her teeth.

'Irina. Irina!' Froma threw her head scarf down on the dining table. The scrawny Irina skulked into the room. 'Yes, Mistress.'

'Brandy. Three glasses.'

Irina scuttled out the door and rushed back with three goblets and a decanter on a tray.

'Sugared plums?' Froma said, raising an eyebrow.

'Oh yes, Mistress,' Irina said, placing the tray on the table.

'You are an idiot, girl.' Froma boxed at her ears but she was already out of reach, as she rushed out towards the kitchen.

Froma's veins thumped in her neck and her belly churned. She poured herself a small dram of brandy. The liquor oozed down her throat, soothing her anger and her queasiness. She sighed.

Danis burst through the door. 'Where is this damned brandy, woman?'

'I - I...' Froma said with a gulp, goblet in hand.

'You serve yourself before you serve the men?' He strode up to her. Froma was a tall woman, but he was half a head taller, he scowled down at her and prodded her chest with his finger.

'I was--' Froma stepped back, dropping the goblet from her fingers. The silver cup struck the wooden floor and plum brandy splattered over her slippers.

'Making me look a fool in front of *my* customers? Have you been laying with Vinko while I was away?'

'Of course not,' she spluttered.

'Have you forgotten your place, woman?'

'No...' She raised her arms above her head.

The first blow knocked the hearing from her ears. She swayed from foot to foot, hot pain spreading across her head. The second blow cracked the bridge of her nose, sending waves of nausea through her whole body. The third blow pounded into her eye and she crumpled to the floor, crushing her lips together to smother her cries. But Danis was unconcerned about the eavesdroppers. This was his right as a man.

'Remember your place.' He kicked at her. She curled into a ball. 'Remember.'

'Yes,' she croaked.

'Irina,' he bellowed.

Froma covered her head with her arms, hiding her bleeding face.

Irina's footsteps were cautious.

'Never mind her. Come and serve the brandy.'

'Yes, sir,' Irina said with a wobble in her voice and the door to the shop slammed closed.

From the floor, Froma listened to their laughter through the wall, and all alone, she finally allowed herself to shed a silent tear.

CHAPTER TEN

THE SUN WAS ALMOST OVERHEAD as Rabel hurried for the Seaweed Arms in the Alleys. The midday bells would peal any moment. With the basket on her arm and the coin pouch and Ma's necklace bouncing in her pocket, she picked up her pace. Rabel gnawed at her lip. Was it enough to satisfy Sabet?

She crossed the cobbled Square and passed the grand merchant shop fronts to the narrower streets of the craftsmen. The weavers, the carpenters and rope makers had resumed trade after their year at war. She passed a familiar shopfront, the place where her Pa had twisted hemp for a living and earned the coins for the ill-fated necklace in her pocket.

At the metal workshop, she turned right and stepped into the heart of the Alleys. Buildings loomed high on all sides, blocking the sunlight. Strangers bumped shoulders in the cramped pathways. The ground was slick with filth. Makeshift stalls sold stolen goods and various other sins while shadowy figures stood just out of sight.

Rabel ignored the jeers and touts and elbowed her way through the maze until she spied the hand-painted sign: an octopus made of green seaweed. Rabel paused by the open door. She'd never been inside the Seaweed Arms before. The windows of the crumbling red-brick alehouse were half-boarded up with mismatching planks of wood and bent nails. Apart from Sabet or the wretches of Guts Alley, this was not a place for women.

Rabel stepped inside, her eyes watering at the stink of the sour spilt ale, dirty feet and fish. She swallowed and peered into the dim room, which was lined with long empty wooden benches. A toothless woman tended the well-worn bar, where a few wrinkled men sat hunched over their tankards, drinking alone. Three men in fishermen's tunics threw dice in the corner while a mangy cat chewed angrily at his fleas in the centre of the room.

But Sabet was nowhere to be seen.

'What do you want?' scowled the toothless bar maid, her voice strangely girlish. 'No peddlers in here.'

'I'm lookin' for Sabet?'

'Not here.'

Rabel sighed. 'She told me to meet her here.'

'You just missed her. She was in her spot there by the fire. She left with some man. And her son.'

'Do you know when she'll be back?'

The woman shrugged and turned away to the next person at the bar. 'Another, Ansi?'

The pouch weighed heavy in Rabel's pocket but she couldn't trust anyone with the payment.

'Rabel. Long time, no see. You looking for Iwan?' It was Mirn, a mono-browed oyster diver, a man she and Iwan had known a lifetime ago when Iwan still worked on the boats.

'No,' she said, with narrowed eyes.

'He's here somewhere. I saw him a minute ago.'

Another gap-toothed fisherman at the bar shook his head. 'He went off with Sabet.'

Rabel grabbed her basket and sprinted as fast as she could towards her shack.

The solar door creaked open. Agata straightened, placed her book down and smoothed her skirts with an expectant smile.

'Oh excuse me, m'Lady.'

Agata slumped as the Duke's manservant Wladek entered the room.

'I thought the room was empty,' he said.

'Where is your Master?' Agata asked.

'Did you not see him at breakfast, m'Lady?' Wladek said, a sneer flickering over his lips.

'I have not seen him all morning,' she said as haughtily as she could but the words stung as she said them aloud.

'He left early with Lord Kalin to attend to some pressing business.'

'What business?'

'He did not confide in me, m'Lady,' he replied with a deferential bow. His hooded eyes reminded her of the geckos in her home region. She thought the winters in Ambrovna were too cold for these creatures.

'If he has returned, he may be in his Cabinet rooms,' Wladek offered.

'Alone?'

'I do not know, m'Lady. If you'll excuse me, there are many things to be done to return the castle to normal.'

Agata waved him away, frowning as he closed the hefty door.

Two days ago, she had been the ruler of the Duchy. Now she had to resort to pleading with a valet for news of her husband. Where was he? Why had he avoided her all morning? A year was a long time for a man to be alone and the palace of Sulun was renowned for its bewitching courtesans. Had he found another love in the capital? Under the new King, a wife from the Neven Clan was an embarrassment and a burden and without her brother and father to protect her interests, she could be easily tossed aside.

As she headed upstairs, the midday service bells pealed. Midday was the time when the Father, the Sun, was at his zenith and his power was strongest. All the pious townspeople would be heading to the Temple. Agata avoided services when she could; she could not bear to hear the Scion's talk of women being unclean, unstable, untrustworthy, merely vessels for carrying life. In the lands of the Neven, the women's soil was sacred. How could words from the very same Teachings be twisted in such different ways? Agata sighed again.

As she approached the Duke's Cabinet rooms, the pock-faced guard at the door straightened and reached for the door handle. She raised her hand to stop him.

'Is the Duke inside?'

'Yes, m'Lady.'

She smiled. 'Is he alone?'

'No, m'Lady.'

She pursed her lips and paused, leaning against the door and listening to the raised male voices inside. It was Kalin and the other lords. She chewed her lip. All she wanted was a few precious moments alone with him, a few words shared between a husband and a wife.

'They're a dirty lot, those Nevenish women. They need a firm hand.'

Agata flinched. Lord Egid's loud voice was clearly audible through the door. The guard fidgeted beside her. She paused, waiting for the Duke to speak up in her defence. How could he allow his men to insult his own wife?

But there was only laughter in response. She could even hear Lord Sylwin chuckling with them.

'And their golden skin. Very tasty.'

'If you like that sort of thing!' said Lord Jotek with his low rumble. 'I wouldn't touch them.'

'That's not what you said after the fall of Telan. I saw you in that house. Helping yourself to the spoils of war.'

'That's different. It is your right after a battle.'

Agata covered her hand with her mouth. Every maiden knew to be wary of soldiers after a battle. Warnings passed down from mothers and maids about men who forced themselves on any female in reach. The old, the young, the noble, the peasant, no one was safe. The stories struck fear and obedience into every girl's heart. But was it not just common soldiers and ruffians? Noblemen as well? Even her own husband? Did they all take part?

She shook her head.

She waited again for the Duke to put his lords in their place, but she could hear only more laughter, his voice mixed in with all the others.

A rush of bile burned her throat. She dropped her hand from the handle and hurried away to the privy.

Rabel barrelled inside the open shack door, sweat trickling between her shoulder blades and down her spine. Sabet sat at the table with Aula on her knee. It looked like an innocent scene, a family friend visiting for a cup of tea but Rabel knew better.

'Here she is,' said Iwan, a weasel-like smile on his face. He pointed at the basket. 'I hope that's luncheon.'

'I came lookin' for you,' Rabel said to Sabet.

'Is that right?' Sabet tickled Aula, the little girl squealed and giggled. 'Iwan and I've been havin' a good talk. Haven't we?'

Iwan barked out a laugh. 'Sabet's a very understandin' woman.'

Rabel's eyes darted between Iwan to Sabet, her pulse racing.

'We've struck a deal, Sabet and me. A way to clear all our debts.'

'Your debts,' Rabel said with a shake in her voice.

'She's a pretty one.' Sabet bounced Aula on her knee. 'Look at them curls.'

The little girl giggled. 'More. More.'

'No,' cried Rabel and lunged for her girl but Iwan jumped to his feet and blocked her path.

'It's the only way,' he said, holding Rabel back.

'You can't be serious.' She tried to shoved him away but Iwan grabbed her wrists and thrust her back towards the door.

Nostrils flaring, Rabel came at him again. 'Not my baby.'

Iwan threw her to the floor. Rabel rummaged inside her pocket and grabbed Sira's pouch. 'I've got your payment. You can't take her. Here.' She scuttled along the ground and thumped the pouch onto the table.

Sabet's son stepped out unexpectedly from the shadows. He tipped the contents onto the table and a single silver coin rolled out.

'Where did you get that?' Iwan said, his eyes hard. 'You said you had nothin'.'

Sabet's son tested the coin between his teeth and nodded. Rabel struggled to her feet.

'Not enough. I said thirty-three,' Sabet said with a half-shrug.

'My girl is worth eight coppers?'

'It's eight coppers you don't have. And this payment'll settle the rest of your debts. I'll leave you alone from now on. In the eyes of the Father.' Sabet circled her forehead with a grin. 'That's what we agreed.'

'No deal,' said Rabel, her eyes narrowed.

Iwan gripped her by the arm. 'Don't be stupid. You've already buried two. You've still got the boys. We can always have more.'

'No,' screamed Rabel.

Iwan slapped her across the face. Rabel stumbled backwards, a wildness in her eyes.

'You got a better idea, woman?' he said, looming over her, his spittle spattering on her face.

'Sell your own daughter? You know what they'll do with her.'

'I'm the man of the house. I make the decisions. It's a sacrifice I'm willin' to make.'

'No,' Rabel said quietly but her voice was as hard as a rock.

'Well, you can't afford the payment and so a deal has been struck.' Sabet handed Aula to her son. He held the girl with outstretched arms as though she was jumping with fleas.

'Ma. Ma.' Aula squirmed, reaching out her little arms.

Rabel thrust her hand into her pocket for her Ma's necklace. Sira claimed it was silver. Not enough to cover the whole debt but enough to keep Sabet satisfied for another week. She fumbled around inside but found nothing.

Her heart thundered as she rifled in her other pocket but it was also empty. The necklace must be lying in a puddle in the Alleys. Rabel's breaths were shallow and painful.

'Take me. Take me instead!'

Sabet's son laughed and Sabet merely smiled.

'I don't need another clapped out old boiler. I've got plenty of them already. You're worth nothin'. Not like this lovely thing.' Sabet eased herself to her feet with a groan. 'Come to Aunty Sabet, my pretty. You're goin' to make your Aunty a good purse.'

Rabel's belly curdled as she imagined sinful grubby hands touching her little girl. She spied her kitchen knife on the shelf and with shaking hands, she tried her pocket once more.

'Pleasure doin' business with you,' Sabet said to Iwan, the little girl balanced on her hip. 'Consider your debt repaid.'

She found a small hole in the corner of her pocket. With a grimace, she squeezed her eyes shut and traced the rip with her fingertip. Something cold shifted against her leg.

Metal.

She wrenched her pocket inside out. The silver chain was caught on a thread, dangling inside her skirts.

'No!' she cried out. 'Here. Take this.'

She flung the necklace at the old woman's face and shoved past Iwan, pulling Aula from Sabet's arms. The little girl wrapped her arms around her mother's neck and Rabel scuttled back into the corner of the room, panting.

Sabet pointed to the necklace and her lumbering son picked it up off the floor. He handed it over and Sabet wound the chain around her fingers, stepping towards the door and inspecting it in the light.

'Silver,' Rabel declared, her girl close to her chest.

'Low grade,' Sabet replied with a grumble.

'But is it enough?'

Sabet grunted and gestured to her son. 'Let's go. I'm wastin' coins standin' around here.'

'Are the debts repaid?'

Sabet turned back with a grin. 'No. This tat isn't enough. Nowhere near as valuable as her. You want to repay the whole debt and never see me again? You hand over the child. That's the deal. This...,' she said waving the chain in the air. '...only covers payment for one week.' Sabet raised her eyebrows, waiting for an answer.

'Never,' Rabel replied.

Iwan said nothing.

'Your choice.' Sabet shrugged. 'See you next week. Another thirty-three.'

Sabet and her son left and the shack was silent.

Rabel sat on the bench, stroking Aula's hair and cooing. 'Mama is here.'

'You idiot.' Iwan thumped the table with his fist and Aula started to cry again.

'Me? What kind of father are you?'

'We could've been clear. But you've gone and ruined it. You'll have to find another thirty-three coppers next week. And the week after. And the week after that. Won't you?'

'But it's your debt.'

'I found a way to repay, but you didn't like it. It's your debt now.'

'A father's supposed to protect his children.'

'Like yours did?' Iwan snorted. 'It's goin' to take years before we can make any money out of her. And only if she keeps her looks. Not like you.'

Rabel calmly reached back, her fingers wrapping around the handle of her kitchen knife.

'Go on,' Iwan said with a sneer, tapping on his breastbone. 'Right here. Come on.'

Rabel narrowed her eyes. She tightened her grip and her jaw, but she couldn't move.

'You haven't got the guts.' He scoffed. 'I'm goin' out.'

As the door slammed, Rabel bowed her head, releasing the knife. With trembling hands, she smoothed Aula's hair.

'They're not goin' to take you. I won't let them. Ever.'

Rabel's heart burned as she imagined the pain Aula would have suffered. She pushed aside the memories of her own childhood shame. She'd been able to protect her girl. This time.

Aula cuddled against Rabel's chest and pulled at her loose curls.

One day back from war and Iwan had gambled away all their coins and bartered his own children.

She never imagined he'd come back worse.

This couldn't go on. Something had to change.

CHAPTER ELEVEN

AGATA THREADED HER FINGERS THROUGH her braids, her head whirling. Her brother's head on a spike. The Scion's smirk. The nobles' coarse laughter. Her husband walking away from her bedchamber last night. A single phrase rang in her ears, the voice of her long-gone mother. 'Don't be like me.'

She collapsed on the bench, her body limp and boneless. Two days ago, she could have helped Sira and her sister but now she was as powerless as they were. Like the tapestry with the Ambrovna eel sigil on the wall, she was a chattel of the Duchy but of lesser value.

Burying her face in the cushions, she screamed long and hard until her voice was hoarse and every last wisp of breath left her lungs. How could she have been so foolish? So weak? Why had she imagined her life would be different now?

Agata remembered her eighth summer when she roamed freely on her father's lands. Her father's manor house sat in wild flower strewn meadows filled with piebald cows and buzzing bees, a morning's ride from the nearest township. The sun had shone more in Tramissa than it ever did in Ambrovna. The estate farmed oranges, almonds and olives, and manicured rows of grape vines snaked into the hills.

Her father was often in Sulun at court, her brothers had no patience for a little girl and her mother spent most of her days in a dark room, complaining of headaches and chills. Agata did as she pleased until two events occurred. The first was the arrival of a governess.

Agata had been under the shade of the oak trees with the farm dog's golden puppies and the cook's daughter when the wagon rumbled up the path to the house. Agata had run to meet her new governess, her cheeks flushed, her hair loose and the runt of the litter in her arms.

A hard-faced woman in a cream shift and matching headscarf had stepped down from the wagon, her face puckered as though she disapproved of the country air.

'Agata. This is Madame Fidan,' her mother. 'She is here from Sulun. You are very lucky to have her. She has taught all the best families at court. Even the Duchess Birit herself.'

'Good morning,' Agata said with her best manners while the puppy licked her face. Madame Fidan turned her scrutinising glare to Agata and raised a dark eyebrow. 'Good morning, *Madame Fidan*?'

Agata shifted her weight from foot to foot. 'Good morning, Madame Fidan.'

'Good morning, young lady. And where are your shoes?'

'Shoes?' She looked down at her naked feet.

'It is not proper for a lady to have such dirty feet.'

'But...'

'Or to talk back.'

'Madame Fidan is here to teach you how to be a lady,' her mother said, her breath rattling in her chest. These were the days before the physician found her mother's illness. 'You want to be a lady?'

Agata shrugged, unsure what being a lady actually entailed.

'Of course you do,' said Madame Fidan with a tut. 'And even if you do not, you are from the house of Ulvos. One of the oldest noble families of the Neven Clan. It is your duty.'

Whenever anyone mentioned duty, it sounded dull.

'Please show me to my chamber, Lady Ulvos. I will quickly get settled and then we shall begin our lessons immediately. I seem to have a great deal of work to do.' She peered down her nose. 'Now Lady Agata, put that dog down this instant. Dogs are riddled with fleas.'

Agata stroked the puppy's head then put the dog down. She glanced at the bottoms of her blackened feet. The feeling of the wet grass and cool mud between her toes were so much nicer than the hard leather of her boots.

As they walked inside, the newcomer inspected every inch of the manor's panelled Great Hall, with an ever-present sneer. Agata, loitering behind them, stayed within earshot.

'You allow her to associate with the servant children?' Madame Fidan said. 'We must stop her running about like a peasant girl.'

Agata's mother wheezed. 'I know. I have not had the strength. She is a good girl, though. Kind and clever.'

'Never mind. I am here now. You do not need to worry.'

'You will be teaching her the sciences and numbers? The Earl agreed.' Agata's mother stopped to lean against the wall, her hand at her forehead, her golden skin ashen. 'I want Agata to learn the things I did not.'

Madame Fidan pursed her lips. 'We shall start with the basics.'

Within the hour, Madame Fidan had given her a vigorous scrubbing with a rough cloth and dressed her in uncomfortable shoes and an ankle length tunic. The day had been golden and glorious outside the window, with birds trilling and insects humming but Agata was stuck inside the cold dark Hall while Madame Fidan prodded and corrected.

'Sit up straight.'

'Look at your fingernails.'

'Young ladies do not yawn openly.'

'Stop staring out the window.'

The lessons stretched for hours and hours and Agata wriggled in her hard chair. She snuck longing looks outside as the sun began to dip and grey clouds rolled in from the North.

'That is sufficient for today.'

Agata sprang to her feet, but rather than heading upstairs to the solar, she headed out to the kitchens to find Yeta scrubbing turnips. The two girls scampered out into the early evening behind Yeta's mother's back.

'She is horrible,' Agata said. 'She says all these silly things. Rule after rule. I never want to go back.'

Yeta nodded.

'If only Father was here. He would stop Madame Fidan. Do you think there will be any raspberries left?'

The girls picked up speed, running over the fields and past the lake towards the orchards where wild raspberries grew between the trees. They'd reached the orange grove with their branches sagging with fruit, when the first drops of rain splashed onto the dirt. Only then did they notice the darkness of the sky, the clouds veiling the remaining daylight.

A crack of thunder echoed down the valley and rattled the ground. Rain pelt down, heavy drops hit the ground like stones.

'Let's go back,' said Yeta. 'We'll get in trouble.'

They gazed back towards the manor. They'd run so far.

'We can wait out the storm under the trees,' said Agata.

Yeta shook her head. 'It's not safe.'

A slash of white lightning pierced the dark sky and struck a nearby hill. The air bristled with energy. Agata's eyes widened and Yeta grabbed her arm. A second thunderclap boomed across the sky. Rain trickled down their faces between the leaves, soaking their hair and dresses, the wet cold cloth sticking to their skin.

More lightning sliced the sky. White light struck a nearby orange tree with a sizzle. Agata's heartbeat thumped in her ears and her knees trembled. Hard rain slapped against the leaves.

'Run!' yelled Yeta.

Agata did not hear the branch break but she felt the pain.

When she woke up, the rain still lashed against the glass but she was tucked up under her own eiderdown. Her head throbbed. She slipped a finger under the wet cloth draped over her head and felt the lump on the side of her head.

'Oh my little--' Her mother wrung her hands.

'You silly child,' Madame Fidan interrupted. 'You could have been killed.'

'You have been very foolish,' said a deep familiar voice.

'Father.' Agata smiled as he had lain his large warm hand on her shoulder.

'The men searched all night for you.' His brow furrowed, his face dark with concern. 'You were hit by a tree.'

'Yeta?' Agata said.

'The servant girl? She ran away, coward,' said Madame Fidan. 'But we caught her. She will be punished. Severely.'

'It wasn't her fault. It was me,' Agata said, barely louder than a murmur, her head aching with every word.

'Listen to the way Lady Agata speaks, my Lord.' Madame Fidan continued. 'Like a peasant. The servant girl has had too much influence. We must make an example of the child. Abandoning your daughter this way.'

Agata's father nodded.

'But--' Agata tried to sit up but the room whirled.

Her father breathed out through clenched teeth. 'Daughter. You frightened us all. I see now I have been too lenient with you. Your childish ways must stop. You are a lady of the house of Ulvos and you must behave as such. Your poor mother...you know how fragile she is.'

'It wasn't Yeta's fault,' Agata said over and over, too tired to hold her head off the pillow.

'She will be punished in the morning,' her father said.

'May I suggest that Agata is present?' said Madame Fidan.

'No,' said her mother firmly.

'The child must see actions have consequences,' Madame Fidan said.

'My Lord?' her mother said as she grabbed his forearm, her eyes wide. 'She is only a child.'

Her father pressed his lips together hard, then nodded. 'You tried, dear wife but you are weak. We have been neglectful in our duties. Agata must learn the truth about the world and her place in it. The sooner the better.'

'But husband--' her mother said.

'I will hear nothing more.' Her father had left the room. Madame Fidan followed him, leaving Agata and her mother alone.

'I am sorry,' her mother said through her tears. 'If only I was stronger.'

Agata closed her eyes, trying to hold back the throbbing in her head.

'When the Father finally blessed us with a daughter, I was filled with so much light and hope, I thought I would burst. I told myself you would not be like me. You would be courageous and loyal and strong. My Agata would speak her mind and make them listen. But I was naive. History is repeating as I feared. Please. If you only do one thing for me... do not be like me. Please.'

Agata had not understood then but those five words had rung in her ears. 'Do not be like me.'

The next morning, the sky had cleared. Madame Fidan summoned Agata from her bed and marched her to the courtyard behind the kitchens where the chickens ran free pecking grubs in the dirt.

In the centre of the courtyard, Yeta stood stripped naked to the waist. Two farm labourers held back her scrawny arms as a third man flicked a birch rod. The thin wood snapped and cracked as it flexed. Agata's father stood by the house, his face stern. Her mother was nowhere to be seen.

'No,' cried Agata, surging forward. Madame Fidan grabbed her by the shoulders and held her back.

'Yeta must learn her place,' Agata's father said. 'She should not have led the lady of the estate out into the fields and left her injured in a storm.'

'She didn't!' Agata screeched. 'Father, it was me.'

'Quiet,' said Madame Fidan.

'Ten strikes, Brno.'

'Yes, m'Lord.'

Agata froze, unsure what to do.

Time slowed down as the muscular man hoisted the switch over his head. The birch hummed as it travelled through the air and slapping hard against Yeta's bare back.

Yeta's first howl was a sound Agata would never forget. Her friend's scream scraped up her spine, shredded her skin and rattled her brain. Agata covered her eyes but Madame Fidan tore her hands away.

'You cannot look away,' she hissed. 'This is your fault.'

Agata saw Yeta's ripped flesh and the streams of blood trickling down her back. She collapsed to the dirt screeching. Madame Fidan left her this time, and with eyes firmly shut, Agata did not see the continued punishment but heard every birch strike and scream that followed.

Agata never spoke to Yeta again. She could never meet her eyes, the weight of her cowardice too great. She had learned a lesson that day. No one would listen no matter how she screamed.

Leaving the cushioned bench, Agata struggled to her feet and wiped away her tears old and new. 'I am exactly like my mother.' She stared at the luncheon spread on the table, her appetite gone. An insect rested on the edge of the jam pot and an idea lit up her mind.

She shooed away the wasp and traced her bottom lip with her thumb, her eyes brightening as she rolled the notion around in her head. She was no longer a child. Did she want a life of silence and cowering in regret? But thoughts without action were meaningless. Could she be like Queen Magnilla and be the courageous woman her mother hoped she'd be? Defiance invited serious consequences.

CHAPTER TWELVE

S IRA COMPLETED HER CHORES IN a daze. She darned
hose, mended slippers and polished the Duchess's jewellery, all
the while wondering whether the necklace and silver had satisfied
Sabet. Fairness was not a trait shared by debt collectors. As the shadows
spread and there was no news from the Alleys, she headed down to the
laundry to collect the Duchess's Spawning Festival gown.

The wooden laundry shack, which sat on the edge of the castle bailey,
backed onto the high craggy red cliffs alongside the kitchens and the buttery.
White steam and cackles of laughter spewed from the open door. Sira smiled
a little as she approached, wondering who was the victim of the day.

Hot white clouds enveloped her as she stepped inside. A pink-
cheeked laundress with a large mole on her chin looked up from a
steaming vat. 'Ah, perhaps Sira can tell us.'

Sira frowned. After all these years, Gitthe and the others should
know better than to expect castle gossip from her. Secrets were hard to
keep from the women who washed the town's sheets.

'Is the Duchess's gown ready, Gitthe?'

'We've just heard about Rabel,' another laundress said, pummelling
with her flabby arms. 'Terrible.'

Sira's stomach dropped.

'That Sabet's a real piece of work.'

If Gitthe knew, then the whole town would know her sister's woes.
Sira rubbed the back of her neck.

'What a monster.' Gitthe shook her head.

'What kind of person does that? Their own little one?' The fat laundress slapped her paddle against a bundle of wet cloth.

Sira frowned, glancing from face to face.

'She doesn't know,' the fat woman said with a grimace.

Gitthe placed a moist hand on Sira's shoulder. 'He tried to sell their little girl to Sabet. Rabel got home just in time. There was all kinds of screamin' going on. Half the Alleys heard it.'

Sira bunched her fists, tighter and tighter as Gitthe's words seeped in. Her heartbeat thundered, drowning out their voices and the foggy room spun.

'Sorry to share the bad news,' Gitthe said, straining a smile.

'No. Thank you,' Sira said, her voice distant. 'But she stopped him?'

'That's what we heard.' Gitthe shrugged. 'Somehow.'

'Good,' Sira said through clenched teeth.

Gitthe carefully handed over the smoothed-out gown and Sira farewelled the laundresses but her walk back to the castle keep was a blur. She was in the Duchess's bower before she realised.

She laid the dress on the Duchess's bed and sat on the coverlet embroidered with eels, her head pounding. She should've been there. She should've stopped him. Her jaw ached as her head whirled with thoughts of how she could have fought off Iwan and Sabet. If only she'd been there.

Sira slumped. What could she really have done? When Rabel defied their Pa, she made a choice. She set a path for herself and she must follow it. Sira wished the eel on the coverlet would spring to life and swallow her up.

The wooden door scraped open and Sira jumped to her feet, wiping her nose without looking up. She turned and laid out the laundered gown, smoothing the terracotta silk and inspecting for leftover stains.

'My gown,' the Duchess sighed, her eyes puffy. She stood at Sira's side and glanced over at her.

Sira averted her eyes.

'I see I am not the only one with heavy thoughts. Tell me, Sira. What is troubling you?'

'I'm only tired, m'Lady,' Sira said, plastering on her obedient smile. 'I tossed and turned during the night.'

The Duchess grabbed Sira by the shoulders. 'What has happened?' Her dainty hands were stronger than they appeared. 'Do not lie to me. Please. I could not bear it.'

Sira winced. She'd lived her life in the shadowy corners of the room. People diverted their eyes from her stained face, their initial curiosity quickly replaced by disgust. Such close scrutiny made Sira's knees tremble.

'I should not burden you with my problems, m'Lady.'

The Duchess released her fingers. 'I am a good listener.'

She patted the coverlet and sat. Sira followed, perching on the precipice of the bed, wringing her hands.

'Tell me, Sira. If you will not tell me willingly, I will have to order you.'

Sira swallowed, her throat clogged with years of unsaid words.

'I failed Rabel. Again, I failed her. I could not protect her back then and I cannot protect her now. What kind of sister am I?'

'What has happened?'

'Iwan tried to sell their daughter. To pay off his debts.'

'Ogre!' the Duchess gasped, her hand flying to her chest. 'But she stopped him?'

'I believe so. I only know what the laundresses told me. That poor little thing...'

'He cannot be allowed to get away with this.' The Duchess's eyes were narrow and tight, her hand skimmed over her stomach. 'His own children.'

'What can Rabel do, m'Lady?' Sira slumped. 'She cannot leave him. This is her fate.'

'To live with a monster?'

'I should have stopped her...before--'

'It is not your fault. Or her fault. He is the one to blame.'

'She chose a thorny path,' Sira sighed.

The Duchess rose to her feet and paced the length of the room. 'How can they be permitted to act as they please while we are treated no better than goats?'

Sira wrung her hands. 'We women are destined to suffer. This is what the Scion teaches. Our rewards will come in the Land Beyond the Sunset. If the Father allows us in--'

'Ah yes, the all-seeing Protector? Ha. Where was he when Rabel needed his protection?' Spit flew from the Duchess's mouth as her

Nevenish accent thickened. 'What kind of loving Father allows such injustice?'

Sira covered her mouth and traced the eye of the Father on her forehead. The Duchess flinched as she realised what she'd said aloud. She spun around, looking out for eavesdroppers.

'There is no other way, m'Lady.'

'There are always ways,' Agata said firmly.

Sira looked askance at her mistress, goose bumps prickling up her spine.

'I have been thinking.'

Sira's chest tightened. She'd had her share of terrible fancies, thoughts a pious woman should never have, let alone admit to her mistress.

'In Tramissa, there are women. With special knowledge. Who do not play by the rules of the Father. Who would know how to take care of this problem. Permanently.'

'Wasp Women?' Sira breathed, her eyes widening.

The Duchess nodded, lowering her voice to a whisper. 'Some people use this unkind name. The stories are untrue, they are good women. Wise. The Scion and the Fatherhood have muddied people's minds. When my own mother was ill and the physicians could not help, she called a woman down from the mountain. A woman who eased her pain. My mother smiled again in her last few days. We never told my father. He would not have understood.'

'Wisia,' Sira said, her voice drifting away. 'But it's been a very long time.'

The Duchess brightened. 'You know one? Here in Ambrovna? Will she help us?'

'Many years have passed.' Sira shrugged. 'I have to find her first.'

'They know ways. Forgotten secrets.'

Sira nodded, slowly at first, her nods picking up pace as she allowed a real smile to cross her lips. 'This is a way to make amends.'

'And I will help.'

The Duchess reached out but Sira slipped her hand away and shook her head. 'No, m'Lady. Please. This is my problem. It is best you play no part. You have already done enough and you have more to lose than I do. No one cares about an ugly Singlewoman like me.'

'We are not so different. You and I,' the Duchess laughed but her eyes were sad. 'I am just the bigger fool. This is one way I can help.'

'No, m'Lady.' Sira's voice was low, unexpectedly steely.

The Duchess scraped her fingers down her cheeks and neck. 'But I cannot stand going back to being so useless.'

Sira pressed her lips together. She had her own troubles without taking on the added burden of her mistress. She straightened her spine. 'I am thankful, m'Lady. I will be forever thankful but I must go alone.'

The Duchess sighed and patted Sira's hand. 'I understand. But come to me if you need anything. This will be our secret. No one else shall know.'

Sira nodded and closed her mouth. There was one person who already knew everything.

The Father.

A sin in thought is as true as words and deeds.

An icy chill slid down her spine. No matter what Sira did next, whether she found the Wasp Woman or forgot the whole scheme, the sin was there and she would be forever damned in his eyes.

CHAPTER THIRTEEN

O N WINTER NIGHTS DURING THE war, when the castle was half-empty and long dark evenings stretched forever, Agata had sat in her husband's chair in his Cabinet room. At first, she'd felt unsettled, all alone in the room where Nyvard men had ruled over Ambrovna ever since the sun first rose. On some nights when her mind whirred with troubles, she had hoped the Duke's fading scent and the ghosts of his ancestors would provide guidance.

Behind his desk stood rows of books, leather-bound with crinkled pages and richly-inked illustrations; *The Chronicles of the Five River Clans*, *The Teachings of the Father* and *The History of Ambrovna*. These books were a far cry from the safe romantic poetry ladies were permitted to read.

With no one to disapprove, Agata devoured every volume, soaked up their knowledge with her evening meals, and before spring had blossomed, she'd read them all.

On one particularly cold night she searched through the shelves again, hoping to find an overlooked volume and an excuse to stay away from the solar and embroidery with Sira.

She ran her fingers along the spines until she noticed something new. A slim red volume, a quarter the size of the other books with no inscription on the spine, was squashed into the corner of the top shelf. Agata grabbed the book and opened to the first page. The words were scratchy, hurried, unlike the precise calligraphy of the history books. Was this a personal diary? Her stomach flipped as she read the first line.

'*The Tale of Magnilla: The Heretic and Warrior Queen of the Akull.*'

Agata's eyes had widened. She poured herself another goblet of wine, drew her knees up against her chest and read:

Herein lies the account of my travels to the Akull lands, the faraway lands of the Fifth River Clan. As a Cousin, I was sent to spread the word of the Father in the North. My name before I took my oath was Japer and I grew up in a small village in Nithese in the lands of the Neven. All through my childhood I had heard fireside tales of the fierce Akull Clansmen. Forged strong by the ice and wind of their homeland, their hair was said to be long and white, their cheekbones high, their eyes like the almonds in our trees but as colourless as mountain streams. I knew of their viciousness but until I visited their lands for myself, and met their queen, I had never heard a word spoken about their women.

I will never forget the queen, not in all my time here in this realm nor when the Father takes me to the Land Beyond the Sunset. I spent a mere three days in her hospitality, a time so strange, so confusing, so otherworldly, it compelled me to write this account in order to try to make sense of my experience. When I returned, no one would listen. They claimed me a liar, said the snows had sent me mad and I was bewitched by barbarians. This is my attempt to record the truth for my own sanity. It is the story of a woman playing the role of a man, but she was nothing like a man. She was something else entirely.

PART TWO

THE PLAN

CHAPTER FOURTEEN

I N THE WEAK LIGHT OF a cheap spluttering candle, Rabel
patched Teo's threadbare tunic. Her three babes slept the sound
sleep of the young while a mouse scurried over the floor, looking
for crumbs.

Rabel stabbed her finger with the needle and flinched, her mind a
thousand miles from her stitches.

A gentle knock sounded on the shack door and her pulse quickened.
Good news was rare at this hour. Whoever it was knocked once more
and she groaned to her feet, inching the door open a crack.

'Sira? What are you doin' here?' she whispered as she opened the
door. 'It's not safe this time of night.' Word of her run-in with Sabet
must have reached the castle. The shack walls were too thin for secrets.

'We must talk.' Sira rushed inside, her cheeks flushed almost the
same shade as her birth blemish. 'Where is he?'

'Out.' Rabel placed her finger to her dry lips. 'They're sleepin'.'

'Where can we go?'

Rabel flung her shawl over her head and shoulders and beckoned
to a loose wall panel at the back of the shack. She led her sister into
the stables next door. The horses fussed and brayed as she unlatched
the lock and the sisters snuck inside but they quickly returned to their
hay. Rabel and Sira found a stall with a placid dappled grey mare and
huddled inside.

'I was goin' to come and tell you, but--' Rabel sighed.

'Never mind, are you alright?'

Rabel shrugged. 'Aula's fine. That's all that matters.'

'We must do something,' Sira said, an unfamiliar zeal in her eyes. 'I have been speaking with...we, I have an idea, an answer to your problem.'

'My problem?' Rabel spluttered.

'A way to make it go away.'

Rabel's heart quickened. 'What do you mean?'

A grin lit up her sister's round face. 'Wisia.'

Rabel's eyes widened. 'But she...no.'

Sira nodded. 'She has the knowledge we need. She'll know a way to fix everything. I can find her.'

'It's been so long ...' Rabel shook her head. 'No. It's not right.'

'And what he did is right?' Sira hissed.

Rabel was slack-jawed, her eyes downcast. She avoided her sister's gaze. 'You know the punishment.'

Sira gripped Rabel's hand. 'What choice do we have? Think of your children. Who knows what he will do tomorrow? You cannot watch them every moment.'

Rabel rubbed her neck as Sira's words tumbled around her head. Was this an answer to her prayers? But how desperately did she want it? How far was she willing to go? Something must be done but not this. Not this way. Iwan was her husband no matter what. She shuddered, imagining the Father eavesdropping on her thoughts. But what about Teo, Aula and Jorn? Could she? Should she?

Rabel grimaced. 'I don't--'

Sira grabbed her elbow. 'I can help you. I will do whatever you want.' She sighed. 'If only I had been here.'

'You couldn't have stopped him.' Rabel shook her head.

'But I can help now. You're right, we must be careful. But think about it. Please. '

Rabel gazed at her sister, her mouth dry, her eyes unfocussed.

'It is late. I must get back to the castle,' Sira said, squeezing Rabel's arm. 'It was only an idea. But in the end, this is your decision.'

Rabel blinked. 'No,' she replied, firmly but quietly. A wave of queasiness rushing over her as the words left her mouth. 'It's wrong.'

'I understand.' Sira smiled bitterly. 'This is your family. I only wanted to help if I could.'

'Thank you. You are a good sister. But--'

'Send word if you need me. There is much to do tomorrow with the Duchess's and her women's circle in the morning and preparations for the Spawning Festival. If you change your mind...'

Rabel led her sister out of the stables, back through the shack and into the muddy alley. They embraced.

'Remember, if you need me,' Sira whispered, then she disappeared into the shadows.

Rabel slumped against the closed door and sucked in a shaky breath. She'd made the right choice. She must be strong, find compassion and love for her husband, the way the Father taught a wife should be. She traced a circle on her forehead. She deserved this path.

Rabel closed her eyes. Once she'd been happy, as she stood on the jetty, holding her Pa's rough rope maker's hand and watching white-sailed boats rolling out into the open sea. That was the last time she remembered feeling as free and light as the careening gulls in the sky.

Her Pa had not believed in schooling for girls, except for the Teachings at the Temple. But the solemn words of the Father confused the young Rabel. '*A woman's body is sinful. A woman's thoughts, words and actions must be as pure as the sun. She must think of her family, her Father and serving her men first. A woman shall not question her husband or her father as they are the representatives of the Father on this soil. There is a place in the Land of Eternal Darkness for the unclean who do not abide by these rules.*'

Until one day a new Cousin arrived, his eyes as green as seaweed and his smile as warm as the sun. When he started taking the Children's Service, Rabel looked especially forward to these Second Day afternoons.

'Is it Second Day yet?' she would ask her Ma and her Ma would pat her hair.

'You are a good girl. You love the Father, don't you?'

'I want to be a Cousin.' She'd nod.

'Silly girl. Women can't be Cousins. You'll find yourself a good husband and serve him well, givin' him lots of sons,' she said. 'Not like me.'

Rabel would screw up her face. 'Why can't I be a Cousin?'

'You just can't,' Ma would reply then asked her to help with the chickens or the mending or the peas.

Rabel had not believed her Ma. She decided she could become a Cousin, if she tried hard enough.

She determined to wait and talk with the Cousin with the sea green eyes after the next Second Day Service. He would understand.

Her heart thundered as she approached the altar with the twinkling little lights and the Cousin in his bronze-coloured dress. The Temple was so big and white, she could feel the Father's love coming down from the ceiling. She waited for all the boys to leave. The girls sat at the back of the room and had to wait until every last boy was gone before they could go. She'd practised her speech all day but when the moment came, her words tumbled out clumsily.

'I want to be like you.'

She was dazzled when the Cousin smiled. Her mind went blank.

'Your name is Rabel?'

She nodded, her nerves clogging up her mouth.

'And you love the Father?'

She nodded even harder.

'This is good. The Father needs as many good-hearted followers as possible in the world. The more good in the world, the more love. Do you understand?'

Rabel nodded again, but not quite understanding.

'The Father is grateful for your commitment. There is a role for you with the Father. Not as a Cousin. But I have something. Something special you can help with. Would you like to help the Father?'

Special. No one ever had said she was special. Rabel beamed and nodded vigorously.

'Your father is the rope maker?'

'Yes.'

'A very pious man. A credit to the Father. But you cannot tell him. This is a secret between you and me and the Father. Do you understand?'

A secret sounded exciting and keeping secrets from her Pa sounded even more fun. But weren't secrets a sin? Rabel weighed it up in her head. If a Cousin suggested it, it must be good and pious. The Cousin laid his hand on her shoulder. She looked up at him, her heart thumping.

'Have you taken confession before?'

She nodded. She stole an apple from the orchard and Pa made her take confession. He paraded her through the streets with her hands tied behind her back, calling out 'Thief' and marching her right to the Temple doors.

'First we must take confession.'

Rabel nodded and shrugged.

'I will see you in a moment.'

She smiled and hurried off, opening the door into the small dark room and closing the door behind her. It smelled of dust and tobacco, like old men. She sat on the seat and wondered what the surprise was. She hoped it was sugared plums.

When the Cousin entered, Rabel had been confused. This must have been a different type of confession. Last time, the Cousin had not come into the same small room with her.

'Remember this is our secret,' the Cousin had said. 'In the eyes of the Father.'

'In the eyes of the Father,' she repeated. She did not understand what happened next.

Rabel had kept her silence but when Second Day came the next week, she tried to hide in the chicken shed. Pa had dragged her to the town Square. She had entered the Temple and hidden right at the back.

'A woman's sin can infect a man,' the green-eyed Cousin had said. 'She must be pure not to entice him.' The boys in the front giggled and elbowed each other.

As soon as the Cousin finished speaking, Rabel scrambled to her feet and ran home. She spent the rest of the week looking for an excuse not to attend again.

She pretended to be sick the following week, and Ma fed her eel oil. The foul tasting of the oil was better than having to see the Cousin again. She wrapped herself up in her blanket and stared at the ceiling, pleased with herself. After a few hours, she went back out to the kitchen for dinner, only to find the Cousin sitting at the table with her Pa.

'Say hello to the Cousin, Rabel,' Pa said.

'You look much better,' said Ma.

But she did not feel better. Not now.

'Hello,' she said, her head bowed.

'Say it properly. What's got into you?' her Pa said with a grumble. 'She is usually a very good girl.'

'I know,' said the Cousin with his white smile. 'We missed you today at the Children's Service.'

'Hear that, Ma,' Pa said, his chest puffed while Ma nodded and beamed.

'Your Pa was telling me all about your chickens and how you like to look after them,' the Cousin said.

'Show the Cousin your chickens,' said Pa. 'If you'll excuse me, I have one last order for the day.'

'A man's work is never done. I understand,' the Cousin said. 'Rabel can show me around, can't you?'

Rabel screwed up her face, trying to squeeze the tears back into her eyes.

'What's wrong, girl?' Her Pa said. 'Go.'

Rabel dragged herself to her feet and the Cousin followed her out into the shed. She pointed out her favourite red hen with a lacklustre shake of her wrist.

'I am pleased you have kept our secret,' the Cousin whispered. 'The Father is pleased too. He does not look kindly on those who break their promises.'

Rabel whimpered as the Cousin closed the door of the chicken shed.

CHAPTER FIFTEEN

THE SHARP BLADE PRESSED AGAINST the Duke's throat.

'I know all about you,' the wiry man sneered.

'No. No,' the Duke pleaded.

'I'll tell 'em all. Your friends. Your subjects. Your wife.'

'What do you want? I will give you anything. You know I have wealth.'

'You'll be the laughin' stock.'

'Anything,' the Duke choked.

'Pathetic,' said the man. The knife pierced through his skin with a pop, slicing at the cords of his neck.

'My Lord. My Lord,' said a different male voice as a hand gently shook his shoulder.

The Duke gasped awake, his hair plastered against his forehead.

'Bad dream, my Lord?' Wladek said, a candlestick in his hand.

The Duke blinked as his eyes adjusted.

'Nightmares are no surprise after war. The things we saw.... I'll get you a mug of warm milk, your Lordship. My mother always fed us milk when we had troubling dreams.'

The Duke said nothing as his valet slipped away. His nightmares could not be blamed on the bloody battlefield.

Wiping away his sweat, he took deep breaths and calmed his galloping heart. Luckily, he was alone in his own bedchamber and his ramblings had not woken Agata. He pushed himself upright, staring out across the bed into the dark room. There was a man who knew his secret and he was here somewhere in Ambrovna.

The Duke chewed at his torn fingernails. He sighed, his lungs loaded with stones. If he told Scion Zavis the truth, would he find relief? Would the dreams stop? The Father, all-seeing, already knew exactly what happened on the battlefield. The Scion held a sacred duty to secrecy but the Duke shuddered to imagine Scion Zavis's scalding expression as he confessed. He couldn't bear the prospect of facing the Scion's disgust every day for the rest of his life.

Wladek returned with a tankard. The lukewarm milk was soothing as it flowed down his throat, but it turned rancid as it hit his stomach.

If he searched the homes and streets of Ambrovna, could he track down the man, speak with him, reason with him, bargain with him? There was no one he could trust to assist him, not even Kalin. Especially not Kalin. The Duke exhaled. A Duke going door to door around the town? This would only raise eyebrows and give fuel to gossiping tongues. But what gossip could be worse than the truth?

The Duke lay staring at the patterned canopy of his bed until the grey light trickled over the horizon. As the first cocks crowed, he was bone tired and no closer to a plan of action.

Froma sat stony-faced at the breakfast table with her head bare and chin lifted, all her bruises on display. Froma forced a thin slice of apple through her lips and down into her bilious stomach. Irina stood by the dining room door, her head bowed.

Heavy boots clumped along the wooden floors, and despite her resolve, Froma flinched. Froma straightened to her full height, her body rigid, head high as Danis's silhouette darkened the doorway, his sour sweat filling her nostrils. She would not allow him the pleasure of seeing her fear, no matter how much her knees trembled under the table.

Danis grunted a greeting as he took his seat. His eyelids were red, his teeth stained. He immediately grabbed for his goblet and started drinking all over again.

Irina darted forward with a plate of ham and white cheese and sliced him a hunk of bread. He nodded but said nothing. Froma narrowed her one good eye as a tiny smile flickered over the serving girl's mouth.

Danis glanced at Froma, his white eyeballs cracked with red, but he instantly looked away.

'Did you rest well, wife?' He said, his voice low and considered.

'Given the circumstances,' she replied.

They lapsed into a stifling silence.

Froma sipped her honey-wine and watched Danis as he focused all his attention on his breakfast plate. Irina stood behind him, the smirk still present on her face.

'Vinko is a wily man,' Danis mumbled as he buttered his bread. 'He is giving me trouble.'

'He certainly knows how to bargain.'

'The war is over and everything is returning to normal but the stocks are low. And so are prices.'

'Prices should be high, husband.'

He shook his head. 'The quality.'

'You can still fetch a good price...' Froma leaned forward but she caught herself and stopped. She closed her mouth and rested back in her chair.

Danis carved off a chunk of ham. 'Continue, wife,' he said between chews.

Froma raised an eyebrow before sweeping all emotions from her face. 'The flocks are sparse. Most were requisitioned for meat to feed the armies. If traders want mohair this season, they do not have much choice.' Froma's words were hesitant at first, poised for his interruption but Danis watched on from the other end of the table, his face impassive but not angry.

'The fall shearing is already late but if we...you...can secure the yield from this season and help the herders. They will be thankful.'

Danis scratched his ear with the hilt of his knife.

'The herders returning from war need coins now,' she continued. 'Their farms are in disarray after a year of neglect. Not everyone was lucky enough to have their businesses looked after while they were fighting.' She braced herself for his retort but he only took another bite of bread.

'If you are clever, they will welcome any price. You could bargain to even lower than normal. And increase your profit when you sell to Vinko at a higher price.'

Danis pursed his lips. 'If Vinko wants to buy--'

'Of course, Vinko wants to buy. That's why he is here. Our...your mohair is the best. Next season, when the improved wool comes, the herders will remember your deal and come to you first. Then you can demand an even higher price from Vinko and others. If you think ahead, husband, it can be very lucrative.'

Danis grunted again and slurped from his goblet. Froma took another small slice of apple and stared down the table at him, waiting, forcing a calm expression on her face while underneath her heart beat frantically.

'Interesting,' Danis mumbled.

Froma's breath caught in her throat. This was a blow she did not expect.

'Perhaps, I should bring you to my next meeting with Vinko.'

Froma blinked and scrutinised Danis's red face. She waited for the inevitable insult but Danis returned to his breakfast.

'More ham, Irina.' He waved and Irina dutifully scurried away. 'I have forgotten how good our ham is.'

'You have woken in a fine mood this morning, husband,' Froma said, clearing her throat.

'I am home from war. I am alive. Father be praised.' Danis looked Froma in the eye. She glanced back stoically. Again Danis dropped his gaze first.

Froma hid a smile behind her napkin as she wiped her mouth. Perhaps war had changed Danis. This morning his eyes were open to his prosperous future. Or more likely, guilt consumed him as he glanced at her battered face. She could not recall the last time he'd praised the Father unprompted.

'In the eyes of the Father,' she said, lifting her chin high. 'I will be pleased to help you, husband.'

Froma gathered the veil from across her shoulders and wound the cloth around her head, hiding her face away.

Rabel turned back to the shack with her filled water jug. At this grey hour, the queue for the well was short, without the usual banter and laughter. Women whispered behind their hands as she passed and her heart sank. She must be the subject of Alleys talk today.

Some days as she walked back from the well and past the gruel man slopping out ladles of thick beige mush, Rabel dreamed of a small plot of her own. She didn't need much, just enough dirt to grow carrots, onions and parsley, and raise fat hens again. She wouldn't mind paying her share to the Duchy and the Fatherhood because there'd be enough left for her family and she'd be able to feed her babes with food she'd grown from her own hard work. With a little piece of land, Iwan would be different, she was sure of it. He'd be like he was once again.

She shook her head. No one would give Iwan land to tend and she'd never get land on her own. But her little daydream helped to push aside thoughts of Sira's late night visit. Rabel had made the right decision. Hadn't she?

'Where've you been?' grumbled Iwan.

She placed the jug down on the table and said nothing.

'I'm talkin' to you,' he said, his eyes narrowed.

Rabel sucked in a deep breath. 'The well.'

'You left me here with this lot.' He pointed at the twins, their faces dirty with dried tears. 'They've been whingein' and cryin'. What kind of mother are you?'

'Mama,' Aula wailed, her arms outstretched.

'They're hungry,' she said.

'They're not the only ones.' Iwan, reeking of last night's ale, rested his head in his hands. 'Where's breakfast?'

Rabel brought out the remains of the two-day-old bread. She poured water into a chipped bowl and dampened a cloth before wiping their faces clean.

'Hungry,' snivelled Jorn as his sister writhed.

'I know.'

She turned to cut a slice for the twins, but the bread was gone. Rabel frowned. She'd put the bread out, hadn't she? Or was her head still in the clouds?

Then she saw Iwan shove the last mouthful into his face.

'The children?' She said, mouth open.

'They can wait.'

Rabel clenched her jaw.

'Who comes first in this house? The war time has made you forgetful of your duties as a wife. What does the Scion teach?'

'Hungry,' wailed Jorn then Aula began to cry, too.

Iwan covered his ears. 'Shut 'em up or I'll do it.'

'Quiet, babes,' Rabel said, patting their heads, her heart racing.

'Bread!' Jorn said.

'Later,' she said, smoothing his hair, furtively glancing at Iwan's face. His cheeks flushed redder by the moment.

'Now!' The little boy belted out an ear-splitting screech.

Iwan jumped to his feet and glowered at Rabel, his knife in hand. 'I told you!'

Rabel wrapped her arms around the twins as his blade glinted in the light.

'No,' she shouted.

The children sobbed against her breast and her pulse thumped in her throat.

'They need to learn.'

Jorn poked his head out from under Rabel's arm. 'Bad man. Go away, bad man.'

'What did you say, you little shit?' Iwan lunged forward with his knife, the tip aimed directly at the boy's face. She tugged the children away from his reach but lost her balance and tumbled backwards.

'He didn't mean it.' Rabel twisted to shield the twins with her body.

Iwan's eyes were wild. 'This is what I get. After a year riskin' my life, seeing death every day, wonderin' if I'm next. I come home to this? You need a lesson.'

'Not the little ones.'

Iwan crouched beside her. 'I didn't mean them.' His breath reeked of sour beer and the cold metal grazed her skin. 'This will remind you who is head of this house. I come first. Me. Not the children. Understand?'

Rabel nodded feverishly as the sharp tip pressed into the hollow of her cheek.

'Next time, it won't be you. It'll be one of them.'

Iwan took the knife away and stood up. Rabel breathed in and a tear escaped. Just as she assured herself that Iwan would never go that far, for all his bluster, he was a good man underneath, Iwan slashed her left cheek.

Rabel gasped, first with shock and then with pain. Blood dribbled down her face. A drop splashed onto Aula's nose and the little girl shrieked.

Iwan slammed the door, leaving Rabel alone, bleeding. She cuddled her twins tightly and ground her teeth as they sobbed against her breast.

But Rabel didn't cry, her mind was suddenly clear. She must get word to Sira, the sooner the better.

CHAPTER SIXTEEN

AGATA PULLED THE SLIM VOLUME out of her needlework basket and smiled as she opened the pages to read the story of Magnilla once again.

My Scion sent me to the land of the Akull to teach their people the ways of the Father. The Akull were the last remaining Clan where the Fatherhood did not sit alongside the rulers in his rightful place, providing nobles and their people moral guidance on the proper way to live.

Some said the Father did not reside in the North. That this was why the ground was covered by ice and snow for most of the year, but I was filled with the love and hope of the Father. Deep in my bones, I knew the people of the Akull would embrace the Father and his Teachings once they heard his word. As I had. I knew I would succeed in bringing the light of the Father to the wintry north. Although, if I am truthful, which I must be as a sworn oath taker of the Father, I must admit there was fear in my heart. That fear grew bigger and blacker as we travelled, as the green forests thinned and the snow deepened.

I hoped, after my many years of service and when I returned triumphant, I would receive a province of my own as reward. Not for my own good but for the good of the people. Nothing would have pleased me more than to speak the word of the Father three times a day to my own congregation. I dreamed of my own Temple keeping me warm as our mud-soaked boots grew heavy and we skidded on the ice. I sought the Father's blessing for strong and sturdy legs and for the quick healing of our blisters and chilblains but these minor irritations did not dampen my spirits.

We were a band of three Cousins. I was the elder, the two others barely with whiskers on their cheeks. One had jug handles for ears and the other, a nose like a bulb of garlic. We had food, our cloaks, a hand-drawn map and our Teachings of the Father. We needed nothing else. My beard grew long and my hair grew for the first time since I swore my oath and life to the Father.

As we travelled north, through the lands of the Neven and the Vorosy, the bandits let us be. They recognised our bronze robes and knew we were Cousins renounced of all possessions. We were not worth the bother or the extra sin of laying a hand on a man under the Father's oath.

But it was not the case when we reached the snow lands. We had been travelling along a well-worn road through a grassy plain covered in patchy snow, the monotonous landscape broken here and there by groves of evergreen pines. In the distance, the silhouette of vague white hills stung my eyes.

To pass the time along miles and miles of furrowed tracks, I insisted my companions recite the Teachings of the Father. My Scion had taught me the Teachings by heart and I wanted to pass on this tradition. Memorising the Words was the best way to fully absorb the true wisdom of the Father.

'It is a sin to let a man go hungry. It is a sin to let a man go thirsty. It is a sin--'

A whistling pierced the air and the garlic-nosed Cousin crashed to the snowy ground with a thud and a wet gurgle. The remaining Cousin and I cast our eyes about, heartbeats thumping in our throats. The fletching of an arrow jutted straight out of the bloody hole in our fallen Cousin's neck. Three men charged towards us, clad head to toe in white, seemingly transparent against the snow. I choked with fear as they approached, my head filled with foolish thoughts of ghosts. I admonished myself. Ghosts were superstitious nonsense, the tales of lowbred old women. The three horsemen stopped in front of us, bows on their shoulders. Their horses in similar white coats that seemed to fade into the snow.

'We are Cousins! Men of the Fatherhood! Don't you recognise us?' my companion said, a shake in his voice.

I hushed him as the leader came closer. Not only was he dressed in white but his hair was the same shade as the surrounding snow. A long braid ran down his back like a tail and his beard was neatly trimmed despite reaching down to the middle of his chest, far longer than the fashion in the South. I held my hands in the air as their horses encircled us. 'We have nothing to steal, sir,' I said, hoping I was using the right respectful words. Before my journey, my Scion had given me very little information about the North and I'd rarely travelled out of Nithese before. 'As my fellow Cousin said, we are merely men of the Fatherhood.'

The man grunted and gesticulated for us to follow, his eyes as hard as frost.

'What is happening?' The young Cousin hissed.

I shushed him. 'Where are you taking us?' I asked.

The leader spoke in a rough tongue I did not understand and the men on horses prodded us with their long-handled whips.

I tried again. 'Are you taking us to your leader?'

The man nodded, his voice deep and peculiar. 'Meeraq.'

I turned to my fellow Cousin and nodded with a raised eyebrow. We were on our way to the leader of the Akull, exactly as I hoped. At the time, I thought this was a sign that the Father was smiling on our journey. I thought my mission would be easy.

What a fool I was.

CHAPTER SEVENTEEN

H ER HANDS SHOULD HAVE TREMBLED, but Rabel knocked on the door with a lightness in her chest, her backbone straight.

She had left the twins with Dorot, a tiny raisin of a woman with a bellow which could gut fish. Hers was the one place they'd be safe for a few minutes. Even Iwan was not stupid enough to cross Dorot. But Dorot was as impatient as she was terrifying so Rabel's time was short.

Irina answered the door with her usual bowed head but her eyes narrowed to slits when she recognised Rabel. 'What do you want?'

'Is Mistress Plesec home?'

'Wait here.' Irina huffed and closed the door, leaving Rabel to wait in the street chewing on her fingers. Rabel shivered as the autumnal winds with a hint of winter blew away the last breaths of summer. In two days' time, Ambrovna would celebrate the Spawning Festival, which blessed the new eel season. In the coming weeks, the fishermen's nets would be full, but the Festival also meant the downward spiral to winter.

The door opened again and Froma filled the frame. Her lower face was wrapped in a turquoise veil but her eyes were exposed. Her left eye was swollen half-closed and the surrounding skin was mottled with wine-coloured bruises.

Rabel's fingers flew to her mouth. 'Mistress Plesec?'

'I was attacked,' she replied flatly, her chin held high. 'Bashed and my purse ripped away by some vagabond. The Master of the Shield is investigating.'

'I'm sorry, Mistress.'

'The physician said I will heal within a few days. I do not have much time. I'm expected at the castle,' Froma said, with a toss of her head. 'What do you want?'

Rabel's mouth was gluey, the tight band returned to her chest. Her body seemed to fight to keep her words inside. 'I was wondering--'

Froma sighed. 'I told you before, I have no work for you. Ucin has returned and he needs to feed his family.' Froma started to close the door.

'Wait. Please.' Rabel's heart clattered.

Froma glared at Rabel with her unblemished eye.

'You're going to the castle? You are a member of the women's circle?'

'This is no concern of yours.' Froma sniffed.

'You were so kind to me during the war--'

'I did what I could.'

'And I'll always remember how well you treated me. And my children.' Rabel bowed her head. 'May I ask a favour, Mistress Plesec?'

Froma rolled her eyes and pushed the door but Rabel stopped it with her hand. 'I need to get a message to Sira.'

Froma stopped. 'Your sister? The one with the stained face?'

Rabel nodded. 'Can you tell her...' She swallowed hard. 'Can you tell her...I agree.' Rabel winced, expecting the Father to strike her down as the words left her mouth.

'You agree?' Froma raised an eyebrow.

'Yes.'

'That is all? The whole message?'

'Yes. If you'd be so kind. I'd be very grateful and any time you need help around the house. Any chores. I don't mind.'

'Why not go yourself?'

'I've got to get back to my children. I can't leave them alone for too long. And Sira is very busy.'

Froma frowned. 'All you want me to say is 'Rabel agrees'.'

'Yes.'

'Are you in trouble?' The veiled woman traced her own cheek with a finger, following the same line as the fresh cut on Rabel's face.

'You haven't heard,' Rabel murmured. 'I thought it was all over town.'

'I am not some fishwife. I do not listen to the gossip on the street. Your husband I presume?'

Rabel hung her head and nodded.

Froma let out a long slow breath and steepled her fingers in front of her veiled mouth.

Rabel's heart thumped as she waited. It was a foolish idea to come to Mistress Plesec for help. Why would she care?

'I will do this for you.'

Rabel gasped. She saw a surprising softness in Froma's eyes as she gushed, 'Thank you. Thank you. Please do not tell another living soul. Please, Mistress Plesec.'

'I understand.'

'And if you ever need me for anything. Just ask. Thank you again.'

Froma closed the door and Rabel rushed back into the Alleys. With each step, the knot in her belly hardened. The message was on its way to Sira. The flame was lit.

Froma covered her face as best she could. She had felt Rabel's pitying glances and did not want to invite disdain from the Circle members. Songs had been written about her mother's chestnut hair, which glistened like auburn flames in the sunlight but Froma was her father's daughter. From ten summers old, Froma had stood shoulder to shoulder with her father and brothers and all the admiration flowed to her sister, Anuka with her pale skin, small hands and rust-red hair. Her father had joked at the dining table, 'I should thank the Father. I'll only have one dowry to pay for.' Her brothers had guffawed while her mother patted her hand. Froma had narrowed her eyes and tossed her head but inside, her heart crumbled.

'At least you are useful, girl,' her father would say. 'And I do not have to worry about you running off with some mummer. Anyway, you are valuable. You know the abacus better than me.'

While other girls courted and found husbands, Froma distracted herself with the accounts and the yield on barley from the fields of Ledvor. Eventually, she stopped imagining her betrothal and resigned herself to a life in the port town of Veigur helping her father, the merchant. As he had said, she was an asset, unlike those other featherbrains. Until one day, Danis had appeared.

Satisfied with her wrapping, Froma left for the castle, her mind churning with Rabel's secret message. The mystery was a welcome respite from her own troubles. Yet this morning Danis had seemed different, like a warm breeze blowing through the house. She sighed and shook her head at her own simple-mindedness. Of all people, she should know a few kind words did not make a reformed man.

She bustled into the Square, past the Old Man Tree and up the Avenue. When the guards ushered her straight through the gatehouse, she smiled under her veil and strode at her full height. A rat-faced guard escorted her across the bailey, through the thick arched oak doors and up the stairs into the solar.

The sky outside the windows rippled with threatening clouds in white, silver and steel while winds battered the ancient red-brick walls. A fire crackled in the iron grate but the heat failed to spread and Froma did not remove her cloak.

'Ah, Mistress Plesec. Please take --' the Duchess stopped short. Karolien gasped loudly and Randvi and Clawa muttered behind their hands.

Froma tossed her head. 'I was attacked near the Alleys yesterday, my Lady. He ripped my purse from my hands and struck me across the face.'

'How terrible,' the Duchess said, hand pressed against her breastbone.

'I should have been more careful.' Froma shrugged. 'I'd forgotten to take care in the slums. Things have returned to normal, it appears.'

'This is unacceptable. Has Lord Kalin been informed?'

'I reported it immediately,' Froma lied, taking a seat on the cushioned bench. A serving girl poured her a goblet of wine but Froma kept her veil in place. 'The Shield are searching the Alleys for the culprit.'

'Are you in pain?' the Duchess asked.

Froma tingled as the Duchess fussed over her well-being. 'The marks will fade, my Lady. I will be fully recovered once the brute is in the dungeon.'

'We all hope the man is arrested soon and you are quickly healed,' the Duchess said, smiling sweetly before turning back to the others.

Gala, the fleshy grocer's wife, pursed her lips but said nothing. Froma glanced past the other Circle members, and found Sira in her usual corner, stitching. Froma had often wondered why the Duchess did not insist on full veils or at least head scarves for her servants, even the Singlewomen.

'Very well. Let's begin. Yesterday we spoke about other ways we can help the war widows. Has anyone had any ideas?'

The dour Karolien piped up first. 'We should ask the Scion to pray for them...'

Froma stopped listening and turned back to Sira whose head was bowed over her needlework. She searched Sira's birth-stained face for clues. What were the sisters plotting? The Duchess's maid, all piety and constant smile, did not appear the type for conspiracy but every person held a secret beneath their chemise.

'We need a tally of the fallen men and the families left behind,' said the Duchess.

'Do we keep such records?' Gala asked.

'The Seneschal will know.' Froma returned to the conversation. 'There are population numbers in the ledger for taxation. Although it is too soon after the men's return. I doubt he will have an accurate number yet.'

'Some good-for-nothing men use war as an excuse to abandon their families,' said Gala, with a shake of her double chins. 'My aunt was left to bring up six babes in poverty. And then the old goat turned up twenty years later. Very much alive.'

'It is the path of we women,' said Karolien, her brow furrowed. 'To suffer.'

Froma clenched her teeth. Why were men so free to abandon their responsibilities? A woman could not stray ten steps from her home without raising suspicion and Father forbid if she spoke her mind. Her father had told her many times with her homely looks and loose tongue she'd be lucky to find a husband at all. And sometimes she wished...

'In the eyes of the Father,' the others murmured, circling their forehead. Froma copied, covering up her blasphemous thoughts as she sighed behind her veil.

'Your food basket idea is good, Gala. Let us hand out the first baskets as part of the Spawning,' the Duchess said, rubbing her hands together.

'Will you speak with the Scion?' Karolien said meekly. 'For his blessing?'

The other women nodded in agreement.

The Duchess blinked. 'I will discuss it with the Scion. Who will join me?'

'I will,' blurted Froma before anyone else could speak. The other Circle members narrowed their eyes at her but she smirked under her veil. One had to be quick to take advantage of favourable circumstances.

'Wonderful, Mistress Plesec,' the Duchess said. 'We should go as soon as possible. Are you free now?'

'Of course, my Lady,' Froma replied.

'Excellent. I thank everyone again for coming along this morning. Gala?'

'I'll talk with the other grocers. They'll want to help.'

'And I'll speak to Anarr,' said Jadzia. 'The fishermen follow anything he says.'

'Let us meet again tomorrow at the same time and, Father willing, we will have everything ready for the widows at the Spawning.' The Duchess gently clapped her hands and grinned.

The women left their seats and, with a rustling of tunics, tossed cloaks over their shoulders. The less mannered of the Circle drained their goblets and wolfed down a few more almond cakes before departing for their own chores.

The Duchess stood by the door, farewelling each Circle member one by one. As she comforted Clawa, the new widow, Froma grabbed her chance and headed for Sira in the corner.

'I have a message for you,' Froma said, her voice low. 'From Rabel.'

Sira glanced up from her needlework with wide eyes.

'She asked me to tell you. She agrees.'

Blinking, Sira calmly put down her needle and rested her hands in her lap, Froma scrutinised her face as her eyelids flickered. The Duchess's maid nodded slowly.

'What is it, Sira?' the Duchess said as she closed the door and the three women were alone. 'You look quite pale.'

'Only a headache, m'Lady,' Sira said as she stood and tidied away her needlework. 'No cause for your concern.'

'I will decide what is my concern.' The Duchess frowned and Froma pursed her lips.

'It is nothing, m'Lady.' Sira bowed her head, her right cheek now as red as her left.

'Do not lie to me, Sira.' The Duchess folded her arms. 'I will not put up with disobedience.'

'No, m'Lady,' Sira said, her eyes downcast, her face blank.

She flicked her hand with a huff. 'Go to the Seneschal and tell him I want to see him after luncheon. Mistress Plesec and I will visit the Scion now.'

'As you wish, m'Lady.' Sira scuttled out of the room and the Duchess flopped into a chair with a sigh.

'Servants can be very frustrating,' Froma said but the Duchess's attention was lost outside the window.

Froma thought the naive Duchess was too soft-hearted. She would never tolerate such cheek from Irina. Perhaps the Neven treated their servants differently.

'I cannot abide lies and deception,' the Duchess muttered.

'Perhaps she does not want to involve you,' said Froma. 'And perhaps this is wise, my Lady. You do not want to be involved,'

The Duchess recoiled. 'What do you know?'

'I do not want to break any confidences,' Froma said, smirking under her veil.

'Please tell me.' The Duchess fiddled with her necklace.

'I only know a little.'

The Duchess leaned in and placed a hand on Froma's arm.

'Her sister asked me to pass on a message to Sira.'

'And? What did she say?'

'It was quite a riddle. Something about Rabel agreeing.'

The Duchess's face creased. 'To what?'

'I do not know, my Lady. Sira said nothing when I passed it on.'

'Is that all? Was that the whole message?'

'Did you hear the gossip?' Froma asked. She asked Irina what gossip there was of Rabel after she left and her sulky kitchen maid had been only too willing to oblige. 'Her husband tried to sell their daughter.'

'My stars!' the Duchess said. 'To who?'

'I do not know. But there are many wicked people in Ambrovna. I shudder to think what such sinners would do with a young girl.'

The Duchess's face drained. 'Thank you for confiding in me. There is more depravity in this town than I ever realised.'

'Left without guidance, people are no better than animals,' Froma said. 'In the eyes of the Father.'

'Poor Rabel,' the Duchess sighed. 'How can we help?'

This time, Froma grasped the Duchess's hand. 'May I give you some advice, my Lady. Do not get involved. This could be dangerous. You are the Duchess and the rules are quite different for you.'

The Duchess blinked and pressing her lips together in a weak smile. 'It pains me to sit by idly, but you are wise, Mistress Plesec,' she said. 'Please tell me if you hear any more. I need to know if my servants are in trouble. I feel a responsibility towards them.'

Froma nodded.

'But we have another matter to attend to.' She rose and smoothed her braids. 'I am so glad you offered to accompany me...'

The Duchess looped her arm through Froma's as they headed out the door. Froma grinned. Her veil had so many uses.

CHAPTER EIGHTEEN

SIRA'S FACE SOFTENED INTO A secret smile when she left the solar. Rabel had agreed. Sira hurried along the corridors towards the Seneschal's room as butterflies swarmed in her belly. It was now up to her.

Sira hoped she had diverted Mistress Plesec from their plan. She grimaced and hoped she'd not been too disrespectful. The Duchess's anger had been part of the act. If only Rabel had chosen a more trustworthy person to pass on her message. Sira knew the haughty wool merchant's wife would betray their confidence the moment Sira left the room.

With each step along the corridor, Sira's plan and their sin became as real as the bricks below her feet. She shivered, picturing the Father's wrath. The butterflies turned to stones in her stomach.

All her life she'd been taught to fear the Land of Eternal Darkness, a place in the coldest depths of the bottom of the sea where no light or hope could reach. It was the realm of the worst sinners where thousands were free to satisfy their every wicked desire. A place where screams would never be heard.

But Sira's plan observed the Teachings. Didn't the Scion say "a woman always places her family first in all her words and actions"? As a Singlewoman with her Pa and Ma long cold, Rabel was her only kin. She was helping her family. Shouldn't the Father approve?

Sira knocked on the Seneschal's thick wooden door.

'Enter.'

She blinked and shivered as she stepped inside the gloomy room. Weak candlelight strained over three broad tables covered in leather-bound ledgers. The twig-like Seneschal stooped over a large book, a quill in his hand, and a young boy on a ladder slotted books into the shelves behind him.

'What do you want?' He scowled, a deep divot running between his eyebrows.

'The Duchess would like to see you after luncheon, Sir.'

'What does she want?' He continued scribing. 'These ledgers were left in a disgraceful state by some damned fool woman.'

'She wants the count of war widows left in Ambrovna.'

The Seneschal snorted. 'Good luck. Taxation is not due until the end of the Spawning season. And even then, she will need the Duke's permission.'

'I'm sure he will be forthcoming, sir,' Sira said.

'I will talk to her once the Duke has granted permission and not before. Such matters are not her concern. Now, out.'

He flicked his fingers. Sira lowered her head and backed out of the room.

'Wait. Now you have interrupted my work you can make yourself useful. Bring me some ale and cakes.'

Sira gritted her teeth but plastered on a smile. 'Yes, sir.'

Sira headed for the kitchens through the bailey, ignoring the hubbub of rowdy men all around her. Was there another way? Could she speak to a Cousin on Rabel's behalf? Ask for his assistance with Iwan? She exhaled and shook her head. A Cousin would only tell Rabel to persevere. Sira chewed her lip. How much would it cost to hire an Alleys thug to give Iwan his comeuppance? She sighed. Her last silver coin was already in Sabet's filthy hands.

Sira had made a promise to her sister and according to the Scion, a promise was golden. In the eyes of the Father.

'Ale and cakes for the Seneschal,' Sira said as she passed the row of bare-armed kitchen girls rolling out sheets of white dough.

'More?' said Majvi, wiping her hands on her apron and reaching for the thick brass key swinging from her neck. 'Greedy old goat.'

Sira chuckled as the tiny cook stood on tip-toes and unlocked the spice cabinet. Her body always softened in Majvi's company.

'Remember Mida,' Sira said as Majvi shaved a nugget of nutmeg into her large bowl.

'That's goin' back years.'

'She used to say some strange things.'

Mida, a charwoman with three teeth left in her head, would ramble into young Sira's ears. 'See 'em spices,' she'd point to the very same spice cabinet and then to the bushels of crispy leaves hanging from the rafters. 'And them 'erbs. They got more uses than makin' cakes taste good.'

Sira would shrug nervously and continue her turnip peeling.

'No one wants to listen anymore but the cunning lives on. People shoo away the wasp but she brings much more than a sting.' Mida tapped the side of her nose. 'When the world was young, the wasp brought fire to the people. She stole it from the sun and brought it down to earth. But you don't want to anger her. A wasp can sting more than once.'

Majvi tested her batter with a slurp from her spoon. 'I never listened. She was one of them. Wasn't she?'

Sira shrugged.

While no one dared mention them, the old ways were not truly lost. There was one place, one person who still knew. A person who could be trusted to keep a secret. But twenty years had passed since Sira last saw her younger sister.

Even as a child, Wisia was like a ghost, slim and ethereal, dancing lightly over the world. She said the sparrows spoke to her and the bricked walls of their house hummed lullabies. Even before her first bleeding, she'd disappear from home for days on end, returning only with a mysterious smile.

The last time she saw her sister, Wisia was standing over her bed. Somehow she had bypassed the guards and locked castle gates and slipped into Sira's sleeping quarters without waking the other snoring serving women. Although bone-tired servants usually slept like the dead.

'I must go, dear sister. They don't understand,' Wisia had said.

'They love you in their hearts but they are too scared to admit it. They only know the Teachings.'

'They're weak. They put the Father before us. But I'm strong.'

'Where will you go?'

'The hills. A place only you can find me.'

'The Shimmering Spring?'

'It'll make me a fine home.'

'I will visit you.'

'No. You know what they say about me. I don't want to tarnish you.'

Sira had wished she could disagree, but Wisia was right. Their parents were not the only weak ones.

'Only come to me if you must. Life or death.'

'But...'

'Promise?'

'I promise.'

'Don't worry about me. The hills and the forest'll look after me. There is nothing for me here in this town of the Father.'

With these words, her sister disappeared into the shadows. For twenty years Sira had kept her word. But now the moment of life and death had arrived.

CHAPTER NINETEEN

THE SMALL PROCESSION OF THREE crossed the town Square and headed towards the Temple, Agata in her terracotta dress, Froma in her veil and a weak-chinned guard with the eel sigil on his chest. Agata was glad for Froma's company. The merchant's wife was quite the formidable sight, towering over her.

In the early days, Agata had found Froma's airs and strong opinions intimidating and thorny. But she was loyal and her keen mind invaluable and now Agata was willing to give her the benefit of the doubt, and in truth, she had no one else.

It was the hour before the midday service and the market Square was deserted. A lone peddler hawked pies half-heartedly and the wind whipped the tattered terracotta pennants tangled in the Old Man Tree. The stoic Tree snubbed its nose at the stiff breeze while two men sat underneath, heads close together plotting or philosophising. It was hard to tell at a distance and often there was little difference anyway.

As her toes touched the first steps into the Temple, Agata hoisted herself to her full noble posture, bracing for an interaction with the Scion. The weak-chinned guard followed the Duchess and Froma, as close and as silent as a shadow. The Temple walls were built from the same local red brick as the castle, but the interior was painted buttermilk yellow and the bricks underfoot were worn to a rosy pink. Outside, the Square was quiet but inside the hefty arched doors, there was not a breath of sound. Agata felt she was disturbing the Father with her mere presence.

'My Lady, what a pleasant surprise,' said a Cousin. His hands were folded away inside his simple bronze-coloured cotton gown, his dark eyebrows met in the centre. 'Are you here for midday service? You are early. But you are very welcome to wait in the Temple. It's always an honour to receive the wife of our Duke.'

The Cousin gestured through the open doorway where a thousand tiny candles twinkled underneath the circular symbol of the Father etched into the wall.

'I am here to see the Scion.'

'He is quite busy, my Lady. As always. The work of the Father is never complete.'

'I am sure he can find time to see the Duchess,' said Froma.

'Perhaps,' the Cousin said. He beckoned to a younger Cousin and whispered in his ear before sending him away. 'Would you like to wait in the Temple, my Lady? I am available to hear your sins if you feel the need to unburden your soul to the Father?'

'We will wait,' Agata said with a patient smile.

She missed her childhood Scion, a rotund man with deep wrinkles from a lifetime of smiling. Scion Geitor had preached of a wise and kindly Father, a grandfatherly figure who bathed his people with the golden light of his love. Ambrovna's pale yellow paint could not remove the chill from the Temple air.

Agata paced the length of the antechamber, her boot heels clattering against the bricks. When she reached the far end of the entrance, she noticed a doorway. The Cousin rushed in front of her with a sweep of his tunic, blocking her path before she finished her first step towards it.

'My Lady,' he stuttered. 'Women are not permitted in the Cloisters.'

'Not even the Unwanted?' Agata raised an eyebrow.

'This is where we sleep and study. The Unwanted are allowed only in the gardens and kitchens. We do not allow them in our quarters.'

The young Cousin reappeared and whispered into the Cousin's ear.

'The Scion thanks you for visiting but unfortunately, my Lady, he has many pressing matters to attend to. He hopes you will attend the midday service.'

Agata narrowed her eyes. 'Will he see me after the service? I have my own pressing matter to discuss with him.'

The single-browed Cousin shook his head. 'I am sorry, my Lady. He is meeting with the Duke. There is so much to do to bring life back to normal.'

Agata gritted her teeth.

Froma leaned in. 'Did you explain properly, Cousin? We are here to--' She stopped as Agata placed a hand on her arm.

'Very well,' Agata replied. 'The Scion is not alone. I also have much to do.'

'Of course, my Lady.' The Cousin gestured to the door. 'As you wish.'

Neither Agata nor Froma spoke until their feet touched the cobbles of the town Square.

'I must go, my Lady,' Froma said.

Agata nodded, her jaw tight. 'Thank you for your help. In both matters.'

'Please call on me if ever you need me.' Froma strode away across the Square, turquoise veil flapping, leaving Agata with her taciturn guard by the Old Man Tree.

Agata sighed.

Back inside the castle, she heard male laughter as she approached the solar door. Nausea rippled across her belly as she wondered what she might overhear today.

A different guard, with a severe widow's peak, knocked and pushed open the door. The Duke sat on the cushioned bench with his usual noblemen; Kalin, Jotek and Egid. Each had goblets in hand and the table was laden with bread trenchers and platters of beef, chicken legs and silver sardines. Agata pulled back her shoulders and entered, forcing a smile.

'Ah, the beautiful Duchess,' said Lord Egid. His pointed salt and pepper beard was meticulously oiled. 'Come and join us.'

'I do not want to interrupt,' she said.

'Only if you do not mind listening to us reliving our triumphs on the battlefield,' Egid said.

Agata swallowed.

The Duke slurped down another mouthful of wine, barely glancing in Agata's direction.

'How have you been busying yourself today, my Lady,' Egid continued. 'Dresses or needlework?'

The others laughed.

'I visited the Scion,' she replied, her fingers gripping at her necklace.

Kalin rolled his eyes and chuckled as he grabbed a chicken leg. 'Lucky you.'

'To discuss charitable works for the war widows.'

'Very good. Very good,' said the Duke, finally registering her. 'We must do more for the families of the lost men.'

Her heart swelled at the sight of approval on his face. 'I tried, my Lord. But he did not have the time to see me.'

Egid grunted. 'I saw the Scion this morning. He was talking of an Allotment.'

'A sensible idea, my Lord.' The weak-chinned Jotek nodded. 'An Allotment was performed after the last war.'

'I heard the story from my own father,' the Duke said, pinching his bottom lip between his fingers.

Agata glanced from face to face, her brow furrowed. 'What is--?'

The Duke held up his hand. 'I shall explain later.'

Agata closed her mouth and the room settled into an awkward silence, disturbed only by slurping and chewing. She remained standing behind the men and the Duke did not invite her to join him. Heat blazed across her décolletage and spread up her neck as she waited, but he said nothing.

'I'll take my leave, my Lord,' she said finally, curtseying to hide her eyes.

The Duke nodded curtly and reached for a piece of bread.

Her heart pinched inside her chest as she closed the door behind her. She bit down on her lip and turned to rush up the stairs, as far away as she could.

'My Lady.'

Lord Sylwin lurched along the corridor on his bad leg.

'Lord Sylwin.' She conjured up a weak smile as a serving girl approached with a food-laden tray. 'I will take my luncheon in my bower.'

The girl nodded and hurried away towards Agata's rooms.

'Let me walk you there,' Lord Sylwin said, taking her arm. 'How are you keeping, my Lady? It has only been a few days since the men returned but I have barely seen you. I had grown used to seeing your lovely face several times a day.'

'It is an adjustment,' Agata said, pressing her lips. 'For all of us.'

'War is hard to describe to those who have not experienced it.'

'But I want to hear about it. I want to help lighten the burden.'

'There are things about war you can never understand through mere words.'

Agata swallowed.

'I feel like we are strangers once more.'

'Give it time, my Lady,' he sighed. 'If only my sister were alive to advise you but you have only me.'

Agata patted his arm. 'You are the best counsel I could ask for.'

'She would have had much to teach you. The Old Duke was a hard man but a touch of her hand on his arm and her voice in his ear and he would bend like seaweed in the tide.'

Agata smiled weakly.

'Be patient, my Lady.'

Agata nodded. 'Please join me for luncheon? I would like to hear more about my husband's mother. She sounds truly wise.'

Sylwin shook his silver head. 'The Duke requested my company in the solar. But I promise I will come to visit you tomorrow. I do not like to see you frown.'

She nodded solemnly as he hobbled away. Once again, left all alone.

CHAPTER TWENTY

O NCE AGATA'S LUNCHEON WAS LAID out and the wine poured, the serving girl curtseyed and closed the bedchamber door. Agata curled up on the bench, reached for an almond cake and opened the tale of Magnilla once again.

The weak sun was already in the west as we reached the summit. The Cousin and I had stumbled and panted up the rocky and icy incline like bent old women, while the Akull men on their horses were fresh as maidens on a morning stroll. I had repeated my prayer under my breath all the while, 'O Father, Protector. O Father, my keeper. My life is yours. Keep me safe.' I rested on a lichen-covered boulder and gazed into the valley below where I caught my first glimpse of Meeraq. The town sat behind a high wall of compressed ice. As large as any big town in Nithese, Meeraq glistened in the grey afternoon light, its shingled roofs caked in snow.

The three Akull men led us towards a gate built of solid logs where we met a guard twice my size, gobbling on a drumstick. My stomach rumbled and my fellow Cousin moaned aloud. This was the first meat we'd seen in weeks but we said nothing. I circled my forehead. The Father constantly tests us.

The Akull leader said something in his rough tongue and the mountainous gatekeeper opened the gate. We continued into a wide street, flanked by three storey pine dwellings with carved eaves and shutters, and tiled mosaics in blues and pale yellows. The craftsmanship intrigued me but on closer inspection, I saw sin on full display. One of the repeating motifs was a naked female form. I gasped and averted my eyes. We had been right to come here. Our work and the Father were sorely needed. The people of Meeraq would know His wisdom soon. It was never too late.

We continued deeper into the heart of Meeraq past doorways where fur pelts and hunks of wine-coloured dried meat hung alongside wooden contraptions with straight rails rather than wheels. Pale-faced but well-fed children stopped and pointed at us open-mouthed, while roaming wolf-like dogs sniffed at our legs. We turned the corner into another street and then down a narrow alleyway until we stopped outside a house like all the others, with blue and pale yellow tiled walls and pine cones and birds carved into the eaves. The door was opened and the three men escorted us into a small room.

The Cousin and I stepped inside. The leader said a few more unintelligible words from the doorway and closed the door behind him, leaving us all alone. I tried not to think the worst when I heard the latch close. I looked around the stark room and to my surprise, found a bowl of steaming water and a towel. Such luxury in this desolate place? Hot water was not even provided at the castle of Prince Andaras in Nithese. I praised the Father aloud as I splashed my face. My nose and cheeks burned as they thawed and I grinned. But my fellow Cousin refused to wash, his eyes never resting.

'We cannot escape,' he said, shaking his head. 'I knew I should never have come.'

'Why should we escape? We came here to meet with the Akull Clansmen and teach them of the Father. This is our duty.'

'Look what happened to the other Cousin,' he said, in the lowest voice.

I tutted. 'He died spreading the word. A pious death. He is with the Father in the Land Beyond the Sunset right now. There is no reason to be sad. He is receiving his reward. I hope when my time comes, I am on a mission for the Father.'

'It might come very soon,' the Cousin said, slumping onto a cot.

I took my Teachings out and prepared for the moment we would be called to meet their King. I did not sit but I paced the small room with a lightness in my chest, awaiting my chance to prove my true devotion to the Father. How pleased He would be when the Akull turned to Him.

The door opened.

'Come.' A different man in white spoke our language with a thick accent, his white hair piled on his head in a bun like a maiden. 'She is ready for you.'

I smiled but then my brow furrowed. Did he say 'she'? I shrugged, assuming my ears were blocked after the whistling winds of the plains.

But I was wrong.

We followed him through narrower streets banked by snow. 'See the Father is with us,' I said, pointing to the late afternoon sunlight and the glowing golden snow but the other Cousin merely grumbled. I clutched my Teachings to my chest. My heart swelled with hope and as we walked, I searched for the perfect passage from the Teachings to begin with.

Then we turned a corner and I gasped at the tall wooden tower unlike anything I'd seen before. It was not cylindrical like the four towers of the Sulun palace but broad and fat at the base with curved walls and a domed roof, like an acorn. The dark-stained exterior was painted with soaring eagles, diving fish, giant bears and some mysterious creature with a horn on its forehead. The other Cousin took in a similar sharp intake of breath, but his comment was not as complimentary.

'Heretics,' he muttered.

'I think it is glorious,' I said as we started up the wide row of steps towards a massive sliding door. Outside the entrance, a muscular guard with a long white moustache stood under an awning. Wooden racks ran along the wall filled with boots of different shapes and sizes. The door frame was decorated with depictions of the sun, moon and stars and Akull warriors with flowing white hair.

I took a step forward towards the door and the guard yelled, the force of his voice stopping me dead. I shrugged with a trembling smile. He pointed at our feet and shook his head, frowning. Hesitantly I removed my boots, my feet ripe after months on the road, but I followed his orders and he slid open the heavy door.

Like the exterior, the interior took the breath from my lungs. The pine walls of the vast room stretched into a dome in the sky, the ceiling seeming to soar up forever, buttressed by white rafters. To my left and right lay fire pits, which spat sparks and poured out heat. In the centre of the room was an enormous chair carved from a single mammoth tusk, intricately patterned with motifs of icicles and swords and eagles and inlaid with black onyx. I blinked twice, then three times and then I knew I had heard our guide correctly. She sat on the throne while her white-headed court sat at her feet on fringed cushions and rugs.

'Bow when Queen Magnilla speaks to you,' said the educated man who spoke our language.

The room rippled with murmurs as we approached the throne.

'She is beautiful,' whispered the other Cousin, his mouth agape. I did not know much of women but she was luminescent. Her white hair was pinned back from her face with combs of yellowing bone and shone like a shower of ice rippling down her back. Dressed immodestly in eggshell-coloured leather hose and a clinging leather tunic, she slung sideways over the arm of her throne rather than sitting upright. Her silver eyes were inquisitive as she tilted her head with a slight smile. Some might say her smile was cruel but I saw only curiosity. And her curiosity was returned, I longed to know everything about this woman.

'Who are you, strangers?' she said.

CHAPTER TWENTY-ONE

T HE MIDDAY SUN STREAMED THROUGH the solar
windows as the Duke took a long draught of wine and settled
back, listening to Lord Kalin regaling the room with another of
his Sulun conquest stories.

'The most luscious thighs you'd ever seen. Soft as clotted cream.'

Lords Egid and Jotek roared with laughter.

'If nothing else, you have returned with good tales,' said Lord
Sylwin, wiping tears from his eyes. 'I wish I could have joined you.
This cursed old body.'

Kalin topped up his goblet with a sigh. 'But life is back to normal.
Goat stealers and fights in the Inns.'

The Duke chuckled as he sliced sausage with his pocket knife.

'You have not told your tale, my Lord,' Sylwin said.

The Duke glanced up at his great uncle, his pulse quickening. He
produced a smile. 'It's a very simple story. Nothing like my old friend
Kalin's tales over here.'

'What can I say?' Kalin leaned back with his hands behind his head.
'Damsels love me.'

Guffawing, Sylwin replenished the Duke's wine. 'My Lord, don't be so
modest. Battlefield stories are always interesting. Indulge your old Uncle.'

All eyes were on the Duke.

'Very well,' he said, clearing his throat.

He took the goblet from Sylwin's hand and emptied the contents in
a single draft. He longed to loosen his tunic. 'My enemy was a Hende.'

'The Hende,' scoffed Kalin. 'Their skills are in the forges, not on the battlefields.'

'Rightly so. With the sharpest sword I've ever seen. It sang through the air. Cleaving right through to the bone with a single swipe. The physician proclaimed it was the cleanest cut he'd ever seen.'

His great uncle whistled through his yellow teeth.

'I foolishly allowed him one clear strike.' He continued, patting his empty hose. 'But the Father blessed me that day and I am here to tell the tale. In the eyes of the Father.'

'Luck and years of training.' Jotek winked.

'You did not give in, my Lord,' Sylwin nodded.

'All your hours of swordsmanship lessons came back to me, Uncle. Like second nature,' the Duke said and the old man bowed his head. He took another sip of wine, pausing to piece together a believable story from all the battlefield tales he'd heard since childhood. He wished he was more like Kalin, a natural storyteller.

'Go on, my Lord,' Sylwin said.

The Duke tugged at his tunic neck and gestured to Wladek, pointing to the window. 'His keen blade found my thigh, slicing right through to the bone. But I managed to stay in the saddle and Mortu and I pushed forward, thrusting at him. Oh my beloved horse,' he sighed. 'Then the Hende churl struck once again. This time, Mortu felt his blade and my faithful old steed collapsed to the ground, and I came crashing down with him.'

Sylwin pursed his lips and nodded solemnly. 'Such courage, my Lord.'

'I slid from the saddle and we fought hand to hand in the mud.' The Duke waved his arm for extra effect. The Lords and his great uncle were silent, their eyes glistening and alert, fixed on him. He licked his lips and carried on. 'We wrestled in the dirt, rolling over and over. Him on top. Then me. Spitting and grunting. Once or twice I feared our battle would be my last. I can still see his fiery eyes glaring down at me. That wicked grin.'

'But your leg? The pain, my Lord? The blood?'

'It was strange. At the time, all I could hear was the thundering of my own heart. It felt as if I was peering through a tunnel and my black-clad opponent was all I could see.'

'And how did you finish him off?' Sylwin rubbed his hands.

'My trusty sword did not let me down. I grunted and strained and somehow managed to overcome him. Then the point of my blade found his heart and I plunged in deep with all my remaining strength and it was all over. Another victory for the Vorosy Clansmen.'

'But with the loss of your leg.'

'Tis nothing.' The Duke feigned a smile but his belly plummeted each time he remembered he was now only half a man. *The Father's revenge is swift and absolute.* 'The victory was worth my small trouble.'

The men murmured in agreement.

'Although...,' the Duke said with a laugh. 'I shudder every time I see a man with an axe. Believe me, a battlefield surgeon's blow is more frightening than a Henden sword.'

The Lords nodded and chuckled along with him.

'We are all grateful for your healthy return,' Sylwin said. 'Your battle scar will be a constant reminder of your bravery and your sacrifice for your people.'

'Hear, hear.' Kalin raised his glass and the other lords charged their goblets into the air but the Duke's mind drifted away.

The men seemed satisfied, even impressed. Only one other man knew the whole mortifying truth. His chest tightened. How long would he be silent? When would his secret be revealed to the world?

CHAPTER TWENTY-TWO

T HE BOWER WAS QUIET ALL evening. The Duchess was wrapped up in the pages of a small book as Sira went about her chores without distraction or conversation. Sira was glad. She had feared if she started to speak, she'd talk and talk until she talked herself out of the plan.

Then the moment arrived.

'I am going now,' she said as she slid the bed-warmer under the coverlet. Her heartbeat quickened as she said the words aloud.

The Duchess squeezed her hand. 'Good luck. What you are doing is right.'

Sira nodded, her stomach did not agree.

Snuggling into her boiled-wool cloak, Sira secured the plum cake under her arm as the cart rolled out of the town Square. Sira had cornered Stali the butcher during his late delivery to the kitchens and slipped him a copper for his trouble and his silence.

'I'll take you as far as the valley,' Stali had said and he stayed quiet during the ride, only bidding her farewell as she slid off the back of his cart at the crossroad where the valley met the hills. She hoped the copper was enough to hold his tongue, otherwise stories of Sira's late night visits to her goat-herder lover would be all over Ambrovna by midday service. But there were far worse sins to be accused of.

The hills rose sharply and Sira started up a winding path between the rocks. The sky was strewn with wisps of cloud, pin-pricked with starlight.

The autumn wind carried stray sounds towards her, singing and laughter from the herders' huts, barking dogs and clanging goat bells. Sira climbed higher with only the wan moonlight to guide her. She squeezed through the narrow passes between boulders, every single footstep requiring concentration. The craggy terrain was perfect for goats but one fumbled step and a tumble and she'd be lost up here alone and injured until a goat boy found her – if the wolves did not find her first.

Sira had once known these hills. While her Pa earned a decent livelihood as a rope-maker, he had enjoyed hunting like his Pa before him with Wisia, Rabel and Sira tagging along. He said trapping rabbits brought him closer to the Father. Sira and her sisters were of little help, which gave Pa another excuse to lament his lack of sons so he left them to amuse themselves. They'd wander among the rocks, picking wildflowers, singing songs and playing make-believe. Wisia came alive in the open air. The hills were her place. In the town she was withdrawn and dreamy. She worsened as she approached womanhood, always in trouble for her queer ways and absences.

Then one day Wisia had left, never to return.

Over the years, Sira heard rumours about Wisia's whereabouts. Her sister had been seen frequenting Guts Alley, making coppers the only way a desperate woman could, or she'd married a goat herder and now hid away in a hut in the valleys, or even the elegantly dressed Wisia had been seen in the court of the dead King Rados, living a grand life as a successful and influential silver merchant. But the most popular story was that she was a Wasp Woman living in the hills.

Sira had kept her word and never sought out her sister. Somehow within her bones she knew that wherever Wisia was, she was safe. She was home.

Sira rested her aching calves and looked back over Ambrovna and the castle tower silhouetted against the sea. Tiny specks of light flickered in keep windows. Her home and the town was so far away. The wind moaned through the crooked trees and squat shrubs. Something screamed in the distance. She shivered, hoping it was a fox. The keening sounded similar to a child in pain. With a gulp, she wrapped her cloak tighter around her shoulders and set off again.

Many years had passed since Sira's childhood walks and the hills had a way of changing. Boulders had slipped down slopes, trees had grown tall or rotted and fell, paths had been washed away by rain and forest fires had destroyed everything in their path. The hills felt familiar and confusing at once, like grasping for meaning inside a dream, but Sira pressed on, higher and higher. She felt she'd been climbing for hours, yet she was no closer to the Shimmering Spring.

A blister burst on her heel and she slumped on a rock, head in her hands, mouth sticky. Was she mad? Wandering out in the hills at night on a whim? Was Wisia still out here? Twenty years was a long time. What if she couldn't find her? Was she still alive? The longer Sira sat alone in the dark, the more she convinced herself she was destined to fail Rabel all over again.

A stream of air rushed overhead and Sira ducked. A white owl swept through the night, over the red boulders and scrub until it landed on a tree in the distance. Her heart leapt as she scrambled to her feet and hurried to the owl perched on a gnarled walnut tree. She patted the corrugated bark as if greeting an old friend.

'Thank you,' she whispered to the owl. Now she knew exactly where she was. The owl blinked its black eyes in reply.

A smile spread over Sira's face as she passed the last boulder, glimpsing the calm waters of the pool and the cliffs looming on three sides. She didn't know if the spring had a proper name. It had always been the Shimmering Spring to Sira, Wisia and Rabel.

Sira bent down, trailing her fingers through the icy water, stinging her teeth as she took a sip. The waters reflected the stars and moon above but there was no sign of Wisia or a dwelling: only black water, green reeds, rumbling frogs and red rocks.

Sira unlaced her boots and dipped her aching feet in the water with a half-relieved, half-frustrated sigh. This was a foolish trip.

She leaned back on a rock and clenched her jaw. There was nothing here and it would be a long journey home to the castle by foot. She sighed. What would she say to Rabel?

Sira switched the plum cake from hand to hand and wonder whether she should take a bite, when a tune popped into her head. The old song burst free from the back corridors of her mind, her lips remembering every word.

The Sun, the Moon, the rain, the wind,
The life, the flowers, the trees begin,
The leaves will fall, they turn to earth,
There's always death and there's always birth.

Sira sang Wisia's little song as she dried her feet on her cloak and gathered her strength for the long trek home. There would be no sleep for her tonight.

'Here you are, dear sister.'

Sira jumped as a woman appeared beside her, her skin crinkled and bronzed by the sun, her hair cropped short against her skull, her wiry body wrapped in goatskins but the eyes and the grin were the same.

'Wisia.'

'It's been a long time, beloved Sira.'

Sira breathed out. 'I am so happy to see you. I thought you were gone.'

'And yet here I am. Come. I've been waitin'.' Wisia held out a grubby hand and helped Sira to her feet. Sira rushed into her boots and followed Wisia between the rocks. They traced the shore of the spring, a hut came into view, set against the furthest rock wall.

'That hut was not there a moment ago,' Sira said, pursing her lips as they approached a windowless pile of mismatched stones with a grass thatched roof.

'Maybe. Maybe not. Perhaps you weren't lookin' properly,' Wisia said, pushing open the door made from bundles of birch trunks.

A fire snapped in the corner and goat, fox and rabbit pelts hung from the beams. Fresh scented rushes lined the floor. The hut was more comfortable than the horse stable Rabel called home.

Wisia gestured to an upturned log and Sira sat, pulling the plum cake from beneath her cloak. 'I brought this for you.'

Wisia hesitantly took the cake and inspected it from all angles before lifting it to her nose and taking a long sniff of the crust. 'So many years since I've seen one of these. One of Majvi's?' She smiled with a raised eyebrow before snapping the cake in two and handing half to Sira. 'Now, tell me why you've come to me, dear sister. Why tonight?'

Sira shifted on her seat. Wisia stared unrelentingly as she tore into the cake. Sira averted her eyes and squinted at the collection of skulls on a shelf high up on the wall. Not all the leering jaws were animal shaped.

Sira cleared her throat. 'You said you were waiting?'

Her sister reached over and stirred the pot on the fire. She pulled a handful of dried leaves from a sack and crushed them in her palm, tossing the flakes into a wood-hewn cup. Then she scooped something pink and soft, suspiciously like animal innards, from the steaming pot into the cup.

Sira sniffed hesitantly as Wisia handed it over. 'What is this?'

'The Great Mother shows me many things.'

Heart thumping, Sira took a sip and the hot tincture blasted her nostrils. She spluttered and her sister chuckled, her open mouth lined with perfectly white teeth.

Sira rubbed her watering eyes and noticed strange rusty-red markings on the walls. She peered closer. The first painting was of a woman with her legs spread and all her sinful parts on full display. Another showed the outline of a dog or a fox sliced open from mouth to tail, all its bones and guts documented. Over in the corner, under a sketch of a ghoulish grinning face, the blade of a scythe glinted in the firelight. Sira gulped, her hands clammy despite the heat.

'You haven't answered me, sister. Why now?'

Sira's heart pattered in her chest. Wisia's stare was like the Scion's. She looked straight through her, past her mask and into her lies, seeing the true sin inside. Sira swallowed, her mouth sour with the tincture. 'I need your help.'

'But not for yourself? This much I know.'

'I need your knowledge.'

'Ha.' Wisia barked and bit into the cake. 'I live in the hills like an animal. An ignorant sinner. Isn't that what they say? Isn't that what you think?'

'I never...I have come for your wisdom: knowledge which is lost to the rest of us.'

Wisia raised her eyebrow with a smirk. 'Knowledge not respected in the town. But you need me?'

'Rabel.'

'Our other dear sister.' Wisia nodded wistfully. 'She's in pain?'

Sira smiled weakly and Wisia wolfed down the rest of the cake, licking the crumbs from her fingers.

'She's sick? You need medicine?'

Sira's throat was tight, the words reluctant to come out. 'Not quite,' she cleared her throat and croaked. 'Her husband.'

'It's his life you wish to save?'

'She needs to be...' Sira shook her head and chewed her lip. 'Rid of him.'

'Ah.' Wisia raised her eyebrow. 'And you think I can help?'

'I hoped.'

'Tell me more.' Wisia wiped her mouth and pointed to Sira's untouched half of the cake. 'You want this?' Sira shook her head and Wisia grabbed the cake.

'He is a bad man, a bad father. He gambles away all their coins, and leaves Rabel's family poor and hungry.'

Wisia scoffed. 'Coins. Such a cause of pain. Scraps of metal, they mean nothin'.'

'He went to war but came back in one piece, only to start his gambling again. Yesterday, he tried to hand over his own daughter to a flesh merchant to repay his debts.'

'And you think I can help? Remove him from Rabel's life? Take the annoying little thorn from her paw?'

'It is more than that!' Sira blurted.

'She should run away from him. But of course, your Fatherhood and his blind children wouldn't approve. But you know the Father doesn't know everything. Not like they claim he does.'

'What would she do? Hide in the hills, like you?'

Wisia shrugged, waving her hand around her hut. 'I'm free. I do as I please. I'd never return to Ambrovna.'

'We need your help.'

'You underestimate yourself, sister. You never listen to the truth in your heart.'

Sira suppressed a gasp and shifted in her seat.

'You want to meddle with life and death? The Father might spread his untruths about everlastin' life but everythin' must die.'

Sira leaned forward, her eyes large. 'Can you help?'

'Of course.' Wisia said, settling back with her arms folded, chewing the last mouthful of cake.

Apart from the fire crackling in the corner and Wisia smacking her lips, the hut was quiet. Sira wrung her hands.

'But will you help?'

Wisia smiled. 'The right question, sister. You took your time but you finally reached it.'

CHAPTER TWENTY-THREE

T HE BATTALION OF VOROSY CLANSMEN faced their Hende enemies on the low foggy plains of Truinn. Since first light, the battle had raged, black tunics versus red. The clang of forged swords against thickened shields, the frenzied battle cries and gurgled death rattles. On a hillock, the mounted Duke peered through the smoky gloom, his heart in his throat, his eyes blurry and burning. His man-servant, Wladek was out there, somewhere on the plains carrying a message back to Prince Absalom and likewise, his best friend Lord Kalin had insisted on leading the first phalanx into the fray.

It had been a simple plan: push the Hende men back towards the Persilek River and fence them in, freeing the Eastern passage along the plains into Sulun. Other Clans were known for their cruelty or their brute strength but the Hende bred the most skilled craftsmen in the kingdom. The black-clad soldiers were always the first with new weaponry. In comparison, the Duke's men were everyday men conscripted from towns, farms and villages. Most were without a single day of training. They fought with sharp scythes, heavy hammers and barbed hooks: whatever weapons they had brought from home.

The Duke rubbed his hand across his face. The dry yellow grass was splattered with blood and entrails and red-clad bodies littered the ground. To the South, a handful of red uniforms fled from the fight into the thick forest.

'Deserters, my Lord?' stuttered Curtnas, the long-haired squire.

The Duke chewed his lip, his heart wrenching as he watched another sword slice through one of his men. The Hende steadily encroached, taking back precious land, one body at a time.

'My Lord? What is your command?'

The Duke gulped and slumped. He stood out of reach without a scratch while the blood of his men flowed freely. Why was he so weak?

'Do we retreat, my Lord?'

The Old Duke had raised him on tales from the last Civil War but none of his father's stories had prepared him for defeat. The other nobles and squires on the hillock watched, judged, waited. If only the Old Duke was here by his side.

Digging deep, he found his voice. The fear of appearing cowardly and the sideways glances of his peers were greater than his fear of death. 'No,' he said vehemently. 'We must reach the barricades. Prince Absalom is relying on us.'

'But, my Lord?' the young squire said, his voice crackling with fear.

He tried to fill his lungs with courage. 'Onward,' he called in the loudest voice he could muster. 'Towards the river.'

The squire blasted his horn.

With a gentle touch of the reins, his steed Mortu charged into the crowd, never shying when sharp blades met soft flesh. If only his horse's fearlessness would rub off on him.

Swallowed by the blanket of smoke, the Duke could barely see more than a few feet ahead. Black and red shapes swarmed. Grunts and roars sounded from all directions. Steel clashed against steel and the wounded wailed for their mothers and pleaded for the Father's mercy.

Mortu crashed into a throng of brawling men. The Duke clutched his sword tightly as faces and swords emerged out of the fog. A black-clad soldier ran towards him and the Duke swung his blade. The sharp edge hummed through the air and slammed into the Hende man's neck. The man hit the grass with a wet slap. One down.

Up ahead a red-clad man was winning against three men dressed in black, swinging his sword with a grin.

'Well done, my good man,' the Duke cheered, foolishly taking his eyes off his own surroundings. The pain was the first thing he noticed.

The blade sliced through hose, skin and meat, shuddering to a stop when the metal collided with his thigh bone. The black-clad man drew back his sword and the Duke fell from his saddle, crashing to the hard-trampled dirt.

'Physician,' the Duke croaked but the swordsman lunged again, this time slashing at Mortu, sending the white stallion toppling to the ground.

Lying on the ground, Mortu thrashed and whinnied beside him, blood frothing around his muzzle. Tears clogged the Duke's throat as he reached out to stroke his beloved horse. As he moved he saw the blood, darkening and saturating his hose leg. He fingered the warm red liquid and his mind scrambled. Mortu's blood or his own?

He tried to move his half-severed leg. As he tugged, he felt no pain, only a gnawing, spreading cold. His leg obeyed reluctantly, his useless foot trailing along the grass like a sulky child.

'Physician!' he called again but his voice was drowned out by the chaos of battle.

The man in black loomed over him, his twisted smile showed broken brown teeth. The Duke tried to drag himself backwards but the effort ripped his wound wider. The pain hit like a torrent, overwhelming and blinding. His skin blazed hot but his body trembled, sweaty and feverish. This must be a dream, a nightmare and he would soon wake safely tucked up in his castle bower.

Mortu flailed his last, his intestines spooling onto the dirt and the man lifted his sword above his head. The Duke's eyes widened, mesmerised. Caked with blood, the weapon looked ordinary but it had carved effortlessly through both man and horse. What chance did he have against this special blade?

'I have coin,' the Duke spluttered.

The man guffawed. He was not big or intimidating; if anything he was smaller than average and somehow this made it worse. 'I want your head on a spike. That's worth more than any of your Vorosy silver.'

'You know who I am. I am rich,' he replied with a wince, unable to stop the words tumbling from his mouth. 'Please. I would be a valuable prisoner.'

'It's time to meet the Father.'

The Duke braced his arms over his head and waited for the blow. 'Please do not kill me.'

'Coward.'

He was supposed to be a nobleman, the leader of a battalion and yet he whimpered like a maiden. All his life, swords had felt heavy and awkward in his hands but he'd had no choice. He was born into this life. Perhaps, deep inside he'd always suspected his life would end this way. His privileged life about to be cut short by a small man with rotten teeth and a sharp sword.

'Please,' he said, sickened by his own pathetic voice.

The man laughed. The Duke shut his eyes and waited. He deserved nothing better.

There was a clash of swords and the Duke prised open his eyes. A red-clad soldier had come to his rescue. The wiry hero brandished a dagger half the size of the frightening broad sword. He darted left and right, dodging blows before kicking the swordsman's legs out from under him and swiftly slitting his throat. The man in black gurgled and clutched at his neck, his blood spilled down his shirt like an overfilling goblet.

The man wiped his dagger and hurried to the Duke's side.

'Thank you,' the Duke said as the man helped him to his feet.

His rescuer said nothing.

The Duke cringed. How much had he heard? Did he know the full extent of his cowardice?

'I am eternally grateful to you.'

They hobbled together across the grass but his strength was fading with each step as the blood drained from his body and the world swam before his eyes.

'My Lord!' The Duke fluttered his eyes open to see Lord Kalin's pained face in front of him. A surgeon with a broad-axe at his side.

He gulped as his men swamped him, pushing aside the man with the dagger.

'Get back to the line,' ordered Kalin. 'Stop lazing about.'

The man's cold staring eyes sent shivers through the Duke's body. He knew he should have intervened, should have said something in the man's defence. That man was the hero after all. The Duke could have blamed the pain for his silence but he looked away, knowing full well what he was doing.

The Duke woke up hours later in a tent with a physician tying bandages where his thigh used to be.

'The man,' he said, bolting upright. 'Where is he?'

'Rest, my Lord,' said the physician, handing over a goblet of wine.

'I must thank...' His voice trailed off as his stump thumped with pain. 'Who was the man who brought me here?'

'I did not see, my Lord.' The physician shrugged.

'Some peasant. They all look the same,' Kalin said from a chair in the corner. 'Look at you. Proper battle scars. The Old Duke would be proud. Was it one of those new swords? I've heard it takes weeks to fold the steel. Ingenious. We need to capture one of their smiths.'

'Mortu is gone,' he sighed.

Kalin shook his head. 'A fine horse.'

'Did we triumph?'

'We suffered many losses but yes, now the path to Sulun is clear. The final push is tomorrow. If Prince Celso and the Neven have not already run from the Palace with their tails between their legs.'

'Excellent,' the Duke said, collapsing wearily into the cot. Where was he, that man with the dagger? Was he in the camp, celebrating? Telling all of the cowardly Duke who bargained for his life?

Kalin leaned forward in his chair. 'Come on, my Lord. I have been waiting here all night to hear what happened.'

The Duke had wished Kalin would leave him to his pain and cowardice but the tale must be told sooner or later. It was time to start spinning the lies. The more he told his story, the more he convinced himself. Almost. But a part of him always scoured the room for that small man. Months had passed without a glimpse of him and he had started to tell himself a new story: there was nothing to fear. His saviour must have been killed in the Battle of Truinn, along with countless other foot soldiers. He was safe and no one would ever know the truth.

But the Duke was wrong. The man was here, somewhere in Ambrovna and at any moment, his secret could be revealed.

The Duke gestured for more wine, in the vain hope that one more goblet would cure his nightmares.

CHAPTER TWENTY-FOUR

W ILL YOU HELP US?' SIRA said, leaning forward from
her tree stump seat. 'The world will be better off without
him.'

'You believe that but is it the truth? Only the Great Mother chooses
where and when. And who.'

'Rabel is suffering. Your own sister. And your niece. Your nephews.
Your blood.'

'Takin' a life? You want that on your conscience? What would your
Father say?'

'But He is wrong,' Sira blurted, quickly made a circle on her
forehead. 'I mean Iwan. Not the Father.'

'The Great Mother doesn't have right and wrong. No good. No bad.
Just what is. There's only one certainty in life. Death. There's a time
when death comes for every one of us. A time. A day. Only she knows
when and she doesn't like it when we meddle in her plans.'

'What about justice?'

'Justice? Another made-up story. Is there justice in the weather? You
build a home to keep out the rain and the wind. For thirty years your
little house proves itself until one day the Weather Daughter blows in
a storm and destroys it all. Is that good or bad? Everyone, everything
must die.'

'We are not animals. We must live by what is right,' Sira said.

'Survival or death. That's all.'

'Life is not so simple.'

'You and the town people like to complicate the world. But if you look closely, your rules are all contrived for their gain. Your Father is dreamed up by men in bronze gowns.'

Sira winced and checked over her shoulder, even though they were alone in the hut.

'We can't change anythin' by sayin' nonsense verses,' Wisia continued. 'I'm glad I'm free of Him and all your rules. I float with the wind because there's no point fightin' it.'

Sira wiped her palm over her face. Her sister reached out and patted her knee. 'This isn't what you want to hear, I know.'

'I am sorry,' Sira said, lowering her eyes. 'I did not help you. Back then.'

Wisia chuckled and shook her head. 'I didn't need your help.'

'I should have stopped them. All the terrible things they said about you. I should have...' Sira dropped her head. 'But I did nothing. And when the same thing happened, I did not help Rabel. But I can make amends. I will make it right this time. All I need is your help.' She sniffled into her sleeve.

'And I'll help you. If I can. But understand that the Great Mother doesn't promise you'll get the result you want.'

Sira's face brightened. 'I am willing to take the risk.'

'But...' Wisia tugged at her lower lip.

Sira swallowed. This was what she feared. She glanced at the grinning skulls on the shelf. 'What do you want in return?'

'I already ate your cake. But you must promise me somethin'.'

'Anything if you will help.'

'Anything?'

'Anything.'

'Promise me you're listenin' to your heart? If you are, that is all I need.'

Sira's heart thumped in reply. The question was like an arrow to her chest. What did Wisia see?

'I am,' she spluttered.

'Your whole heart?' Wisia lifted an eyebrow.

Sira nodded jerkily and Wisia jumped to her feet. 'Come,' she said and Sira stood, groaning as she straightened her stiff knees.

Wisia led her back into the night, under tree branches, between boulders and across ankle-deep streams. A thin sliver of a waxing moon gleamed overhead.

Following as best she could, Sira pondered Wisia's puzzling words. But she breathed easier, feeling as if her apology had set her free after so many years.

They continued along a narrow ridge overlooking perilous cliffs and finally stopped at a grove of walnut trees whose outstretched branches interlocked into a leafy tunnel over the winding path. The ground was carpeted with damp leaves and half-chewed nuts.

'We're here. This is the right time.'

Squatting and rummaging among the layers of red and yellow leaves, Wisia dug into the brown compost, releasing the fertile smells underneath. She plucked out a white-capped fungus and stood up, inspecting it in the dim light.

'Only good for eatin'.'

She pocketed it and moved to the next tree, sweeping aside more mounds of leaves, and uncovering a handful of white puffballs.

'Ah ha.'

Wisia plucked out the smallest one, the size of a daisy eye.

'Puffballs?' Sira frowned as her sister wrapped it in a square of goat hide and handed it over. The fur parcel, secured shut with a thin strap of leather, weighed nothing in her palm.

'Much worse. I've given you enough to slay five large men.'

'Will he taste it?'

'He'll never notice.'

Sira gingerly slipped the pouch into her dress. The all-important contents hummed through the cloth, vibrating against her leg. Life or death in her pocket.

She clasped Wisia's rough hand tightly. 'Thank you, dear sister.'

'Remember what I said.'

Sira nodded and her stomach roiled. She was too afraid to ask which part her sister meant.

But the details did not matter, Sira had what she came for. She would not let Rabel down this time.

CHAPTER TWENTY-FIVE

G ET OFF ME,' THE BOY squealed, his voice bouncing off the brick walls and down the dungeon corridor.

'In here, you little toerag,' grunted Seliv.

A tubby guard in a terracotta tunic dragged the kicking boy into the room. The boy skidded on the well-worn bricks and slipped to the ground.

'Takes two of you, eh Seliv? How old is he? Eight?' Lord Kalin said with his boots on the table.

'I'm nine.' The hare-lipped kid scowled. His hessian shirt was stained and ripped under one arm.

'Nine, *m'Lord*,' the fat guard spat. 'Don't they teach you no manners?'

'I gather this is the culprit.' Kalin rolled his eyes.

'Yes, my Lord. Caught Wilken here red-handed,' Seliv said.

Seliv handed Kalin a slip of paper. He unfolded the ink-smudged note, which was covered in clumsy lettering.

'*You aren't what you seem, Duke. I'll tell them all unless you pay.*'

'What do you have to say for yourself, boy?'

Wilken stuck out his tongue.

'Answer the Master of the Shield, you little turd.' The guard clipped him across the ear.

'Ow!' The boy clutched his head. 'I've done nothin' wrong.'

'Where did you get this letter?' Kalin waved the paper in his face.

'What letter?'

Kalin narrowed his eyes. 'Do you know how serious this is?'

'It's just a bit of paper,' Wilken said with a shrug of his scrawny shoulders.

'Just a bit of paper, *my Lord*.' Seliv prodded a hard finger into the kid's chest.

'Do you know what this means? This is treason. A threat to the Duke.'

Wilken lifted his head. 'Treason?' His voice shook. 'But it's just words.'

'Of course. You cannot read. Can you?'

'Look at him, sir,' Seliv said.

The boy bowed his head, all his swagger gone. He suddenly seemed much younger than nine. 'I didn't know, m'Lord,' he murmured, his bottom lip quivering. 'He gave me a copper and asked me to deliver it. Easy coin. That's all.'

'Who?'

The boy shrugged. 'He hangs around the Alleys. Near the Seaweed Arms. Don't know his name. There's lots of new faces back from the war. He gave me a copper. I didn't ask.'

'Details, boy. Old? Young? Tall? Short?'

'Not tall, not short...' he said, his voice wobbling.

'You can do better than that, Wilken,' Seliv said.

The boy pouted.

'Where is your mother? Maybe she can make you talk,' Kalin said.

'Probably on Guts Alley,' chuckled the guard.

'You shut up.' The boy turned and jabbed him in the ballocks.

The guard groaned and doubled over. Seliv guffawed and Kalin let out a little smile.

'You little...' the guard wheezed. He lunged with his doughy forearms outstretched.

Kalin held out his hand and the guard stopped short.

'Would you remember the man again, boy? If you saw him?'

Wilken nodded his head vigorously. 'Yes, m'Lord.'

'Guard. Go with him,' Kalin exhaled. 'Walk around the Alleys. Find this man. And do not tell anyone about this, Wilken. Otherwise we shall bring your mother back here, too. And we will not be as kind. We must find him. Understand?'

'Yes, m'Lord,' the boy repeated.

The guard grabbed Wilken by the shirt and pulled him down the corridor with Seliv following behind.

Alone in the room, Kalin rubbed the back of his neck. He unfolded the note and read it again, chuckling as he pictured the Duke's little indiscretions and remembered a few of his own. The Duke was a man after all, and as a noble, he could do as he pleased. But he wondered why his friend had withheld the details of his colourful adventures.

Kalin headed through the dungeon gate and towards the keep, his head filled with memories of the plump brown-eyed Ishilde from his favourite Sulun pleasure house. He did not hear the Seneschal approach.

'Lord Kalin, I was hoping to catch you.'

His lusty daydream spoiled, Kalin scowled and turned to head in the opposite direction.

'Lord Kalin, I must speak with you. Most urgently. About your expenses.' The stooping coin counter waved his hand, his heavy chain necklace rattling.

Kalin rushed towards the Avenue, calling back over his shoulder. 'I have an urgent matter to attend, Seneschal. I will come to see you this evening.'

'You said that yesterday,' the Seneschal grumbled.

Kalin strode down the Avenue and into the Square. It had been a long time since he'd led an investigation and a little adventure in the Alleys would make for an amusing tale at this evening's meal. If he hurried, he'd easily catch them.

CHAPTER TWENTY-SIX

F OR HOURS RABEL HAD STARED into the darkness, waiting for first light of day to peek through the holes in the thatched roof. When she had managed to doze off, her scraps of sleep were haunted by angry, sweaty dreams. Her eyes were already open when someone knocked gently at the door. She slipped from under the scratchy blanket, careful not to disturb Iwan or the sleeping babes intertwined on the leaf-stuffed mattress. Rubbing her sore eyes and covering her thin shift with her shawl, she cracked open the door to see Sira.

'Good. You're awake,' Sira whispered.

Rabel swallowed hard and closing the door softly behind her as she stepped barefoot into the dirt street.

Sira grabbed her hand and placed a fur pouch into her palm, wrapping her fingers around it. Sira started to speak but Rabel's mind drifted away. The fur was soft against her skin but the gravity of the contents pulsed through her veins. Rabel blinked and tried to listen to her sister.

'More than enough. It will take half a day,' Sira said gently, keeping her voice low.

Rabel gulped. 'How was she? What did she want in return?'

'Nothing. I think,' Sira said, pulling at her bottom lip. 'She did not ask for anything. All those years alone in the hills have made her even stranger.'

'How does she live? What did she say?'

'I must go. There will be plenty of time to explain later. But you have it now. Will you do it today?'

Rabel clutched the pouch to her chest, her hand clammy against the fur. 'Thank you.'

The sisters hugged and Sira slipped her a couple of coppers before disappearing down the puddle-filled Alleys. Rabel stood in the cold, staring at her hand. The answer was here, laying in her palm.

Could she ever be as strong as her sisters? She felt unworthy of their sacrifice, risking eternal damnation to help her. The all-seeing Father knew their devious plans and thoughts, no matter how they repented. Even if her cowardice overwhelmed her and she changed her mind.

'Mornin' Goodwife,' said the rabbit-faced stable hand, unlocking the stable door. 'Out and about early?'

Rabel flinched, shoving the fur pouch into her pocket. 'Mornin' Porvid.'

'Nice day, isn't it?'

Smiling weakly, Rabel looked up at the thin strip of clear sky between the broken roof shingles and squirrel-gnawed thatches. The linen-coloured sky turned bluer by the moment.

Today.

Could she do it today?

She rubbed her hand across her forehead as one of the twins began to cry on the other side of the flimsy wall. She reached for the shack door, the question still resting unanswered on her tongue.

With a child in each hand, Rabel headed for the Square. She bypassed the shiny red apples, the green-topped turnips and the clear-eyed cod from the grocers and turned down the alley, tip-toeing over a rivulet of dirty water. She knocked on the back doors of the shops, just as she did every day.

The stallholders sighed, hands on their hips, wary as soon as they saw her familiar face.

'I can pay. I'm not beggin'.' She'd say, holding out a copper. No one believed her until they saw the coin in her palm. 'Stale bread? Old milk? Rotten vegetables? I'll take it off your hands?' Her search for food could take the whole day as she knocked on door after door.

Sometimes she came away with nothing, their produce sold out before she arrived. On other days, she was lucky if she got mouldy cheese, a blackened cabbage or rock-hard bread. Food they couldn't sell to anyone else.

Today she was lucky. Today a single copper bought her stinky fish heads, rubbery parsnips and a caraway cob loaf with a suspicious bite out of one end. Enough for a decent midday meal and a copper left over for tomorrow.

'Come along.' She dragged her twins from their game in the dirty water and wiped them down, ignoring the sneering stall girls who leaned against the laneway walls. Rabel hurried the twins into the town Square and her mind wandered to the pouch hidden inside her pocket.

'Good morning.'

Rabel flinched. Mistress Plesec's face was covered nose to chin by a cream coloured veil, but her black eye was on full display. She had a sullen Irina in tow.

'Mornin', Mistress Plesec.' Rabel cleared her throat. 'A fine day.'

'It is indeed. Irina, go get a round of cheese from Dyntr and do not pay more than six coppers. No matter what he says.'

Bowing her head with a sneer, Irina scuttled off. Mistress Plesec grabbed Rabel by the elbow and pulled her into a corner, away from the earshot of others. Rabel's breath snagged in her throat.

'I passed on your message,' she whispered. Their faces were so close, Rabel sniffed the plum brandy on her breath. 'Has Sira come to see you?'

'I'm very thankful.'

The veiled woman's good eye gleamed. 'Everything is in place?'

Rabel hesitated, her stomach clenching. How much had Sira told her? Did she know about the contents of her pocket?

'I am here to help,' Mistress Plesec said. 'You know you can trust me.'

Rabel nodded, unsure what to say. She kicked the dirt with her boots.

'That's settled.' The merchant's wife raised her voice, loud enough for any passer-by to hear. 'Please come to see me tomorrow morning, Rabel. I may have work for you.'

'I will, Mistress Plesec,' Rabel replied at a similar volume. 'Thank you.'

The merchant's wife tossed her head and strode through the market, calling out for Irina.

Rabel collapsed against the wall, her knees trembling, Aula tugged at her skirts. 'Ma?'

Leaning her cheek against the cool rough bricks, Rabel caught her breath and took a few moments before returning home to prepare the midday meal. The meal that would solve all her problems. She had everything she needed. Everything except the most important thing.

Courage.

CHAPTER TWENTY-SEVEN

K ALIN FINALLY FOUND SELIV AND Wilken in the Alleys
among the shacks and stalls built from patched sails and broken
doors. He tutted as he passed grubby men and women hawking
grey gruel, shabby trinkets, moonshine and suspect stolen goods. In the
past year without the men of the Shield, the Alleys' denizens had spread
like vines. Women were just as capable of petty crime as men. He resolved
to return and clean up the Alleys, but first the small matter of blackmail.

'What have you discovered?' he said, striding up to them.

'Nothing as yet, m'Lord,' Seliv said, his meaty fist firmly attached
to the writhing Wilken's collar.

'I told you. He's not around.'

'Are you sure you want to be down here, m'Lord?' Seliv whispered.

'Why ever not? Solving a little crime is exactly what I need to help
me return to my duties as Master of the Shield. The old head gets a little
rusty with fighting alone.'

'It's only...' Seliv chewed on his lip.

Kalin rolled his eyes. 'Spit it out.'

'You stand out a bit, m'Lord.'

He lifted his head to see two of the nearby stalls had suddenly packed
up and disappeared. Only a pair of holed boots and an empty jug remained
discarded in the mud. As people squeezed past him, they hid their faces.

'I should be more visible in the Alleys. It will force these people to
smarten up their acts. It's no better than a pigsty down here.'

'M'Lord, people might not be so forthcomin' with you around.'

'Rubbish. Lead on. Where to next? This tavern? All this walking makes a man thirsty.'

'This way, sir,' Seliv sighed and he dragged Wilken like a sulky dog along the winding crowded passages.

'Oi! What're you doin' with my Wilken? Take your hands off 'im.' A scrawny woman dressed only in a stained shift elbowed her way through the crowd.

'And who are you, erm...Goodwife?' Seliv said.

'Get out of here, Ma.' Wilken rushed forward but the big man tugged him back.

'What's he done?' She said, eyes flashing.

'Your son is helping the Shield like a decent townsman,' Kalin said. 'None of your concern.'

'Sorry, m'Lord. I didn't see you there.' The woman smoothed her hair with a smile and dropped into a wobbly curtsey. 'You can call me Eeva,'

'We shall bring your son back when we are done with our search,' Kalin said, ignoring her batting eyelids. 'As long as he co-operates.'

'Of course, m'Lord. He's a good boy, really.' Eeva stepped forward and he grimaced at the scent of her sickly cider breath. 'Maybe you'll come and find me when you're done with him.'

He pressed his lips together. 'Let's go, Seliv.'

'I saw him earlier...' she added as they walked away. 'Talking to a skinny man who used to be on the boats years ago. I can't remember his name.'

'Ma!' Wilken said through clenched teeth. 'Don't.'

'What?' She shrugged her bony shoulders. 'I'm helpin' the Shield.'

'Could you describe him?' Seliv said.

'He likes the Seaweed Arms. And the cock fights. Back from the war like you.'

'Would you recognise him if you saw him again?'

'Oh yes, m'Lord. Maybe he's there now. We could go and check.'

Seliv scowled at him but Kalin half-shrugged.

'The more information the better.'

The gaunt woman grinned and Kalin sighed.

'This way,' she said.

CHAPTER TWENTY-EIGHT

EVERY FEW MOMENTS RABEL STIRRED the pot. The stew didn't need stirring but it was the only way to stop her hands from shaking. The fur parcel in her pocket throbbed against her leg. What strange Wasp Woman magic lay inside?

At the table, Iwan picked his teeth with a knife and the twins sat alongside him on the bench, a row of honey-brown heads. The sight of her family together hit Rabel like a slap across her face and she changed her mind for the thirtieth time. Iwan was the father of her children. He'd been the centre of her life since she was fifteen summers old.

At first, she had been flattered by the wiry sandy-headed lad who stopped by the cheese merchants every single day and ordered the smallest sliver of cheese. He'd only had eyes for Rabel. In those days, he'd worked on the boats, coming back from sea early each afternoon with plenty of time to walk her home. He smelled of fish but he gave her jonquils and told her she was the prettiest girl in Ambrovna, and for a while, she believed him. Back then Iwan had been a good man. He stood by her when her bleeding stopped and Pa threw her out. They were betrothed within days and she almost fooled herself his love had rinsed away her sins.

Life was good until the Great Storm came and smashed the town's fishing boats against the sharp red cliffs, leaving Iwan without work. The storm took a toll on the whole of Ambrovna and without fish, food was scarce. To begin with Iwan had tried hard to find work, but as the weeks and months passed with nothing but an hour of work here and there, Iwan started to squander his free days, and his coins, in the Inns on the wrestling and the cock fights.

Iwan used to stroke her cheek and hold her in his arms but he became a stranger who no longer brought her jonquils or kind words. She ignored the gossip about his losses until the debt collectors knocked at the door and took whatever they could carry. She told herself that if she tried harder, perhaps he'd be that man again.

Sighing, she continued to stir the pot.

Why had the Father forsaken her? A good honest death on the battlefield could have avoided all of this. Teo and Jorn would have grown up thinking their father was a war hero, whatever the truth. Thousands of other men lay dead, why save him?

If only the war had changed him and brought back the young Iwan she'd married. Older women had said a war was good for an idle man, that closeness to death reminded him of the important things in life.

It was just like Iwan to prove them wrong.

Over the past year she proved to herself she could manage alone, although in truth, she'd been alone for many years.

Aula climbed up onto the table and knocked over Iwan's tankard, spilling ale over the tabletop and onto the ground.

'You little--' Iwan jumped to his feet, trying to salvage his booze. Aula wailed. 'I should have sold you when I had the chance. Maybe Sabet'll still take you.'

Iwan shoved her off the table Her head thumped against the wooden bench and the little girl unleashed another ear-splitting wail as a thin stream of blood ran down her face.

'Aula,' Rabel said, her voice so weak. Sickened, she rushed for her but Aula scuttled away and hid in the corner of the room behind the mattress. 'Come out. Please.'

'She'll live,' Iwan shouted. 'Where's my food?'

Glaring, Rabel changed her mind for the thirty-first time.

'Now! Are you deaf?'

Rabel turned back to the pot and with shaking hands ladled stew into a carved wooden bowl. Aula shrieked once again from the corner and Rabel flinched, splattering stew onto the ground.

'Shut up!' Iwan yelled at Aula, without moving from his seat.

Rabel's heartbeat thundered in her ears as she angled her body to hide her hands. She unwrapped the pouch and stared down at the tiny white puffball. It was so small. She remembered what Sira had said and chopped it in two, pocketing the other half. A lump swelled in her throat as she finely sliced the mushroom. She glanced over at Iwan with his contorted ugly face and watched him ignore his own crying children.

Her hand, which held the innocent-looking white shreds, hovered over Iwan's bowl. Rabel looked over at Jorn with his trembling chin and listened to Aula's muffled sobs in the background. She dropped the white flecks into his bowl and stirred. Ever so slowly, she turned towards the table, expecting something or someone to stop her. But the Father did nothing to intervene.

'About time. I'm bloody starvin' to death over here.'

Iwan grabbed the bowl from her shaking hands. Rabel swallowed hard, waiting beside him as he took a long slurp. He winced, his lips curling in disgust.

Rabel's heart squeezed.

'Fish head stew. Urgh.' Iwan stuck out his coated tongue then he took another gulp.

'All we can afford,' she said, a wobble in her voice. He grunted, lifting the bowl to his chin.

The door opened and Teo hurried in, a wide smile on his face and a sprig of straw sticking out of his hair.

'Get paid today, lad?' Iwan said, before belching loudly and slamming his empty bowl down on the table.

'Not till tomorrow,' Teo said. She handed him his bowl and grabbed for the straw in his hair but the boy jerked his head out of her reach.

'Tomorrow.' Iwan got to his feet and Rabel's eyes widened as she watched his every movement. 'I'll expect to see those coins tomorrow, lad. Understand?'

'Yes, Pa,' the boy said, his eyes on his stew.

'Good lad.' He clapped Teo's shoulder while Rabel's knees shook. So far, he seemed normal. Did it work?

'I'm goin' out. I've got to see a man about some business.' He grinned. 'I think my prospects are lookin' up. We won't be eatin' this shit for much longer.'

'Will you be home for dinner?' she said brightly, trying to cover her quivering lip.

Iwan shrugged and swaggered off, slamming the door behind him. It was done.

Gripping the table edge, she gulped for breaths, her pulse galloping. If it worked as Sira said, he would never walk through that door again.

A slight smile blossomed on her face.

'I did get paid today, Ma,' Teo said, sliding a handful of coppers along the tabletop.

Rabel grinned, her face shining as she tousled Teo's hair.

'Any word from Rabel?' the Duchess said.

'Nothing, m'Lady,' Sira replied, unpicking another wayward stitch with a sigh. 'Wisia said the mushroom should take quick effect. Is the lack of news good or bad?'

Agata pressed her lips together.

A gentle knock on the bedchamber door made both women jump. The Duke hobbled into the room on his iron crutch, his empty hose leg swinging.

Agata's heart swelled with delight. 'My Lord.'

Sira curtseyed and disappeared to her adjoining room.

Agata put aside her needlework and rose to her feet to help him but he waved his hand dismissively and found his own way beside her on the cushioned bench.

'I came to see how you are faring,' the Duke said. 'My Uncle mentioned you were feeling poorly.'

Agata clenched her fists in her lap and sucked in a breath before replying. Poorly was not the right word and it had been almost an entire day since she had last seen Lord Sylwin. 'I am much better, my Lord.'

'I am glad.'

He held out his arms. His eyes were soft but she hesitated, staying firmly in her seat. She longed to run to him but where had he been all day? And all night? He'd been home for days, but had barely spent two moments in her presence.

Agata caught a hint of his warm scent, the familiar smell of the man she loved, a smell she had missed so much. But she straightened her shoulders. 'Wine, my Lord?'

He folded his arms across his chest and nodded curtly. Lord Sylwin's words were true, his eyes were different. Her husband was the same man, but there was something new in his eyes, a change she could not articulate. The war had stolen more than his leg.

Agata poured his wine from the decanter and brought a glass dish of sugar-dusted plums. He took the goblet from her hand and their fingers touched. Her cheeks reddened and her mouth ran dry. They were husband and wife yet strangers all over again. She took a sip of wine.

'You are so beautiful, my wife,' he said.

'I have missed you, dear husband.' She reached for him, finding only the empty fabric where his leg used to be.

He flinched and Agata bit her lip. He stiffened and glanced away towards the window.

With another gulp of wine, she squashed her vexation, drew in a breath and grabbed his hand. 'Please do not push me away, my Lord. I am your wife. I declared before the Father to stay by your side until I was taken to the Land Beyond the Sunset. No matter what.'

He sighed. 'So much has changed--'

'Not for me. Ambrovna is the same. Your castle is still here. Your people are still here. I am still here.'

'But my ....'

'I do not care.'

'If only it were so simple.'

'Why is it complicated, my Lord? What could be simpler than a husband and his wife?'

'What you must think of me--' He averted his eyes.

'I am proud of you.' Agata dropped to her knees in front of him and clasped his hands in hers. 'Enduring such pain.'

'I am wrapped in my own misery.' He shook his head. 'My own pathetic thoughts.'

'We can be happy again, my Lord.'

'You pity me.' He pulled his hands away. 'This is not the way for a man and wife.'

'No, my Lord. I did not understand at first. I was blinded by my own selfishness. But Lord Sylwin provided wise counsel. He told me to consider the horrors you'd experienced.'

'Some days were bleak.' He nodded. 'I find it hard to drive the memories from my mind.'

'Let me help you.'

'I am not the man I was.'

'I have changed, too.'

He paused and she gently bit her lip, her eyes never leaving his.

The fire crackled in the grate as they sat in a thick silence until finally he unleashed a long slow sigh.

'I fear that I cannot sire heirs.'

Agata clamped her mouth shut and stifled her cry. With all her musing and reasoning, this possibility had never occurred to her.

'The physicians in Sulun said it should not affect my ability to father but I am--'

Beneath her dress, Agata's belly shrivelled but she reached for him and squeezed his hand. 'You must put your faith in the healers, my Lord. The Father will reward your faith and loyalty on the battlefield.'

The Duke shook his head, Agata's heart tearing at the sight of his vacant eyes. Gently she took his bearded chin in her hands and forced him to look at her. She smiled wider as she gazed into his face. No matter what she had overheard through the solar door, he was not like the others. At his core, this man was good.

'Let us see whether the physicians were right.'

She leaned in and kissed him. At first, he did not return the kiss but Agata persisted. Then he softened, his lips opening, a gentle moan escaping his throat. She pressed her body weight against him, her chest against his. He wrapped his arms around her neck and pulled her close. She gasped as he tightened his embrace. His arms were lean and muscular, his grip as though he never wanted to let her go.

'My Agata.' He pulled back from the kiss and whispered in her ear, pushing aside her stray curls and caressing her earlobes. A delicious shiver ran down her spine. His kisses grew more insistent and he nibbled at her neck. She unfastened his tunic, her fingers stroking the fine hairs on his chest.

His fingertips traced down her neck and across her chest, smoothing over the roundness of her breasts, tracing gently over her skin. He tugged at her belt, slipped the gown from her body, lifted her chemise and cupping her bare skin in his hands. He found the sensitive tips of her nipples with his tongue. She panted as he licked one side and then the other and threaded her fingers through his hair. She tingled, longing for him to be inside her.

This time she was careful as she ran her hand along his right leg. His thigh was strong from months on horseback. He continued, nuzzling at her chest as she inched her fingers up his inner thigh. His drawers tightened and she smiled. His fears were unfounded.

Agata loosened his ties and he lifted his hips as she yanked his drawers down. Her hands slipped under his chemise, along his naked torso and over his hip to the end of his left thigh, reaching the bandage-covered stump.

He stopped cold.

'No. No,' she said softly in his ear. 'Please.'

'But I am no longer the man you married,' he said.

'I disagree, my Lord,' she said, as her fingers found him.

He gasped. 'My lovely,' he murmured as she took him in her hand. He was hard and ready.

She lay back on the bench and opened herself. He slid over her, his eyes gleaming, his breath heavy. She cried out with his first thrust. It had been a year since he was last inside her.

'Did I hurt you?' he said.

'No.' She kissed him forcefully and he smiled as he entered her again. She arched her back, grabbing fistfuls of his hair as they writhed together. He grunted and pushed harder, she leaned her head back and he bit at her throat. His fingers explored her, finding again the special spot they had discovered in their first weeks together. She inhaled sharply, her eyes shining as he rubbed, rippling back and forwards and the tingling spread down her legs and flowed up into her chest, her breath catching in her breast.

'A little more. A little more,' she moaned, her heart thundering in her ears. The room dissolved until there was only his hands, his smell, his beard against her skin. She burst out, the pleasure rushing over her, her body undulating. He held her tightly against him and thrust harder and harder. Their bodies glowed with sweat as they slapped together. She kissed him feverishly, gripping hard at his shoulders as he pushed and strained. He spluttered, cried out and clutched her to his chest. She could feel his heart beating against her own ribcage.

'I told you, husband.' She smoothed his hair as they regained their breath. 'The physicians were right. You will bless me with many children.'

He nestled his head into her shoulder, his body trembling. Agata's brow creased as she rubbed his back and held him tight, his hot tears splashed against her skin.

'I am yours,' she said, rocking him like her own child.

'My love,' he said, his voice muffled against her chest.

Agata smiled.

CHAPTER TWENTY-NINE

'QUIET!' RABEL TRAWLED HER FINGERS through her hair.

'Mama. Mama,' cried Aula.

Rabel paced, wearing a path in the dirt floor, a cloud of dust trailing her skirts. She rubbed her shoulders and watched the door.

'I shouldn't have done it,' she muttered, tearing at her scalp. 'I'm wicked. I must confess.'

She opened the front door. It should have happened by now. Outside the day was fading into night.

'Waiting for Pa?' said Teo, appearing from the stables next door.

'Yes,' Rabel said, covering her mouth with her hands.

Her oldest boy came inside and slumped on the bench. 'I hope he never comes home.'

Rabel said nothing as she closed the door and lit the candle stub in the centre of the table, all the while keeping one eye on the door.

'I'll put on the stew,' she said.

'Not hungry, Ma.'

Rabel turned from the hearth with a frown, his face was paler than usual. Almost green.

'I feel bad.'

Teo squeezed his eyes shut, hunching his narrow shoulders as he clutched at his belly. Rabel laid her hand on his forehead.

'You're burnin'. You must eat. Then straight to sleep.'

'No, Ma...'

His words were cut short by a rush of vomit, gushing from his mouth and splashing all over the dirt floor. Rabel rubbed his back.

'There. There. Let it out.'

'My belly, Ma,' he said weakly, red froth bubbling around his lips. His shirt stained crimson. He gagged again, red liquid surging from his mouth, his eyes straining in their sockets.

'Did you eat something bad?' she said, the rancid smell singeing her nostrils. Then her words hit her. 'No,' she whispered, clutching at her throat. 'No.'

Teo crumpled to the ground, spluttering, his thin arms jerking.

She turned, crashing full force into the table as she rushed to slop water into a bowl. She pulled back Teo's head and forced water into his mouth. Teo shoved the bowl away and spewed again, choking and sobbing like one of the twins.

She stared helplessly at him. 'She didn't tell me how to stop it.' Tears streamed down her face. 'No. Teo. My boy. Not you.'

He writhed on the dirt floor in his own bloody vomit, arms thrashing, whole body convulsing.

Rabel fell to her knees, cradling her boy to her breast, her eyes skywards. 'No. No, Father. Take me instead.'

Teo slapped her in the face with his flailing hands. She only felt her heart being ripped from her chest.

The twins wailed, and Rabel howled along with them. She called his name but Teo did not respond as more blood poured from his mouth.

Then Teo stopped shuddering. So very still.

'No,' she screamed, shaking him but his head lolled.

'No!'

His open sightless eyes stared at her, accusing, unrelenting.

Rabel ignored the knocking on the door, burying her head in his chest, sobbing.

The door opened. Her heart plummeted. Iwan was home. She'd mixed up the bowls somehow. She should have known this was how it would end.

'Goodwife?'

Rabel jerked her head up and stared.

Two strangers stood in the doorway, propping up Iwan. He was dead drunk, his head flopping forward against his chest. Hot tears stung her eyes, Teo was gone but her no-good husband was back.

'Put him over there,' she croaked.

The two men dropped Iwan onto the bed.

'He was sick...' the bald one started.

Iwan's head rolled back, his face covered in red smears, his lips colourless.

Rabel's breath froze in her throat. Everything slowed down. It was as if she was travelling through tar.

'Iwan?' she whispered.

'What happened to the boy?' the bald man asked.

She placed Teo's head gently down on the ground and struggled to her feet.

The bearded man clutched his hands in front of his chest. 'He had a fit in the tavern. Spewed great loads of blood and he never got up again. In the eyes of the Father.'

The two men made the sign of the Father on their foreheads.

'Let's get out of here.' The bearded one pointed at Teo's body. 'They've all got it.'

The men hurried out and slammed the door, leaving Rabel alone with two dead bodies and two small children. She darted between Teo and Iwan. Teo. Iwan. Both bodies were growing colder by the moment.

Rabel slumped to the ground, wrapped her arms around her head and screamed.

She had got what she wanted. She had got what she deserved.

CHAPTER THIRTY

T HE DUKE SNORED SOFTLY IN her bed but Agata was wide awake. She slipped over to the window and opened up the book, leaning against the windowsill to catch the light of the moon.

The radiant Queen angled her head, her snowy hair shimmering in the candlelight.

'Who are you?' she said, speaking our language with a musical lilt. I bowed my head as I was told. 'Simple men of the faith from the lands of Vorosy. Visiting your lands to share the wise Teachings of the Father with your people.'

'Whose Father?' she scoffed.

'He is Father of all. The one true Father. Creator, Protector, the all-seeing.'

Her forehead furrowed. 'One Father? For all of us?'

'Yes.'

The guide kicked at the back of my knee. 'Address Queen Magnilla with respect.'

I cleared my throat. 'Yes, Queen Magnilla.'

'You are here to teach us of your Father?'

'Yes.'

'With no weapons.'

'I do not need a sword. I have his Teachings.' I held up my book.

'You are here to conquer me with your papers?' She burst out laughing and her courtiers on the cushions around the firepits, laughed along with her. It was then I noticed, her court had equal numbers of men and women. These were not the unsavoury flesh-baring women of the taverns or noble women sitting in the shadows. They sat alongside the men. I tore my eyes away from these strange sights and answered the Queen's question.

'I am not here to conquer you, gracious Queen. I am here to share the Father's love. So you and all your people can benefit from His wisdom. Like thousands of your countrymen in the other Four Clans.'

She sneered. 'Countrymen? What is this word? There are not only men here. Is the Father only for your men or do women love your Father too?'

This was not a matter I had ever considered. It was too obvious to ever question. Our women followed the men, this is what the Father taught. I opened my mouth to answer.

She waited, head tilted.

'The Father loves all equally,' I said, finally finding my tongue.

She blinked very slowly then gestured for more wine. A young man poured a clear drink into her goblet. Do the Akull Clansmen drink only water?

She turned to her court and asked a question in her own language. I looked to the other Cousin and he shrugged back. The educated man stepped forward and translated into my ear.

'Queen Magnilla said 'what shall I do with them?''

Shouts of reply filled the dome and I could not understand a word.

Our translator pointed to a man missing a front tooth and repeated his words. 'Banish 'em.'

He next pointed to a woman with wide rosy cheeks. 'She said 'leave 'em in the snows.''

'And he...' The translator gestured to a man whose face

was crumpled with age. 'He said 'take off their 'eads. And send 'em back to Sulun. A gift from Meeraq.''

I gasped.

Then a slim girl, barely old enough to be away from her mother, spoke. Her words were unfamiliar but her voice was clear and thoughtful, in a way I had rarely heard from a woman before. She was like a man but not like a man.

The translator repeated her words. 'Let them speak,' she said.

My heart thundered in my chest. My fellow Cousin grasped my sleeve. Queen Magnilla held out her hands for silence and the ruckus stopped.

The educated man continued to translate the Queen's words. 'Why should I let them speak, Senu?'

The young girl, slender and white-haired like a lily, smiled as she rose to her feet and bowed. 'Let us hear their ways, so we can learn.'

The silver haired man grumbled.

Queen Magnilla nodded. 'I too am curious, too.' She turned back to us and spoke in our language. 'Sit.'

The guards cleared a space on the floor by her throne and the Cousin and I lowered ourselves onto the cushions with creaking knees. I accepted a goblet but it was not water at all. The burning liquid was stronger than any home-stilled brandy. My fellow Cousin spluttered out the first mouthful, much to the delight of the courtiers. I refused a second cup, as men of the Fatherhood should, but my Cousin was not as pious. He asked for more when his goblet ran dry.

'Tell me more of this Father of yours,' the Queen said.

I took a deep breath and began with a smile. 'The Father created all.' I waited as the Queen listened intently and the educated man repeated my words to the rest of the court. 'From the dirt to the sky. Every animal. Every man. The rain. The sea. The snow. All come from Him.'

'How does a man give life?' Magnilla said, with a squint. 'Do men birth babies in the South Rivers?'

'Of course not. His seed started it all. He is the originator. That's why we call him the Father.'

'But who births the people? Who nurtures them?'

'Females, of course. But they are only the vessel for the male seed.'

'Only?' She narrowed her eyes. 'Can two men have a baby?'

I tried not to grimace at the mere suggestion of such a union. The other Cousin guffawed and slobbered in my ear. 'She is an imbecile.'

I pushed him and his sour breath away. 'Of course, two men cannot have a baby. A woman is needed like a bowl to carry the water. Men cannot lay with one another. It is forbidden.'

'Why?'

'It is unnatural.'

'But you said, men loving other men is part of the Fatherhood. Do you not love the Father?'

'Not in that way.'

She shrugged. 'Why is it different?'

'It is a sin.'

'But why? Your sin is just a word. There must be a reason. I thought your Father encouraged love.'

I opened my mouth but no words came forth. She leaned back in her throne with a smirk.

'So, where does this Father live?'

'In the sky. In the Land Beyond the Sunset.'

'What does he look like? Does he speak to you?'

'Not directly.' I scratched my head. I could not tell whether her questions were mocking or not. 'He cannot be seen. Only sensed through his love and his power.'

'Is he here now?'

'Of course. He is in this room. He is inside you and me.'

She laughed. 'He's not inside me.'

'Oh, but he is.'

She shook her head. 'I would not allow it. It's unnatural.'

Her courtiers burst out laughing.

The Cousin grunted and I opened my mouth to protest, heat prickling up my neck, but I calmed my ire with deep breaths. I knew converting unbelievers to the light of the Father would not be easy. I had to be patient. This was only another test of my faith.

The Queen loomed over me. I gulped as I looked up into her silver eyes, unable to read her face. 'I am tired of this talk,' she said with a flourish of her hand. 'I do not yet understand your love for the man in the sky. It does not make sense. Come back with better reasons tomorrow.'

'Yes, Queen Magnilla,' I said as she swept from the room. I wiped the sweat from my brow and began preparing passages for the next evening in my head. The first step was complete, I had her curiosity and I knew the Father would win her heart, in time.

CHAPTER THIRTY-ONE

THE STENCH OF STALE ALE, vomit and fish guts struck Kalin as he stepped inside the Seaweed Arms. The red-brick drinking house was as shabby as its patrons.

'Get a round of ales, Seliv,' he said, hoping a drink would drown out the scent.

'Thank you kindly, m'Lord,' Eeva tittered.

Kalin eyed her coldly. 'And ask the landlord about this churl.'

He squinted at three men hunched over the bar, staring into their tankards, the room shadowy with cheap struggling candles. Over to the side, a group of fishermen stopped their game of King's Table and whispered. Off to the side, in an adjoining smaller room, an old woman and a younger man sat by the hearth. In ordinary company, the man would be considered burly but not compared to a mountain like Seliv.

'Well? Is he here?' Kalin turned to the boy and his mother.

Wilken shrugged while Eeva took her time to look. 'It doesn't look like it.'

Kalin raised his eyebrows as he took a slurp from the wooden tankard Seliv handed him, but the ale was fresh. He'd tasted far worse in his time. He took another sip as Eeva emptied her tankard in a single draft.

'The landlord was useless,' Seliv said. 'But our description is very muddy.'

Kalin marched past the bar and through into the room with the hearth, waving Seliv over.

'Old woman. You know who I am?'

The grey-haired woman raised her head and smiled without missing a beat of her knitting. 'Yes, Lord Kalin.'

'We are looking for a man.'

'Always glad to help the Duchy, my Lord.'

'Excellent. You boy, tell her.'

Seliv thrust Wilken forward, the boy stared down at his holed boots and muttered.

'Speak up.' Kalin clipped him.

Eeva jumped in. 'A skinny man. Used to work on the boats. Likes his cock fights.'

'Could be anyone.' The old woman shrugged. 'Plenty like that in here.'

Kalin sighed. 'Get another round.'

'How very kind of you, my Lord,' the old woman said. 'But I am getting on in years. My memory is not quite what it was. Soon the Father will take me, hopefully, to the Land Beyond the Sunset.'

Kalin rolled his eyes but kept his hands away from his purse.

The tavern door opened and Kalin spun around. But the man was tall and fleshy, the complete opposite to the one they were looking for. The man approached the bar, dressed in a fine coat of brown wool unlike the other drinkers, and waited for the landlord to finish serving Seliv.

Kalin started for the bar, his eyes narrowed.

'I might know...' the old lady said as he walked away.

'Master Plesec?' Kalin said.

Plesec flinched. 'Lord Kalin. What are you doing in here?' He said, flushing red.

'I was wondering the same thing about you.'

'Passing by,' he said with an awkward chuckle. 'I heard their ale is not bad.'

'It is surprisingly drinkable. You have business in the Alleys?' Kalin frowned.

'Meeting a goat-farmer, my Lord.'

Kalin nodded, not believing a word.

The door opened again, but before Kalin could catch sight of him, someone in the room yelled, 'Shield!'

The door slammed shut.

Kalin glanced around. 'Who said that?' he shouted.

Everyone bowed their heads.

Seliv offered Kalin another tankard.

'No time for that,' growled Kalin. 'After him!'

CHAPTER THIRTY-TWO

AFTER ANOTHER SULLEN DINNER, FROMA retired to a chair by the fire to inspect the household accounts.

'Wife!' Danis's bellow echoed down the wood-panelled hallway. Froma cringed.

'Come here now!'

Froma scurried from the hall to his Cabinet room, her heart pattering. She paused before the doorway, pulling herself up to her full height and clearing her throat.

'What is this gibberish?' Danis was sitting behind his hefty wooden desk, his big fingers jabbing at a page in the ledger, a goblet in his other hand.

'What is it, husband?' Froma stepped forward with her head high, trying to hide the tremble in her knees.

'This.' He pointed. 'What is this?'

Froma stood beside him, leaning over to read the entry. He reached up and gripped her by the throat, his fingers crushing her windpipe, pulling her face down to the page, an inch above the print.

'This is your scribing?'

She gagged and he loosened his grip. 'Yes, husband. Who else would it be?' she croaked.

'I should have never lost that bet. Who needs a wife who can read? Especially one as ugly as you.' His breath was thick with wine. 'There. What price did you sell to Vinko?'

Froma stuttered and he slammed her head onto the page hard, the shock splintered across her face, the room swayed before her eyes.

'Are you deaf? What price?'

She blinked rapidly. 'Thirteen coppers a pound.'

'What?' he roared, shoving her away. She tripped and hit the floor with a thud. He tossed his wine into her face, followed by the goblet. The pewter cup ricocheted off her head and clattered to the ground. 'You sow. What kind of price is that?'

Froma scuttled backwards, red wine streaming down her face. 'It was second rate wool. Vinko was one of our only buyers. It was a fair price.'

'And now he will not pay any more.' Danis loomed over her. 'I thought the snake was lying to me. But here it is and it's all your fault. I should have known. You spoiled a good client. Stupid woman.'

'If you let me talk to him. As you suggested at breakfast,' Froma said cowering, her hands in the air protecting her face.

He guffawed. 'After what you have done?'

Danis grabbed her around the throat, his thumbs pressing hard against her windpipe. Her ears thumped as he squeezed, the sound of struggling blood.

'Idiot. I come home to this. A year of men being slaughtered all around me. A sea of blood and guts. Shit and mud. Grown men screaming and crying like babies. And now it's all over. And my business in ruins!'

Froma tore at his hands, gouged with her fingernails but his sword-hardened grip was too strong. She tried to call out for help, but all she could do was gurgle. No one would come to her aid anyway. Irina had been deaf and blind for years.

'Stupid, stupid woman.' Danis gritted his teeth as he pressed harder. 'I could kill you right now.'

Danis, the furniture, the walls, the whole room blurred. Froma's pain and panic subsided, and a lightness, a sense of peace, descended over her. Froma was no longer in his Cabinet room. She was up above, looking down on a woman who looked like her but she was safe, somewhere far away. The room darkened, her eyelids were so heavy and she wanted to sleep. If only he'd let her sleep.

Froma fell in a heap. Danis stepped back and sat at his desk, scraping his chair along the floorboards. Froma spluttered and coughed as she rubbed at her bruised throat, her cheek resting against the cool wood.

'Get out of my sight.' He grumbled and poured himself more wine.

Froma dragged herself to her feet without a word. She corked her tears, lifted her chin and stumbled out of the room. She fled up the stairs and closed her chamber door firmly behind her. With a whimper, she collapsed onto her bed and curled into a ball, gingerly tracing the tender marks on her neck.

A few days back from war and once again, she must mask her bruises. There was no new leaf.

She could not live this way. She would not. Her fists tightened around her eiderdown as her tears dried on her cheeks.

CHAPTER THIRTY-THREE

KALIN DRUMMED HIS FINGERS ON the arm of his chair and stared into the crackling fire. He clenched his jaw. Night had fallen and Seliv had not returned with news from the Alleys.

Eleven years ago, Kalin had taken his oath as Master of the Shield, Protector of the Duchy and, most importantly, Protector of the Duke himself. Eleven long, quiet years he'd served his friend. And the one day when the Duke truly needed him, he had not been by his side. His failure to prevent the soldier's blow haunted him day and night.

'M'Lord.' Seliv took up most of the doorway. 'Sorry to disturb you.'

'Where have you been?' Kalin glanced up from the fire. 'I presume you found the churl?'

'No, my Lord. No sign of him.'

Kalin grunted. 'What is it then?'

'Another incident this evening in another tavern in the Alleys. A man is dead. They are saying he was bleeding from the mouth.'

Kalin's eyebrows soared. 'The red death?'

'It could be, m'Lord.'

'Was a physician called?'

Seliv shrugged. 'Alley people, m'Lord.'

Kalin tugged at his beard. Ambrovna had been lucky until now. Other towns across the Four Rivers Kingdom had lost thousands of otherwise healthy people from the illness. On his long journey to the battlefields, Kalin had passed through wastelands of weed-filled villages with empty huts and untended fields, regions so stricken there were no men left to pledge for the war effort.

'Who was this man?' Kalin groaned as he stood. He'd returned from war an old man.

'Some sluggard back from the war like the rest of us.'

'He probably brought it back with him.' Kalin grimaced. 'We should have scrubbed every man clean before they came over the hills.' He shuddered to think what other illnesses the men had brought back with them. He scratched his own groin, pondering the cleanliness of Sulun's pleasure houses.

'Shall I call Tveldt?'

He shook his head. 'Dispose of the body. If it is the red death, burning will get rid of the illness. Hopefully he's the only one.' Kalin rubbed his chin. 'And tell no one. Quash any rumours. We do not want panic.'

'In the eyes of the Father. Will you inform the Duke?'

'Not this evening. With the Allotment and the Spawning Festival, the Duke has plenty on his mind.'

Seliv bowed his big head.

'But if you hear even a whisper about any other infections, come to me immediately. A second case is a completely different matter.'

Rabel's shack was suddenly filled with a blur of unfamiliar faces covered in kerchiefs. Aula and Jorn wailed as men in terracotta uniforms shouted into Rabel's face, waving flaming torches. Cowering, she covered her eyes. She would put up no resistance, she decided. She deserved this.

But no one touched her.

Rabel wrenched open her eyes to find the men wrapping Iwan and Teo in hessian.

'Red death,' someone said. 'Two?'

Rabel clutched at her belly. The red death? 'Where are you taking them?' she croaked but no one replied.

The men picked up the shrouds and carried them out of the door. Rabel scuttled to block their path and screeched, her fingers extended like claws. 'Where are you taking them?'

A guard shoved her aside with an elbow, sending her stumbling back against the wall. She scurried after them through the open door and into the night.

'Help me,' she yelled into the dark alleys. Her neighbour's homes were too quiet, everyone peered from the shadows but no one came to help.

In her bare feet, Rabel followed the guards with eels on their chest down the narrow alleys, onto the main street.

'Stop! What are you doin' with them?' she screamed, tugging at their tunics but the masked guards ignored her. Old Orvald ushering them inside the Brickworks where smoke plumed from the kiln.

'No!' she screeched.

A guard, smaller than the others with hair like a hedgehog, turned and pushed her back with the butt of his pike, careful not to lay a finger on her. 'It has to be done,' he said, his voice muffled under his kerchief.

She watched, arms hanging heavy, as the guards tipped the two bodies into the roaring flames and clamped the door shut.

Rabel's face contorted in anguish, but her eyes remained dry. An innocent like Teo deserved better than this. Even Iwan. Where would they go without the proper words from a Cousin to guide them to the Father?

The guards farewelled Orvald, wiped their hands and turned back towards the town. With shoulders hunched, Rabel waited for them to grab her by the arm and take her to the dungeons.

'Go home, woman,' one of the guards growled.

Rabel paused, anticipating the heavy hand on her shoulder.

'Are you deaf? Go on. Get out of here.'

The guards marched ahead of her into the dark, chuckling as they took off their kerchiefs.

Rabel wandered home alone, slow and numb.

CHAPTER THIRTY-FOUR

The next day, to our surprise, the lock on our room was unlatched and we were free to wander about Meeraq. My fellow Cousin was nursing a powerful headache from the poison water and he grumbled at my heels.

As we stepped out of our room, a sour-faced woman with cropped white hair appeared.

'I shall be your guide today,' she said in our language and the Cousin grumbled quietly by my side. I too would have preferred to explore the town without an escort but I nodded.

'This way,' she said curtly.

Meeraq was unlike any town I'd visited before. Women were everywhere we went. They were stony-eyed guards with swords by their sides, silver-tongued traders and soot-covered blacksmiths hammering shields while the men happily carried babies and fussed over children. And not one person seemed richer than another. I saw no lords or ladies, peasants or barefoot urchins. Even Queen Magnilla dressed modestly compared to the gold and jewels of Queen Hendriet of Sulun.

I remarked on my observations to the Cousin as we partook in a pot of the local milky tea, but he only grunted.

The woman running the tea-stall assured us with gestures that the strong sour drink was a cure for my Cousin's pounding head. While we enjoyed our tea, our gruff translator sat separately, smoking a pipe with two other Akull guards in leather jerkins. Every now and then they looked up, eying us suspiciously.

Throughout the day as we wandered, I poured over the Teachings in my head, searching for the perfect passages to convince Queen Magnilla of the wisdom of the Father. I think best when I walk, so when we finished our tea, we continued to roam until we found ourselves outside the pine-cone-shaped dome again, the Umbaz as the Meeraq people called it. A queue of people streamed out down the steps, men and women, young and old.

'What is happening?' I asked our translator.

She pursed her lips and answered. 'Today is Court Day. The Queen is presiding.'

'Over what?'

'Disputes. Administrative matters.'

I blinked and lifted my eyebrows. 'She is a good ruler?' I said, trying to hide the doubt in my voice. I had presumed Magnilla was a figurehead and that other men did the true work of the nobility.

'Of course,' the woman said, rolling her eyes.

'I know little of your history. Is Magnilla your first Queen? Did the King die and leave no heirs?'

The woman tutted. 'The first child is always ruler. Woman or man.'

I rubbed my chin. 'And she is not irrational or weak?'

'She is the wisest of us all.' The woman folded her arms.

'Does she preside over crimes? Murders? Not subjects suitable for ladies.'

'You have some strange ideas, Southerner,' said our female translator shaking her head. 'Come and see for yourself.'

I was keen to witness the Queen's deliberations. We climbed the steps and peered through the open doorway.

A long queue snaked inside. Magnilla sat on her throne, dressed in bone-coloured tunic and trousers, her white hair coiled around her head. A silver icicle-shaped pendant swung from her neck.

'Go in,' said our stony-faced escort. 'But no talking.'

I nodded and slipped off my boots while my Cousin chose to remain outside. I approached the throne and stood to the side. The Queen glanced at me briefly. I smiled but she looked away, her face unchanged. Two men stood before her, one fat with straggly thin hair, the other elderly with a walleye. Both were grimacing, caps in hand.

The translator sidled up to me. As Magnilla spoke in her native tongue, she interpreted quietly into my ear.

'Knag. You bring shame on your family with your spite. You will pay fourteen coins to Lempi. I will hear no more of your bickering about the wall. You must learn to live as neighbours.'

Knag, the balding fat man, lowered his head. 'I only--'

'Enough excuses. This is my final judgement. Pay the fine and work with Lempi. The Clan cannot allow such quarrelling. We must work together and resolve our differences.'

He nodded but pursed his lips.

'Thank you, my Queen,' said the white-haired man as he bowed his head. The two turned without another word and the next man in line approached the throne.

'What is your complaint?'

The young man straightened his spine and lifted his chin high. 'I am Borild, apprentice sled-maker. I wish to complain about Alu Biar.'

The Queen raised an eyebrow. 'And what is the nature of your complaint?'

'She broke our contract.' The young man's neck flushed as he spoke. 'I want you to enforce our agreement.'

'What contract?'

'She agreed to be my bride...' he said, thrusting out his chest. 'But she has thrown me aside for Balbin Canu.'

Two grey-headed women, next in line, sniggered. I raised my eyebrows. A woman refusing a betrothal? Unheard of. Her father must have intervened to prevent the union.

'What do you want me to do about it?' the Queen scoffed.

'Enforce it, my Queen.'

'You want to force her when she does not want to be your wife?' the Queen asked, her face straight.

'But she agreed...'

I shook my head. A woman reneging on her betrothal? This was a serious matter. A girl should be happy to be chosen by any man for his wife. To be a wife and mother is the true path of a woman's life. Perhaps the Akull women were not so different; they still lacked the logic to make decisions. This is why they needed men.

'I will not enforce your contract,' the Queen said. 'She is free to choose who she loves. You cannot force another to love you, no matter how you try.'

As the guide translated, I gasped and covered my mouth. Borild's face was scarlet. His eyes flashed as he dropped his head and turned away from the throne. A stocky male guard blocked Borild's path with his sword. 'Remember your place, apprentice. Give thanks to your Queen.'

He stopped, screwing up his face. 'Thank you, my Queen,' he said through gritted teeth.

The Queen narrowed her eyes. 'If I hear of you making trouble between Alu and Balbin, there will be consequences. Understand?'

Borild bowed his head. 'Yes, my Queen.'

The Queen shook her head as Borild stomped away. She whispered into the ear of her stocky guard who saluted and followed the jilted man out of the Umbaz. I decided to follow them and our translator trailed behind me.

I found the guard speaking intensely but quietly to Borild, who was staring at his boots, shifting his weight like a boy receiving a scolding from his father. Borild's lips were tight, his shoulders high. The heavyset guard jabbed his finger into Borild's chest and walked away. Borild spat on the ground, but only once the guard was gone.

I turned to my guide. 'Help me speak to him,' I said. She squinted but agreed. We approached Borild, who glared at me, arms folded. The guide interpreted as I spoke. 'I understand your anger, young man. You have been slighted,' I said.

'You are from the South?' His eyes lit up.

'The Neven Clan.' I nodded. 'I have come to teach your people about my Father. Our Protector in the sky.' I smiled as I recognised a welcome ear. 'This would never be allowed to happen in my land.'

'She lied,' Borild said. 'Made a fool of me.'

'Where I am from, women know their place. They support the men. They do not choose.'

The guide frowned and cleared her throat before she spoke, I had to trust she passed on my words truthfully. Borild's face was keen with interest.

A tall man shoved his way between us. 'Don't listen to this fool,' he said to Borild.

Borild deflated and turned away, but I did not give up so easily. My Scion said persistence was my most admirable trait.

'If you need someone to talk to, I am a good listener. Or if you wish to hear more of the Father's Teachings, come and find me. Day or night. I know you will find solace in His wisdom as I have.' My last sentences were shouted, calling out after Borild as he disappeared out of view and into the crowd. The guide dutifully repeated my words and the other townspeople waiting in the queue at the Umbaz glared at me. Some folded their arms. 'The offer is open to everyone,' I said loudly, looking into every single face. 'I am here if you wish to learn about the Father and his glorious love.'

Someone laughed.

'Southern scum,' a man said in my tongue, barely intelligible.

A drop of rain hit me on the cheek and I glanced up into the sky, flicking the raindrop away with my fingers but the sky was clear. More drops hit my face and then I realised the women were spitting on me.

CHAPTER THIRTY-FIVE

THE NEXT MORNING, AGATA SWEPT into the Great Hall, beaming at her husband at the head of the table. The sun shone through the lead-lined windows illuminating the long table with criss-cross patterns. A sapphire sky outside.

'My love,' the Duke said, and she went to him, despite the guards and the servants lining the walls. He threaded his arm around her waist and pulled her to his lips. 'My flower.'

Giggling and blushing, she untangled herself from his embrace and with a longing look under her eyelashes, she took her seat. Her stomach grumbled and she waved to the serving girl to pile her plate with bread.

'There is a matter I wish to discuss with you, dear husband,' Agata said, slathering her bread with soft white cheese. For some unknown reason, figs were banned in Ambrovna. She dearly missed her homeland breakfasts of the luscious fruit. Tomorrow she would ask the Duke why and try to convince him to change the ban but today there were more important matters to discuss.

'The war widows--'

'The Scion has already--'

The doors opened and Kalin entered like a cold wind, his sword clanging by his side, his jaw set. The Seneschal followed closely behind, thin and stooping like a river reed.

'Good morning, my Lord,' Kalin said as he bowed.

'And to you, Lord Kalin. Sit. Eat.'

Agata suppressed a frown, their time alone was over for another day.

Kalin scraped his chair across the brick floor and a homely serving girl instantly offered a plate as she stifled a little giggle.

Agata squinted. What did other women see in the pompous Master of the Shield?

'How do you look so refreshed, Kalin?' The Duke enquired. 'I feel as though Death spat me back into this world.'

'Practice, my Lord. You must be ageing.'

'Pfft. How dare you insult your Duke in this way?' the Duke grinned.

'I only speak the truth, my Lord. This is why you appreciate my service.'

The Duke laughed riotously and Agata forced a smile but as always Kalin paid her no attention.

Even before the war, Kalin barely acknowledged Agata's existence and on the rare and fleeting occasions he met her eyes, he glared with animosity. Since the defeat of her Clansmen and the rumours about her brother, her political value had turned to dust and she was certain he spoke ill of her to the Duke. Kalin had ample opportunity to whisper poison in his ears or make hateful jokes during their long nights of drinking.

Agata took another piece of bread and chewed silently. She would not allow him to drive a rift between them.

'Is everything prepared for this morning?' her husband said.

'My men are already on their way, but first my Lord, I bring troubling news from the Alleys. Two deaths overnight, a man and a young boy. There are rumours of the red death.'

'No,' the Duke gasped.

Agata's mouth dropped open. They said the red death hits suddenly, turning into a torrent of bleeding from every orifice until the body ran dry. Towns and villages in other parts of the Kingdom had built high walls to contain the spread.

'We burned the bodies last night. To stop the blight.'

'Who were the dead?'

'Some good-for-nothing and his son. Of no importance. No leasehold or stable employment.'

'It could easily spread through the Alleys. Are there others? What of his family?'

'A wife and two babes. My men said they showed no signs of sickness but I have a guard outside their hut, waiting for your instructions.'

The Duke sucked in a breath through clenched teeth. Agata's belly churned. She was glad she no longer sat in the Duke's place this morning.

Her husband rubbed his chin. 'We cannot take any chances. I want them removed from Ambrovna.'

'A wise decision in the best interests of your people. Consider it done.'

'What will you do with them?' Agata said as she pushed her plate away, her appetite gone.

Kalin took a long sip of ale and turned to her with hard grey eyes. 'It is none of your concern.'

'I will leave it to your judgement as Master of the Shield,' the Duke said, buttering a hunk of bread.

'Thank you, my Lord. The problem will be dealt with.'

Agata shivered as she wondering what fate awaited the poor widow. 'Who is she, Lord Kalin?'

'What does it matter?'

'Please indulge me, my Lord.'

Kalin grumbled but the Duke nodded.

'I believe she did some work for the Plesec merchants during the war.' Kalin shrugged. 'One step up from Guts Alley.'

Hot bile shot up the back of Agata's throat. Rabel? Was he talking about Rabel? Was it the red death or was it something else? Didn't he mention two deaths? She scrubbed her face with her hands.

'Deal with it before midday service,' the Duke instructed. 'Nothing should spoil tomorrow's Spawning Festival.'

'Think nothing further of it, my Lord.'

Agata rose to her feet, a tremble in her knees. 'Please excuse me, my Lord,' she said curtseying.

'I will see you for luncheon, my love,' the Duke replied. Kalin chewed cold meat from his knife, not even glancing in her direction.

Agata controlled herself, making sure to walk through the Great Hall at a casual pace while her heart thumped. As the door closed behind her, she bolted, almost knocking over the elderly Lord Sylwin as she skidded around a corner.

'Why the hurry, my Lady?' he said, grasping her by the shoulders to right his balance. 'Is there a crisis? Is it my nephew?'

'My apologies, Lord Sylwin,' she said, calling over her shoulder. 'All is well. I need to find Sira.'

Closing her bower door firmly behind her, Agata struggled to catch her breath after taking the stairs two at a time. 'Rabel,' she croaked.

Sira dropped her mending and jumped to her feet, her eyes wide. 'Is there news, m'Lady?'

'The Shield guards are coming for her.'

'How did they find out?' Sira gasped, hands at her throat.

Agata shook her head. 'They think she is carrying the red death.'

'I don't understand.'

'Kalin said there were two deaths.'

Sira blinked, furrowing her brow. 'Two?'

'A boy and a man.'

'Teo? Jorn?' Her voice cracked, her fists bunching by her sides. 'What happened?'

'You must go now. Tell her to run.'

'But where will she go, m'Lady? Can we hide her here?'

'It's not safe.'

'Where then?'

The two women stopped, searching for answers in each other's fear-filled faces.

'What will they do to her?' Sira said with a gulp.

Chewing on her fingertip, Agata counted all the people she knew in Ambrovna. Once finished, she counted out a much shorter list: the names of the people she could trust.

'Go to your sister. I have an idea.'

Rabel felt like a gutted fish as she stared at the black stain on the dirt floor. The last remnant of her oldest boy. Teo. Gone. Killed with her own hand. She wanted to cry again but she had nothing left. Her throat was raw and empty, her nostrils still coated with the smoke from the Brickworks kiln. The one-room shack seemed so large without the two of them, a cavernous hole where they used to be.

180

Three times during the night, her hand had reached for her pocket and the goat fur pouch but three times she had stopped, looking back at the other two sleeping heads, so small and very much alive.

Rabel had got what she wanted. Iwan was gone but she should have known the Father would insist on a price. Why would her life suddenly be any different?

'Ma.' Aula snuggled up to her side, her small body soothing and warm. Somehow the little ones knew what their mother needed. Her little boy, now her only boy, joined his sister and nestled in. 'Hungry.'

Rabel sighed and struggled to her feet, her flesh had been replaced with stone overnight. She shuffled to the shelf and found a small crust of dark bread, days old and rock hard.

The knife shattered the bread into crumbs as she tried to slice it but she filled her fist and fed her twins. Aula and Jorn lifted their heads like baby birds in a nest, craning for more. They giggled as crumbs bounced off their chins and onto the floor.

Rabel found herself smiling, Aula and Jorn needed their mother. For months, years, she'd dreamed of a life without Iwan and now the day was here. The first day in their new life. There were a few coppers left but they wouldn't last. She must plan a new beginning, her little hut in the valley with the chickens. But without Teo.

Someone knocked, hard and insistently, on the shack door. Rabel frowned as she crossed the room to answer it.

CHAPTER THIRTY-SIX

AGATA LEFT THE CASTLE WEARING a dress borrowed from Sira, her slender figure swamped by extra fabric. Inspired by Froma, she covered her face. The veil rendered her so anonymous, a rat-faced guard tried to paw her as she passed through the gate. She slipped from his grasp, but took note of his face.

Agata sneaked through the streets until she arrived at a side door entrance to the Plesec residence. A scrawny girl with skittish eyes answered. 'Yes,' she said in a wobbly voice.

'Is Mistress Plesec at home?' Agata said, unwrapping her veil. The serving girl gasped. Agata placed a finger over her lips and the girl curtseyed long and low.

'M'Lady,' the girl whispered, gesturing for her to enter. Agata followed her along a dark hallway lined with intricately carved wooden walls and into the solar. It was almost as lavish as her castle quarters with its cheery fire roaring in the grate, emerald velvet curtains framing the windows and a large tapestry depicting a deer hunt covering an entire wall. It was true what they said. Merchants had the riches of the nobles without the responsibilities these days.

Within seconds, Froma swept into the room, tying the end of her veil around her face. But she was too slow and Agata glimpsed her face and throat, mottled with purple bruises.

'My Lady. What a surprise. If only you'd given me a chance to prepare,' Froma rasped. 'Irina, wine for our guest.'

Agata waited until Irina left the room. 'Please excuse my ill manners, Mistress Plesec. But there was no time.'

Froma arched an eyebrow.

'I wanted to speak with you alone. Without your husband knowing. Or anyone else. No one must know I was here.'

Agata's mouth drained. She inhaled slowly, taking one last moment to gauge the merchant's wife before she spoke. 'I need your help,' she said.

Froma tilted her head and smoothed the edges of the veil around her face. 'Of course, my Lady.' She folded her hands demurely in her lap and straightened her posture. 'How may I be of assistance?'

Agata swallowed. 'You have provided wise counsel over the past year. Helped me greatly with those confusing ledgers. You are a valuable member of my Circle.'

'Thank you for your kind words. But it was my duty to serve.'

'I hope you see me as more than a member of the Duchy. I hope after all we experienced in the past year, I hope we are...friends.'

'Absolutely, my Lady.'

Agata watched Mistress Plesec's eyes, wishing she'd remove her veil.

'It is an honour to be considered as a friend.'

'I am glad,' Agata proceeded cautiously. 'People do not realise it is not easy to make friends in my position.'

'I understand,' Froma said softly, before coughing and returning her voice to its usual reserved tone. 'You said you needed my help?'

Agata leaned in, lowering her voice. 'It is rather delicate. A matter best kept between you and I.'

Froma nodded slowly but the door opened. Irina entered, carrying wine and a tiered platter piled with lemon cakes. Agata and Froma straightened their spines, assuming the formal postures required. Froma unwrapped her veil to sip her wine and Agata politely averted her eyes.

Irina handed Agata a cake on a delicate white plate. 'How lovely,' she said, her finger tracing the familiar swirling peacock-blue pattern.

'The plates were a gift from one of our traders in Tramissa.'

'My home region,' Agata murmured. She took a generous bite. The delicacy was moist and crumbly, the perfect balance of tart and sweet. 'Did you make these?' She asked Irina, loitering by the door and the girl timidly nodded.

Agata ate another two cakes as she fought the urge to jump to her feet and run from the Plesec house. She had not yet fully explained and confessed her involvement in two murders to anyone. But if she truly wanted to help the women of Ambrovna, be the woman her mother wanted, she must act.

Watching Froma sip her wine, the truth hit Agata like a splash of cold water. There was no one else. She had no true friends in Ambrovna, no one she could trust. Froma was her only hope. Agata gulped and placed her half-eaten cake back on the plate.

'You have to go.' Sira rushed inside and closed the door behind her. 'Get the children and leave. Now. The Shield are coming for you.'

Rabel stared back at her sister, open-mouthed.

'They believe you're carrying the red death.'

Thoughts swarmed like flies inside Rabel's head. Red vomit. Burning bodies. What should she take? A pot, a blanket, wooden blocks for the twins? Where would she go?

'Stop dilly-dallying!' Sira tugged at her arm. 'Don't worry about your belongings. The Duke ordered them to get rid of you.'

'But--' Rabel glanced around the shack.

Sira took Aula by the hand. 'Let's go.'

Rabel opened her mouth but no words came out.

'We'll find you somewhere safe. But you must leave now. There was a guard outside but I slipped one of the girls a copper to distract him for a few minutes. But he's only young. He won't take long.'

Rabel's body felt limp and heavy. She stared at the black stain on the ground.

'Come on.' Sira frowned.

'I've done somethin' terrible,' Rabel whispered. 'I should be punished.'

'You did what was right.'

'But Teo,' she choked.

Sira squeezed her sister's arm, her eyes moist.

'I never meant...I don't know what happened.' Rabel rubbed her forehead and swallowed hard. 'I can't do this.'

'I can't be seen with you,' Sira handed Rabel her shawl. 'Wrap your face and go down by the wharves. I'll come and find you after midday service.'

'I could find a boat, someone to take me faraway.' Rabel said. 'It'd be safer for you.'

'My Lady will find you somewhere to hide.'

'And then what? I can't hide forever.'

'There's no time for this,' Sira huffed. 'Wait any longer and the Shield will make the decision for you.'

Sira opened the door and checked up and down the alley.

'Go.'

Children in hand and her face hidden, Rabel slipped next door through the gates into the stables. She wanted to glance back at her shack one last time, but she couldn't risk it. She turned the corner and headed through the Alleys towards the bay. With no husband, no Teo, no home and the Shield after her. She sighed, clutching the only things she had left in the world, her babes.

Agata's stomach roiled the entire time she and Froma chatted about the weather and her gown for tomorrow's Spawning Festival. Then Irina left the room.

'If we are exchanging favours, my Lady, please call me Froma at the very least.'

'Thank you, Froma.' Agata rolled the name around in her mouth. Solid and unyielding as it was, it suited her.

Agata moved next to Froma where no one could eavesdrop. 'Is your husband at home?'

'He is in the shop. Meeting with a trader. He will not come back into the house until luncheon. Business always comes first with Master Plesec.'

Agata nodded. 'So we are alone?'

'You may speak freely, my Lady.'

'I have your word? To keep our conversation between ourselves?'

Froma traced a circle on her forehead. 'In the eyes of the Father.'

Agata tightened her lips as she recalled the Scion's snub. When she returned to the castle, she must discuss the war widows with the Duke. But first.

'Goodwife Rabel Ejvind worked for you during the war?'

'You haven't involved yourself with Sira and her sister, have you?' Froma asked. 'I did warn you, my Lady.'

Agata waved her hand. 'Rabel is in a spot of trouble. She needs a place to stay. Secretly. Would you be willing to house her for a few days?'

Froma's eyes narrowed. 'Is she a fugitive?'

'It is better if you do not know all the details.'

'You presume I do not already know.' Froma lifted her chin. 'You are not the only one who has asked for a favour in the last few days.'

Agata leaned back and scrutinised Froma's full profile. Had the sisters shared their plan with her? Sira had said nothing about this.

'Rabel was very open with me. I was not sure whether Rabel and Sira had confided fully in you, my Lady. You say, this is a delicate matter and you have just as much to lose. I did not want to expose you to harm.'

'Can I be more open?'

'Most certainly, my Lady.'

Agata gazed at Froma as she bit the inside of her cheek.

'You can trust me,' Froma insisted.

Fidgeting with the tassel at her belt, Agata sipped her wine and Froma never averted her gaze. Agata patted her mouth dry and when she spoke, her voice was barely audible. 'She did it. Last night. He is gone.'

Froma leaned in, her eyes shining. 'What was the method?'

'A mushroom, I believe.'

Froma blinked.

'But now Lord Kalin thinks she carries the red death. And they are coming for her.'

'The red death?' Froma recoiled. 'But you did not speak to the Duke? Set him straight and ask for clemency?'

Agata's hand flew to her chest. She had never considered telling him. Had she underestimated her husband? Was all this deceit unnecessary? But in her belly, she knew. 'He has his position to protect and we all know the punishment for poison.'

Froma shuddered.

Agata clasped Froma's hand. 'I would be most grateful if you could help her, Froma.'

'I am honoured you have come to me for help,' Froma said. 'However...what would Danis say if he found out? We also have a position to protect.'

'Please, Mistress Plesec.'

Froma looked back at Agata with a steady probing gaze. Agata gulped and squeezed Froma's hand.

Froma sighed. 'I can find her a place in the stables for a few nights, a week at the very most.'

'Thank you,' Agatha said breathily, her palm pressed to her heart.

Froma held up her index finger. 'But if there is a public call for her, you will need to hide her somewhere else, my Lady.'

'A few days is all we need. This is a good deed you are doing.'

'I doubt the Father would see it the same way,' Froma said with one eyebrow raised.

Agata knew the Father would be far from happy but she was also convinced his negligence caused the problem in the first place. 'Thank you for your generosity. We shall send her to you after midday service.' Agata stood to leave.

'One moment, my Lady.' Froma placed her goblet on the table with a clang. 'As you know, I am a woman of trade.'

'And a very good one from what I've seen.'

'You flatter me,' Froma replied. 'In trade, there is negotiation. A price is paid and goods are exchanged.'

Agata frowned, hairs prickling along the back of her neck. 'You want coins?'

'No, my Lady. Nothing like that.' Froma held up her hand. 'I have a favour to ask in return.'

Agata's heart thumped as she narrowed her eyes. 'Yes?'

Froma paused, her eyes icy.

'I want a mushroom.'

CHAPTER THIRTY-SEVEN

SELIV DUCKED HIS BIG HEAD, his arms raised as he waited for the blow but Kalin slammed his fist into the table instead.

'She was gone, my Lord.'

'Churls,' Kalin grumbled. 'So how are you planning to fix this mess?'

'He's on slop bowl duty now, m'Lord.'

'Not him. The woman!'

'I came to you first.' Seliv shrugged.

'Did you lose your brain in the war, Seliv? You are supposed to be my second in command. Not some feather-headed peasant. How can you lose a damned woman and her two babies? You realise she's out there now, spreading her dirty sickness across the whole town. Everyone will be spewing blood by dusk service and it will be all your fault. You hear? The deaths will be on your useless head.'

Seliv cowered.

'Go. Take all the men. Search the Alleys and the wharf. Find her now! And that blackmailer, too, while you're out there. Otherwise, you will be joining that other churl on slop duty.'

'But the Allotment, m'Lord?'

Kalin groaned, keeping his blasphemy to himself. 'Use whoever you have left. Find her.'

The large man scuttled out of the room and Kalin kicked the table leg. He sucked a breath through his clenched teeth and headed straight for the wine. He gulped down a goblet in a single draft then slammed the empty cup onto the table. Then he trudged out of his room, rubbing his forehead, wondering how he would explain the mistake to the Duke.

Rabel hauled her cargo of children through the narrow Alleys market, past the patchwork stalls built from all types of flotsam, her face sweaty under her shawl. Rabel blended easily into the crowd. No one glanced twice at a wrapped woman. The air was thick with frying oil, fish guts and moonshine as stallholders touted, bartered, even begged.

'Watch where you're goin',' grumbled a stubby olive-skinned man.

There was barely space for two people to pass side by side. Rabel stumbled as she tried to squeeze past him and a scowling ebony-haired woman gave her a sharp elbow to the ribs.

At least the babes were quiet. Her little ones somehow understood the seriousness of their situation without her explaining a word. Rabel thanked the Father for each moment of their silence though she doubted he'd be listening. Still, it did not stop her silent prayer. Sniffing, she found the salt of the sea through the Alleys stench and headed in the right direction to meet Sira.

'Pies. Pies. A copper a pie,' a wrinkled almond-eyed woman said as she offered her tray of golden-topped meat pies.

Rabel's stomach rumbled loud enough for others to hear but she'd had plenty of practice setting aside her hunger. She knew she might need the few coppers jangling in her pocket for something else. Swatting away an inquisitive wasp, Rabel continued past tinkers selling dented saucepans, second-hand boots and poor-quality candles, holding her nose against the reek of piss from the tanneries.

'New shawl. New shawl.' A black moustached man grabbed at her arm, almost pulling her off her feet. 'Good price. Real mohair.'

'Get off.' She wrenched away from him and crashed into another woman.

'Beautiful children,' the woman said, her scabby fingers reaching for Aula.

'Don't touch.' Rabel clutched her twins close to her chest.

'Such beautiful 'air,' she said, her grin too wide. 'The colour of 'oney.'

'I said don't touch!'

'I'll give you fifteen coppers for the hair,' she said. 'Both of them. Baby 'air. So soft. So pretty. It'd make a fine wig for some rich bitch.'

'No.' Rabel covered their heads with her hands.

'Fifteen coppers. Easy coins. A good deal,' the woman said, pointing to a covered stall. 'Just come through 'ere, I'll cut it myself. They're young. It'll grow back quick.'

Rabel shook her head and hurried towards the smell of the sea.

'Alright. Twenty,' the woman called after her.

As Rabel hurried around the next dog-leg corner, she spotted two terracotta uniforms up ahead. They'd stopped another woman with a similar build to her own, whose shoulders were hunched and her eyes wide as they spoke quietly, their fingers poking at her collarbone.

Rabel gulped and backtracked, her heart walloping. The wig woman stood in the same spot with the same unnatural smile.

'Changed your mind?'

'Twenty coppers? Let's go.'

The woman ushered her through another curtain into a windowless room. A prune-like grey-haired woman sat perched on a small stool, sewing chunks of hair onto a fabric cap, a large mound of chestnut brown hair at her feet. The seamstress hummed an old folk song about the mermaid and the fishermen with the golden net as she stitched without looking up.

'How much for my hair?' Rabel said as she sat down on a stool and balanced the twins on her knees, gripping them so tight, they squirmed.

The woman wheezed a sigh. 'That wasn't the deal.' She lit a pipe and sucked in hard. 'But show me.'

Rabel unfurled her shawl and unbraided her hair.

The wig woman cackled and coughed. 'No one would buy that!'

Rabel's heart sank. As a girl she'd had fine hair the colour of cedar, but now it was brittle and shot with grey.

'Only the babes.'

Rabel stroked Aula's honey coloured hair. Twenty coppers was enough to buy passage on a boat out of Ambrovna. She couldn't, could she?

'Let go, Ma.' Aula wriggled.

'I want walk,' said Jorn, slipping out of her arms.

'No. Be good for Mama.'

'Hungry.'

'Soon. I'll get some food in a minute.' Rabel scooped up her grumbling children and stood.

'Not so fast. We 'ad an agreement.'

'I changed my mind.'

'I don't like people who go back on their word.'

'What are you going to do?' Rabel sneered, looking at the skinny woman and the old lady.

The wig woman raised an eyebrow. 'Jaco!'

The door flap flew open and a bald man, the size of a bull, filled the doorway.

Rabel took a step back away from the door.

The wig woman smiled.

'The mushroom?'

Froma nodded. 'One small thing is all I ask. A little favour in return.'

Agata blinked. 'You mean to kill someone?'

'You are shocked?' Froma said, lifting an eyebrow, her goblet to her lips.

'You know the consequences?'

'Am I so different to Rabel?'

Agata covered her mouth with her hand. Who did Froma have in her sights?

'This is my offer.' Froma shrugged. 'I will harbour Rabel if I can have what she has. I am putting myself in danger for you, my Lady. It is only fair.'

Agata stared across the solar and rubbed her forehead. Another death on her hands?

'I do not have it,' she stuttered. 'I am not sure there is any left.'

'I am sure you can get hold of it. Or more if you need. I have faith in you, my Lady. If anyone can obtain it, you can.' Froma's eyes were steady.

Agata chewed on her lip. This deal would have deadly consequences.

'Do we have an agreement?' Froma said, slowly and precisely. 'My Lady.'

'Yes,' Agata spluttered, regretting the words as soon as they left her lips.

'Good. It is settled. Bring me the item and I'll prepare a place for Rabel.'

Agata rose to her feet, the floor and walls undulating as she stood. She clutched the back of the chair until her vision cleared. 'Thank you for seeing me so unexpectedly.'

'Thank you for visiting my humble home, my Lady. I only hope my hospitality was adequate at such short notice.'

'Your hospitality was without fault. The cakes were delightful, Mistress Plesec,' Agata said, the walls of formality rising between them once again.

'Will I see you again today?'

She shook her head. 'I shall send Sira.'

Froma nodded. 'I will make the arrangements.'

Agata wrapped her face and headed out into the late morning. She drifted through the throngs of people. This misadventure was spreading like a vine, snaking and creeping out of her control, wrapping around her chest and squeezing her ribs until she could barely breathe.

In the Square, carpenters hammered and sawed, finalising the stage for the mummers and troubadours to entertain the town as Ambrovna celebrated the coming Eel season. In front of the Temple, more men laid out long planks of wood. Agata squinted. She recalling nothing about a dais near the Temple in the Festival plans. What was the Scion up to?

Under the Old Man Tree, a woman kneeled with her head bowed and hands cupped, two snotty-faced babes sitting alongside her. Another war widow. Agata fumbled in her pocket but she did not carry coins and a smile of pity was useless to the woman. Two young terracotta guards loomed over the woman and she glanced up at them glumly. Agata paused to watch. Should she intervene? Then she remembered her disguise. A group of Cousins walked towards her, among them the single-browed Cousin who yesterday prevented her from seeing the Scion.

She bowed her head to hide her face and with clenched fists, she turned away and continued up the Avenue, vowing to speak with her husband about the welfare of the town's widows before luncheon. After she'd spoken with Sira.

She unwrapped her face and straightened her posture as she approached the castle gates. The sullen pot-bellied guard looked puzzled as she swept through the gatehouse but he did not stop her.

She hesitated as she passed him. 'What is the construction outside the Temple? Who authorised it?'

'It's for the Allotment, m'Lady,' he replied. 'Lord Kalin.'

Agata narrowed her eyes. She remembered Gala and Jadzia talking about an Allotment. The word seemed familiar. She chewed her lip. There had been a passing reference to an Allotment in the History of Ambrovna, a book on the shelves of the Duke's Cabinet. Here was yet another reason to visit her husband.

She strode across the inner bailey towards the keep, her belly knotting as she recalled Froma's bargain. This mess was all her doing and if she did not agree to Froma's demands, what would become of Rabel? Agata wrung her hands as she continued to her chambers.

'My Lady.'

Agata jumped.

The furrows in Lord Sylwin's brow were as deep as moats. 'Are you well?'

Agata smile and reached for his hand. 'Yes, my Lord.'

'You are pale, my Lady. Should I call for the physician?'

'I am not ill, my Lord. Merely busy. There is much to do for tomorrow's festivities. Have you seen Sira?'

'I saw her in the outer bailey a few minutes ago. Bustling about from step to stair. I said she must have a very demanding mistress.' Sylwin grinned.

'I must go.'

'Wait.' Sylwin placed his hand on her arm. 'You seem troubled, my dear. Is it the Duke? Should I be concerned about his health? Is it what we talked about?'

Perhaps she'd forgotten another friend. The kindly old great uncle had been her counsel and support during the year of war. She glanced up and down the brick-walled corridor, checking for any big-eared guards or servants.

She sighed. 'I appear to be in an...interesting...position.'

He pulled her aside, his voice low. 'You know you can trust me, my Lady.'

She nodded.

'Are you in trouble?'

She chewed her lip. 'What would you do if you had to hurt one person to help another?'

He leaned in, his white eyebrows knitting together. 'A difficult matter indeed. If you spoke to the Scion, he would say a good act does not erase a sin.'

Agata swallowed. 'What if you had no choice?'.

'This would not be an excuse in the eyes of the Father. You must have the strength to do what is right.'

'But what is right?' Agata said in a faraway voice.

'Now you have me worried, my Lady. But you are stronger than you think. Unfortunately, I must rush. Your husband has called me to his Cabinet but please come to talk with me this afternoon.'

'Yes, my Lord,' Agata said with a tiny smile. The tight band across her chest loosened a notch as the old man squeezed her hand. Agata hurried towards her chambers where Sira was waiting by the window, wringing her hands.

'M'Lady?' She clutched a hand to her bosom.

'We have a problem,' Agata said.

Sira's shoulders sank. 'She wouldn't help.'

Agata shook her head. 'She will. But with one condition.'

'What does she want?' Sira frowned.

'Do you have any of the poison left?'

Sira tutted. 'Of course. Rabel is not the only one who suffers. Master Plesec always had a terrible temper. You've seen her face.'

'She said it was robbers!'

'You need to spend more time in the laundry, m'Lady,' Sira said. 'To learn the truth about life in Ambrovna.'

'We cannot help her.'

Sira's cheeks blazed. 'What of Rabel?'

'We cannot be complicit in another man's death.'

'I already have two on my conscience.' Sira's shoulders slumped. 'I'm already bound for the Land of Eternal Darkness.'

'I won't allow it.'

'You are innocent so far, m'Lady. If this helps my sister, I am willing.'

'I don't feel innocent,' Agata said, tugging at the tassel around her waist.

'What Mistress Plesec does is not my concern. I only care about my family.'

'But you know what she will do. We cannot trade lives.'

'I am at peace with my sins.' Sira held her head high.

'I will have no more deaths. There must be another way.'

'But, m'Lady. Think of the little ones,' Sira said, her voice thick with tears as she grasped Agata's arm with desperate fingers.

'I can't,' Agata said, patting Sira's hand.

Sira pursed her lips, a spark of anger flashing in her eyes.

'I understand your sister means everything to you but this is my final answer. It must end here.' Agata's heart tore as she watched Sira's downcast face.

'As you wish, m'Lady,' Sira said, her voice turning as cold as a winter wind. 'May I leave? I must go and find her. Before the guards do.'

'Be quick.'

'Thank you, m'Lady.' Sira's blank servant's smile was once again in place as she curtseyed. 'Is there anything else you need?'

Agata pinched the bridge of her nose and squeezed her eyes shut, the decision weighing heavily on her chest. She drifted to the window, overlooking the Square.

'Before you go. Explain to me about the Allotment. Is this part of the Spawning Festival? We didn't do it last year.'

Sira gasped, eyes bulging. 'Sorry, m'Lady. Did you say Allotment?'

'The Scion mentioned it a few days ago and I read a reference to an Allotment in a history chronicle. There are men in the Square preparing for it. Down there in front of the Temple.'

Sira ran to her side by the window. 'Oh no.'

'What is it?'

'They're coming.' Sira pointed to a row of carts entering the Square. 'You must stop it.'

CHAPTER THIRTY-EIGHT

FROMA KNOCKED ON CLAWA'S DOOR and waited, smoothing her veil as she tapped her foot. A mousy serving girl eventually answered.

'Is your mistress in?' Froma said.

'Yes, Mistress, but...' the girl replied, her eyes lowered.

'But what?' Froma frowned. I am here on business from the Duchess.' She never tired of saying these words.

'My Mistress is not well. The news of our Master's death has hit her hard and today is worse than yesterday.'

'Of course but she will see me. Mistress Plesec.'

Froma barged past the girl, through the doorway into Clawa's house. She needed to be quick, she did not want to miss Sira and her delivery from the Duchess.

She followed the light into a well-appointed hall with gleaming wooden furniture and rich tapestries rivalling her own. Clawa was sitting at a long table, stirring a spoonful of honey into her porridge and staring glassy-eyed into the bowl.

'Mistress Plesec to see you, Mistress?' the serving girl said.

Clawa nodded without looking up. 'Hagnis wouldn't approve,' she muttered, her lip trembling as she continued to stir. 'He insisted porridge should only be eaten with salt.'

Froma nodded as she sat down. She watched Clawa closely, studying her grief. Even the discussion of porridge brought fresh tears to the widow's eyes. A merchant's wife should show more restraint. She locked away the observation in her mind. She may need it very soon.

'I am terribly sorry for your loss, Clawa. But I am here about --.'

'The house is so empty without him,' Clawa said with a sniff. 'And my Bergdis is shut up in her chamber. The poor child. Her bad news was two-fold.'

'Your daughter?'

'Her father and her betrothed. Both killed in the war.'

'Oh, the poor girl. In the eyes of the Father.' Froma circled her forehead.

'No father, no husband and barely sixteen years old.'

Someone thumped at the side door but Clawa didn't raise her head, she kept stirring and mumbling. The person knocked again, this time twice as loud.

The serving girl scurried down the hallway and opened the door to yelling. Heavy boots clumped inside. Clawa lifted her head and Froma's eyes widened as three terracotta guards stormed into the room.

'Clawa Gunde?' asked the largest of the three, his face covered by a thick beard.

'Yes,' she squeaked.

A blond guard and one with hair like a hedgehog grabbed Clawa by the elbows, sending her chair clattering backwards and lifting her to her feet.

'Take your hands off her,' Froma said, shooting up from her chair as the guards dragged Clawa towards the door.

'Quiet,' the bearded guard snapped. He approached Clawa, her eyes round and wet. 'Where can I find Bergdis Gunde?'

'S-s-she's not here,' Clawa stuttered. 'She is away. In Ledvor.'

The bearded man backhanded Clawa across the face. 'Liar. Where is your daughter?'

Bloody spit dribbled onto Clawa's tunic as she shook her head.

'How dare you!' Froma said, grabbing the bearded guard by the arm. 'Mistress Clawa is a respectable woman--'

'I told you to be quiet,' the guard said, wrenching his hand out of Froma's grasp and jabbing his finger into her face. 'This is none of your business. Unless you want to come too.'

She stood her ground, her hands on her hips. 'How dare you speak to me in this manner. I shall report you to the Duchess.'

'Go ahead. This is an order from the Duke himself.'

Clawa gasped. 'The Allotment?'

The big guard grinned. 'Where is your daughter?'

Clawa shook her head and he raised his big hand once more.

'Upstairs!' the serving girl yelped.

The big man nodded to the blond guard who rushed out of the room and thumped up the stairs.

'What is going on, Clawa? What is an Allotment?' Froma asked.

'Bergdis!' Clawa shouted. 'Leave her alone.' She moaned as the guards tied her hands behind her back.

'Another word and we'll gag you,' the big guard growled.

Froma stood frozen and nauseous, glancing from the guards to Clawa and back again.

Sounds of screaming, banging and crashing floated down the stairs.

Clawa shrieked. 'Don't hurt her...please. Go to my husband's room. Take all the coins you want. Or wine? Take the wine. Anything you want.'

The blond guard appeared in the doorway with Bergdis flung over his shoulder, her long walnut-coloured hair covering her face, her bare toes kicking him in the back. 'Put me down, you churl.'

Froma pushed past Clawa and the guards and rushed to the hallway, blocking the blond guard's path. 'I demand you put her down. Now.'

The blond guard rammed into Froma, shoving her aside like a skittle. The bearded guard laughed as she crashed into the wall with a groan.

'Take them both to the cart.'

'Hurry,' Sira panted as they rushed down the steep Avenue.

'What is it?' Agata shaded her eyes against the midday sun as three carts rumbled into the Square. 'Tell me.'

The carpenters fell silent, their hammers hanging in mid-air. The boys playing in the Old Man Tree stopped laughing as everyone pointed and stared. A hush descended over Ambrovna as the carts rolled in.

Agata's jaw dropped open.

Rather than livestock, the three horse-drawn carts were filled with women. Young and middle-aged, tall and small, stout and slim. In coarse tunics with dirty faces, in veils, in finely embroidered silk. Some cried, some stared blankly, others squeezed their eyes firmly shut, but all were ashen-faced. The women were not alone. They came with newborns in their arms, toddlers at their feet and children, some taller than their mothers.

The carts travelled across the Square and stopped outside the Temple where waiting guards opened the wooden gate. Now it made sense. The Scion's timber construction was a holding pen with high walls and a narrow entry gate.

Agata called out across the Square, her voice bouncing off the bricks. 'What is going on?'

A terracotta clad full-bearded guard dropped his reins and jumped down. Agata lifted her skirts and hurried to take a position between the cart and the pen.

'I asked you a question, guard. Answer your Duchess,' she said, hands on hips as she made her slender frame as large as possible.

The bearded guard bowed his head. 'M'Lady. Please move out of the way.' He kept his eyes on the ground as he spoke.

'Not until you tell me what is going on?'

'Please, m'Lady. I'm only following orders.'

'From who.'

'Me.' Lord Kalin and his guards approached from the rear, his peacock-blue surcoat flapping as he strode towards the pen. 'Unload them.'

'I demand an explanation, Lord Kalin.'

The guards unfastened the cart doors and yanked the women and children by the arms, tossing them into the pen. The Square rang with shrieks for mercy and howls of indignation. A woman in a rough hessian shift tripped and three others toppled over her. The guards laughed and elbowed one another.

'I demand you stop at once. You're hurting them. What is going on?'

Kalin shrugged. 'These are the orders of the Duke. The Allotment will take place tomorrow at the Spawning.'

The women huddled together in the centre of the pen, their children clasped to their chests. A few squinted with fire in their eyes.

'What is the Allotment?'

Lord Kalin laughed. 'I forgot you are a stranger here. You will find out tomorrow.'

'My Lady! My Lady!' said a familiar voice.

'Clawa?' Agata reached through the railings as a pock-faced guard shoved the merchant's widow into the pen.

'Help me,' she said feebly, her button-nose bloodied.

'This woman is one of my Circle. A respectable woman.' Agata's eyes flashed.

'A widow,' Lord Kalin said. 'With a few more child-bearing years in her. Still useful. She'll be given to a new husband by sunset tomorrow.'

'Her husband was a Guild member. A war hero. Have you no respect? You are treating her like a goat!'

'It could be worse. She could end up with the Unwanted.'

'This is barbaric.'

'I'd watch your tongue if I were you, my Lady. The Allotment keeps our town and the families strong. Perhaps traditions and unity are values you Neven people cannot understand--'

'Where is my husband?' Agata spat.

'With the Scion in his Cabinet. Making the last arrangements.'

Agata ground her teeth.

'I must go, my Lady,' Sira whispered and Agata waved her maid away.

'I will stop this,' she said as she lifted her skirts and stomped towards the Avenue.

'Give my regards to the Scion,' Kalin chuckled after her.

Meanwhile, a fourth cart rolled into the Square.

Rabel gulped as the bovine man blocked the doorway of the wig woman's stall.

'What's goin' on?' he boomed.

'I'm leavin',' Rabel said, pulling herself to her full height, surprised by the iron in her voice.

'This tart is trying to back out of our deal and we don't like that. Do we, Jaco?'

The man moved towards Rabel but she stood firm, despite her thumping heart. She glanced around, looked for another way out and pulled Aula and Jorn closer.

'Now, be a good girl and sit down,' Jaco said.

The wig woman gestured to a stool next to the old seamstress. 'It will only take a few moments.'

Rabel shook her head violently. The wig woman and Jaco came towards her, closer and closer, one from the left and one from the right. The wig woman reached for Aula's head and Jaco stretched his meaty fingers for Rabel's shoulder. She swung around but there was only one way out.

'Red death,' Rabel blurted.

Jaco recoiled, his palms in the air.

'What did you say?' the wig woman stuttered.

'You don't want to touch us. We've got the red death.'

The wig woman and Jaco exchanged frantic glances. 'Tripe,' the wig woman said, a tremor in her voice.

Rabel shrugged. 'You don't have to believe me.'

The wig woman backed away slowly.

'Are you thick? Listen to 'er. Let 'em go,' barked the old seamstress from the corner. 'And quick, go get some marigolds and a hen,'

'Get out of 'ere,' the wig woman spat, her eyes flashing as Jaco disappeared through the door.

'For my troubles, I'll take this.' Rabel grabbed a large mud-brown shawl from the table, her pulse racing. The wig woman opened her mouth to protest but said nothing once Rabel's fingers had touched the wool.

'Thank you kindly.' Rabel wrapped it over her head, the blanket-sized shawl falling right down to her knees and covering Jorn and Aula. The children giggled. 'We're playing castles, Ma.'

'A good game, little ones.' Rabel found herself smiling, too.

'Out,' the wig woman snarled.

Rabel hurried away through the flap, back into the markets, her chest tight with fresh worries.

What if the wig woman raised the alarm?

The guards were one problem but what would the Alleys people do to her if they thought she carried the red death? It was time to start afresh, on her own. Her sisters had done so much already. Rabel weighed up her choices. Leaving Ambrovna seemed the only way. She'd tell Sira she no longer needed her help. But first she needed coins and food. The blanket game would only distract the twins for so long.

Finding a clear patch of ground between a stall selling wilted bunches of nettles and a woman selling wart-cures, she bent down. She splashed her hands in a puddle and smeared her face with mud and did the same to the twins. They giggled and wriggled, enjoying this new game. With the blanket covering her hair and shoulders, she kneeled with her head bowed and her hands cupped in the air.

For so many years, she'd resisted begging, but she was out of choices. It was this or Guts Alley. She said nothing, only held out her hands with her twins by her side. Even if she wanted to speak, a boulder-sized lump in her throat held back her words.

'Piss off out of 'ere,' said one man.

'Dirty slut,' laughed a young boy. 'I'll pay you a copper to suck me'.

'Get a job,' said a woman

Head down and hands up, Rabel didn't raise her eyes until she felt the bounce of a copper hitting her shawl. 'In the eyes of the Father,' she muttered, snaffling the coin before another greedy Alleys hand beat her to it.

'Here you go, little ones,' said a woman's voice.

Rabel glanced up to see a rosy-cheeked woman handing over two broken oat cakes. The twins grabbed the biscuits and gobbled them down, crumbs covering their dirty faces.

'Thank you, Goodwife,' Rabel croaked.

'Haven't you heard what's happenin' today? It's not safe out here. They'll round you up too,' the woman said. 'Go and hide.'

Rabel frowned.

'Another one!'

Rabel's eyes widened, her heart yanked from her chest as a big-eared terracotta guard pointed at her.

'Go,' the woman said, before vanishing into the crowd.

Rabel grabbed the twins and scrambled to her feet. 'Come on.'

'More biscuits, Ma?' Jorn said with a pout.

'We're goin' to get more, Jorn,' she said, her voice cracking. 'This way.'

'Not so fast.'

The big-eared guard blocked her path, his arms outstretched. She gripped her children's hands, her knees shaking.

A second rodent-faced guard approached her. 'Where's your husband, woman? Have you got one?'

'Look at her. Who'd want her?' The guard with the ears chuckled and then squeezed his nostrils. 'Will they wash them before the ceremony?'

Rabel flitted from face to face, narrowing her eyes.

'You're comin' with us.'

'Where?'

'You'll find out.'

She dragged her children against her bony chest. Did the guards know who she was? No one had mentioned the red death or Iwan. What was the oat-cake woman talking about? What was going on?

The rat-faced guard grabbed her by the elbow. She tugged her arm away.

'Are you comin' willingly? Otherwise we'll have to force you.'

Rabel bit down on her lip and held back tears. She had nowhere left to run. She stared at the muddy ground and nodded. No point fighting. She must face her actions and accept the Father's judgement.

She took her twins by the hands. 'Come along, little ones.'

'Biscuit?' Jorn said, with eyes wide.

Rabel nodded weakly and with her head bowed, she followed the uniforms through the market, wondering what was in store for them.

'Stop.'

Rabel's heart jumped once more but this time she smiled.

'It's the Duchess's ugly maid,' hissed the big-eared guard.

'Seliv is looking for you two.' Sira pushed through the crowd towards them. 'I don't know what you've done. But he's fuming.'

The guards grimaced at each other.

'He's in the Square.'

'What have you done now?' the rat-faced guard asked his companion.

'I didn't do nothin'.' The other guard flung his hands in the air. 'Maybe it was you.'

'You better hurry,' Sira warned.

With eyes narrowed at each other, the guards turned and pushed their way back through the crowd. 'Get out of our way.'

'Sira,' Rabel breathed once they were gone.

'Come. Now. Before they find out I'm lying.'

CHAPTER THIRTY-NINE

AGATA BARGED THROUGH THE CABINET door, her blood like fire under her skin.

'There you are, my dear. I was going to send for you.' The Duke said as he sat at his carved desk, a warm smile on his lips.

She pointed at the lead-lined window and spat out her words before she could temper herself. 'My Lord. What is going on out there? Women in pens?'

His smile evaporated, his face turning as hard as the brick walls. 'The Allotment is a tradition.'

'Here in Ambrovna we believe in the sanctity of the family,' the Scion said. Agata spun around with a scowl, finding the bald Scion and his two Cousins standing behind her.

Agata glanced at her husband, but he nodded with his hands steepled on the desk. 'My father ordered the same after the last Civil War.'

'It is obvious the adherence to the Teachings is lax in Tramissa,' the Scion continued.

'Thank you for your concern about my education, Scion Zavis.' Agata straightened her spine and drew in a breath through her nostrils. 'However, I know my Teachings well. There is nothing in the text about treating your subjects like livestock.'

'It is an old way, not often used but referenced in the ancient versions of the Teachings.' The Scion swept past her and stood at the Duke's shoulder. 'After the last war, the old Duke and I thought it was the best approach. The needs of the greater family were at stake.'

'Please, sit and rest, my dear. You seem rather overwrought. The preparations for the Spawning Festival must be putting a strain on you. Fetch the Duchess some wine.' The Duke waved at a serving boy.

Agata narrowed her eyes.

'You do not need to concern yourself with these matters.'

'But while the men were at war, we women proved ourselves capable. You must agree that the town is in an acceptable state, my Lord? These women are more than goats at market.'

'Stability is needed. The family must be upheld. Homes must be headed by a man. The Scion came to me and I thought it was an excellent idea.'

Agata's cheeks burned, her fists bunched by her sides.

'The Allotment allows men to take multiple wives. Good breeding stock should never be wasted,' the Scion continued. 'Particularly brothers who are prepared to take their sisters-in-law. The older ones are useless, only good to join the Unwanted. The Allotment turned out well last time, strengthened the town. And it shows our commitment to the Father and his Teachings. Proving Ambrovna is a pious town.'

'But the women have no say,' Agata blurted.

'It is for their benefit. And the benefit of their children. The Fatherhood knows best. I'm sure the Duke will agree.'

The Duke nodded. 'And the people will enjoy the ceremony. A happy celebration of the family.'

'But the women should be able to make this choice for themselves. They have brains, they have hearts.'

'If they do not have husbands, they will starve. Who will employ them? There are more than enough washerwomen and seamstresses. I cannot allow my people to starve.'

'Your people are starving now, my Lord.' Agata's voice wavered as her words poured out unfiltered. 'When did you last visit to the Alleys and see the way they live?'

'You wish to allow these women to remain in poverty when we have a way for them to live a better life?' Her husband stared back with emotionless grey eyes.

'You appear surprised?' The Scion tilted his head. 'Did you have any say in the selection of the Duke as your husband?'

Agata pressed her lips. The politics of the Kingdom and the Five River Clans had taken precedence over a young girl's wishes. She had been lucky with her father's selection. She could have easily been handed over to some cruel but important noble, old enough to be her grandfather.

The Scion stared at her unblinking.

'The ceremony will take place tomorrow during the Spawning Festival,' the Duke continued. 'Arrangements must be made for a mass betrothal as part of the festivities. The Scion will lead the vows, obviously. But I need you to gather the veils and posies, whatever things women need.'

Agata gritted her teeth.

'The tinsmith is working on a number of rings but many of the women are widows. We shall use their old betrothal bands.'

Agata found herself twisting her own band of gold.

'Mid-morning is the best time for a betrothal,' said the Scion. 'While the sun is coming up in the sky.'

'Are my instructions clear, my Lady?' the Duke said.

Agata swallowed, wanting to say so much more.

'My decision has been made. Please commence preparations. You may not understand, but it is your duty. As the Duchess of Ambrovna.'

'Do you understand what it is like? To have no say over your own life? Your own husband? Your own body?' Agata grumbled. 'Of course, you don't.'

'You are not yourself. Boy, call the physician.'

Leaning over the desk, Agata stared into her husband's face. 'You are not listening to me. I am not ill. I am angry. Angry at the way you treat women. Including me.' She jabbed a finger into her own chest.

'You are not making any sense. Go and rest, my dear. The stress of the last few days must be taking its toll on you.'

'Because I am speaking my mind for the first time?'

'Enough.' He folded his arms tightly across his chest, red blotches on his cheeks. 'I understand you are upset but there is no need to be so shrill. I should have known this would happen in my absence. You have become too emotionally attached to the townswomen. Go now. Calm yourself. There is much work to be done.'

Agata lowered her head. She would not waste another breath. 'Yes, my Lord,' she said.

If the Scion had eyebrows, he would have raised one. A glimmer of a smile passed over his lips.

'I will see you for the Blessing of the Spawn at dusk,' the Duke said with a wave of his hand.

With a curtsey, she left the Cabinet room but paused in the doorway.

'Call together my Women's Circle,' she said to the guard with the widow's peak. 'Bring them here. Now. Preparations must be made on the Duke's orders.'

'Yes, m'Lady.' The guard bowed and hurried away.

Agata chewed her lip. He was right. There was much to be done and little time to stop the Allotment.

Pacing her bedchamber, Froma squeezed her upper arms as she waited for the knock at the side door. She smiled at her luck, the solution to her misfortune had fallen right into her lap.

As soon as the Duchess had left, Froma had marched out to inspect the stables and clambered up a ladder to find a perfect hiding place among the hay bales. The snuffles and squawks of the livestock in the neighbouring shed would mask any sign of people. As long as the children kept quiet.

Irina only had eyes for Danis. She'd relish any chance to stir up trouble between them.

A rap sounded at the door and Froma's heart leapt. She rushed downstairs two steps at a time, holding her breath as Irina answered the door.

'Is Mistress Plesec receiving company?'

Froma licked her lips and stepped out from her eavesdropping spot. 'Good morning Sira. Come into the hall,' she said.

The Duchess's maid nodded, her stained face bland. An experienced servant hid every thought.

'Irina, leave us. Your Master will be expecting his luncheon.'

They entered the hall but did not sit down. Froma waited until Irina was safely out of the main house before she spoke.

'Do you have it?'

Without a word, Sira handed over a Square of grey-brown fur. Froma snatched the pouch and plunged it deep into her pocket.

'There is one small piece left but it is more than enough, Mistress,' Sira said flatly. 'Are you prepared for her?'

'Do I simply add it to the food?'

'I am told it is tasteless. Where should I send Rabel?'

'How long does it take?'

'If you use it soon, it should work by nightfall.'

Froma's heart thundered in her chest. By morning, she'd be free.

'Mistress Plesec?' Sira's brow furrowed. 'Rabel?'

'Yes. Yes. I have a place for her. As long as she is quiet.'

'She is waiting in the next alleyway.'

'Meet me at the back gate but she must be discreet. No one can know she is here.'

'I am so grateful.'

'Thank you, Sira,' said Froma. 'We understand one another. We are not afraid to do what needs to be done. Take matters into our own hands.'

Sira pursed her lips. 'I did this for my sister and her children, Mistress Plesec.'

Froma's nostrils flared.

The maid shrugged her shoulders. 'It is not my place to judge you.'

'You have no idea what I have suffered.' Froma narrowed her eyes to slits.

'Suffering is our fate as women. Mistress Plesec. I must be back at the castle. Please excuse me.' Sira turned on her heel. 'Rabel will be at the gate.'

Froma gritted her teeth as Sira. How dare a servant judge her? A low born woman acting innocent and righteous, but equally stained with sin. But Froma's smile returned when her fingertips touched the fur in her pocket. The maid was of no consequence. She no longer needed her or the Duchess, or anyone else. Life reminded her again and again she could only rely on herself.

Froma bustled to the kitchen hut.

CHAPTER FORTY

A GATA MARCHED INTO THE SOLAR. 'I am glad you could all come at such short notice. I will be quick so you can return to your luncheons.'

Skinny Jadzia and plump Gala perched on the edge of the cushioned bench, arms folded as they leaned forward.

'There is an urgent matter we must attend to...' Agata took a seat alongside them, a flutter in her veins. Sira sat in her place by the wall at the back of the room.

The door opened and Froma bustled in. 'Apologies, my Lady.' Froma's face was veiled but there was an expectant gleam in her eye.

'No need for apologies, Mistress Plesec. I had not yet begun.' Agata's belly lurched. She had considered excluding Froma from the meeting but they were all too entangled now. Her demand for poison must wait.

'Randvi and Karolien are not here yet?' said Gala. 'And Clawa.'

'I did not invite them,' she replied. Gala and Jadzia shared glances. 'And this concerns Clawa.'

'How may we assist you, my Lady?' Froma said.

'It is sensitive,' Agata said leaning forward, searching the women's faces. Could she trust them? 'This concerns the Allotment.'

'I saw them outside the Temple.' Jadzia shook her head and sighed. 'They took my kitchen woman.'

'And one of the laundresses.' Gala nodded.

'And Clawa. I saw her myself,' Agata said. 'Being dragged into the pen.'

'I was there when they took her,' Froma said flatly.

Gala and Jadzia gasped.

'How does this *tradition* make you feel?'

'Bloody angry,' Jadzia blurted and then covered her mouth. Gala grunted with a nod. Froma said nothing.

'I agree. I am furious. This is a terrible wrong against grieving widows. I am glad, I am not alone. This is why I did not ask for Karolien and the others. I have an idea but I need people I can trust. People who are willing to help me stop this.'

Gala breathed out long and low with a sideways glance. 'Are you suggesting we go against the Scion? Your own husband? The whole town?'

'It's not right, Gala. You can't deny it,' Jadzia said. 'We should help them.'

'But how? Look at us. We're only a handful of women.'

Agata tutted. 'Women who ran this town alone for an entire year.'

Gala chewed her lip.

'We must help them escape. Somewhere out of reach of the Fatherhood and the Master of the Shield.'

Froma shook her veiled head. 'The Fatherhood is everywhere.'

'But the Allotment is not. I doubt the Chief Scion in Sulun would approve. If I am frank, this is a backwards practice,' Agata said.

Jadzia and Gala grinned and covered their mouths like mischievous little girls.

'What about the hills?' Agata said. 'Sira, would she help?'

'You don't mean Wisia?' said Gala with a frown. 'But she's a ...'

'There are too many of them to hide, m'Lady,' Sira replied. 'They'd be easily found.'

Jadzia rubbed her sharp chin. 'Ships leave every night.'

'Would the seamen help us?' Agata asked, eyes wide.

'For the right price, m'Lady, you can get anything you want,' Jadzia said.

Agata had never carried coins but upstairs, hidden inside a trunk, she had a brooch. It was a simple twisted branch made of gold once owned by her mother. No one would notice if it went missing. Her heart clenched at the idea of handing her mother's jewellery over to a street peddler but if the coins meant safe passage for a group of women in need, her mother would definitely approve.

'We couldn't guarantee their safety at the other end.' Jadzia grimaced. 'You know what sailors are like.'

'Could their fate be any worse?'

Agata glanced at her Circle members. Gala and Jadzia clasped their hands tightly, their eyes gleaming but Froma was a closed door.

'What about weapons?' Gala asked.

'I don't want anyone hurt.' Agata shook her head.

'With respect, m'Lady. You can't do this without bloodshed,' Gala replied. 'My brother is a blade-smith. I can get whatever we need.'

'Even with blades, we'll never win with pure force,' Jadzia said. 'We have to be cunning.'

Agata rubbed her forehead and her stomach roiled. There was another option. 'Sira. Do you have any left? What happens with a smaller dose? Is it less effective?'

'Yes, m'Lady,' Sira said.

Agata watched Froma share a curious glance with Sira. Clever Froma understood she was being denied. Agata hoped she could see the greater good, but her stomach doubted it.

'Excellent.' She clapped her hands and forced a smile. 'We have the makings of a plan. Here's what we should do...'

CHAPTER FORTY-ONE

I prepared myself to return to the Umbaz again that evening, ready to win over the Queen and her court with the Father's insightful words. As the sun was setting, one of Magnilla's female guards arrived at our door to collect us, a sword jangling at her hip. But she led us past the Umbaz to an adjoining building with many-sided walls like a honeycomb.

'Where are you taking us?' grumbled the Cousin.

Without replying, the guard ushered us through a sliding wooden door. My belly fluttered as we entered an open room with a shingled ceiling. Each wooden tile was edged with gold paint. In the flicker of candlelight, the ceiling undulated like a gilded snake. Overlapping woven carpets were strewn with embroidered cushions and oblong pillows of blue and pale yellow.

The queen lay on a long wooden bench, inches off the ground with a handful of her white-haired people lounging at her feet, sipping spirits and eating roasted meat from silver platters.

I smiled. A private audience was a most promising sign.

'My visitors,' the Queen said. 'Sit. Eat. Drink.'

This time, my fellow Cousin avoided the clear fire water and we both took only small morsels of meat.

'Tell me of your day in Meeraq, visitors,' she said. 'What did you see and hear? What impressed you?'

'Your judgements, my Queen,' I replied, my words spilling out before I had thought my answer through. The translator with the white bun repeated my words to the others at Magnilla's feet.

She raised a white eyebrow. 'Our squabbles over land and livestock interest you?'

'Your ways are...different.'

'How are your quarrels decided?'

'By a noble in a similar way, but he is always a man. You are a rarity.'

'Me?' the Queen laughed and shook her head. 'You are the rare one here. I am only the latest in a long line of female rulers. There were many before me and there will be many after me. Whoever the Great Mother decides to birth into my family. The next ruler will be a King.'

'You have been raised to be a ruler.' I nodded. 'Raised as a man.'

The Queen's brow furrowed. 'Man or woman, it does not matter. No one is better. We are all capable. We have different strengths, but all of us are able.'

'But what of times of war? You lack the physical strength to lead an army into battle.'

'Your King fights on the field like a common soldier? If physical strength was all that mattered, then the strongest man would be your King. Is your King the strongest man? Did he fight all to get his crown? One on one?'

'We are beyond such things. Our King is intelligent. Women lack the...experience... for battle strategy.'

'Are there not stupid men? And clever women? Are there no clever women in the Neven lands?'

I pursed my lips. Queen Gwynfor was known for her skills on the lute but I shook my head at the very idea of Gwynfor spearheading an army.

'Do you know any women? Have you ever known a woman?' The other guests chuckled lustfully as my cheeks flamed red. 'You raise your women to be livestock. You smother their flames. Here we welcome women and fan their fires to burn bright and hot.'

'Our women take their roles willingly.' Heat spread across my cheeks, sweat prickled my brow.

'Have you asked them what they want?'

'There is no need. It is obvious. They want the same as the men. To serve the Father.'

'Is it truly in their hearts? If you beat a dog often enough, he cowers when you raise your hand.'

'They love the Father.'

'But the Father does not love them.'

I jumped to my feet and words gushed from my mouth. 'That is untrue. The Father loves all his followers. He is kind and wise. He looks after us all. He forgives our faults.'

The wiry female guard stepped forward, her blade in hand. I gulped as Magnilla waved her down. The guard narrowed her eyes as she rested back, her gaze like the dagger she longed to point into my heart.

'He does not love women. He uses them.'

'How dare...' my fellow Cousin blurted as he stumbled upright. I placed my hand on his arm but he shook me away, fists bunched. 'You know nothing of what you speak.'

'You call Queen a liar?' A broad-shouldered man said clumsily in our tongue. He rose to his feet, his hands on his hips. The other courtiers glared at me from their places on the ground and I glared back.

I took in gulps of breath as I tried to cool my blood. The Father's love for his followers was an undeniable truth. Despite the q]Queen's ignorance, this was her land and I was a guest in her home. I had to show respect, no matter how much I wanted to retort. The room became uncomfortably still. The courtiers watched and waited, the broad-shouldered man and the guards like cats ready to pounce.

My heart thumped.

'I can see you are troubled by my words,' Queen Magnilla said with a casual blink of her eyes, dismissing me like any other servant. 'Leave now.'

'Thank you, Queen Magnilla' I said, bowing my head as etiquette demanded. I would return tomorrow night armed with the perfect passages to convince her and her people of the wisdom and love of the Father. 'We can continue our discussion tomorrow.

'No,' she replied. 'I am bored with you and your ignorance. You will leave my land.'

My mouth dropped open.

'You may stay one more night. But you will return to your homelands tomorrow. I do not want to hear any more of your nonsense. I heard about your meddling and the commotion outside the Umbaz this afternoon. I have given you a chance to explain yourself, have shown you nothing but hospitality but you do not respect our ways. I want you gone.'

My fellow Cousin lunged forward, fire in his eyes. I held him back but had no one to hold me back. Only the Father. I begged Him for strength and steadied myself enough to speak calmly. I bowed my head. 'I am sad you are not willing to listen to the Father's Teachings. You are missing a chance to learn about His true love and reform your sinful ways.'

The courtiers guffawed and elbowed one another. Even the Queen cracked a smirk.

'But I will not stay where my faith is not welcome. Come, Cousin.'

We walked from the room, our heads held high, the heat of the Cousin's anger exuding from his skin. Or was it my own?

'Heathens,' he spat once we were out in the cool night air. 'How dare they throw us out? The Father will strike revenge on their town and their people. We must send word to King Heribert to plan an attack.'

I rubbed my chin and sighed as my companion blew out his steam. How would I explain this failure to my Scion?

A sharp whistle from a shadowy laneway on my left pierced the air. I furrowed my brow and squinted as a man stepped into the light. It was Borild, the forsaken man from the Umbaz hearing.

'I knew you would come back to hear more of the love of the Father,' I said as he beckoned us into the laneway.

As I stepped into the shadows, a fist struck me above the ear. The powerful knock rattled my senses and sent me stumbling blindly. My fellow Cousin grunted and hit the ground with a heavy thud. Boots stamped all around us. I blinked and as my vision returned. Our attackers were three men and two women. One woman, the size of a child came toe-to-toe and glared up at my face.

'We do not fight,' I said, looking down at her, forcing a smile on my trembling lips. 'It is not the way of the Fatherhood.'

She laughed and replied in our tongue. 'We do.'

Her first blow hit me square in the nose and with it came a shot of scalding pain. She returned with a second, slamming my septum into my skull. The others cheered as her third blow struck me across the jaw.

'Take back these scars and show them what Akull Women can do,' she whispered in my ear then everything went black.

CHAPTER FORTY-TWO

THE MEETING IN THE SOLAR was over and the women went their separate ways.

Sira scurried down the corridor. 'Mistress Plesec!'

Froma turned, her eyebrow arched.

'May I speak with you?' Sira panted, her voice low.

'Ah, Sira. Lying to your own mistress? Hmm?' she said, the smirk visible in her eyes.

'I gave you more than enough...'

'It is mine now.' Mistress Plesec turned on her heel.

'Please. If you gave me back half...'

The merchant's wife snorted.

Sira reached out, grasping her arm. 'What do you want? Please tell me.'

'Get your hands off me. I have what I want.'

'But think of the women?'

Mistress Plesec barked out a laugh. 'You are not thinking of them. You only wish to save yourself. The Duchess would banish you from the castle if she found out you had lied to her. Wouldn't she?'

Sira swallowed.

'Go to your Wasp Woman and get yourself more. This is mine.'

'There's no time.'

'We had a bargain. I upheld my side. Do you want me to have a quiet word to a guard on the way out? Tell him about a certain woman hiding in a loft. I can do that easily.'

'No. No. Surely there is something you want from me.'

The Mistress narrowed her eyes. 'Perhaps...'

'Anything.'

'Anything?'

'Anything,' Sira said, clutching her hands.

Mistress Plesec smoothed the edges of her veil. 'You are the eyes and ears of the Duchess. I want you to tell me everything that goes on here in the castle. Every word, every visit.'

Sira dropped her head.

'You will come to me once a week with a report.'

Sira slumped. Betray her mistress or lose her livelihood?

'Do we have an agreement?' Mistress Plesec raised an eyebrow.

CHAPTER FORTY-THREE

WATCHING DANIS WOLF DOWN HIS luncheon that day was one of the most pleasurable moments of Froma's life. Irina's goat stew was rich and perfectly salted. A small white mushroom had slipped easily unnoticed into her husband's bowl.

Danis grunted in reply, globs of brown gravy congealing on the bristles of his moustache. He finished off his meal with several more goblets of red wine then wiped his mouth on the tablecloth and clumped back to the shop front.

All afternoon, Froma tried to busy her mind. First, she embroidered a new cushion, gold and green to match the tapestry on the wall but as she bungled stitch after stitch, she tossed her needlework aside in disgust.

She found herself gazing out the window, waiting for the hours to pass. Her eyes gleamed, dreaming of tomorrow, of a future of haggling deals with weavers and dyers, of producing the finest mohair and the most glorious colours in all the Five Rivers.

Unlike other women, Froma was lucky. A merchant's widow inherited her dead husband's business. The Fatherhood turned a blind eye to merchant women whose riches lined the Temple's pockets. Men would leave her alone to prosper, as long as she was careful where she trod. And now as part of the Duchess's inner circle, she would not be denied. Blood stained all their hands.

A furious knock sounded at the side door. Froma flinched and tore down the hallway to see Irina opening the door to the bandy-legged balding Master Tveldt.

'This way, sir,' Irina said, hurrying him towards Danis's study.

'What is going on?' Froma frowned. 'Irina?'

Irina cowered as Master Tveldt marched inside, followed a young boy who struggled with a cumbersome leather bag.

'The Master is sick. He called for Master Tveldt.'

'Why was I not informed?'

She shrugged. 'I was carin' for the Master.'

'Stupid girl,' Froma said, striking out as she passed but Irina ducked in time. Froma pursed her lips and bustled towards the study, her heart thundering. Irina prepared the meals. She would be blamed for the poison. Nothing would shine suspicion on Froma.

In his study, Danis lay slumped over his desk. Tveldt rushed to his side. His assistant lifted Danis's big head to reveal his face was sweaty and wan, tinged with green.

'What ails my husband, Master Tveldt?' Froma said, wringing her hands.

'Let me examine him,' the doctor replied. 'There is word of the red death in Ambrovna. We must be very careful.'

Froma gasped and covered her mouth with her hands, making a grand show of her concern. 'We have only been reunited for a few short days. Can you save him?'

Tveldt peeled back Danis's eyelids, inspected his eyeballs and mumbled incomprehensibly to his assistant. The assistant opened the bag and pulled out a glass vial.

'What is that?' Froma said, hovering close by.

'Please leave us, Mistress Plesec. I must be allowed to perform my examination without interruption. Time is precious.'

Froma nodded and left the room. She loitered outside, pacing the hallway.

'Is the Master going to die?' Irina sniffled as she stood with her back flat against the hallway wall.

'Why didn't you come to me first?' Froma hissed.

Irina shrugged her skinny shoulders and Froma narrowed her eyes. Irina would learn to regret her disloyalty. She'd be out on the streets the moment Danis was gone.

If Tveldt didn't spoil everything.

Froma wished she could peer inside the physician's mind as she paced and wrung her hands. Ordinarily in moments like this, she'd call on the mercy of the Father but not today. The Father did not reward sinners.

Froma told herself she needn't worry. Tveldt suspected the red death. She was safe. The same poison would produce the same results.

Both Irina and Froma rushed forward as the door opened. Tveldt and his assistant lugged Danis through the door, his head lolling loosely.

'Mistress, where is your bedchamber?'

'Upstairs.'

Danis gurgled and a fountain of red vomit gushed from his mouth, splattering up the walls.

'The red death!' Irina squealed and ran.

'Get a bucket,' Froma yelled but the girl was already gone.

The two men hauled Danis up the stairs, the young boy and the older man groaning under his weight.

'Is she right?' Froma asked with a shake in her voice as they forced Danis through the door and onto the bed.

'It appears like the red death in some ways. But not others,' Tveldt panted. 'I must bleed him to clear his humours and then I will know better. Can you fetch hot water?'

Froma nodded, her shoulders tightening as she headed for the kitchen hut to find Irina. The poison and her plot may not be uncovered but Froma faced a greater problem.

Tveldt might save him.

CHAPTER FORTY-FOUR

S IRA CLASPED HER HANDS TOGETHER, her knuckles colourless with the pressure. 'Perhaps there is another way, m'Lady?'

The Duchess shook her head, standing with her arms folded by her bedchamber window.

'But more lives?'

'You told me it was not enough to kill?'

'I am not sure, m'Lady. Rabel only had a small amount left,' Sira lied. There was only a quarter of the tiny puffball left after she'd split the remaining half with Mistress Plesec.

'I will hear no more arguments, Sira,' the Duchess said, her friendly face vanishing. 'Go. This is an order.'

Sira plastered on a smile and curtseyed, biting her lip as she left the room. She dawdled towards the kitchens, hoping for an interruption, anything to stop her along the way. With Iwan, her actions had felt righteous but this time her stomach gurgled like boiling oil.

She trudged into the kitchens and with a sigh, sidled up to Majvi. 'Are they ready?'

Majvi pulled a covered basket out from below the table, her lips pressed white as she handed it over.

'She thanks you,' Sira whispered.

'And you don't?'

Sira shrugged, taking the basket in her hands. 'It doesn't matter what I think.'

'You worry me,' Majvi said with soft eyes, her a hand on Sira's forearm. Her touch tingled against Sira's skin but Sira looked away. Without another word, she left the kitchens.

The basket burdened her arm as she continued across the bailey, the weight of the Father's displeasure weighing heavier on her shoulders with every step.

'What have you got there?' A lanky guard blocked her path in front of the gate.

Sira slapped his hand away.

'We demand a tax,' said another with a red nose as he reached for the cloth.

The guards smirked at one another as the tall skinny one grabbed the basket. The load on her conscience lifted as he took possession of it. If they stole the cakes from her, she was no longer responsible.

'Give it back,' she said half-heartedly.

The one with the drinker's nose lifted the cloth and breathed in deeply. 'No one will notice a few missing,' he said.

'No--'

'Herwin. Seppu,' said a stern voice. 'Hand it back.' Lord Kalin strode up to the gate, his sword jangling.

'Yes, m'Lord.' The guards cowered.

'Some of Majvi's baking?' Lord Kalin raised the cloth and stared at the golden almond cakes.

Sira held her breath.

He reached down.

Should she stop him? He was the one who ordered Rabel's arrest.

'Lord Kalin?' Seliv, his second in command lumbered up to him. 'I must speak with you.'

Kalin's hand hovered over a cake.

Sira held her breath as she watched, her full lungs almost bursting, her face red hot. The Father was interfering with their plans. What fate did he have in mind?

Kalin jerked his head and snatched his hand away. Empty. 'What now?' He turned with a sigh and followed Seliv.

Sira let out her breath. She clutched the iron gate and wiped her brow. Once her heartbeat calmed, she continued down the Avenue, following her orders. But her pulse picking up speed again when she saw the Allotment women and their children huddled together in the pen.

They reminded her of the Unwanted, the women hidden behind the walls of the Temple, destined to a life of serving the Fatherhood. Sira had only seen them once or twice in her entire life. They looked as lifeless as husks with their hair cropped like shorn sheep, their dead eyes and grain sacks for tunics.

Three young guards stood by the gate of the pen, fulfilling their duty as a man of Ambrovna. One blond and pale, one big-eared and one pimple-cheeked. Only a few summers ago, these guards were boys. Had they done anything to deserve this? Were they pure in the eyes of the Father? Like Teo? Sira's heart crumpled. She'd already killed twice.

'What do you want?' the spotty one snarled.

She paused. Should she turn and run? Dump the cakes in the sea and lie to her mistress? Would a falsehood to save lives redeem her in the eyes of the Father? She pulled the basket close to her chest.

'Are you dumb?' he said.

'She sure is ugly,' the blond guard laughed.

'Shh. Don't you know who she is? She's *her* maid,' the big-eared one said.

'What do you want, Singlewoman?' the spotty guard said slowly as if speaking to a simpleton.

She shrugged and turned away, heart pounding. The Father had delivered her a reprieve. As she spun around, Sira latched eyes with a lanky brown-haired girl in the pen. Around nine years old, she gripped the hands of a younger boy and girl. She stared back at Sira with defiance in her eyes and a purple stain on her cheek, much like Sira's own. The little boy pulled at her hand, his face scrunched with tears but she patted him and whispered soothing words into his ear.

Sucking in a breath, Sira turned and pulled back the cloth cover to reveal the almond cakes. 'The Duchess asked me to bring you these.'

The three guards huddled around her, grinning. Their greedy hands did not need a second invitation.

CHAPTER FORTY-FIVE

ALL AFTERNOON DANIS HAD THRASHED and moaned, tying his sheets in knots and spewing blood-filled vomit down the bedside.

'He will get better, won't he?' Froma asked as she sat on the bed, feeding him broth.

'I do not know,' Tveldt grimaced. 'I've done all I can. It is with the Father now.'

'You must eat, husband,' Froma said through gritted her teeth as she forcing another spoonful through his thick protesting lips.

Tveldt sat on the opposite side of the bedchamber while his assistant scuttled off for more supplies. Froma had sent the sniffling Irina down to the kitchen to prepare a meal for the physician, knowing any meal she prepared would be heavily garnished with her tears.

Conscious of Tveldt's beady eyes following her every move, Froma smoothed Danis's sparse sweaty hair across his forehead. She twisted her hands and blinked back tears for the doctor's benefit while inside her chest swelled with hope. Tveldt was only a country physician, she told herself. He knew nothing more than leeches and bleeding. Poison and the old ways were lost to men like him.

Danis's face was grey and slick with sweat, but Froma felt neither pity nor regret as she watched him. Not for a single moment. There was no love left for Danis in her heart, the man who married her after losing a bet.

Danis had been a widower, a regular visitor to the port of Veigur, Froma's hometown further down the coast. He had also been her Papa's drinking friend. One day at breakfast, her Papa had announced his Singlewoman daughter was finally to be married. Froma had known of Danis's thick fish-lips and gruff demeanour, but the prospect still excited her. She would become a merchant's wife, live in a grand house with servants to boss about and have a wardrobe of fine gowns befitting her position. Finally, her chance for respect had arrived.

After a betrothal that was more like a business deal, Froma came to Ambrovna. Years rolled by without an heir and Danis's malice crept up on her like a vine. A snide comment here. A push and shove there. Then a fist and a boot. Until one day, after another of his failed deals, when she covered her face to venture out in public, Froma realised what she'd become.

She'd had nowhere to go but back home to Veigur, to a life of waiting on her Papa and Mama. She would have been an embarrassment and a blight on her family. And a small greedy part of her couldn't bear to walk away from the comforts Danis provided.

She told herself that once the fleece rot was cured, once the spring came, once the war was over, he'd change. But she had been wrong. He was never going to stop his cruelty on his own.

Danis sat upright and reached out with his hands. 'The mohair is first grade, Sir. You'll find nothing better,' he said loudly then he slumped back against the pillows, his eyes closed.

'Is he improving?' she asked.

Tveldt's brow furrowed.

Danis wailed and scratched savagely at his belly.

'Master Tveldt!' Froma's hands wrapped around her throat. 'Do something!' But underneath her veil, she smirked as he convulsed. The end was nigh and her own nightmare was almost over.

Red froth bubbled from Danis's mouth, the whites of his eyes curdled into pink. The young assistant appeared at the door and rushed over, joining Tveldt at Danis's side.

'Help him. Help him,' Froma squealed, backing away from the bedside as Danis gurgled.

'Open his mouth.' Tveldt took a pinch of grey sand from a vial.

The assistant wiped away the red muck around Danis's mouth and forced open his jaw. Danis grunted, his eyes rolling. Tveldt tossed the sand into his mouth and the two men slammed his jaw shut.

Danis spewed violently, a wave of blood gushing from his mouth. Tveldt and the boy recoiled.

When the shower of vomit and convulsions stopped, Danis leaned forward, his mouth agape. His tongue lolled blue and swollen and blood trickled down his chin. Danis then collapsed face-forward like a felled tree.

'Danis!'

Tveldt and the assistant pulled him upright but Danis stared straight ahead, unseeing.

Froma gulped down a sob. He was gone.

A low-class woman would have screamed and cried but a woman of her standing had to be stoic. Her subdued emotion would be perfectly acceptable.

'Go!' Tveldt yelled the assistant ran out the door, his boots clumping down the stairs.

'What do we do now?' Froma said, forcing a wobble into her voice. 'Should I call for the Scion?'

Tveldt closed Danis's eyelids and laid him back on the bed. He looked so peaceful, except for the blood crusted around his nose and mouth.

Froma feigned a whimper. He would never strike her again. She tilted her head at the sound of footsteps stomping up the stairs. Two men in terracotta tunics entered, one with a red-nose, the other lanky and tall. Did the Shield guards attend every death in the town?

'Arrest her,' Tveldt said.

Froma stared, open-mouthed. The guards took an arm each and lifted her off her feet.

'Take your hands off me!' Froma spat and struggled. 'This moment! What do you think you are doing?'

The guards ignored her.

'My husband has just died. Have some respect,' she said as she tried to tug herself free but their hold was too strong. 'Master Tveldt? I don't understand.'

'Take her away. She poisoned her husband.' Tveldt pointed an accusing finger and the men dragged Froma to the door.

'This man is a liar. He's no physician. Look! He couldn't save...I didn't...' The guards wrestled Froma along the corridor and down the stairs. 'Unhand me. I've done nothing wrong. Master Tveldt is the one you should arrest.'

The guards yanked her through the side door and into the street.

'I demand you let me go. Where are you taking me?'

'Where do you think?' The red-nosed guard sneered.

Froma gulped.

CHAPTER FORTY-SIX

A GATA SHIFTED IN HER SEAT. The Duke sat stiffly by her side in the front row of the Temple and not a single word passed between them as they waited for the Blessing of the Spawn to begin.

Every seat was taken, even the aisles were full and the doors were wide open so others could listen from the steps and the Square. The foyer of the Temple was piled high with offerings for the Fatherhood: baskets of hazelnuts and rosy apples; bales of mohair; dark bottles of wine; leather saddles; knitted blankets; ropes and dried fish encrusted with salt.

As the last Temple bell sounded and the final clang faded away, the buzz of chatter hushed. The Scion appeared. Unlike other Scions, he entered the Temple through the same entrance as all the other townspeople. As he wove his way through the crowd, people reached out to touch his gown but he tugged the cloth from their hands with a stern look. The Scion seemed to consider himself a simple man, no better than the rest of the townspeople and yet he was incapable of showing even the slightest hint of compassion.

By the time he reached the Temple table, the room was quiet. The Scion turned to face the people with his Cousins in lines to his left and right, their heads bowed. Thousands of tiny candles behind him glistened and flickered. The Scion glanced over at Agata and the Duke in the front row. She met the Scion's eyes steadily, denying him the benefit of deference. Beside her, the Duke nodded in response.

The Scion stood perfectly still, staring out at the people. He waited through the coughs, the shuffling of feet, stray comments from naughty children. Once there was absolute silence, he began. 'In the eyes of the Father.'

'In the eyes of the Father,' the people repeated after him, their voices echoing into the Temple's high ceilings. The Scion nodded gravely and Agata wondered whether the old man ever smiled.

'Today we gather for the most important time of the year in Ambrovna, the Blessing of the Spawn when we seek the Father's blessing for the coming Spawning Season, so he may fill our nets with the bounty of the sea. In the eyes of the Father.'

'In the eyes of the Father.'

'The Father thanks all those who provided offerings to the Fatherhood. Your kindness allows the Cousins and myself to devote ourselves to the spiritual welfare of Ambrovna. We thank you. Your generosity makes the Father proud of his children. And you are all his children. Every one of you.'

'As we all know with families, there can be troubles and disagreements, but in the end there is always love. The Father will reward your kindness.'

'We have all been through a trying time. At last year's Blessing, the men left and the women prayed for the return of our soldiers. Just as the eels return every year from the Spawning grounds. But unlike the eels, our men did not venture on a trip towards abundance and the bringing of new life. Instead theirs was a trip towards death.'

Agata smiled painfully as she listened to the sound of muffled tears in the crowd behind her. The Scion paused and nodded.

'But like the eels on their journey to the Spawning grounds, all journeys contain risks. Like the eels, it is the duty of men to protect and continue the line of their family. This is the true way of the Father. All men must make sacrifices to perpetuate their line and become fathers in His image. They must take the role of the Father in their own households and be willing to fight any threat.'

'We may have a new King in Sulun but our ways are unchanged. The eels still spawn, the sun still rises in the East, the winter comes and the Father still reigns supreme, in the Temple and in the home. This is the way it has always been and the way it always will be. Everything has a place under the Father, be it man, woman, fisherman, the eel, the sky, the weather, the cliffs, the Fatherhood.

This is what our Father expects from us. If we stray, we make the Father unhappy. We do not know what will happen then. Some of the older among us have known lean seasons followed by times when people have tried to change the ways. The Father has showed his disappointment in the winds, through rough seas and forest fires, which tore through the valleys.

The Father is kind and loving and wise, but he expects obedience. He knows we are but children, in need of a guiding hand to learn. We need discipline when we wander like all small children do.'

Agata clenched her fists.

'This is a time when we give thanks for all we have. On the eve of the Festival, we must judge our own behaviour. Ask yourselves, "have I been pious?" "Have I obeyed the Father and my own father?" "Have I confessed my sins?"'

'In the eyes of the Father.'

The Scion stared into the faces of the people. All around, Agata felt the townspeople fidget under his unrelenting gaze.

'Men, have you provided for your families? Been wise and strong? Been an example to your children and women? In the image of the Father himself?'

'In the eyes of the Father,' boomed the men.

'Women, have you obeyed your husbands? Been pious and demure? Provided a warm home for your men?'

'In the eyes of the Father,' the women chorused.

The Scion's eyes rested on Agata. She stared back, chin lifted, answering his questions with a slight smile.

'Unfortunately, war brings death. Not all our brave soldiers returned. They left grieving widows and children adrift without protection. To strengthen our families in Ambrovna and show our commitment to the Father, the Allotment will take place tomorrow at mid-morning. You all saw the Allotment women outside. All unmarried men and widowers who wish for a new wife must see the Seneschal to take part. After this ceremony, we hope the Father will be happy with our actions and bless us with a mild winter and a rich eel season. And our women and children will find the protection they need. In the eyes of the Father.'

Agata pressed her lips together tightly. The Allotment must be stopped.

CHAPTER FORTY-SEVEN

F ROMA LAY IN THE MUCKY straw, her cheeks flaming as the cart bounced across the cobbles.

'How dare they!' she cursed under her breath. Didn't they know she was? She was a merchant's wife and a friend of the Duchess.

As the dusk rolled in, the round white face of the moon stared down at her in judgement. The streets were crowded with people late for the Blessing. They peered into the cart with curious faces. Froma ducked her head as the guards took the familiar path to the castle, through the Square and past the Old Man Tree. But rather than taking the steep Avenue to the main gatehouse, the cart continued straight ahead towards a gate she'd never noticed before, a door hidden at the base of the castle walls.

The two guards dragged her out of the cart, through a screeching iron gate and a third guard, pot-bellied and bug-eyed, led the way into the bowels of the castle. The stink of body waste, rotting straw and decay hit her as they hauled her down a sparsely lit corridor.

'I demand to see the Duke,' she said, lifting her chin as the fat guard jangled his keys and unlocked an iron-barred door. The guard cackled as he shoved her inside and locked the door behind her.

Froma stuck her head through the bars. 'Now. You hear. This is a mistake. You will be sorry once the Duke finds out.'

'Shut up,' yelled a man from another cell.

The guards disappeared into the darkness. Froma shook the door with all her might but it barely moved. She grunted. She bared her teeth. She slammed her fists against the bars and bellowed. But no one came.

Clutching the sides of her head, she slumped against the cold wall. A thin gap between the bricks cast a narrow strip of moonlight onto the straw floor and a hole in the wall let in a breath of sea air, a vague respite from the stench. But the rest of her cell was pure darkness. Something rustled in the shadows.

'Hello,' she said, her pulse quickening. What kind of ruffian would she meet in the castle dungeons? Someone who truly belonged here. Unlike her.

A fat rat scampered out of the dark and stopped in the rectangle of light to clean his whiskers. Froma shooed the rodent away with a flick of her skirts.

Alone again, she paced but as time passed and no one came to free her, the truth of her predicament dawned on her. Froma slid to the ground in the rotting straw and wrapped her arms around her knees against the chill. Here she was, imprisoned in the dungeon under the castle, facing a charge of murder by poisoning. Her own husband. Who would help her? Her chin trembled and the tears began to fall.

No one.

Kalin topped up the Duke's goblet with a gleam in his eye. 'I have a little story to tell. But no need to thank me. It's merely part of my job as your humble servant.'

The Duke chuckled and settled back in his chair.

'Since we returned home from Sulun, a few notes have arrived here at the castle--'

'Notes?' the Duke said, a golden eyebrow raised. 'More love letters from your pining conquests?'

'Not quite,' Kalin replied. 'Anonymous notes. Threats towards you.'

The Duke spluttered and cleared his throat. He barked out a laugh to cover his reaction. 'Me?'

Kalin shrugged. 'Some fool trying his hand at blackmail.'

The Duke's heartbeat galloped in his ears. He gripped his goblet tight. 'What do the notes say?'

'Some nonsense about "knowing what you did",' Kalin smirked.

The Duke's stomach plummeted. His nightmare was coming true. How much would this man demand for his silence?

'I do not need to know the full story, my Lord. Although if it involves that delicious red-head from Ledvor, I might insist on hearing all the details.'

The Duke forced another laugh. 'I am a married man.'

'And?' Kalin grinned.

'Have you caught him?' the Duke said, rubbing the back of his neck.

'I didn't want to concern you with such trifles,' Kalin said. 'After fighting all day, every day, and then the excitement and lovely distractions of Sulun...' He paused, a faraway smile on his face. 'I have to admit I was a bit bored and so I decided to find out the truth for myself. But no need to worry, the whole situation is resolved.'

'What did he say?' The Duke's heart thundered as he examined his friend's face for clues. Did the man reveal his cowardly secret? Did Kalin now know a pathetic pretender sat on the Ambrovnan throne?

'The problem solved itself, my Lord. It turns out the note writer died.'

'Died?' The Duke smiled as he let out a slow, quiet exhale. His rescuer was dead, taking the Duke's secret with him.

The room grew brighter, more sweetly scented than he remembered. The Duke's fingers and toes tingled, his whole body felt as light as a kite. He felt he could kiss his oldest friend but he grinned instead.

'His wife got rid of your problem for you.'

'He was killed by a woman?'

Kalin nodded. 'The blackmailer was Danis Plesec.'

The Duke squinted. 'Plesec? Big man? Thick lips?'

'Fish face. That's him. At the ford battle at Hambane.'

The Duke pictured Plesec's meaty face and his stomach dropped. Plesec was not the man who had saved him on the battlefield. His saviour was rodent-like, slight and fast, not a lumbering whale like Plesec. The Duke wheezed and clutched at his heart.

'He was probably deep in debt. It's always about coins with these merchants. I caught him hanging about the Seaweed Arms, an alehouse of ill repute in the Alleys, engaging others to do his dirty work, of course. But you are off the hook, my liege. Thanks to me.'

'What a relief,' the Duke produced a half-hearted smile. 'How did you discover it was Plesec?'

'Alley people turn on each other at the glimpse of a copper.' Kalin waved his hand.

The Duke downed his wine and held out his goblet for another. The real man was still out there. Perhaps he had been working with Plesec and was right now in the Alleys joking about the cowardly Duke.

'Cheer up, my Lord. I saved you from paying out a few coppers to a crooked churl. It's not the end of the world. And it's Spawning Festival tomorrow.'

The Duke swallowed. 'You are right. All this talk of death is bringing down the mood. Please lift my spirits. Tell me another of your tales.'

'Did I tell you about the camel merchant's wife in Oukib...'

The Duke's mind whirred as he settled back against the cushions and pretended to listen as Kalin treated him to another story. How long would it be before another letter arrived and Kalin realised he was wrong? How could he quietly stop this without anyone finding out the truth?

The Duke gulped down another wine and asked for more.

Froma patrolled her cell, her footsteps wearing a track through the straw. She blamed the Duchess, blamed Danis, blamed Sira and her sister. It was all their fault. They'd driven her to it. She could not be blamed.

Boots clumped down the corridor and stopped outside her cell. A pair of hairy-knuckled hands shoved a mug and plate through the iron bars.

'Wait.' She veiled her face and rushed to the bars. 'I am a rich woman. I can pay you.'

The fat guard ignored her and continued his delivery to the other cells.

'Shut your face, bitch,' said a voice further down the corridor. Someone else laughed.

Froma crammed her lips together. Then she noticed her cellmate, the fat rat, gnawing at her dinner.

'Curse you,' she said as she kicked and the round-bellied rodent scurried away.

She unwrapped her face and gulped down the sour-tasting water, gobbling down the stale bread in three bites. Then she sighed and rested against the cold wall. The distraction of food was over too quickly. She slid her heavy body down to the floor.

Eventually, Froma dozed off but Danis came for her in her dreams, howling for revenge, blood pouring from his mouth. He charged at her with hard knuckles. She jerked awake, panting, her chest damp with icy sweat.

It was not her fault.

After hours in the dark, a key rattled in the lock. Froma scrambled to her feet, replacing her veil as a torch lit up the cell and the fat guard stomped in. Another auburn-haired guard followed him inside.

'I knew you were cleverer than the others,' she said, attempting a welcoming smile. 'I tell the truth, I have silver,' 'One piece for each of you?'

They grabbed hold of her arms and bustled her along the corridor.

'Let me go,' she hissed. 'No one need know. I can make it worth your trouble.'

The fat guard spat on the ground. 'I don't take blood coin.'

'I am innocent. Master Tveldt was wrong.'

'That's what they all say,' he sneered.

The guards led Froma up a winding stone staircase and into a blindingly bright red-brick room that was filled with the warm smell of melting beeswax, and men.

Froma blinked as the guards thrust her into a wooden chair. Three men sat at a long table in front of her and five or six other terracotta uniforms stood in a circle behind her.

'Mistress Plesec,' said Lord Kalin, one of the three seated men. Kalin was a fine-looking man with his steel-grey eyes and dark hair fading silver at the temples but his expression was as severe as his reputation.

'You are under arrest for breaching a law of the Kingdom of the Four Rivers and the Duchy of Ambrovna. And in accordance with the laws of our land, you have been called before the Initial Council. The first step in this process is the hearing of your accusation. This is your chance to plea your case before the three. We are the Master of the Shield, a representative of the Fatherhood and a representative of the townspeople named by the Duke himself. Do you understand?'

Alongside Lord Kalin sat an unfamiliar Cousin. Like many in the Fatherhood, he was bald and dressed in a bronze-coloured tunic. His eyes were curiously small. The third man was the pointy-bearded Lord Egid, husband of Lady Reyna, the woman who had always been too refined to fraternise with a merchant's wife.

'If you do not confess and we determine the accusation has merit, you will be summoned to appear before the Duke for a full trial that will be open to the townspeople of Ambrovna.'

Froma's stomach churned as she pictured the town's tongues wagging, a guilty judgment already passed by every washerwoman and fisherman. Town gossip would sting more than cold stares of these men on the panel.

'At a trial, the Duke makes the final decision on your fate. Do you understand the accusation and how we will proceed, Mistress Plesec?'

'Perfectly, my Lord. But I have a question,' she said, narrowing her eyes. 'Is this how you treat grieving widows?'

'Such impertinence will win you no favours,' Egid scoffed.

'This is how we treat murderers, Mistress Plesec,' said Kalin. 'It is in your best interest to confess.'

Froma folded her arms across her chest and lifted her nose high. 'There is no proof.'

'There are accusations,' Kalin said. 'Claims of poisoning.'

'Tveldt,' she sneered and placed her hands demurely in her lap. 'A small-town physician. A more educated physician would recognise the red death.'

'Master Tveldt is a well-respected man.'

'If he's wrong and it was the red death, I would be carrying the sickness right now. At this moment. Spreading my illness to all the men here in this room. Including you, my Lord.'

The guards shuffled their feet and exchanged skittish glances. Froma smirked under her veil.

'He is a liar. My husband fell sick and died. Tveldt could not save him. He is covering up his incompetence. Or perhaps he murdered Danis himself.'

'What reason would he have to murder Master Plesec?' said Egid. 'Unlike you.'

'What are you implying, my Lord?' Froma said.

'Your husband was a wealthy man. And you would be a wealthy widow.'

'You do not appear upset, Mistress Plesec,' said the Cousin. 'Where are your tears?'

'I have not had a chance to grieve, Cousin. I am too busy protesting my innocence and being outraged at my treatment. I am too angry to be sad at this moment.'

Egid guffawed and shook his head.

'The Father does not look kindly on those who do not confess to their sins,' the Cousin said.

Froma compressed her lips. Hard.

'Think very carefully, Mistress Plesec.' Kalin said as he leaned forward, his elbows resting on the table. 'You have a chance to confess. If you admit your guilt now, we can deal with this matter quickly. The Duke may show mercy.'

'Why would I choose to make a false confession?'

With a roll of his eyes, Kalin pushed back in his chair and waved his hand with a flourish. 'Then you will stand trial and be judged by the Duke with all Ambrovna watching. Is that what you want?'

Froma breathed out fiercely, her nostrils flaring.

'You are not from Ambrovna, Mistress Plesec? Are you?' Kalin said.

'Veigur is my hometown, my Lord. But I have been a resident for more than ten years.'

'So, you know our ways. Do you know the punishment for death by poisoning?' Kalin asked, his eyes stony.

Froma jutted her chin to hide her gulp.

'It is best if you confess, my child,' the Cousin said, compassion in his eyes. 'The Father looks kindly on confessors. If you are pious and confess all, you may still be granted entry into the Land Beyond the Sunset. You can redeem yourself.'

Froma began to sweat under the heat of their accusing eyes. She wiped her damp palms and exhaled slowly. 'What if he deserved it, my Lord? What if my husband was not the good man he should have been?'

'There is no excuse for murder,' Kalin replied.

'You show no respect, woman.' Egid furrowed his brow. 'Your husband was a man of good character. A war hero. I will not allow you to speak ill of the dead.'

Froma reached under her chin and unwrapped the veil from her face. As the fabric dropped, the Cousin gasped. Lord Egid averted his gaze and even Kalin let a grimace pass over his face. "Good character?" she said.

'A wife must obey her husband. As the Father teaches,' the Cousin said with a croak and Egid nodded.

Froma narrowed her eyes and opened her mouth to speak but how could the Lords and the Cousin understand what she'd been through? They would never listen to reason. Froma shut her mouth and leaned back against the hard chair. There would be no justice for her today. But she would not let them win.

'I am giving you one last chance to confess before we bring you before the Duke.'

'What if I told you I did not act alone?'

'There are more of you?' Kalin baulked.

The room fell silent as every man leaned forward, eyes wide.

Froma tried not to smile.

'I can name three others.'

CHAPTER FORTY-EIGHT

RABEL STROKED JORN'S HONEY COLOURED hair. 'Hungry, Ma,' he moaned.

Her little boy was not alone, Rabel's stomach also yowled. 'I know,' she cooed. 'Be a good boy and stay quiet for me? Food will be here soon.'

Jorn's lip trembled but he nodded.

Mistress Plesec had promised a meal but there had been no sign of her. The house was silent, now. A few hours earlier, it had been a ruckus with people coming and going, shouting and slamming doors. At the time, Rabel had hugged her children tight, expecting a Shield guardsman to discover them at any moment, but no one came to the shed.

With nothing to do but think, Rabel began to plan. She was a wanted woman. There was nothing left for her in Ambrovna. At dawn she'd sneak down to the quay and barter for berth on a boat, the destination did not matter. They'd leave the memory of Iwan and her poor Teo behind. Get a fresh start in a new town. Rabel sighed and clutched her chest as a million knives stabbed holes into her heart. Her boy. Her first-born.

But she couldn't leave without sending a message to Sira. Where was Mistress Plesec? One day she would repay everyone's kindness.

Voices bounced across the courtyard and Rabel flinched, herding her children into the corner. Boots clumped towards her hiding place, growing louder and louder.

'Quick. Under the straw.' She wriggled down into the bales and covered their heads and bodies.

'Itchy, Ma,' grizzled Jorn.

'Shh. We're playing a game. We can't let them hear us. Understand?'

Jorn grumbled but buried himself deep into the straw. Rabel waited, her heartbeat thundering in her ears.

'In here?' said a young girl's voice. Irina. 'I haven't heard anythin'.'

The footsteps were right underneath her. Rabel held her children close, their little heartbeats clattering against her chest.

Someone started up the ladder. Rabel bit down hard on her lip and drew blood. The footsteps stomped on the loft's wooden floor. Rabel tensed so tightly, she began to shake.

'Nothing,' a man yelled.

'Look properly,' said another brusque voice. The first man grunted and kicked at the bales of hay.

Aula let out a little giggle and Rabel rustled through the straw, clamping a hand over her mouth. The footsteps came nearer. With a rush of air, the straw swept away from her face and she looked directly into the eyes of a smirking red-nosed guard.

'You're comin' with me,' he said. 'Got her!'

Rabel froze, her eyes wide. The guard grabbed her by the arm and pulled her to her feet. She let go of the children.

'Come on,' he said as he lugged her towards the ladder.

'Wait. My babes!' she yelled. 'Let me pick them up.'

Two bewildered faces half-buried in the straw stared at her.

'I only have orders for you,' he grunted.

'Mama,' cried Aula, her arms reaching out.

Rabel grabbed at the floor, the hay, anything to stop him from dragging her away but she failed to get purchase. 'Look how small they are! They need me.' She struggled and writhed, her fingernails scraping against the wooden floor.

Jorn wailed.

'You must take them, too,' she pleaded.

'Not my problem.' The guard gripped her by the arm and dragged her like a sack of salt across the floor towards the ladder.

'I'm not leavin' without them!' Rabel thrust out her free hand, wedging herself inside the trapdoor.

The man yanked hard, jolting her arm from the socket.

'No!' she groaned through gritted teeth. She pressed a foot against the floor but the guard was stronger, inching her down the ladder headfirst.

'You're comin' with me.'

A second bearded guard stood at the base of the ladder.

'My children,' Rabel screamed to him. 'I'll come. Willingly. But you must bring them.'

'She's a feisty one,' laughed the bearded guard. 'Watch her. She'll sting you.'

Rabel stopped short. What did the guard mean? Distracted, she didn't notice she'd loosened her grip.

'Got you.' The red-nosed guard chuckled as he tugged and she slipped down the ladder, missing half the rungs. She crashed into him before hitting the ground hard.

'My babes,' she wailed.

'You make me sick.' The bearded one wrenched her to her feet and marched her through the courtyard. 'Play acting like you're worried about your children. What about your boy? The one you killed?'

'My children,' she howled. 'Teo'. All strength drained from her body.

'Shut up.' The bearded guard spat on the cobbles and jumped into the cart beside her. 'Murderess.'

Rabel curled up and sobbed as the cart rumbling down the street.

The Father's revenge is swift and absolute.

The Duke stood by his Cabinet window overlooking the lit up Square below. The roast chestnut seller was at his kettle fire, serving a gang of peckish carpenters while other traders set up their stalls in preparation for an early start in the morning.

Two Cousins were scrubbing the already spotless Temple facade and beside them in the Allotment pen, the women clustered together in the chilly evening air. A nimble girl had scaled the high walls of the pen and one of the young guards was stabbing his pike at her from the outside. The Duke watched as the girl surrendered. She let go of her grip and jumped back down to the ground, her shoulders rounding as she rejoined the others.

A sharp knock sounded at the door.

'Enter.'

Kalin strode into the room.

'I'm looking forward to the Festival,' the Duke said, rubbing his hands. 'The Duchess has done well. Everything seems in place.'

The Master of the Shield paused in the centre of the room, his lips pursed.

The Duke frowned. Ordinarily, his friend's face was a blank page but Kalin's eyes darted about the room as he scratched at his beard.

'What's wrong, my friend?' the Duke hobbled over to his desk and tumbled into his seat, grimacing at his own lack of grace.

Kalin cleared his throat and adjusted his tunic. The Duke's stomach flipped. The blackmailer.

'I have a very delicate matter to discuss with you, my Lord.'

The word must be out, thought the Duke. All of Ambrovna would be whispering about his cowardice.

'Do we need wine?'

'Most definitely, my Lord.'

Kalin poured two goblets and both men took a hearty gulp.

'What is troubling you?' the Duke asked.

Kalin sat with a sigh. 'It concerns the Duchess.'

'Is she hurt?' he gasped.

'Your wife has been accused of a serious crime, my Lord.'

'Ridiculous,' the Duke snorted with relief. 'Who is the accuser?'

'The Plesec woman. The one who poisoned your blackmailer. She claims the Duchess gave her the poison.'

The Duke chuckled and shook his head.

'She named the Duchess, her maid and the maid's sister and said all three were involved in the poisoning of her husband.'

'A conspiracy?' The Duke leaned back in his chair and sipped his wine. 'A fine tale for the ale houses. I admit my wife was a little upset earlier today. Women can be like that. But a murderess?'

'People are already calling them Wasp Women.'

The Duke frowned. This was a term he had not heard in years. 'People?'

'Mistress Plesec made her accusation in front of the Initial Council, which included a number of guards. I warned them to keep their mouths closed but--'

'Add treason to the list of the merchant's wife's accusations. I will not allow anyone to spread such lies about my wife.'

Kalin chewed on his lip. 'Perhaps there is some truth to it, my Lord. I have always wondered about Sira with that witch-mark. And they say Wasp Women are like weeds in Tramissa.'

'How dare you!' the Duke said, slamming his fist on the table. 'You may be my friend but remember your place! I will not have my wife's name besmirched.'

'There is a connection between all four women.' Kalin held his hands up. 'And there is evidence.'

The Duke folded his arms tightly. 'Go on.'

'Sira's sister is the woman we suspected of spreading the red death – the matter I brought to you this morning. But it appears the deaths were due to poison, not the red death at all.'

'Is there any proof of the Duchess's involvement? Beside this vile woman's words?'

'No. But there were witnesses to Sira conspiring with her sister. The sister is in the dungeons and my men are looking for Sira as we speak.'

'Three murderesses,' the Duke said with a sigh.

'Three victims. Two dead husbands, both war veterans, and a boy. Her own son. The Scion will call for the strictest of punishments, that is certain.'

The Duke nodded. 'And I agree. We cannot allow this type of behaviour to go unpunished. Wasp Women cannot be allowed to flourish again.'

'Including the Duchess?'

The Duke waved his hand. 'Can you imagine my Lady poisoning anyone?' He laughed but Kalin did not join him. 'These are the venomous words of a guilty woman backed into a corner, trying to save herself. Bring my Lady here. I am sure she will find this matter quite amusing.'

'I looked in her bower and the solar but I could not find her, my Lord.'

'She's probably busy with final preparations for the Spawning,' the Duke said with a shrug. 'When will the merchant woman be put to trial? The rest of the town must witness justice in action, and it must be swift. There will be no leniency.'

'The day after tomorrow, my Lord,' Kalin said. 'It will be bigger than the Spawning Festival itself. Ambrovna has not had a good trial in many years. Women murdering their husbands! Imagine the crowd.'

The Duke grimaced. 'Why do we revel in others' misfortunes?'

There was a gentle knock sounded and the pock-faced guard cracked open the door.

'Not now,' the Duke snapped.

The Scion and three Cousins swept into the room, like a hen and her chicks.

'Scion Zavis, what an unexpected pleasure,' the Duke said, straightening his posture as his stomach churned.

'We need to discuss an urgent matter,' the Scion barked.

The Duke suppressed a gulp and waved for the Fatherhood group to sit. Even now as a fully-grown man and ruler of the Duchy, Zavis made him feel like a half-witted child.

'I prefer to stand,' the Scion said.

The Duke's heart thundered. 'What did you want to discuss?'

'Your wife and her involvement with the Wasp Women,' the Scion said.

'False accusations,' the Duke replied with a half-shrug.

'Three brutal murders.' The Scion stood straight as an arrow, his three subordinates in a line behind him. 'The perpetrators must be smoked out.'

The Duke leaned against the table to hide his trembling hands. 'There is no evidence. Only the words of a bitter woman. We have interred one of the sisters and the mohair merchant's wife.'

'The Father will judge the Duchess if you do not have the strength to judge her yourself,' the Scion boomed, his voice filling the Cabinet in the same way it filled the Temple during a service.

The Duke flinched.

'Your wife is of no concern. Her judgement has been set and she will pay for her sins.'

The Scion then lowered his voice and spoke with unusual softness. 'I am disappointed in you.'

The Duke's belly plummeted. The Scion's words were stronger than any blow. He faked a smile. 'I am thankful for your concern, Scion. But until there is real proof--'

'Has she used her Wasp Woman magic on you, too? Curdled your mind?'

'My mind is very clear, Scion Zavis,' the Duke lied.

'You know my view on the subject of your betrothal from the very beginning. Taking a Neven wife was a poor decision. Fatherless sinners!'

he spat. 'I said that bringing one of their women here would wreck the morals of the whole Duchy and I was right. While you were at war, she and her band of so-called women blatantly ignored the Teachings of the Father. I had to put a stop to their schemes on a number of occasions. For the good of the town. You invited a Queen Wasp to Ambrovna and left her in charge. You are lucky I was here to keep order.'

'From what I have seen, Ambrovna was well governed in my absence.' The Duke set his jaw, his cheek muscles taut as ship ropes. 'I am blessed with a wife who is more than a pretty bird in a cage. She may be spirited, but I am proud of her.'

Zavis lifted a hairless eyebrow. 'She undermines you. And she will be your downfall. Underneath, all women are the same.'

'This could be your opportunity to be rid of her, my Lord,' Kalin offered. 'With the rumours of her brother and Absalom on the throne, you no longer need her. You have no children. You could annul the betrothal and pack her off back to Tramissa. Your problem will disappear.'

'No,' said the Duke and the Scion in unison.

The Scion continued. 'You made a choice. A commitment to the Father when you took her as a wife. This cannot be broken. You are joined until death. You must deal with the consequences of your poor decisions.'

'I am aware of my situation and I appreciate your concern but there is no proof to support these accusations,' the Duke insisted.

'It is my role to provide counsel on your spiritual welfare, my Lord. Your people will yield to you but it is my duty to tell you the truth. However hurtful.'

The Duke's tunic itched against his skin. He rubbed his neckline as his throat burned red hot.

'Your troubles reached my ears through official channels. How many others will hear the story in less salubrious ways? Tomorrow at the Spawning Festival, will your people snigger behind their hands at you? The Duke on the throne, a man without the strength to bring his wife to justice? They will question everything about you. And quite rightly.'

'I am sure you are busy preparing for the Allotment, Scion Zavis,' the Duke spoke carefully, trying to temper the shudder in his voice. 'I thank you for your time and counsel. But until there is actual proof--'

'The proof may be closer than you think.'

The Duke blinked rapidly and frowned. 'I will consider your advice.'

'We will pray for you. That the Father will guide you to the right path.'

Scion Zavis and his Cousins left the room and the Duke dropped his head into his hands with a sigh. 'What foolishness.'

'Your love is blinding you,' Kalin said. 'Perhaps there is some truth in the accusations. And perhaps you were to be their next victim.'

'That is absurd,' the Duke chuckled half-heartedly. 'My wife, a murderess? A Wasp Woman? Mixing spells and cavorting with the Great Mother? No.'

The room slid into silence. The Duke wiped his forehead as the brick walls and bookshelves whirled before his eyes. It couldn't possibly be true. Could it?

Every child in Ambrovna was fed on tales of the Wasp Women with their riddles and poisons. As a noble child the Duke had been no different. His nursemaid and his grandfather had told him of the days, hundreds of years ago, when Wasp Women were strong. One day the Fatherhood arrived to teach ignorant people about the love and wisdom of the Father and the true place of a woman in the world. As the word of the Father spread, the Wasp Women struck back, revealing their true evil nature as they turned against their own townspeople. They sent sickness to the new believers, blackened their crops, and threatened to poison the seas. Despite the Wasp Women's efforts, the whole town became enlightened and the Fatherhood prevailed.

The first Scion of Ambrovna had driven the Wasp Women and their wickedness into hiding. But that was not the end of it. The women continued their campaign of violence in secret. No one knew whether beneath their cloaks, a mother or sister or daughter worshipped the barbaric Great Mother. The men had worked tirelessly to uncover their nests until every last Wasp Woman was driven into the hills or executed in the Square. The last remaining Wasp Woman, Ysopa, was hanged from the Old Man Tree. Her body was left to rot there as a reminder to all. Now, every child learned the story of Ysopa and shuddered in their beds at the thought of the Wasp Women's return. Unlike a bee with its single sacrificial sting, a wasp could sting over and over, again and again.

The Duke raked his fingers along his scalp.

'I agree with the Scion,' Kalin chewed his lip.

The Duke sighed again. 'What do you suggest I do?'

'If you are unwilling to cast her aside, make her answer these accusations. Let her prove her innocence.'

The Duke nodded reluctantly. 'Zavis said there was more proof. Make enquiries. But be subtle. And find my wife.'

CHAPTER FORTY-NINE

AGATA PACED THE NARROW ALLEY behind Gala's shopfront. 'Where is Froma?'

Sira shrugged.

'He can only take twelve at the most. He's going to Blek,' Jadzia said.

'Blek?' Gala shuddered. 'We better give them blades before they go.'

'And he can't wait all night.'

'Twelve is better than nothing,' Agata said, her eyes still watching the entry to the alley. Where was Froma? Was this Froma's revenge after Agata refused to hand the poison over to her? 'What did you tell him?'

'Not much. I said they were kidnapped during the war. To be honest, I could have said anything. Once he saw the glimmer of the silver--'

'We cannot wait any longer for Mistress Plesec,' Agata said, pressing her lips together. 'Ready?'

'Yes, m'Lady,' said Sira. Jadzia and Gala nodded.

'I am proud of you all,' she said, her voice then lowered to a mutter. 'We are doing a good thing. No matter what happens.'

Jadzia gulped.

'They'll sing ballads about us one day,' Gala said, her smile a little forced.

'One day, perhaps,' Agata sighed.

Agata tugged at her hose, she was swimming inside the pilfered terracotta guard's uniform. The others were similarly disguised. Sira hid her blemished face under a hood, the plump Gala filled out her surcoat better than the others and Jadzia was the height of a small man. But it was lucky the sun had set. In full daylight they'd have fooled no one.

'Remember we are supposed to be guards.'

The four women left the alley and marched into the town Square, Agata's heart thundering, and her chest was tight. Fear and excitement wrestled in her belly.

Wind whipped in from the sea, making the handful of torches in the Square flicker and the pennants in the Old Man Tree flap. Unlike the capital Sulun or her home region of Tramissa where people made merry in the warm evenings until the moon sank, the Square was deserted. The clear dark sky was peppered with stars.

On the far side by the Temple, the Allotment women huddled together for warmth in their makeshift pen. They ranged in age from barely marriageable to the edges of middle life. All were quiet, dour, even the babies.

'We wait here until we see the sign,' Agata whispered and the four women stopped in the shadows by the dais.

'What's the sign?' Jadzia asked. Agata shushed her with a finger to her lips.

Three guards leaned on their pikes at the narrow pen gate, gossiping and laughing. One was blond and pale, one had protruding ears and the third was cursed with a rash of pimples across his face.

Agata steeled herself but her belly fluttered. She still had time to back out and sneak into the castle, pretend nothing happened. No one would know. Except for the other women. And they would understand. Wouldn't they?

But if she didn't act now, would this moment play on her mind forever? Weigh her down? Would her mother be shaking her head from the Land Beyond the Sunset?

The pale blond guard coughed.

'It's happening,' Agata whispered and Sira replied with a pained smile.

His cough echoed around the empty Square. Then he doubled over.

Then the pimple-cheeked guard wheezed and spluttered and leaned over his pike as he struggled for breath.

'You alright?' asked the boyish big-eared guard, his eyes bulging with concern.

The pale-faced man groaned. His vomit splattered to the ground. The boyish guard jumped out of range, while on his left the pimply guard spewed.

Agata's hand flew to her mouth and glanced across at Sira, who nodded. 'Rabel said it was awful.'

'There wasn't enough to kill them? Was there?' Agata stuttered.

Sira shrugged.

'What's happening?' Jadzia asked, her eyebrows lowered.

'It's time,' Agata said, her heart walloping. She grimaced as the guards convulsed. Their suffering was all her doing. Someone in the pen screamed.

'It's the red death!'

The pale-faced guard keeled over.

Shrieks echoed across the Square.

'It's the sickness. Get away from them,' screeched a freckle-faced woman with a baby clutched to her bosom.

'We're going to die!' shouted a red-head.

The penned women scrambled to their feet and yanked their children by the wrists, scurrying away from the gate.

'Let us go,' they cried.

Frightened babies and children caterwauled.

'Quiet,' yelled the big-eared guard. His voice reedy and shrill.

'Have mercy! Think of the children.'

The women rushed to the back corner of the pen, pushing and trampling one another as they cried out in fear and pain.

'You'll infect us all,' the red-head woman screeched.

The shouting echoed around the Square.

'Silence,' squawked the guard but no one listened.

The pimple-covered guard hurtled towards the Old Man Tree. Half way across the Square, he dropped on to his hands and knees. His body twitched and jolted. He lifted his head and puke surged from his mouth.

Gala and Jadzia exchanged frowns.

'Now!' yelled Agata.

'But... the red death?' Gala blurted.

'This is the sign.'

'There is one left, m'Lady.' Sira said.

But Agata didn't wait. She sprinted towards the pen, delighting in the ease of movement a man's hose and surcoat afforded. It reminded her of her childhood days running through her father's fields.

'Calm down. All of you.' The young guard with the large ears shouted, darting left and right in front of the panicked Allotment women, his pike firmly gripped in his skinny hand. 'Calm down.' But even he seemed unconvinced by his own words.

Agata reached the gate first.

'Open the gate,' Agata said, her voice firm.

Sira and Jadzia picked up the fallen guards' pikes.

'Who are you? I have orders...' he squinted in the torchlight, his brow furrowing. 'Wait? You're women?'

'Step aside.' Agata drew to her full height. 'Sira?'

Sira thrust the pike into his face.

'Wasp Women.' He recoiled.

Gala narrowed her eyes. 'What did he say?'

Agata gulped. She'd heard exactly what he'd said. Where did he get such an idea?

CHAPTER FIFTY

I woke as morning crept into the laneway, a grey dim light that bleached away all colours. Huddled beside me in a ball, my fellow Cousin's face was a mess of crusted blood. I presumed mine was similar and I shivered, wondering how we had managed to sleep in a bed of snow. Grabbing at my ribs, I moaned as I tried to stand. I roused my companion, helped him to his feet and we hobbled through the streets to the gates of Meeraq. We did not stop for anything, not even water. I even left my copy of the Teachings behind in the room. As we started our journey South, my heart was as bruised as my face. We were but a few miles out of Meeraq when we heard the thundering of hooves and my heart bolted.

'Quick,' the Cousin said. 'They are coming to finish us off.'

We ran but our feet, unaccustomed to the icy road, slid and slipped. The Akull Clansmen closed in on us swiftly.

'The Father will protect us,' I said. 'The Father will protect us.'

Three horses surrounded us in a flurry of snow. I looked into the white smiles of the Queen's guards, my knees trembling. A fourth horse pulled up, ridden by the Queen herself. My heart stalled.

'*Father men. You leave without saying goodbye? This is not the way in the land of the Akull.*'

'*Apologies, Queen Magnilla.*' *I bowed my head.* '*I thought you wanted rid of us.*'

She waved her hand. '*My guards tell me there was another incident. Last night. After you left my quarters.*' *Her eyes scoured my face.*

'*We ran into a disagreement.*'

'*Thugs!*' *said the other Cousin.*

'*I wanted to apologise for them. They have been rounded up and will be punished for disgracing our clan.*'

I shuffled back a step.

She smiled. '*You think this strange?*'

'*Nobles do not often ask forgiveness,*' *I said.*

'*Queens and kings are as flawed as anyone. My people's behaviour was wrong. I do not want you to leave my land with this taste in your mouth.*' *Her silver eyes sparkled under her white lashes.* '*We are warriors but we do not treat guests with such dishonour.*'

'*I thank you for your apology, Queen.*'

'*You and I may disagree, but we are the same. Every person deserves respect, regardless. I do not believe in your man in the sky and I do not control your thoughts. Nor should I. You are free to think as you please, as long as you do not hurt others.*'

I nodded, her words spinning in my head.

'*Good travels, Father men.*'

With a cry, she slapped her horse and galloped away, kicking up clouds of white powder.

The Cousin and I were left open-mouthed. An Akull man on horseback tossed a satchel onto the ice. We stood, watching them disappear into the distance. I opened the bag to find dried meat and water, provisions for our journey. I threw it over my shoulder and we continued our trek home, so many miles away. On the long trip South,

I had much time to think. The all-seeing Father would understand how we tried to share his word. I only hoped that my Scion would be as understanding.

Rather than returning triumphant after bringing the light of the Father to the cold North, I came back to Sulun with my head bowed low like a dog. My fellow Cousin left the Fatherhood as soon as we reached the capital. I heard he became a candle maker. But I remained. I kept my oath but no one let me forget my failure. My fellow Cousins ridiculed me daily, openly laughing at my failure to convert a woman. But I pursed my lips, they did not understand the different world of the Akull.

Not all was lost. My Scion awarded me a congregation of sorts. I was placed in charge of the Unwanted, given a chance to redeem myself. I sometimes watched the Unwanted with their dull eyes and broken spirits. I wondered whether any of them could become a Queen. As wise, brave and truly noble as she was. But my answer was always a resounding 'no.' Queen Magnilla was a one-off, a lucky find, a two-yolked egg.

Or was she?

CHAPTER FIFTY-ONE

AGATA SWALLOWED. THERE WAS NO time to find out how the guard knew about the Wasp Women.

'Open the gate,' she ordered and Jadzia raised her weapon. With two pikes aimed at his scrawny throat, he lifted the latch with fumbling hands and stepped aside.

'Come on!' Jadzia called, beckoning the women to the open gate. 'You are free to go.'

'Get away from us,' yelled a pock-faced woman, tugging her three children close.

'You'll infect us,' screamed another, her eyes wild. 'Go away.'

'We're here to help you,' said Gala, pulling down her hood to show her face. 'We're not guards. We're women.'

But the captives refused to listen.

'Leave us be,' wailed one woman who crumpled to the cobbles sobbing. 'I don't want to die. Oh Father, please protect us.'

'Come with us.' Jadzia urged as she approached three women with weather-worn faces and plain linen shifts but they screeched and ran in the opposite direction. Two able-bodied women climbed up and over the fence walls, cheering as they hit the ground and bolted away.

Someone threw a boot, the leather sole clocking Sira in the head. Gala threw up her hands. 'Why won't they listen? Why don't they trust us?'

Jadzia shrugged. 'We have a ship!' she yelled.

'Get out of our way.' A woman and her two sons barrelled towards Agata, who was standing at the open gate. They crashed into her with sharp elbows and closed fists, knocking her down. Agata yelped as she landed heavily on the bricks. She cowered as the boys and their mother took turns kicking her. Agata covered her face, flinching and groaning as their boots pounded her again and again.

'Get off her,' Sira yelled and the pain stopped. Agata uncovered her eyes to see the boys and their mother running off into the night.

'My Lady.' Sira pointed as a stream of guards sprinted down the Avenue towards the Square. 'We have to go!'

Jadzia and Gala glanced up, their eyes widening.

'Hurry,' Agata croaked. Sira helped her stumble upright then rushed into the crowd of women who were huddled against the back of the pen. Sira studied each face in the cowering group.

'Let's go.' Jadzia shepherded a flock of women and children towards the gate.

'Did you see a girl with a mark on her face like me?' Sira asked.

The others shook their heads.

'She must be here somewhere,' Sira fussed.

'We cannot force them to come,' Agata said, placing her hand on Sira's shoulder.

'Fools,' Gala sighed.

'Frightened,' Sira mumbled. 'I would be, too.'

Agata turned to their charges with a smile. 'We will take you away from all this.'

'Duchess? Is that you?' said a young buck-toothed girl, her eyes gleaming.

Agata grinned, her finger pressed to her lips. 'Quickly.'

The small group of heroines and fugitives ran to the entrance of the pen. The big-eared guard stood by like a statue, staring at his boots, ignoring the pushing and yelling around him. The other two stricken guards lay flat on the cobbles, moaning but still alive.

'This way,' said Jadzia.

'Stop!' called a voice as the guards entered the Square and ran towards them.

The women and children skirted out of their way and behind the Old Man Tree but its gnarled branches had hidden the approach of another group.

'What is going on here?' asked a familiar voice.

Agata looked up in horror at the bronze tunics and bald heads. Her hood was down, her face fully exposed.

'You?' the Scion said. 'What on earth do you think you are doing?'

'Run,' Agata yelled to the others but she did not move. Agata lifted her chin and waited alongside the Scion. Zavis or the Cousins would never lay a finger on any woman, regardless of class.

Jadzia and Gala side-stepped the bronze-frocked Fatherhood and kept running. Hand in hand with the rescued women, children on their hips and backs, they hurried towards the promise of a new life at the pier.

Sira hesitated, stuck to the spot alongside her mistress.

'Go!' Agata hissed but Sira stood as still as the Old Man Tree, her eyes darting between Agata, the Scion and the runaways.

As the women and children reached the pier's wooden boards, Agata smiled and raised a dark eyebrow at the Scion. But her smile did not last long as pike-waving guards poured from the castle and swiftly headed off the women and children.

'You thought you could outsmart us?' the Scion said.

Agata hoisted her nose high but beneath the surface, her backbone crumbled into dust. In a single moment, heroines had become fools and her courageous ballad turned into the punchline for a bawdy joke.

Seliv closed in, four guards at his side. 'Come with me, my Lady.' His words were awkward rather than authoritative, but there was no surprise on his face.

'Take me to the Duke,' she said, tossing her head.

'Those are not my orders, m'Lady.'

Agata folded her arms. 'And what are your orders?'

'Please, m'Lady.'

Like the Fatherhood, Seliv dared not touch her. Instead, he waved her in the direction of the Avenue. The guards tried to herd Jadzia, Gala and the others back towards the Square and into the pen but the women spat and clawed like cats.

'Secure the gate and call the physician,' Seliv yelled as the poisoned guards gulped down water from skins. Agata released a long thin breath as the pimple-faced guard rose shakily to his feet.

'M'Lady. Come,' Seliv said, this time with a little more iron in his voice. 'You too, Singlewoman.'

Agata straightened and followed willingly with the Scion and Sira close behind her. With each step towards her husband and the castle, her stomach tightened. She'd defied him, plotted against him, embarrassed him in front of his guards, his people, the whole town. What would he say? During their short betrothal, she'd never witnessed the full force of his ire. Would he understand? Would he even listen? She rubbed her forehead, searching for persuasive words.

Deep in his heart, he must realise the Allotment was wrong. He must. He had to.

The guards turned left at the iron gates towards to a door Agata did not recognise.

'Where are you taking me?' Her brow furrowed.

'Where do you think?' said the Scion from behind. 'After what you've done.'

The iron gate screeched open and Seliv led her into a dark moist corridor. 'Put the Singlewoman with the others.'

'Others?' Agata recoiled, a flush of heat rising up her neck. Sira shrugged as they led her away.

'You wait here, m'Lady.'

Seliv rapped on a carved door before sticking his head inside.

'Bring her in.'

Smoothing back her hair, she stepped through the doorway and bracing herself for the blow of his disappointed face. The rescue had nothing to do with him, or them. Her love for him was unchanged. She only hoped he would understand that. Stepping inside the room, her heart dropped like a bird pushed from its nest. Lord Kalin sat alone with his feet on the table and the soles of his boots facing her.

'So it is true,' he said. 'Although I am not entirely surprised.'

'She was trying to free the Allotment women,' the Scion interjected. 'I witnessed their attempted escape.'

'The accusations are piling up, my Lady.'

'Where is my husband?'

'He does not wish to see you.'

'I will go to him myself.' Agata swivelled on her heel towards the door.

'Even if he did want to see you, I would not allow it. I must keep him safe.'

Seliv blocked her exit with his bulky frame.

'I am the Duchess of Ambrovna. I demand to see my husband,' Agata roared. 'Move.'

But Seliv stood like a boulder in her path. 'I cannot, m'Lady,' he said, eyes downturned.

Agata's cheeks blazed. 'Move! I will not tell you again.'

Kalin cocked an eyebrow and Seliv remained in place. Agata gritted her teeth and jabbed her finger into the giant's Square chin. 'Now!'

'Please control yourself,' Kalin said. 'You will not solve anything by getting hysterical,'

'I am not hysterical!' she said with an unintended screech and Kalin smirked.

Agata clenched her fists, slowed her breath and softened her tone. 'I am perfectly calm. Only confused by the situation. If you'd please explain.'

'You will see him. At your trial. The day after the Spawning Festival.'

'Trial? You cannot place me on trial without an Initial Council. What are the charges?'

'Once you have calmed down, I will educate you on the law. Take her to a cell.'

'I don't understand.' She clawed at her hair as the brick walls swirled before her. The mouldy damp smell crawled down her throat, stifling her. 'Let me see him, I can explain.'

Kalin snorted. 'Take her away,' he said as he flicked his hand.

A fat toad-like guard gripped her by the elbow and wrenched her out the door.

'My Lord!' she yelled, her voice bouncing off the slimy-bricked corridor. She wailed, unfamiliar howls pouring from her mouth. 'My Lord!'

'Shut up,' said the guard.

'Gerthorn!' she screamed.

But she knew the Duke, who was sitting four floors above her, would never hear her cries.

CHAPTER FIFTY-TWO

F ROMA LOST COUNT OF THE hours in the dungeon with nothing to see but brick walls and the rat, nothing to distract her from her thoughts until a set of keys clunked in the door and Lord Kalin strode in.

'About time,' she smirked, pulling herself upright and smoothing her dress.

'Mistress Plesec.'

Froma studied the Master of the Shield's steely eyes and tight calves and she blushed like a ninny. Her life as a wealthy widow lay before her. A new life without Danis.

'Your trial date has been determined,' he said and she instantly shook away her fancies. She narrowed her eyes.

'You will appear before the Duke the day after tomorrow. Along with the other three accused.'

'A full trial?' She blurted.

Despite her fine clothes, Froma's constitution was strong. Her people were bred for the fields and her bones knew how to survive hardship. But a full trial meant the risk of death. 'You said I could expect leniency if I confessed. I gave you their names. Do I get nothing in return?'

'Mistress Plesec, you disappointed me. You did not tell all. The truth has come out and naturally matters have taken a more serious turn. A full trial is necessary.'

'More serious than murder?' Her eyebrows knitted together as sweat beaded at her hairline. Her mind whirred.

'There is no need to play the innocent. Accusations have been made and all four of you will stand trial.'

'I do not follow you, Lord Kalin. Has someone been feeding you lies?' Froma asked, her belly cramping as she felt the situation slipping through her fingers.

'There was a conspiracy to kill the Duke and take over the Duchy,' Kalin said flatly. 'You will have your chance the day after tomorrow.'

'But--'

Kalin stormed out of the cell before she could utter another word. The door clunked behind him.

Froma slammed her fists against the locked door as a chill crept into her heart.

'This is not my fault,' she muttered to herself. She snarled at the blank wall. 'It was them.'

Faces flickered through her mind, Danis, the smug Scion, the Cousins, the pathetic Duke, the vain Duchess, Rabel, the self-righteous Sira, even the useless Irina. They had all driven her to it. All of them. She was the innocent victim here. No one understood her suffering. She should be rewarded, not punished. Where was the Father to protect his children?

A different set of thoughts hissed in her ear. Quiet at first, the voice grew steadily more insistent.

'You got what you deserved.'

'You brought it on yourself.'

'No one cares about you, not now, not ever.'

She remembered familiar laughter. Her father, Danis, her brother, the sneering boys from the muddy streets of Veigur.

'Ugly. Unlovable. Barren.'

The snigger of Lady Reyna. *'Commoner.'*

'Be quiet,' She clutched at her hair, crying aloud. 'Leave me alone.'

'Worthless. Useless.'

'You got what you deserve.'

Froma slumped against the wall. 'It is not true,' she said until her voice faded to nothing and only her lips moved, silently repeating. 'It is not true.'

'The day after tomorrow,' Kalin said as he left Sira's cell and the guard locked the door behind him. Sira scuttled back into the corner, away from the other two prisoners in the cell, a wizened shirtless old man and a light-fingered boy, or perhaps it was a girl, Sira could not tell. At least they were quiet and kept their hands to themselves.

With her back flat against the soothing cold wall, Sira stared through the narrow window slit into the night sky. She'd never missed a Spawning Festival before even though her hair was shot with grey and her days of dancing and revelling until dawn were long gone. These days she celebrated the new eel season with a few sips of wine and too many cakes before retiring to her room early to avoid the rowdy crowds. Now she missed every wine-soaked face and wished she could jig until her heels were red with blisters.

She didn't scream like the others, their voices carrying down the corridor into her cell. Sira watched herself from above. Hers was a life of obedience. The good sister, the good child, the good servant. And her one rebellious act had landed her in the dungeons. She chuckled, a smile dawning on her face as Wisia's riddles unravelled.

If only she'd listened to her heart and had the courage to act earlier, chased down her heart's desires, reached out her hand when temptation burned, told Majvi how beautiful she was. Maybe she could have known love.

The world was rid of Iwan. After so many years of shame over her failure to defend her sister, the dragging remorse was finally gone from her belly. But it had been replaced by a new regret. Teo. She wished she could have saved him. She sighed at the thought of his terror and pain. Her only consolation was his innocence. The Father would see a young boy untouched by sin and invite him into the Land Beyond the Sunset without question. He would run carefree in the meadows and eat ripe peaches and smile by the Father's side.

Sira's fate lay in the hands of a man she'd spent her whole life serving. A decent young man. Thankfully, he had not inherited his dead father's wandering hands. But as Wisia had said, a price must be paid, and Sira was ready and willing to face punishment for her part in their deaths. The Duke, the Master of Shield and the Scion might not understand the virtue in her actions, but she had acted with love and compassion. Like them, she fought against the threat to her people, her family, but the men would never understand.

Watching silver clouds pass by the moon through the slit window, she sat waiting for her fate to be determined for her, as her whole life had been. She understood that the Father must restore the balance.

Rabel ignored the cockroaches scurrying over her dinner and said nothing when her cellmate snatched the stale bread for himself. Like her son and her babes, her fight was gone. Her body limp and heavy, she lay with her cheek pressed into the slimy straw.

The Duke knew everything. About the deaths, the mushroom, her guilt. He would hand out the punishment she deserved. Stupid, rotten to the core, she never learned, leading her to commit the worst sin of all.

'Why, Mama?' called a tiny familiar voice.

Rabel buried her head in her arms, slamming her hands hard over her ears. She hummed, trying to drown out the noise but the voice continued clearly. Loudly.

'Why did you kill me, Mama? Didn't you love me?'

'I did!' she spluttered. 'My Teo. I loved you more than anythin'.'

'Then why did you kill me?' Teo said.

'If only I hadn't turned my back, I could have stopped you.'

'Shut-up!' Rabel's cellmate yelled out from the corner. 'Mad bitch.'

But she only heard the voice of her son.

'I was hungry, Ma,' Teo said.

'I know,' she said between sobs. 'I was tryin' to protect you.'

'It's cold here, Ma. I'm scared.'

She jolted upright. Her eyes wide and wild, searching the darkness. 'Aren't you with the Father?'

There was no reply.

'Teo? Where are you?'

'Quiet!' Her cellmate stomped over and slapped her across the face.

Rabel cowered but said nothing the man. She curled into a ball, rocking back and forth. 'Don't be scared, Teo,' she said. 'Mama is coming. Mama will be with you soon.'

Brushing aside her tears, Agata pacing her dark cell.

'What do I know?' she muttered, grinding her teeth. 'Think.'

She had scant information but she knew the law. As a child, when her father and Madame Fidan were looking the other way, she'd hidden behind a heavy curtain and watched him preside over his local matters in the manor's Great Hall. Just like Queen Magnilla, he'd sat on his throne and resolved disputes among his subjects. The previous King Rados had enforced a single legal code across the entire Four Rivers Kingdom during his long reign. The same procedures applied in Ambrovna as in Tramissa. Only weeks earlier, Agata had flicked through the pages of this code in her husband's Cabinet. It was one of the many books she'd read in the dark nights of the war.

She straightened and lifted her chin high, as footsteps approached.

Lord Kalin entered, followed by the fleshy toad-like guard who placed a lump of black bread and a mug of water on the rotting straw.

In spite of herself, she lunged for the mug and gulped the water greedily. 'I am ready,' she said, wiping her mouth on her sleeve, still dressed in the stolen guard's terracotta uniform with the eel sigil on the chest.

'For what?' Kalin raised an eyebrow.

'My Initial Council. As is my right,' she said.

'There will be no Initial Council.' Kalin's dark eyes were cold as ash.

'But an Initial Council is required.' Agata frowned. 'This is the legal code of the Kingdom of the Four Rivers.'

'I know the code perfectly well. Different rules apply when a person is accused of treason.'

'Treason?' She stumbled backwards, her jaw slackening.

'Treason and three murders. We were lucky to stop you before you reached your fourth intended victim.'

'Four?' She scrubbed her hand across her forehead and counted two. Rabel's husband and son. Who were the others?

'Do not play me for a fool,' Kalin tutted. 'Your conspiracy to murder the Duke and take the throne for yourself. If you understand the legal code as you claim to, you will know your Wasp Women rebellion is treason.'

'I never...This is all lies!' The room lurched as the allegations thumped in her ears. 'I would never hurt him.'

'Save your protests. I will not be the one determining your fate.'

'But it's not--'

Kalin continued speaking but Agata's thoughts muffled his words. She must see the Duke and explain, untangle these lies. He could not possibly believe she wanted him dead.

'I must speak with the Duke. Alone.'

'You will remain here until your trial with the others.'

'Others?' she stammered.

'You know full well,' Kalin huffed. 'Your ugly maid, her sister and the mohair merchant's wife.'

Agata narrowed her eyes. 'May I ask who made these accusations?'

'I cannot name the source.'

As all the possibilities ran through her head, Agata's eyes never left Kalin's face.

'The Scion,' she said, resisting the urge to spit his name.

'You do not have as many friends as you think. But if you wish to confess, I can arrange for a member of the Fatherhood to visit you? So you may confess your sins?'

Agata barked out a laugh, so angry, even she was shocked by the bitter tone. 'You never approved of me, did you Lord Kalin? You must take great pleasure in bringing me to trial. Tell me. Why do you disapprove of me so much? Is there a particular reason?'

'I have no opinion of you personally.' Kalin blinked, his gaze steady on her face. 'But the Duke should have chosen a Vorosy wife. I counselled him at the time but--'

'You don't like where I come from? Have you cooked up this whole story to be rid of me?'

'You credit me with too much imagination. I have nothing to do with the accusations. I am merely fulfilling my role as Master of the Shield.'

'And enjoying it.'

'In my experience, troubles are avoided when we stick with our own. It turns out I was right. As usual.' He turned for the door. 'I will leave you to consider your accusations. The next time we meet, you will be standing before the Duke and the whole town.'

'If I am not permitted to visit my own husband, can you give the Duke a message from me?'

'I am not a messenger.'

'Tell him, there is some truth but most are lies. I would never hurt him.'

'You can tell him yourself when you are summonsed to the Great Hall.'

'Believe me. I will not allow these lies without a fight.'

Kalin gave a half-shrug. 'As you wish.' He waved to the guard and the door locked behind him.

As soon as he was gone, Agata's knees buckled. She pictured her husband's eyes mirroring Lord Kalin's poisonous glare. If only she'd held her tongue. Kalin would be upstairs now, relaying every spiteful word to him and the Scion.

Agata ripped into the stale bread. The sharp edges grazed the inside of her mouth as tears flowed down her cheeks. She had nowhere to turn. Her father was missing, her brother dead, she had no coins and no friends to rely on. She slurped down the last mouthful of water without tasting a drop and slid down the mossy wall, crumpling to the ground.

CHAPTER FIFTY-THREE

T ODAY, THE WAR WIDOWS OF Ambrovna will be united with new husbands.' The Scion stood at the edge of the wooden dais, his unrelenting glare silencing the crowd across the Square. 'This will reinforce families and demonstrate that we abide by the Teachings of the Father. This is our offering to Him on this auspicious day of the Spawning Festival. We hope this gesture of commitment to the sanctity of the family will lead to a bountiful eel harvest this year. In the eyes of the Father.'

'In the eyes of the Father,' the crowd repeated as reverentially as at any service inside the Temple.

The Duke leaned back in his carved chair and stared at the back of the Scion's bald head. The Allotment women lined up on his right, their faces wrapped with veils of muted blues and pale yellows, their eyes visible and bulging with terror. He rubbed his own raw eyes and tried to concentrate on the betrothal ceremony, but his mind kept wandering down to the dungeon and proceedings scheduled for the following day.

'Bring the new couples together.'

Bronze-gowned Cousins ushered the men from the left and veiled women from the right, bringing them together into couples. Men had queued to take part in the Allotment since the first light of dawn, but first choice went to the men taking their brother's wives, then in descending order, based on class and rank until there were no men left. One woman, widow of a wine merchant, with a daughter of marriageable age and her ability to breed in doubt, was taken away to join the Unwanted.

The allotted couples stood in rows along the front of the dais with hands tied together with rope. The Duke cringed at the sounds of muffled crying.

The Scion raised his arms to the sky. 'We bring these women to these men, all in the eyes of the Father. Their hearts are pure and their commitment to the Father is strong. The light of the Father shining through these men will cleanse the sinful soil of the women. Today as a couple, they make a declaration of unity, as a family, to follow the Teachings. To raise children and bring forth more followers of the Father to continue our glorious way of life. Oh Father, bless these new families with bounty and commitment, and they will, in turn, repay you with their loyalty. And those who do not follow your true path will face the consequences, destined for the Land of Eternal Darkness.'

The Scion turned to the couples. 'Women. Repeat after me. We vow to be pious...'

The women repeated the Scion's words, but their voices were shaky and meek. The Cousin waved his hands, encouraging them to speak up.

'We vow to respect our husbands as the Father of their household, to obey and love him for the rest of our days.'

'In the eyes of the Father.'

The Duke's own betrothal day had been less than two years ago. Like today, it had been a day of new beginnings, of hope. At the time he'd thought his heart would burst with joy. She'd had jonquils in her dark hair and a playful gleam in her cinnamon eyes. But now his foolishness punched him in the solar plexus, the memory forever blackened.

He should be smiling, happy for the newly betrothed but he slumped, his arms and legs heavy as wood. The Scion and Kalin were wrong. Agata would never plot to murder him, would she? Or had he been bewitched as they said? He shuddered and blinked, returning his attention to his people before him. Duty always came first despite the yawning ache in his chest.

'Men. Do you accept the offers of piety, goodness, obedience and love from these women?'

'Yes, Scion Zavis,' the men responded in unison. Some beamed, others had faces as grim as the Duke's. 'In the eyes of the Father.'

'And so, it is sealed, in the eyes of the Father. The couples are united until death.'

The crowd clapped awkwardly as couples left the dais, unlike the usual cheering and dirty jeering at the end of a betrothal ceremony.

Lord Kalin stepped forward. 'Now it is time for the Duke to name the Spawning Queen.' Lifting an eyebrow, he gestured to six giggling girls. Young men in the crowd whistled and hurrahed, but the Duke sighed.

He could not ignore the smirks, the whispering, the furtive glances his way. A scandal in the castle was far more interesting than any ceremony.

Lutes and laughter from the Spawning Festival drifted in through Agata's cell window, the merriment a stark contrast to the year before when she had led a serious toast to all the men on the battlefield and all the women working tirelessly to keep the town running. The women of Ambrovna had stared up at her with a mix of pride and fear in their dark-circled eyes.

The Spawning meant more work bringing in the new season's crop of eels, but despite their aching backs, the traditions were maintained. There was feasting and dancing, women twirling in twos taking turns to lead but after an hour or two, the women all drifted away, seeking the comforts of sleep and their beds.

Agata pictured the dais. Was Lord Kalin sitting alongside the Duke, supping wine and plotting her downfall? Was Kalin whispering in one ear, the Scion in the other, filling the Duke's head with ideas about a new wife. Perhaps there'd be a flaxen-haired lord's daughter, a more appropriate choice with Vorosy blood in her veins. Was Agata from Tramissa already a distant memory?

Or did the Duke sit alone, moping into his wine and staring into the distance, his heart torn in two by his treacherous wife? Or were his cheeks red with shame, embarrassed by his choice of wife, a Wasp Woman who plotted his downfall? How soon before every noble in the kingdom laughed at Nyvard and his marital troubles?

Her speculations were interrupted by a hushed scraping at the lock. Agata's heart thundered as she scrambled to her feet. Was she such an embarrassment that they decided to conduct her trial in secret while the town made merry?

The iron door creaked open and a figure stepped into the cell.

'Duchess,' the stranger said in a muffled male whisper. 'Come with me.'

'Who are you?' She squinted, unable to make out a face.

'Shh. They will hear.'

'Who sent you?' Agata frowned into the darkness as a strong hand grabbed her arm.

'Come. Quickly.'

'Answer me.'

'There is no time. Come.'

Agata paused. She took a single step forward and paused again. 'Was it Lord Kalin who sent you?'

'I can get you out of here,' he said, his tone familiar, but she could not place it.

She pulled her hand away.

'Please trust me. They'll be here soon.'

Agata's head spun and she cupped her cheeks. Should she trust a faceless hand in the dark? Was she being led to an even worse fate? Should she save herself, forget Ambrovna and start anew?

A voice sounded in her head with four familiar words. 'Don't be like me.'

Agata was eight summers old again, back in the courtyard behind her father's manor on the day of Yeta's whipping. She watched her friend struggle and scream as the birch sang through the air. Yeta had not have a voice but Agata did and tomorrow she'd finally have her stage in front of the whole town. She would be Queen Magnilla. Her mother's words filled her with light. She relaxed her shoulders, steadied her breath and lifted her chin.

'Guards!' she yelled at the top of her voice.

'What are you doing?' the figure hissed.

Footsteps ambled down the corridor and the air moved as the faceless person slipped away, closing the door with a quiet thud.

'What?' said a bored lanky guard, his dim face illuminated by a candle between the iron bars.

'Someone tried to attack me. In here. Only moments ago.'

'Is that so?' yawned the guard.

'Push on the door. See. It is open.'

The guard sighed heavily and leaned against the open door. His boots skidded on the slippery bricks as he tumbled into the room.

'Who was it?' he said, shining his candle into all four corners of the room.

'I do not know,' she said, shielding her eyes.

'This better not be a trick,' he grunted. 'I'm not scared of any Wasp Woman,' he said as he locked the door firmly again and lumbered off, his keys jangling.

Agata paced and rubbed her chin, the knot in her belly tightening once more. Had she made a colossal mistake? Tossed away her last chance for freedom?

'Don't be like me.' Her mother's words brought a smile to her lips and untangled that knot. She had a promise to keep.

Peasants and their wives, old and young, whirled around the Square, clapping and slapping their knees while children played chasey. The minstrels tra-la-la'd over the knock of skittles and the banter over tug-of-war.

The Duke's belly was full, the vintage was fine, his best friends were by his side, but he sighed.

The stooped Seneschal presented the newly crowned Spawning Queen to him. She was a plump girl of seventeen with dimpled cream-like skin and straw-coloured hair. The girl fluttered her eyelashes and blushed pink as the Duke kissed her hand while Kalin and his men cat-called and grunted, wine now thick in their veins.

'You cannot go wrong with a Vorosy girl,' Kalin said with a knowing elbow.

Perhaps his friend was right. About many things. 'She is quite pretty,' The Duke replied but his mind wandered to the dungeon.

'Don't look so maudlin, my Lord. Your people will talk. You should be enjoying yourself. Remember the year when we got so drunk you climbed--'

'They are already talking,' the Duke said.

'Do not concern yourself with their prattle,' Kalin replied. 'You have shown courage and commitment to the rule of law, and the Fatherhood. Stand tall.'

The Duke shrugged. If he had acted in the right way, why did his insides churn so much?

'I know the answer. Another drink.'

'Tomorrow...what will I do?' The Duke leaned heavily on his elbow. 'How can I look at her?'

'It's the Spawning Festival for the Father's sake. Drink up. The Father will take care of tomorrow.' Kalin charged his glass into the air. 'You. Boy.'

In the past, the Duke would have swept the cobwebs from his head with dancing. The townswomen would queue to take a turn and he'd dance until the sun rose and his soles were worn through. But tonight he chewed his lip and averted his gaze from his empty hose. Another pleasure taken from him.

Why did the Father test him so? The Duke had always been a loyal follower, treated his people well, loved his wife. The Scion would say there was always a lesson to be learned but the Duke struggled to understand what it could be.

Wladek popped up at the Duke's side and his heart flipped. The Duke glanced at Kalin but his friend was busy, chiding the squire for spilling good wine.

'Is it done?' he whispered.

'She would not come,' his valet said, his voice low, his serpentine eyes darting back and forth.

'She is still there?' he sighed and rubbed his forehead.

His manservant nodded. 'She panicked and called for the guards.'

Sucking down a long draft of wine, the Duke wiped his chin on his sleeve and shook his head. 'Pay the captain off. Easy coin for him. Then join the festivities.'

'As you wish, m'Lord.' Wladek bowed and ducked away.

The Duke flopped into his chair, his eyes fixed on a plank of wood on the stage. 'It is out of my hands,' he mumbled as he slumped once more and glumly raised his tankard for a refill.

PART THREE

THE TRIAL

CHAPTER FIFTY-FOUR

T HE GREAT HALL IS READY, m'Lord,' Wladek said.
The Duke lifted his head from his hands and rubbed his sandy
eyes.

'Have you eaten, m'Lord?'

The plate of golden bread, white cheese and plum jam lay untouched
in front of him.

'For the third time, I am not hungry and you are not my nursemaid,
Wladek!' The Duke scraped his chair along the brick floor, grabbed his
iron crutch and eased himself to his feet with a grunt.

Wladek swooped forward to smooth his surcoat and straighten his
emerald-encrusted belt. The belt was heavy and cumbersome but the
Duke hoped the jewels would bring him the strength and wisdom of his
forebears. He needed every scrap of help he could muster.

'I guess I should go,' the Duke sighed.

'The Father will provide you with wise counsel,' Wladek said
without meeting his eyes.

'He had better hurry,' he replied. 'Time is running out.'

Sira shuffled from the dungeon with her head hanging low, following orders as she'd always done.

'Wasp Woman,' the red-nosed guard hissed in her ear and Sira dropped her head even lower.

The townsmen yelled and pushed as the guards dragged her to the centre of the room. She was guilty before she even opened her mouth, an ungrateful shrew snuffing out a brave man returned from war. But the guards and townsmen did not matter. There was only one person who would make the final judgement and it was not the Duke.

The guard shoved her into a wooden chair. Despite the shouts and scuffles echoing around the Great Hall, a tranquillity settled over her like a warm blanket. She looked up past the thick rafters that lined the ceiling, picturing the wide expanse of sky beyond. She welcomed Him, she was ready for His judgement.

A second woman hit the chair beside her. Her eyes hollow and unseeing. There was a red scratch across her nose and a tuft of straw stuck in her greasy hair.

'Rabel!' Sira grabbed her hand and whispered, smiling, 'Have faith.' Her heart burned as her sister folded over herself like a crumpled leaf.

The guard slapped Sira's hand away.

'He knows the truth in our hearts,' Sira said.

Rabel shook her head. 'He has already decided.'

'Hands off me,' Froma spat. She stood taller than the redheaded boy-guard, but his grip was firm as he steered her through the jeering men.

'Put your veil back on,' said a rough voice and Froma turned her head to find the source, her eyes as cold as icicles.

A man with a prominent brow shuddered. 'Ugly.'

'Watch it. She'll put a spell on you,' lisped a third man.

Froma tossed her head back and strode towards the centre of the room. She matched any stare thrown in her direction with pursed lips. Unimportant churls. Peasant scum.

'Sit,' said the redheaded guard.

She sat with grace and lay her hands in her lap. The truth would come out. The Duke was far more intelligent than that fool Kalin. He would see through the deceit. Unlike the others she would be free before the sun set and would insist on a public apology. She looked forward to Kalin's embarrassment.

Froma glanced at the empty High Table before her and studied the eel sigil on the terracotta and green tapestry that covered the wall. She busied her mind with plans for the future, what she would do once her mohair business was rightfully returned to her.

Agata stepped into the Great Hall of the Eel to the roar of guttural male voices.

'Wasp Women.'

A glob of spit thwacked her cheek. With her hands secured behind her back, she couldn't wipe their disgust away.

Her eyes ignited but she kept her jaw clamped shut.

'Murderess.'

Fishermen stinking of the sea, goat-herders in hessian, callous-handed blacksmiths and even merchants dressed in silk shoved and jostled her as she struggled through the crowd.

'Filth.'

They grabbed her hair, tore at her grubby stolen surcoat, groped at her breasts. Her breath rasped through her clenched teeth, her heartbeat pounded in her ears but she said nothing.

The guards cut her restraints and shoved her into a chair in the centre of the room alongside the others. She grunted as the point of her elbow struck wood. She rubbed her chafed wrists, but sat tall and allowed herself a glimmer of a smile. This was her chance, they would have no choice but to listen to her speak. The Duke would finally hear her. He would understand. Wouldn't he? Her smile wavered.

The ruckus inside the Great Hall died as a guard opened the Court side door and the guards banged their swords against their shields to announce the Duke's entrance. The deafening clang of metal rang in the air, past the candles blazing in tiered chandeliers and up into the highest corners of the vaulted ceiling. All eyes turned to the Duke as he limped towards the low stage and his Chair.

The Duke sat down and forced his shoulders straight and even. He was no longer a man. He was the Duke of Ambrovna, head of the House of Nyvard, alone on the stage in his carved chair. The Scion sat to his left in bronze, Lord Kalin to his right, and directly in front were four bedraggled women.

The first sat with her head hanging down as though she'd been at the wine, the second with her crooked nose high in the air. The third stared straight through him as if he were made of glass and the fourth woman met his gaze, her dark eyebrows raised in a soft questioning look. He glanced away with a gulp.

The guards formed a wall between the accused women and the mob of townsmen who jostled for a better view. Merchants stood next to craftsmen and fisherman still in their smocks after the morning trawl. Three Cousins stood alongside men from the Brick Works, their hair coated in red dust. In the corner, the Seneschal and a grey-bearded scribe sat a table with a quill and knife at the ready. But beside the four accused, there was not another woman in the room. Women were not permitted to attend a trial.

With a nod to Kalin, the Duke shuffled for a comfortable spot in his chair. There was no telling how long this trial would last.

Dressed in his ceremonial tunic, with his beard clipped as precisely as the hedges of Sulun palace, Kalin's voice boomed with all the gravitas of his station. 'Duke Gerthorn Nyvard, the thirty-fourth Duke of Ambrovna is present to hear the accusations made against these four women: Goodwife Rabel Ejvind; Singlewoman Sira Osias; Mistress Froma Plesec and the forty-first Duchess of Ambrovna, Agata Nyvard.'

The Duke's stomach jumped when Kalin mentioned Agata's full title. Unable to meet her eyes, he tried looking beyond her but he still felt the blazing heat of her gaze.

'By the laws of the Kingdom of the Four Rivers, I, as Master of the Shield of Ambrovna, will first state the accusations against each woman. Each accused will have their chance to confess before the Father. If they fail to confess, the trial will begin. Witnesses will be called and evidence presented, subject to permission. During the trial, no one may speak to the Duke directly. But he may ask questions. Once the evidence is complete, I will call for the Voice of the Town.'

The crowd tittered and elbowed one another.

'Then the Duke will make his final judgement.'

'Hang 'em,' yelled a voice from the back and the crowd roared in agreement.

Kalin pointed. 'Eject that man.'

The crowd parted around the speaker. After a short scuffle, the guards dragged the barrel-chested man out the main door.

'Take note,' said Lord Kalin. 'This is how we treat outbursts during a trial.' He scoured the Great Hall with his iron stare. No one said a word.

Pursing his lips, Kalin continued. 'Do you have any further words to say before we begin, my Lord?'

The Duke shook his head, almost imperceptibly. He bunched his fingers into fists, unfurled then tightened them again. Since taking the throne three years earlier, this was his most difficult matter yet, even without his wife's embroilment.

'Thank you, my Lord. We shall begin with the Blessing of the Scion.'

Scion Zavis stood without a single groan or cracking joint. Around the Great Hall, clothing rustled and swords jangled as the guards, onlookers and three of the women kneeled on the hard brick floor. Even Kalin dropped to his knees. Only Agata and the Duke remained seated.

'O Father, you who watch us from beyond the Sunset,' the Scion said, his eyes stern in his wrinkled face.

This man had been a constant presence throughout the Duke's life and perhaps his father's before him. The Duke wondered how old the man was, whether the Father had granted him immortality.

'God of war, god of the sun, of the earth, the sea and of life itself, we offer ourselves as your servants on this land. We look to your Teaching to show us how to live a righteous life. And in turn, we thank you with our worship and love for you. We seek the blessing of your wisdom. Guide us to the truth to ensure the guilty are punished and the innocent go free. Bless the Duke. Ensure he makes true and right decisions on this day, and lets justice prevail. In the eyes of the Father.'

'In the eyes of the Father,' the crowd repeated. Each man present traced the Father's circle on their foreheads.

Agata joined them.

'Thank you Scion Zavis.' Kalin bowed to the Scion and the Duke before turning to address the four women. Kalin cleared his throat. 'Now the accusations. You are all accused of three murders by poisoning, three attempted murders by poisoning, conspiracy to murder the Duke and overthrow the Duchy of Ambrovna. Treason.'

The Duchess's maid screwed up her stained face and exchanged a confused sideways glance with Agata who returned a tight-lipped half-shrug. The scrawny Alleys woman did not even raise her head and the Plesec widow's eyes hardened further.

'Before the trial can rightfully begin, there are two questions for the accused. On your feet, Goodwife Ejvind.'

Sira's sister rose slowly, glancing up with skittish eyes, meek and gaunt like a stray dog.

'Do you have any mortal enemies in Ambrovna?'

She shook her bowed head.

'Singlewoman Osias?'

Sira stood, smiling as always but her blemished face seemed different. There was a light, a confidence in her eyes, an air the Duke had never seen in her before.

'No, m'Lord,' she said without pause.

'Mistress Plesec? Do you have any mortal enemies?'

The large woman drew to her full height then hesitated briefly. The Duke frowned as he noticed the yellow and purple bruising around her puffy eye socket and throat. He hoped his guards were not responsible. She held her nose high and replied, loudly and clearly. 'No, my Lord.'

'Duchess Agata Nyvard?'

The Duke's belly tumbled as his wife rose elegantly. Her hard gaze locked with Kalin for a moment before shifting to the Scion. She licked her lips and raised an eyebrow. 'Enough for someone to accuse me of murder?'

'Answer the question.'

Agata seemed to chew on his words. The room was silent, every man leaning in.

'Aside from Scion Zavis, I have no mortal enemies I am aware of.'

The crowd booed. The loudest roar was from the younger Cousins at the back of the Hall and yet the Scion's face did not flicker.

The Duke shifted his weight in his chair. His heart withered. His wife would never bring the people to her side with such outbursts. She was not helping herself. Or him.

Kalin pursed his lips. 'Aside from your blasphemy, naming the Scion is of no consequence. He is not your accuser and so the trial can commence.'

Agata curled her lip, spoiling her face with an ugly grimace.

'One final question before the trial begins. This is your chance to confess your crimes and stop the trial. Do any of you wish to confess before the Scion and the Father? Are you guilty of three murders and three more attempted murders by poisoning and conspiracy to commit treason?'

'I confess,' the skinny Alleys woman shrieked, collapsing from her seat and splaying out, chest down on the bricked floor. 'It was all my fault.'

'No, Rabel,' Sira said, jumping from her chair and grabbing her sister by the arm.

'Separate them.'

Two guards pulled Sira by the arms back to her seat.

'I confess, too,' she said before she could be pushed back into her seat.

Agata's face twisted.

'You both confess to all accusations?'

'Yes,' wept the Alleys woman, tears and snot dribbling down her face. 'It was me. I killed them.'

'Don't listen. She was not involved,' Sira said.

'Do you confess, Singlewoman?'

'Not to the murder of the Duke and treason. That's all lies. But I admit my part in the poisonings and the release of the Allotment women.'

'Women, are you speaking the truth?' the Scion said, his voice booming around the bricked walls. 'The Father sees all. The Father knows your hearts.'

The skinny woman lay on the ground, howling. 'Oh, Teo.'

'Yes, Scion Zavis.' Sira nodded, meeting his gaze. 'What I say is true. And He knows. In the eyes of the Father.'

Kalin turned to the Duke. Saying nothing, the Duke flicked his fingers for Kalin to continue.

'Goodwife Ejvind and Singlewoman Osias, you are guilty by your own confession. The Duke will consider your punishment at the end of the trial. Put them aside.'

The guards led the sisters away and placed them by the far wall. Agata and Mistress Plesec were now alone in the centre of the room.

'Mistress Plesec? You heard the confessions of your fellow women. This is your last chance to confess and receive the mercy of the Duke and the Father.'

The Plesec woman lifted her lumpy nose higher and compressed her lips until they were invisible. 'I am not guilty. It was them.'

She pointed at Agata and then the two sisters. Agata and Sira glared back in return while the Alleys woman stared at the bricked floor.

'Very well. My Lady? Are you ready to confess in front of the Duke, the Father and the whole town?'

Agata narrowed her eyes.

The Duke's heart thumped slowly, foreboding, like a drum on the battlefield. He sat ramrod straight as he must. Restraint was the only acceptable emotion for a man in his position, no matter how he felt. His wife must know how important her answer was. If she confessed, he might be permitted to show her a little clemency.

'I will not confess,' she said. She folded her arms and sat back down in her chair, a dark eyebrow raised. The Duke swallowed.

'So be it.' Kalin nodded and turned back to the Duke. 'My Lord, we shall now begin the trial.'

CHAPTER FIFTY-FIVE

T HE DUKE CLEARED HIS THROAT and followed the strict formalities according to the laws of the Kingdom. 'May the trial begin. I have heard the accusations brought before me. Are there more than two witnesses to the crimes?'

'Yes, my Lord. We will hear from three witnesses,' Kalin said. 'I call forth the first witness, Master Tveldt.'

The stumpy-legged physician pushed through the townsmen. He straightened his tunic and smoothed his few remaining hairs across his pate as he stood to the left of the High Table, the place for witnesses.

'Master Tveldt. You were a witness to the death of Master Plesec and you are here to provide your testimony. Do you promise to the Father that all your words will be true?'

'I do, my Lord.'

Kalin nodded. 'How long have you been a physician, Master Tveldt?'

'Many years, Lord Kalin. As a mere apprentice boy, I was present at the Duke's own birthing.' He smiled.

'Tell the Duke what you observed.'

'I was summoned to the Plesec household when the Master of the house was feeling unwell and became ill with serious vomiting. Master Plesec is a man of rude health ordinarily, a rugged constitution. And so I knew this was a serious matter.'

'What did you find?' Kalin asked.

'His vomit was thick with blood. At first, I thought it might be the red death. There were rumours of an outbreak in the Alleys.'

'Have you seen the red death before?'

'No, my Lord. Thank the Father. But I have read accounts from other physicians. Much has been written from the experiences in the territory of the Neven. By those who are left.'

The Duke gave a short nod, Master Tveldt was a learned man.

'And when he did not show the boils of the red death under his skin, I became suspicious. Then it all came back to me.' The physician paused and straightened.

The Duke clenched his fists.

'I have seen mushroom poisoning before. My father was a compounder. He stocked a variety of mushrooms in his apothecary and as a child, he gave me strict instructions never to touch those jars. Luckily, I listened to him. The mushroom I suspect in the murder of Master Plesec is small. Like a puffball but deadly. It is known as the 'destroying angel'.'

The crowd gasped and shot disgusted glares at the women.

'And this destroying angel can be found in Ambrovna?'

'The hills are filled with poisonous plants if you know where to look. These days, compounders do not use such ingredients. We heal. We do not kill. You would need someone skilled in un-Fatherly ways to locate it. A Wasp Woman.'

The Duke flinched at the word but if the truth was to be uncovered, references to Wasp Women could not be avoided.

'Boil 'em,' jeered a man.

Kalin glared and pointed and the guards swiftly removed the beady-eyed man without a fuss.

'What makes you suspect...Wasp Women?' Lord Kalin said.

'I was unsure. It was merely a hunch and I try not to listen to the blether of laundresses.' The physician stroked at his beard. 'At first, I suspected an enemy in our town, a Henden compounder perhaps, unhappy with the outcome of the war. This seemed like the most likely answer. Until today. When I saw the other accused women. Those two know exactly how to get their hands on powerful poison.' He pointed at the sisters standing by the wall.

The Duke leaned forward on his elbow. 'How?'

'You are probably too young to remember, my Lord. They have another sister. A notorious Wasp Woman who ran away from Ambrovna decades ago. They say she lives wild in the hills.'

All eyes turned to the sisters. Sira gulped but her sister stared down. The Scion turned to the Duke and nodded sagely.

'Were Singlewoman Osias and Goodwife Ejvind present at the Plesec house?'

'Not when I was treating Master Plesec. At first, I suspected the maid. But I discounted this idea quickly. She was too overwrought and much too feeble-minded. Unless she is a great actress. But there was something amiss about the wife.'

'Mistress Plesec here?' Kalin pointed and the merchant's wife's eyes narrowed to slits.

Tveldt nodded. 'I checked Master Plesec's wine and brandy and found nothing untoward. Then I went to the kitchen shed. The maid apologised profusely. With all her concern for the Master of the House, she had not completed her chores. Lucky for her laziness, his lunch bowls were unwashed. I fed his leftovers to the dog. Within the hour, the dog began vomiting and then I knew. Destroying angel. The little puffball is tasteless but it takes effect quickly. And a dog being smaller than a man, of course.'

'Did you see Mistress Plesec touch the meal?' Kalin asked. 'Or the bowl?'

'No, my Lord.'

'Could someone else have administered the poison?'

'The maid assured me that only she and Mistress Plesec had access to Master Plesec's food.'

The merchant's wife screwed up her face like a dried apple but she remained quiet.

'Are there other possibilities? Master Plesec was a wealthy man. He may have other rivals in business. Enemies. Someone who may want him dead?'

'I did not know him intimately. I was only his physician.'

'Why do you think Mistress Plesec did it?' Kalin asked.

Tveldt rubbed the back of his neck. 'A good question, my Lord. I have been pondering this myself. Who knows what wickedness went on while we were at war. Traders visited Ambrovna like they always did and our women were alone. She must have taken up with another man and hoped Master Plesec would die in battle but when he came back--'

'You do not think she is a Wasp Woman?' Lord Kalin said.

'She did it for the pleasure?' Tveldt said, his eyebrows raised as he contemplated this prospect. 'To appease their savage Mother? I suppose it could be possible. But Mistress Plesec strikes me as a practical woman. I expect there to be a reward for her. A way in which she benefits.'

The Duke shuddered. Mistress Plesec's eyes bulged but she abided by the rules of the trial and said nothing, her lips white. Had a new type of Wasp Woman emerged in his town? Knowledgeable in the ancient ways but also educated and power hungry. Was she the Queen Wasp? The one who had corrupted Agata? A year was plenty of time to enchant and ruin a young woman's mind.

'Thank you, Master Tveldt. My Lord, do you have any questions for the physician?'

The Duke hesitated. He was desperate to ask but fearful of the answer. 'And what of the other accused? Do you know whether the Duchess was involved?'

'Not for certain, my Lord.' Tveldt lowered his eyes. 'But Irina mentioned the Duchess visited the Plesec house on the morning of her Master's death.'

The Duke's eyelid twitched. He sat very still.

Kalin spoke up. 'Irina?'

'The Plesec maid. Singlewoman Vonder.'

'Ah, the lazy one. Do you wish to ask anything further of the physician, my Lord?'

The Duke sucked in a long, deep breath and rubbing his fingers across his chin hairs. 'Bring forth the maid.'

'Very well, my Lord. We have her father's permission. Singlewoman Vonder come forth!'

The physician bowed deeply and scurried off to the side.

Kalin called out once more. 'Singlewoman Vonder.'

The door to the bailey scraped open and the onlookers parted. A scrawny cowed girl with greasy hair approached, dressed in the muddy brown tunic of the serving class. Mistress Plesec harrumphed loudly and Kalin shot her a piercing glare, which she returned with equal ice.

'You are Singlewoman Vonder? Employed as a serving girl at the Plesec house?'

The girl's mouth moved but the Duke could not make out a word.

'Speak louder!' Lord Kalin barked.

The girl cowered. 'Yes, m'Lord.'

'How long have you been serving Master Plesec?'

'Six years, m'Lord.'

'Does your Master treat you well?'

'Oh yes, m'Lord.' Her dull eyes ignited. 'He is a good man. Was...'

'And the mistress of the house?' Kalin asked

The maid shook her head and spat. 'She is not a good woman.'

'In what way?'

'She did not love him. She did not treat the Master the way a wife should.'

'What happened on the day of your Master's death?'

'He called me to his study, m'Lord. He was feeling sickly and then he coughed up blood. I rushed to Master Tveldt and brought him back to make my Master better. But he couldn't.' The girl sniffled, squelching her wet nose against her sleeve.

'How did your Master become sick?'

'I didn't know but Master Tveldt said it was a poison and not the red death.'

'And you believe him?'

'Of course. Master Tveldt is very clever. I looked for poison in my Master's wine but I couldn't see nothin'.'

'Are you familiar with poisons?'

'Oh no, my Lord,' Irina gasped. 'But Master Tveldt does. He found some in a dish. I meant to clean up but I was busy with the people in the shed and looking after Master.'

Mistress Plesec sharply inhaled but clamped her mouth before she spoke, her brow furrowed and mouth pinched.

'By people in the shed you mean Goodwife Ejvind?'

She nodded. 'And her children. Rabel, I mean Goodwife Ejvind, sometimes worked for my Mistress. During the war. My Mistress put them in the loft, above the chickens. I don't know why. She didn't tell me. She doesn't tell me things. Only yells at me.'

'And so, my Lord.' Kalin turned, briefly biting on his lip. 'Here is the connection between Mistress Plesec and Goodwife Ejvind. Mistress Plesec harboured Goodwife Ejvind and her children when your guards were searching for her. When we suspected her of carrying the red death.'

The Duke nodded slowly.

'Goodwife Ejvind came to Mistress Plesec for help? To escape the Shield guards?' Kalin asked.

Irina nodded once more. 'The Duchess asked her to, m'Lord.'

Gasps echoed around the Great Hall. The Duke tightened his fists against the arms of his chair and interjected, his voice roaring louder than he intended. 'How do you know this?'

The girl flinched.

'I overheard them, m'Lord,' she stammered. 'The Duchess came to visit that morning. They thought I was in another room but I have very good ears. I didn't know what they were talkin' about at the time but later I worked it out. They were talkin' of poison and the red death. It is horrible, m'Lord. I didn't want to say but they can't be allowed to get away with such wickedness. It's not right.'

Scrutinising the maid closely, the Duke wiped his damp palms on his chair arm.

The Scion spoke up, his voice kindly. 'You have been very brave, Singlewoman Vonder. It takes courage to speak up against your Masters and tell the truth. The Father will be pleased with your words.'

'Thank you, Scion. He did not deserve to die in such a way.' Irina blew her nose.

'Why do you think your Mistress poisoned him?' Lord Kalin asked. 'Was there another man? Did other men visit your Mistress?'

The maid shook her head. 'She was faithful but she liked him being away.'

Kalin nodded before turning back at the Duke. 'Do you have anything further to ask, my Lord?'

The Duke rubbed his chin and narrowed his eyes at the girl. 'Tell me about the bruises on your Mistress's face? Was he cruel to her?'

Kalin shot him a look of displeasure but the Duke pressed on. There must be a reason for all this death. Violence was not in a woman's nature.

Irina half-shrugged. 'He had a temper. A good wife knows when to be quiet.'

Mistress Plesec rolled her eyes and crossed her arms tightly across her chest.

The Duke compressed his lips. She had not denied the beatings.

'One last question. You overheard your Mistress and the Duchess talking. Did you hear the Duchess speak about my murder? Did you hear them plotting to overthrow me?'

The serving girl stared down at her feet and shuffled from foot to foot, her mouth clamped shut.

The Duke frowned, a sudden heat rising under his tunic. 'I order you to answer me, girl' he said with a glare as sharp as knives.

The maid hid her face behind her lanky hair. 'Yes,' she said, her voice breathy and light, barely louder than a whisper. 'I heard them, m'Lord.'

'You may go.' The Duke leaned back in his chair and wiped his forehead as the blood thumped in the veins. Could it be true? Was Agata a plotting shrew like the merchant's wife? He studied his wife's face, dark as summer storm clouds, saw her eyes follow Irina through the crowd. How well did he truly know the woman he'd married?

'Now my Lord,' Kalin said. 'For our next witnesses, I call Singlewoman Osias and Goodwife Ejvind to give evidence.'

Sira and her sister exchanged frightened glances.

'But first, the matter of permission. In accordance with the customs of Ambrovna, women must have consent to give evidence. Either from their husbands,' the women lowered their heads, 'of which, there are none, or in the absence of a husband, the accused's father. Can your father give permission for you both?'

'Our Pa is in the Land Beyond the Sunset,' Sira said, making the circle of the Father on her forehead.

'In that case, this leaves only the Scion. Scion Zavis, do you grant permission?'

The Scion pressed his lips together. 'Given the confessions of Singlewoman Osias and Goodwife Ejvind, I am willing to permit them to speak. They have shown the strength to admit their sins before the Father. Their repentance is rewarded.'

'Thank you, Scion. Now, your confessions state you obtained poison and colluded to kill Goodman Ejvind and his boy, Teo. An innocent boy of nine...'

Sira's sister lunged forward. 'I did it all, my Lord,' she said, her voice shrill and her eyes savage. 'I killed my husband and my son.'

Sira grabbed her sister's hand but she shook Sira away.

'I did not kill my son on purpose.' The scrawny Alleys woman bent from the waist, clutching her hair in clumps. 'He must have finished my husband's stew when my back was turned. But it is all my fault and I must be punished. My sister had nothin' to do with it.'

Sira stepped forward, pushing in front of her sister. She addressed the Duke directly. 'No, m'Lord. My sister is trying to protect me. I harvested the poison myself. Alone.'

'I can't let you--' Her sister gripped at Sira's shoulder, her face twisted in pain.

'Rabel, please.' Sira shook her head.

'One at a time.' Kalin sighed. 'Singlewoman Osias, you admit to being a Wasp Woman?'

'Never.' Sira clasped her hands at her breastbone. 'I am a devoted follower of the Father. I have heard the tales of the women who follow the Great Mother, like we all have, but I am not a Wasp Woman. I know nothing of their ways. My Pa showed me the mushroom in the hills when I was a child.'

'And what of the third murder by poisoning? The mohair merchant, Danis Plesec. It is claimed you supplied the poison. What do you say in response to these accusations, Singlewoman Osias?'

Sira scrunched her fists by her side and opened her mouth but her sister spoke first. 'It was me.'

'Don't listen to her. It was me,' Sira insisted.

'Silence!' Kalin roared, his voice bouncing off the rafters. The sisters flinched and closed their mouths. He shook his head, muttering over his shoulder to the Duke. 'This is why we should not allow them to speak.' He cleared his throat. 'I need to hear the truth. Who provided the poison to Mistress Plesec?'

'I gave the poison to her, m'Lord,' Sira said. 'But only after she blackmailed me.'

The Duchess recoiled. Mistress Plesec's eyes were without a single flicker of emotion.

'Women,' mumbled the Scion. 'Betraying each other like spoilt children.'

Kalin continued. 'And what was your role in the conspiracy to murder the Duke and take over the Duchy?'

'I know nothing about a rebellion, m'Lord and I would never be part of any such plot. I have served the Duke and his family all my life. I helped to free the Allotment women as I said. But I would never hurt my Lord.'

The Scion walked slowly towards the sisters, his hands clasped behind his back. 'I have known you for many years, Singlewoman Osias. And your family,' he said, his eyes scouring her. 'A murderer? A traitor? The woman I see before me is not the Singlewoman Osias I know.'

Sira shuffled under his glare, her whole face flushed to the colour of her birth-marked cheek. 'I did what I thought was right. My sister and her babes were suffering. And I have confessed my sins.'

'You are not yourself.' He shook his head.

'I do not understand, Scion,' Sira said, her eyebrows pressing together.

'I suspect you have been bewitched.'

Bewildered, she shook her head.

The Duke pressed back slightly in his chair.

'No, Scion. I know what I did. I did it willingly.'

The Scion stroked his chin. 'There are ways to tell. You may not be aware of the spell on you. The Wasp Women should not be underestimated.'

Approval rumbled from the crowd but Kalin held up his hand, his forehead creased. 'With respect, Scion. This is not within the laws of the Four Rivers kingdom. Perhaps in the olden times but not now. We do not follow such practices in the modern day.'

Zavis stared back coldly but said nothing.

The Duke released a breath, glad for Kalin's interjection, the Scion was straying into uncertain grounds.

Kalin continued. 'You are the Duchess's maid, Singlewoman Osias?'

Sira chewed her lip. Kalin and every man in the room knew she was the Duchess's maid.

The Duke's heart clanged like the Temple bell.

'Answer me.'

'Yes, m'Lord. The Duchess was not involved.'

Sira was loyal to the castle and to her sister, but how deep did her loyalty to the Duchess go? His own valet had changed his clothes and emptied his chamber pot ever since he was nine years old. Wladek knew more about him than he did himself. Perhaps the war forged a bond between the women but after less than two years in her service, would Sira lie for her?

'This is your final word. This is the truth?'

'In the eyes of the Father.' Sira nodded.

'You may step back.'

Sira's shoulders dropped, the strain lifting from her face as she retreated from the glare of attention.

'Tell me, my Lord,' her sister cried out, her hands clasped tight at her chest. 'What have you done with my babes? Please. Who is lookin' after them? Not Sabet. Please. Let it not be Sabet.'

'Take them aside.' Kalin frowned.

'Please,' Sira's sister moaned, burying her head in her hands and Sira draped an arm around her shoulders as two guards pushed them back towards the wall.

Kalin turned to the Duke. 'We have one more witness, my lord. Lord Sylwin, please come forward.'

As his silver-haired great uncle limped into the centre of the room, his wife's face brightened. She pressed her hand to her heart with a slow smile and the Duke's damaged heart shattered a little more. From the expression on her face, she had no idea what was coming.

CHAPTER FIFTY-SIX

THE OLD MAN TOOK HIS place, bowed towards his great-nephew then turning to face Lord Kalin. Agata smiled at her grey-haired adviser but he did not meet her eyes. Surely Lord Sylwin would mend the damage. The Duke would certainly give more weight to his words than the spiteful lies of a servant girl.

'Lord Sylwin. You advised the Duchess during the Civil War?' Kalin asked.

'Yes, my Lord. I was her counsel while all you fit young men battled the Hende and Sopter Clans men.'

'She trusted you?'

He nodded. 'I became her confidante.'

Agata licked her dry lips.

'You understand the accusations today? The very serious accusation of treason?'

'I do, my Lord.'

'And do you have any knowledge about the conspiracy to murder the Duke?'

'Yes, my Lord.'

A breath hitched in Agata's throat. She leaned forward.

'Does it relate to any of the accused here in the Great Hall?'

'It concerns the Duchess.'

Agata stared open-mouthed and her heart plummeted. Had she misheard him? She glanced around the room for reassurance.

'Did the Duchess discuss the conspiracy with you?'

'Not directly.'

'But something she said made you suspicious?'

Sylwin pursed his wrinkled lips and nodded. 'I saw her on a number of occasions running through the castle keep. Up and down the stairs, in a manner not befitting a Duchess.'

Agata clenched her fists and dug her fingernails into her palms.

'On one occasion she was frantically searching for Singlewoman Osias. And we have heard Singlewoman Osias's confession today. I believe the Duchess was well aware of the actions of her maid. The Duchess was quite agitated on a number of occasions and made a poor attempt at hiding it.'

The Duchess ground her teeth.

'What did she say specifically?'

'Two days before the Spawning, she spoke of a great conundrum. She was obviously torn between decisions. She told me she must hurt one person for the good of another.'

All across the room, men growled.

Agata lunged forward in her chair, desperate to correct his twisted words, but she held back and obeyed the rules. Her time would come soon and they would all have to listen.

Her husband stared at her blankly.

Sylwin continued. 'I told her in the eyes of the Father, a good deed never erased a sin.'

The Scion nodded emphatically before shooting Agata another one of his stony stares.

'Unfortunately, I was in a hurry but asked her to come to see me later. She never did. If she had, I could have talked her out of this nonsense. As I had a number of times before.'

Agata lowered her head and wished she could cover her ears against his slander.

'What do you think she was referring to?'

'The Duchess enjoyed sitting on the throne while you men were away. A little too much in my view. She clashed with the Scion many times due to her pig-headedness. But now the Duke is back, she has been excluded from decision-making and her foolish pride is damaged. While officially she is next in line to the Duchy, we know she would never be allowed to rule. But she is only a silly young girl. She had probably convinced herself otherwise.'

Tears prickled at Agata's eyes as she gripped her shaking hands between her legs.

Kalin nodded. 'It makes sense. If the accused believed she could do a better job at governing Ambrovna, the only person in her way was the Duke. Or perhaps she is part of a wider conspiracy? The new Kingdom is only in its infancy and the Neven Clan are not known for their honour.'

The Scion lifted an eyebrow. 'Or perhaps she is the ringleader. Ambrovna has been free of cunning women for many years. Then all of a sudden--'

'Wasp Woman,' hissed a voice close behind her, one of the guards who was supposedly protecting her from the rabble.

'And there were other matters,' Sylwin cleared his throat. 'She spoke to me about more intimate and personal troubles. With her husband.'

The crowd seethed. Agata cowered under the weight of scores of eyes, hiding from one pair of grey eyes in particular. How could her words be twisted this way? Betraying a confidence between husband and wife was treachery, whether the man was the Duke or a humble goat-herder.

'Thank you, Lord Sylwin,' Kalin said. 'This ends my questions. Do you have anything further to ask, my Lord?'

Agata peered at him, searching for any glimmer of mercy but the Duke's face was as hard and blank as the dour portraits of his ancestors lining the walls behind him.

'No, Lord Kalin,' he replied.

Every ounce of life drained from her body as her chin lowered to her chest. He believed his great uncle's untruths. Of course, he would. Sylwin was his blood. Unlike her.

'Very well, my Lord. Lord Sylwin was the last of the witnesses. Are there any other questions?'

The old man bowed, and as he turned, Sylwin looked through her as though she were a complete stranger, without a hint of compassion or regret in his face. He shuffled away to join the rest of the onlookers.

'Continue,' the Duke said.

'Now to the Voice of the People.'

Agata lifted her head and scowled, a wave of heat swelling inside her body as she glared at the Duke on his throne. He averted his eyes. Tightening her fists, she jumped to her feet.

'My Lord. You forgot one witness.' Her voice rang out clearly. 'I have not been allowed to speak. I wish to answer the accusations against me.'

'It appears you do not have your husband's permission,' Lord Kalin said with a furtive glance at the Duke.

Agata stared open-mouthed. How could he deny her the chance to defend herself? Did he want to be blind to the truth?

'And your father is missing, presumed dead. Which only leaves the Scion.'

The Scion blinked slowly. 'She is without remorse. Permission is denied.'

Agata had expected nothing less from the Scion but she glanced up at her husband again. She pleaded with her eyes but he inspected his fingernails.

'A decision has been made. Permission refused. Now, sit down. We will move to the Voice of the People,' Kalin commanded.

Gutted like a fish, Agata crumpled in the chair. She was nothing to him. Their time together, their love, the band on her finger had been meaningless. He saw a traitor, not a wife, before him. Her mind clouded as her heartbeat slowed to a dull thud in her chest.

'Lord Kalin. One moment,' the Duke spoke up.

Agata's breath caught in her throat. She leaned in, gently biting her lip. She knew he would not forsake her.

'I wish to hear from Mistress Plesec.'

Agata slumped and prepared herself for another onslaught of falsehoods.

'Mistress Plesec?'

Froma blinked rapidly and composed herself, holding her smile inside. After the hysterics of the sisters and the Duchess's outburst, it was time to convince these fools of her innocence. The Scion had given her an idea.

'Your husband is dead, is your father present?'

'No, my Lord. I am from Veigur.'

'Too far away. Scion Zavis? Do you grant permission for this woman to speak?'

The Scion paused and she held herself very still under his inspection before dropping her mask very briefly and revealing a glimpse of softness. They could be allies. She hoped he understood.

The Scion nodded. 'Permission granted.'

'Stand up, Mistress Plesec.'

She stood slowly and smoothed down her tunic.

'What is your response to the accusations against you?'

Her body tingled but she lifted her eyes humbly.

'Thank you for the chance to speak, my Lord. I have listened to the physician and my serving girl, Irina.' She forced herself to stay composed as she said Irina's name. Anger would not serve her at this moment. 'And the others. Before coming here, I had days in the dungeons to reflect on my sins.'

'And repent?' The Scion tilted his head.

'Of course, Scion Zavis. I have confessed all to the Father. And I will leave the ultimate judgement to him. But it was a comment of yours which perplexed me most.'

The Scion leaned in. 'Yes?'

'I admit I placed the mushroom in the stew. This is true. But who put the thought in my head? I would never have dreamed of killing another person, let alone my own husband. Where did this idea come from?'

The Scion nodded.

'What are you saying?' Kalin squinted. 'You appear to be a woman of your own mind, Mistress Plesec, whatever trouble that may cause.'

'And I am, my Lord. Ordinarily. But something clouded my mind.'

'Greed? You are not alone there.'

'Let her speak,' the Scion said and Kalin frowned, shaking his head.

'It began during the war. Slowly at first. Ideas creeping into my head. New ideas. Sinful ideas. Thoughts and acts I had never considered before. Only now has it become clear. I believe I am bewitched. Just as you suggested, Scion.'

The Scion grunted in agreement and turned to nod at the Duke but the noble's face was blank.

'I do not know where or how. The almond cakes? Wine? But I became her puppet. She moulded me like dough, contorted my mind and I did whatever she asked without question. Even poisoning my own husband.' Froma choked with a sob for effect. 'And if you had not stopped me, I would have joined her to free the Allotment women.'

'She?' Kalin asked.

It was the question every man in the Great Hall wanted answered. All eyes and ears were on Froma as she demurely dabbed at her eyes.

'The Duchess of course. Just as the Scion said. She is the one with the most to gain.'

'You claim you are under the Duchess's spell?' Kalin asked.

Froma nodded solemnly. 'Along with the two sisters. The Scion himself said Singlewoman Osias is acting out of character. I did not understand before but now his words make sense. The veil has lifted from my eyes.'

Kalin guffawed.

'There are tests,' the Scion said. 'Ways we can confirm the bewitching.'

'Witch cakes? It's the stuff of superstitious peasants,' Kalin scoffed.

The Scion glared at him.

'What of your maid's accusation, Mistress Plesec? She presented a reasonable explanation for your actions.'

'I thought it was obvious, my Lord.' Froma replied. 'She wanted my husband for herself but he never looked at her in such a way. He was a good man.' She pursed her lips and treaded carefully.

'A good man?' the Duke said.

Froma's heart thumped. He was the one she must convince of her innocence. 'Irina was right in one way, I did not act like a good wife. But now I understand why. I was under her charm.'

'Very well, Mistress Plesec.' Kalin raised an eyebrow. 'Is there anything further, my Lord?'

The Duke stroked his chin. Froma swallowed. She did not know him well enough to read his face. Had she managed to convince him?

'I have heard enough.' He waved his hand and Froma exhaled discreetly.

'Be seated, Mistress Plesec,' Kalin said and Froma sat, pressing her lips tightly to hold back her smile.

'We have heard from all witnesses, who received permission. If you do not have any further questions, my Lord, it is time for the Voice of the Town.'

The men in the crowd straightened and elbowed one another.

The Duke chewed his lip and squinted.

'Do you wish to hear from any other person, my Lord?'

'Proceed,' the Duke said.

Something hit Agata in the back of the head, hard. She frowned and whirled around in her chair, rubbing the site of the blow. A wall of sneers and narrowed eyes glared back. She turned and slumped. Was there any point in fighting? Smothered tears clogged her throat as she wrapped her arms around herself. She was so alone in a tide of angry men.

'Men of Ambrovna. This is your chance to voice your opinion on the matter before you today.'

The men jeered, eyes gleaming.

'I will choose three men to speak their views.'

Scuffles broke out across the Great Hall as townsmen jostled, waving their arms in the air.

'Quiet! This is not a cock fight!' Kalin shouted.

The mob stopped cold, with many glancing around sheepishly. Kalin raised his finger and pointed. 'You. You and you.'

The chosen three stepped up. The first man wore a peacock-blue wool tunic with gold trim, his chest puffed out. The second, a weather-beaten fisherman pushed through the crowd, grinning. The third was a man in a coarse hemp shirt who inched forward hesitantly.

'State your name and your relation to the accused. If any.'

The fisherman smirked back at his friends, the cart man fidgeted and the merchant stood tall with his shoulders back.

'Iarim, purveyor of the finest nuts and spices in all Ambrovna,' the man in the fine blue coat said with a flourish. 'And no, my Lord. I do not have connections to these women. I knew the late Merchant Plesec through business dealings but I am not acquainted with his wife.'

'Jarku, squid fisherman. No, m'Lord,' said the red-faced man with a bow.

'Aivvet the cart man,' the man in the hemp shirt stammered. 'Me neither, m'Lord.'

'Men. You have heard everyone speak today.'

The three men nodded.

Kalin pointed to Jarku the fisherman. 'What is your opinion on the accusation?'

The florid man breathed out, rubbing at his collar. 'All guilty, m'Lord,' he replied in a deep rumble.

'All four women?'

'Yes, m'Lord,' Jarku said with a definitive nod. 'They deserve the harshest punishment.'

The crowd cheered and Agata sighed, their condemnation like a knife to her chest.

Kalin blinked slowly. 'Iarim?'

The merchant cleared his throat. 'My Lord. This is a matter of grave importance. I served with both men in the Civil War. Merchant Plesec and Goodman Ejvind survived the war, only to come home and be slaughtered by their own wives. This is a great tragedy. As the Scion said earlier, there is no excuse for this behaviour. The maximum punishment must be handed down.' The merchant stepped back, a smug smile on his well-fed face. His words roused more cheers and this time, fists punched in the air.

Lord Kalin moved onto the third man. 'And you? Cart man. What do you say?'

The cart man shuffled forward with a grimace. 'Them over there,' he said, pointing to Sira and Rabel. 'They're guilty. They said as much and they should be punished. But look at the mother. Look at 'er face. She's suffered enough, m'Lord.'

The crowd scoffed behind him.

'You wanted to know what I think.' He raised his hands in the air. 'I don't think she meant to kill her son but she did. By accident. They should get somethin' but not the full punishment.'

'Soft cock,' called out a voice, accompanied by boos and heckles.

He shrugged with a half-smile. 'My Binna always says I'm too soft.'

'And the women here?' Kalin said.

'The merchant woman. She's guilty too. Like these others. It looks like he'd given her a batterin' and that ain't right. But I don't believe her stories about spells.'

Agata tried to suppress a little smile. This cart driver was possibly the smartest man in the room.

'And the Duchess.'

She swallowed.

'This is 'ard, m'Lord.'

The man let out a long sigh. He opened and closed his mouth, wringing his meaty hands. 'She should know better. She's educated. She's not like these peasant women who fuss and carry on. I don't believe she wanted to kill the Duke. No one heard her say it. Out loud, you know. It all sounds like rumours to me. Did she even touch the poison herself?'

Agata wanted to rush forward and kiss his bristled cheek.

'But she did play some part in this. There's some truth. Somewhere. It's 'ard to tell through all these lies. But she should be punished for lettin' the Allotment women go.'

'The full punishment?'

'Oh no, m'Lord.' He shook his head, his lips pulled back and his face contorted. 'No one deserves that. It's too 'orrible.'

But the rest of the town did not agree. Their disapproval filled the Great Hall.

'Weak.'

'They deserve it.'

'Child killer.'

'Black bitch.'

The cart man lowered his head.

'Enough! The Voice of the Town has spoken.' Lord Kalin held up a hand, before turning to the Duke. 'My Lord?'

'Thank you, men, for your honesty,' the Duke said but his face was a mask. 'I shall consider your opinions.'

Had the cart man planted a seed of doubt?

The three townsmen bowed and returned to the crowd. Two with grins and one with a grimace.

Kalin bowed towards the Duke. 'All views have been heard, my Lord and now, it is time for your judgement.'

The Duke pursed his lips.

Time had run out. There was nothing more she could do. She glanced over at the scribe in the corner and from her time with the books in the Cabinet library, she knew exactly how they would portray her. Agata Nyvard, the villainess of the next volume of The History of Ambrovna.

She stared down at her leather boots and blinked back tears. She did not see the change in his expression, she only heard his words.

'One moment, Lord Kalin,' he said. 'I am not quite ready.'

CHAPTER FIFTY-SEVEN

A GATA'S EYES DARTED UP INSTANTLY, her heart leaping.

'Let the Duchess speak,' he said, his voice as flat as the tabletop.

'I advise caution.' The Scion turned swiftly, as though scolding a naughty child.

'Let her speak,' the Duke repeated sharply. 'I am her husband. I can grant her permission.'

'My Lord?' Kalin tilted his head.

'I have made my decision,' the Duke thundered.

Agata rose to her feet, swallowing hard.

'Very well,' Kalin muttered, his eyes narrowed. 'How do you respond to the accusations of murder and conspiracy, Duchess?'

'My Lord. I thank you for allowing me to speak.'

The Duke lowered his head in acknowledgment, his jaw set. Agata sucked in a deep breath to calm the whirlpool in her head and began. 'I came to Ambrovna as a bride from Tramissa in the lands of the Neven.'

'Traitor,' someone whispered behind her.

Holding her head high, she smoothed her unbrushed black hair away from her face. She faced the Duke and him alone, blocking out the rest of the room. The Duke was the only one that mattered. Now and always.

'I knew nothing of my new home but I have grown to love this town in the short time I have been here.'

'Love by poisonin'!' someone in the crowd scoffed.

Kalin gestured to the terracotta guards and the man was quickly ejected from the Hall. A tense silence settled over the room.

'While you, my Lord and Lord Kalin and many of our men risked their lives in the Civil War, I stayed behind to govern the town and protect your interests. I grew to love the people more and more, especially the women of Ambrovna. The women left alone to keep the town afloat while war raged. These women who worked hard, replacing men in all the male jobs. Fishing. Carpentry. Farming. Goat-herding. Merchants.'

She tilted her head towards Froma.

'This is all very pleasant. But please answer the question,' Kalin interjected.

'Like you men on the battlefield, we banded together to ensure that your town, your businesses, your livelihoods were maintained for the day you returned triumphant. All this work was on top of the usual tasks of raising children, preparing food, caring for the elderly and keeping the houses. The women became mother and father. And I defy anyone who says the women did a poor job looking after your town.'

The Scion stared with venomous eyes, her husband half-shrugged and Kalin folded his arms across his chest. But she was unperturbed, she expected nothing less from them.

'The women showed their bravery, their intelligence, their willingness to work hard. They proved they could do the jobs of men.'

Across the room, there were muffled grumbles and grunts of disapproval but no one spoke aloud.

'But then the war ended and we welcomed you home. Our war heroes. But not every story is a ballad and not every man is a hero inside his own home. My maid Sira came to me, in fear for her sister. Her husband was a bad man, a layabout. A gambler, he racked up debts while Rabel struggled to feed her three children. This was a man who took the wages from his nine-year old son to bet on the cocks. Is this a hero?'

No one responded.

'Then Rabel returned one day to find a skin merchant in her home. Her husband was negotiating the sale of their little girl. I ask you, my Lord. Would you call these the acts of a hero?'

The Duke chewed his lip. 'Regardless of the actions of these men, murder is an unreasonable response.'

'What was Rabel to do? Every time her back was turned, her husband plotted, stole the food from her children's mouths. And Mistress Plesec. Her husband beat her black and blue. How long would it have been before he killed her? Is this man a hero?'

'These men fought for their Duchy. They risked their lives and returned. Is this how you repay their sacrifice?' The Duke asked.

'You men knew who your enemies were. They were clothed in black and yellow. You faced them on the battlefields and defended yourselves. These men wanted to kill you. These women,' she gestured to Froma and Rabel, 'faced the threat inside their own homes. Their husbands, men who supposedly loved them and should protect them, turned out to be their greatest enemies. As bad as any Hende Clansman. And now you say these women do not have the right to defend themselves? Like you did on the battlefield?'

'You cannot compare this to war.' Her husband shook his head. 'You have no idea.'

'Do you, my Lord? Do you know what they've been through?'

'This is ridiculous,' the Scion grumbled. 'She has said quite enough,'

'Scion Zavis. What about the Father? The all-seeing Protector? Where was he when these women were beaten and tormented? The Father let down these women.'

'Blasphemy!' The Scion leaped to his feet, pointing a knobbled finger. 'Wasp Woman!'

'If the Father cared for right and wrong, he would have let these men die on the battlefield. He would not have let the circumstances come to this.'

'Silence this woman!' the Scion spat.

'Is this the way you feel about me?' the Duke said, his eyes steely. 'Did I deserve to die on the battlefield, rather than return a cripple to embarrass you?'

Her eyes widened as she shook her head and clutched her hands at her chest. 'Never, my Lord.'

'Is this true?' The Duke directed his question to the other three women. 'Does the Duchess speak the truth?'

Froma tossed her shoulder while Sira nodded fervently and Rabel did not even lift her head in response.

'Your co-conspirators do not fill me with confidence,' he replied.

'Women.' Kalin rolled his eyes. 'No solidarity, my Lord.'

The Duke nodded. 'Did you get a taste for power? Was I an inconvenience?'

'No, my Lord. Believe me. No,' Agata lowered her head, hot tears welling in her eyes. 'This was never about you.'

'And how do you explain the boy? How did he get in your way?' Kalin said.

'It was my fault!' screeched Rabel, startling everyone in the room. 'I deserve to die. I didn't watch him.'

'Silence. I have heard enough.' The Duke's eyes were as cold as midwinter.

Agata stood open-mouthed. She had so much more to say. She searched his face for any inkling of a change of heart. He must believe her, he must. If only she had been allowed to speak to him alone, away from the prying eyes of the town, away from his duties, where he could be her Gerthorn again.

The Duke averted his eyes and nodded to Kalin. The weak-chinned guard rushed to his side and helped him struggle out of his chair. Without a second glance at Agata, he hobbled on his iron crutch towards the side door.

'The trial is complete and all statements have been received. The Duke will retire to consider his judgement.'

Kalin and the Scion followed the Duke out of the Great Hall and the door closed, leaving Agata and the other three women alone in the room with the townsmen.

'Traitorous bitches,' yelled someone from the crowd and others laughed in response. A glob of spit flew across the room and slapped Agata in the face. She swept it away with her hand and glared into the crowd.

'Nevenish scum. You should never have come here.'

'Wasp Women.'

'Hold them back,' yelled Seliv. The guards surged forward to surround Agata and the others as the townsmen pushed and shoved. One of the guards dawdled and another glob of spit landed in her hair.

She gritted her teeth.

All she could do was wait and hope.

CHAPTER FIFTY-EIGHT

A S THE DOOR TO THE Great Hall closed behind them, the Duke let out a long breath, glad to be away from Agata's face with her crumbling hope, her disapproval, her frustration, her pleading eyes. Away from his subjects with their resentment and expectations stifling the air.

His heart was torn in two. On one side, he had the beautiful woman he had married, her gentle words in his ear, her promise of heirs, and the cold nights at war where he thought only of her. And on the other, the same woman and her circle of conspirators had plotted his death.

Was he a fool? Had she bewitched him? Had he invited a Wasp Woman from the Neven Clan into his home and given her his throne?

He lurched across the corridor and up the brick stairs to the solar, the Scion and Kalin closely behind. He stared out at the flawless blue sky, the light sparkling on a gently rolling sea, feeling the direct opposite.

The low table was laid with red grapes and crusty bread, grilled elvers and a wheel of white goat cheese.

'You should eat, my Lord,' said Kalin.

'I suppose,' the Duke mumbled, staring out the window as if an answer would emerge from the waves.

Kalin shrugged and tore into the bread.

The Scion sat, folded his hands and closed his eyes. 'We are grateful for the food you have grown and raised for us. We will repay you with our loyalty and piety. In the eyes of the Father.'

'In the eyes of the Father,' said Kalin with his mouth full. 'You will at least have wine?' he asked.

The freckled serving boy rushed forward with a full goblet and the Duke poured the whole cup straight down his gullet. The wine warmed his throat but not his mood. He sighed and held out his goblet once more. 'If only my father was still alive.'

'We all miss the Old Duke,' the Scion said as he reached for the smallest pieces of bread and an apple. It was then the Duke remembered it was a fasting day. His lack of appetite could appear pious to the Scion but in truth, he could not bear to eat. His impending decision rolled about in his stomach.

'A troublesome matter,' Kalin said, slicing a triangle of white cheese with his knife.

'I disagree,' said the Scion as he picked at his bread. 'It's quite straightforward. The facts speak for themselves.'

The Duke shook his head. 'I wish I had your certainty.'

'Three witnesses including your own Great Uncle. And he said she was tormented by a decision to hurt someone.'

Kalin scratched his beard. 'The merchant's wife is plainly guilty. Stuck-up bitch. What a lot of rot. Bewitched? Spare me.'

'Do not be so dismissive,' said the Scion. 'You do not know everything in this world.'

'Witches? Wasp Women? It was poison, plain and simple. Nothing mystical about it.'

'You have not seen what I have seen.' The Scion pointed with his apple-cutting knife. 'Many years ago, when I first joined the Fatherhood, there was an old Cousin in our Temple, close to death. He would blather on day and night about his encounter with some Akull Queen. Everyone laughed at him. But fifty years after he met her, she still entranced him. Despite a lifetime of devotion to the Father. Women are cunning and insidious. This is why they are so dangerous.'

'Cunning? Absolutely. That Plesec wife was playing you for a fool, Scion. I never thought I'd see the day a woman fooled you.' Kalin smirked. 'And let's be clear, I will not allow any kind of witch bobbing or uncivilised practices while I am Master of the Shield. We have rule of law now. We are beyond all that nonsense.'

The Duke said nothing. Proud, foolish Mistress Plesec reminded him of the traitor Hugon, Agata's brother's friend who challenged his

Clan leader. Despite all his riches and privilege, Hugon blamed others for all his misfortunes. But the bruises on the Plesec woman's face told another side to the story.

'And the other three? Iwan Ejvind was a churl and probably deserved it. It's just a shame the boy ate the wrong stew. But the Duchess...' Kalin sucked at his teeth.

The Duke twisted his mouth.

'She did not confess when you let her speak. Which was very foolish, my Lord. But she still did not claim her innocence,' the Scion said. 'She is guilty as far as I am concerned.'

'We have talked about this subject many times,' Kalin sighed. 'You know I never approved of her, my Lord. I still don't. But do I think she conspired to kill you? No.'

'Do you believe she was involved in the murders of the others?' The Duke narrowed his eyes.

'It is hard to pick out the truth but I suspect she was involved in the attempted murder of my guards. We caught her red-handed with the Allotment women.'

'Then according to the law, she must pay for her involvement,' the Scion said.

'True,' Kalin said, waving a thick slab of ham. 'But what punishment?'

'The right punishment for the crime,' the Scion said. 'Ejvind and Plesec fought for you and the Duchy in the Civil War. Their lives deserve to be avenged. You owe them loyalty for the loyalty they showed you and the whole Vorosy Clan.'

The Duke drew in deeply through his nostrils. 'Could there be a lesser punishment?' His voice emerged shamefully feeble.

'Three men are dead and three more are close to death.'

'Banishment?' he said, tugging on his bottom lip.

'You would be looked upon as weak. You heard the views of the people.'

'Most of them are bloodthirsty idiots looking for a bit of entertainment,' scoffed Kalin. 'But the Scion is right.'

'Haven't I proven myself on the battlefield?' The Duke's hand touched his empty hose leg.

'Perhaps. But that was against our enemies. You need to show equal strength with your subjects,' Kalin said.

'Otherwise you will have a mutiny on your hands.' The Scion nodded.

'My family has held this throne for thousands of years.'

'They want justice. If you are lenient, imagine how other women in Ambrovna will respond. You must enforce our ways.'

'You exaggerate.'

'You witnessed the way they behaved in the Neven. Where the Fatherhood was pushed aside and the people turned their backs on his true Teachings and wisdom. Look what happened to them. They lost the kingdom.'

'The Scion has a point, my Lord. You know how old King Rados and his court were always more interested in politics and art than devotion. That is probably where she got her silly ideas from. And they think us uncivilised fishermen.'

The Scion prodded the table top. 'Thank the Father, the Civil War rid us of the reign of the Neven and the Father is rightfully back in the heart of the Kingdom, as he should be. King Absalom is a pious man. But if you let this matter slip because you do not have the strength to make a tough decision, what will happen to our families? The women will think they can do as they please and the men will blame you.'

The Duke clutched his goblet tightly with a trembling hand.

'If word travels about your weakness and your own people turn against you, you will be an easy target. You can only fight so many men on your own.'

With a bitter laugh, the Duke shook his head and looked to Kalin for support. But his Master of the Shield chewed on his bread with a half-shrug and said nothing.

The Duke swallowed hard and ran his fingers through his hair. 'But if I put innocent women to death, how will the Father look upon me? Aren't I equally as bad?'

'The Father will guide you. You know in your heart what is right,' the Scion said. 'You saw the guilt plain on their faces.'

'You can find another wife,' Kalin said. 'Take my advice this time.'

The Duke slurped the contents of his cup and slammed the silver goblet on the table.

'Well, my friend.' Kalin waved his knife with its piece of ham stuck on the end. 'You had better make a decision soon. They are waiting for your judgement.'

The Duke pursed his lips.

Agata changed her mind with every passing moment. First she wished he would hurry back, then she wished he would take his time. Her confidence soared like an albatross only to plunge into the depths of the sea.

Long shadows fell over the Great Hall but no one came to light the candles. Good beeswax would not be wasted on prisoners and peasants.

'Hurry up,' moaned a man behind her. The anger was long gone and the townsmen were bored.

'I heard there was one trial in the old Duke's day, where it took 'im a week to decide,' a long-nosed man said from the crowd on her left.

'I'm not stayin' here a week,' replied a third man in a high-pitched whine.

'I didn't think it'd take this long. The decision is clear to anyone with eyes.' Long-nose crossed his arms and nodded at Agata.

Then Froma whispered in her ear, croaky and low. 'I should have known Irina would eavesdrop on us. Little liar.'

Agata shook her head. 'You do not see, do you?'

Froma tutted and frowned. 'Of course, I see. It is obvious. That stupid Irina and Tveldt must be in this together.'

'Do you think I am deaf? I was right here when you accused me of bewitching you. It is not all the maid's fault.'

'I think you will find--' Froma said.

'You accused me. You told them about Rabel and Sira. You brought this on us. All of us. I forbade Sira from giving you the poison because I did not trust you. She went behind my back but I was right.'

'I-I-I...' Froma stuttered.

'Even with all this.' Agata gestured to the Great Hall filled with onlookers and guards. 'You cannot admit your fault.'

'He drove me to it.'

With a weak smile, she replied. 'That I believe. I saw your face. You did not deserve to be treated that way. But whatever happens to us, however the decision lands, you must make peace with what you did. You cannot lie to yourself forever.'

Agata turned in her chair away from Froma, her cheeks burning. She heard a huff beside her. Or perhaps it was a sob.

Two footmen entered with flaming torches and the tiered chandeliers were lowered from the ceiling. Agata straightened in her chair, her heart hammering as they lit the wicks. He was coming.

CHAPTER FIFTY-NINE

THE SIDE DOOR OPENED AND the Duke shambled out. Behind him came the Scion with his hands clasped behind his back and Kalin taking large strides. The faces of all three were blank. The air hummed with anticipation as onlookers scrambled for a good vantage point but in the centre of the room, Agata had the best view of all.

'Stand,' Kalin ordered.

Agata shot to her feet but she moved a little too quickly. She grabbed for the back of her chair and drew in a deep breath to settle her spinning head. She must not faint, she must accept her judgement with dignity. No matter what, she was still a noble.

'The Duke will now present his decision with regards to the murders of Goodman Ejvind, his son and Master Plesec by poisoning, the attempted murder by poisoning of three guards and the conspiracy to murder Duke Gerthorn Nyvard and overthrow the Duchy.'

The Duke leaned on his crutch. Agata's knees trembled as she searched his face.

'I have considered the accusations carefully,' the Duke said. He paused and pursed his lips. 'I have listened to the witnesses, the Voice of the Town and taken counsel from the Master of the Shield and the Scion. I have even considered the evidence offered by the accused.'

Agata heard Froma murmuring a prayer to the Father beside her. She squeezed her lips tight. He would not help them now.

'The private relationship between a husband and his wife are not a matter for this Court.' Agata closed her eyes tightly and bit her bottom lip.

'But the crimes committed by the accused are most serious. The taking of life. Here in Ambrovna we believe in the Father. His wisdom guides us in all we do. And according to the Father's Teachings, the family unit is paramount with the man as the leader.'

The Scion stared straight at Agata. Her chest tightened and she dropped her head.

'The man takes the role of the Father in the home, provides protection and wisdom. This is the way we have lived in Ambrovna since the sun first rose in the East. Our strength lies in strong families where everyone knows their role. Without a strong family, there is no trust. And without trust, we are lost.'

Froma let loose a wail, loud enough for the whole room to hear and Agata curled her shoulders. The Duke did not have to explain, his decision was clear and his orders would be followed without question.

'Two of the victims were war heroes, the other an innocent child. Dangerous outlawed poisons were used and the perpetrators lied to the Master of the Shield. This is unacceptable in Ambrovna. After long deliberation, I have come to my decision....'

A slow dull beat thumped in her head, she held her breath.

'...all four women are guilty of all accusations.'

Agata grabbed the top rail of the chair, her knees caving beneath her. The room shimmered as townsmen cheered. Their voices, deafening and joyous, crashed like a wave over them.

The Duke had decided. He did not believe her.

'The guilty will face the maximum punishment for murder by poisoning. Tomorrow. In the Town Square at noon. Let this be a warning to all. Murder will not be tolerated in my Duchy. No matter who you are.'

The Duke headed towards the side door.

Agata stared forward blankly. Beside her, Froma sobbed loudly. The Scion stood, arms folded. He blinked slowly but he did not smile while Kalin rubbed his hand across his bearded chin with a grimace. The two men turned and followed the Duke out of the Hall.

'I'm sorry,' Froma said, her voice small and meek. 'I am so sorry.'

Agata believed her. She took the merchant wife's trembling hand. Maybe it was her own hand that fluttered, it was hard to tell. Froma squeezed back. On the left by the wall, Sira and Rabel were wrapped in each other's arms, their bodies shaking as they sobbed.

Agata did not cry. She slumped limply against the chair, weary and heavy.

He had decided.

CHAPTER SIXTY

THE DUKE DROPPED HIS HEAD, there was nothing more to say. His people jeered and cheered with approval but his belly seethed with nausea. He picked up his iron crutch and shuffled away. 'Forgive me, Father,' he muttered under his breath.

'You found your strength,' the Scion said quietly as they crossed the Great Hall. 'The Father is proud.'

The Duke smiled weakly. He did not feel strong.

A guard opened the side door for him. 'Not always a coward, m'Lord,' the guard whispered as he passed by.

The Duke gasped. He twisted around to face him. The slight frame, the beady eyes, the prominent teeth, the rodent-like face. It was him. In a terracotta uniform. The man who had saved him on the plains of Truinn. His rescuer and blackmailer was dressed in his own eel sigil, the symbol of his family. The Duke stumbled and slammed against the brick wall.

The guard lunged forward, grabbing his elbow. 'Careful, m'Lord.'

The Duke awkwardly found his balance and yanked his arm away from the guard's grip. 'Thank you.'

'My pleasure, m'Lord,' the guard replied with an ice-cold gleam in his eyes. The Duke swallowed hard.

'Are you ill, my Lord?' Kalin rushed to his side.

'Perfectly fine,' the Duke grunted and waved his friend away. His mind whirred as he laboured down the corridor towards the stairs. 'Who was that guard?'

'The one on the door? Vogur? Why? What did he do?'

The Duke stopped. He pressed his lips together. There was one way he could bury his cowardly secret. Forever.

'I want him gone.'

'As you wish, my Lord.' Kalin shrugged. 'I will send him home.'

'No. Gone,' the Duke said precisely, his hands trembling. 'Do you understand?'

Kalin's forehead wrinkled. 'Of course, my Lord. Can I ask why?'

'He is one of them. A conspirator. I heard he tried to free the Duchess last night,' he said, straining to compose his face to hide the lies.

'What?' Kalin's eyebrows hurtled towards the ceiling. 'Why did I not hear of this? You should have informed me immediately.'

The Duke rubbed his forehead. 'Wladek told me of the incident but with all the goings-on today, it slipped my mind. His brother is on guard duty this month and heard it all.'

'Hearsay, my Lord?'

'He is the one responsible. I am sure of it.' The Duke nodded vehemently but Kalin narrowed his eyes.

The Duke pictured the Father in the sky, looking down on him, tutting and shaking his head. This had been another test. A chance to repent for his cowardice on the battlefield. But yet again, he'd failed. Rather than face up to his shortcomings as a pious man would, he'd chosen the path of the weak, ordering another cold-blooded murder to protect his precious honour.

The Duke coughed to clear his throat. He was no better than the women in the dungeons. But he had one advantage. He could get away with it.

'Please deal with the matter.'

'Wouldn't you prefer to make an example of him? There may be others in league with her and the Wasp Women.'

The Duke shook his head. 'Do it quietly. Do not put ideas in the people's heads.'

'But my Lord...'

'No more,' he barked. 'You have my order.'

Kalin paused and lifted an eyebrow. 'As you wish, my Lord.'

The Duke sighed. 'Bring me wine,' he croaked and limped up the stairs toward the solar, but there was not enough wine in Ambrovna to drown out his conscience.

CHAPTER SIXTY-ONE

AGATA STARED THROUGH THE SLIT in the wall at a single lonely star. She craved juicy figs, crumbly almond cakes and golden honey but the toadish guard brought stale black bread and sour-tasting water.

Footsteps approached her cell and her heart skittered as a dim light seeped through the iron door.

Was it him?

A key scraped in the lock and she held her breath, her eyes wide. She'd known he would come to say goodbye. Or better yet, stop this madness. He would give her a proper chance to explain, just the two of them and he would listen. Without Kalin. Without the Scion.

The door opened.

The bald headed Scion entered the cell, accompanied by the quiet weak-chinned guard, holding the torch.

Agata sucked back a sob and her body folded.

'What do you want?' she said weakly.

The Scion clasped his hand behind his back. 'I am afraid your days of giving orders are long gone.'

'Do you want to gloat some more?'

'I did not come here to be insulted.'

'Guard! Get rid of the Scion!'

But the guard did not move.

'I have a matter to discuss with you.'

'What else do you want from me?' Agata said. 'You got your way. You twisted all of them against me. Your precious traditions are preserved.'

The Scion raised an eyebrow. 'You seem to think me the master of a grand plan. I can assure you I did not plot anything.'

'I am sick of hearing from you. You and all the other men. Leave me in peace to enjoy my last night in this world on my own.'

'But I have a proposition for you.'

Agata frowned and crossed her arms.

'This is highly unorthodox, I admit. But the Father would like to offer you a second chance.'

Agata held her breath.

'I can arrange for you to join the Unwanted.'

'Hide?' Agata scoffed. 'How? Every person in Ambrovna knows my face.'

'We will sneak you into the Cloisters. No one except the other Unwanted will ever see you again. We know how to keep secrets. Come and serve the Father and the Fatherhood for the rest of your days. Simply and piously in repentance for your sins.'

'Cook your meals and darn your smocks?'

'Repent. Renounce your Wasp Woman ways. Redeem yourself as a good woman in the eyes of the Father. Every one of the Unwanted is rewarded for their service with entry into the Land Beyond the Sunset.'

'After a life of cleaning out your slop pots.'

'This is my offer.'

'What about tomorrow? The town is looking forward to seeing me suffer.'

'There are always ways. I can supply veils. With your faces covered, no one will know the difference. There is an Unwanted on the verge of death with a similar frame.'

'Does my husband know you are here?'

'No one knows. And no one can know.'

'I would look up at the cliffs to my home every single day?'

'It is your choice. The Unwanted or the Land of Eternal Darkness.' The Scion shrugged.

'Why are you doing this?'

'It is my duty to save souls.'

'Reforming a Wasp Woman will give you additional honour with the Father?'

'It is my role in life to ensure as many people as possible experience the love of the Father.'

'You feel guilty.' She burst out laughing. 'You know I am right. Deep in your heart. You know the ways must change.'

'I am offering you a reprieve. You do not have to take it.'

'Say I am right and I will come with you. Say the words. Admit you are wrong.'

The Scion blinked his eyes slowly. 'Last chance for absolution.'

'Say it. These are my simple terms.'

'You are young. You have many years ahead of you to atone for your sins. It is your choice.'

Agata smiled.

'I will take my own chances with the Father when I meet him tomorrow. I have plenty to say to him.'

CHAPTER SIXTY-TWO

ROM HER DARK CELL, AGATA could not see the position of the sun. For hours, she had lain on her back on the mouldy straw floor, waiting, with no sense of when her time would come. But it was here. Now.

Awaiting her fate, she had floated backwards and forward in time and place. To her childhood home in Tramissa, in the long free days before Madame Fidan and her rules. Before the storm. Racing Yeta through the cool grass. 'Don't be like me,' her mother's voice echoing in her ears.

On the soft carpeted floor of a strange domed structure, lounging at the feet of a smiling woman dressed as a man, with silver eyes and snow-white hair.

Floors above in this very castle built of red bricks snuggled into the cliffs. Where she had tossed and turned in an unfamiliar bed. Frightened and excited, the night before she married him.

Swords clanged against armour as boots clumped down the dungeon corridor. The iron door wrenched open and Lord Kalin stepped inside.

'Get up,' Kalin said gruffly.

Agata was no longer Duchess of the House of Nyvard. She was now an ordinary prisoner destined for death. She blinked at Kalin in his full regalia. His breastplate gleamed in the weak candlelight, yet his eyes were bloodshot. He and the Duke must have celebrated their decision late into the night.

'Can I wash?' she said.

The guards sneered but Kalin did not join in. She covered her face with her dirty hands. She must face the town and the Father bedraggled and unrecognisable in her stained stolen guard's uniform.

Lifting her chin, she straightened her spine. 'You must be happy, Lord Kalin.'

With a rattle of armour, he strode towards her, so close she could feel his warm breath against her cheek. 'I thought I would be,' he whispered. 'But...' He let out a sigh. 'We all have our duties to uphold.'

'Cowards,' she said.

He stepped back, his eyes cold once more. 'Take her away,' he ordered.

The men roped her wrists and tugged her out of the cell by the hands, leading her like a calf to market.

Further along the dank corridor, they stopped to collect Froma, then Sira and finally Rabel. All four women were tied together, one secured behind the other. They were close enough to talk but there was nothing more to say.

The procession of the damned moved out into the stark daylight. The sunshine was blinding after days inside the cells. Agata squinted into another glorious autumnal day. The blue sky was freckled with a few white clouds. The Father must be happy with the result.

The Avenue from the castle to the Square was lined with terracotta-clad guards. 'Wasp Women,' one guard spat and the others snickered. This time, no one stopped them. Agata's eyes blazed like a lit match but then she dropped her head. It no longer mattered what these men thought.

The guards pulled Agata and the others down the slope and into the Square. The crowd roared as the first rows of waiting townsmen caught a glimpse of the condemned women. Agata stopped, wide-eyed, her heart hammering.

'It's time. No escapin'.' The toad-faced guard chuckled and yanked at the rope. She stumbled but continued on.

The townspeople pushed and shoved from every angle as the guards towed them through the throng. Drums thumped, pots banged and horns bleated. People yelled, spat and laughed. Terracotta pennants flapped in the wind and children high in the branches of the Old Man Tree pelted stones at them. She flinched as a sharp stone struck and bounced off her skull. Faces blurred.

The crowd cleared and Agata saw and smelled her punishment.

Four bonfires crackled in front of the dais. Four iron cauldrons, bigger than any cauldron she'd ever seen before, sat above the glowing embers. The oil-filled cauldrons bubbled and plopped.

Froma shrieked.

The heat from the fires hit Agata like the wind on the cruellest summer day. This was the punishment for murder by poisoning.

As the guards dragged them onto the low stage, the crowd roared again, their frenzy like a wave. Agata glanced at the Duke where he sat in full ornamental dress on his high carved chair. His face was pale, his eyes faraway.

Less than a week earlier, she had sat alongside him with a wide smile as they welcomed the men back from war. How naive to think she was embarking on a new era, where husband and wife would share the rule of the Duchy together.

What a fool.

The procession jerked to a stop and Froma dropped to her knees.

'No!' she screeched.

'Get up!' Kalin yelled.

A guard lifted the whimpering Froma up by the armpits and she bumbled to her feet. The guards herded them into the centre of the stage to face the whole town, each woman positioned before a splattering cauldron.

Those thirsty for justice lined up at the front, snarling. A few women stood alongside their men with equal venom in their eyes. But Agata looked beyond the savagery in the front rows. She craned her neck and spied women without any signs of spite or revenge. These were the women she'd led during the war time. These were her women.

With fear-widened eyes and frowns, they shook their heads with disbelief.

The guards untied her hands and she rubbed her raw wrists. Froma snuffled beside her, while the sisters stayed quiet. Agata sensed the Duke's gaze on her back, but she no longer cared to turn and meet his eyes.

He'd made his choice.

Kalin opened his arms wide and the crowd hushed. 'My Lord, Scion Zavis, men of Ambrovna. Today we punish four murderesses and traitors. A fair trial was held and the Duke made a just decision. All four women were found guilty and the full punishment for the crime of murder by poisoning was agreed upon.'

Froma wailed and the men hurrahed.

The guards pushed Agata towards the cauldron. Her cauldron. Two men hoisted her high into the air. From this place in their arms above the crowd, she could see clearly over the jeering men to the clusters of quiet women by the market stalls at the back. Mothers with children on their hips, young servant girls and grey-haired grandmothers shared furtive glances. They were too far away for her to hear their voices but their faces sent her a message. Of anger, of fear, of hope, of pride.

They understood.

All her fears drained away and a smile blossomed across her lips. She didn't struggle. She didn't close her eyes. Her hands were still and her heart beat steadily.

Her mother would be proud.

Queen Magnilla would be proud.

She was proud.

Not today.

But one day.

EPILOGUE

NINE HUNDRED YEARS LATER, GRAND Chancellor Valte stood at the podium, the seal of the Republic behind her. 'Citizens of the Republic of the United Five Rivers. Many of you know the tales of the Wasp Women of Ambrovna, the tale of the four wicked women who betrayed their families, their community and the Fatherhood.'

The camera zoomed in on her cool blue eyes.

'After considerable research by Professor Jelva Agerir of the History Department at Sulun University, the truth about these four women has been uncovered and documented. Today, I am redressing nine hundred years of wrongs perpetrated against the four known as the Wasp Women of Ambrovna.

These women lived in a time when the voices of women were not heard nor were they respected. It was a time when a woman who spoke her mind was branded a witch.

Over the centuries, their story became folklore, a cautionary tale of the terrible consequences if a woman stepped outside her role and acted like a man.'

'Today, because of these four women and their sacrifice, I have the privileged position to right the wrong made nine hundred years ago. Today I announce the formal pardoning of Rabel Ejvind, Sira Osias, Froma Plesec and Agata Nyvard. Without them, the Republic would not be where it is today. And neither would I.'

The Grand Chancellor stared deep into the camera, a slight smile on her lips. In homes, in schools and in workplaces all across the Republic, women smiled with her.

THE END

*Thank you for reading **Women of Wasps and War**.*
If you enjoyed this book, please leave a review or a tell a friend and
share the word.

AUTHOR'S NOTE

Women of Wasps and War is based on a true story and the idea has been rattling around in my head for over twenty years. Sometime in the 1990s, I heard the gruesome tale of the Angel Makers of Nagyrev. The Angel Makers were a group of women from the village of Nagyrev in Hungary who used arsenic to poison over 300 people from 1914 to 1929.

In Hungary at the time, women were forced into arranged marriages and divorce was frowned upon even if the husband was abusive. During the war, Nagyrev was used to house Allied prisoners of war and many of the local women had affairs with foreign men. When the war was over, the husband returned, expecting life to remain the same. But the wives had other ideas. The women used arsenic to rid themselves of husbands, parents and even children. Eventually 26 women were put to trial, eight were sentenced to death but only two were executed.

As is often the case, truth is stranger and more bloodthirsty than fiction.

ACKNOWLEDGEMENTS

I have to thank all the people who helped Women of Wasps and War come to life.

Firstly, thank you to my British Science Fiction Association Orbit critique group members who reviewed early drafts. Thanks to Steve Turnball, Terry Jackson, Dom Dulley, Andy McKell and especially John Keane for their useful pedantry and encouragement.

Thank you to the Monthly Twitter Writing Challenge people for their ongoing support and motivation during the dark days.

I also thank Jo Burnell for her editing and Rebecca Pay for her proofreading and Jake Knight for his copy-editing assistance. And as always thank you to the Deranged Doctor Design team for their cover design and formatting.

ABOUT THE AUTHOR

Madeleine D'Este grew up in Tasmania and is now based in Melbourne. After studying law (but never practising) and travelling the world, Madeleine now lives a double life, working in corporate Australia by day and writing female-led speculative fiction by night. Madeleine also hosts a writing interview podcast *Write Through The Roof* and a weekly book review show on www.artdistrict-radio.com.

Keep in touch with Madeleine for news, reviews and pictures of cake at **www.madeleinedeste.com** or on Twitter at @madeleine_deste.

Published Titles

- Evangeline and the Alchemist
- Evangeline and the Bunyip
- Evangeline and the Spiritualist
- Evangeline and the Mysterious Lights
- The Antics of Evangeline: Collection No.1 (novella series)
- Women of Wasps and War

www.ingramcontent.com/pod-product-compliance
Lightning Source LLC
Chambersburg PA
CBHW030602180626
46816CB00005B/1643